D1452845

Relics, Wrecks, and Ruins. Edited by Aiki Flinthart

Relics,

Wrecks &

Ruins

Anthology of sci-fi, fantasy, and horror short works
Edited by
Aiki Flinthart

Reviews

"The deep messages of this anthology make the very bones hum. Taloned onto the page by resistance and vision, these stories invite us to witness how sacrifice crafts wisdom, and how wisdom opens doors for the next generation."

L.E. Daniels, author of *Serpent's Wake: A Tale for the Bitten*

"Rich, varied, and bittersweet, this anthology is a fitting and triumphant salute to Aiki Flinthart's dauntless spirit and irrepressible moxie."

Geneve Flynn, co-editor of *Black Cranes: Tales of Unquiet Women*

Dedication:

To all the authors out there—both published and aspiring—don't give up. To all the friends, family, and fellow authors who supported me and sometimes even stretched the rules to help me make this anthology happen before end of days…massive thanks.

Relics, Wrecks, & Ruins Edited by Aiki Flinthart

Assistant editors: Gene Flynn, Lauren Daniels
Cover artwork by Daniele Serra
Cover design by Pamela Jeffs
Internal art by Caitlyn McPherson
Published 2021 by CAT Press

All stories are original to this collection or acknowledged as reprints

Cosmic Spring, by Ken Liu - First English publication by *Lightspeed*, March 15, 2018
American Changeling by Mary Robinette Kowal - First English publication in *Daily SF* in September 2010
River of Stars by David Farland—First English publication September 2017.
The Wind and the Rain by Robert Silverberg—First English publication in "Saving Worlds" 1973, Doubleday Books.
Morgan of the Fay by Kate Forsyth—First English publication in "The Road to Camelot", Random House Australia, 2002

A Cataloging-in-Publications entry for this title is available from the National Library of Australia.

ISBN-13: 978-0-6489917-3-1 (Trade Paperback)
ISBN-13: 978-0-6489917-2-4 (e-book)
CAT Press
PO Box 3388, Darra
QLD 4076, Australia

Acknowledgements:
Heartfelt thanks goes to my wonderful, supportive, fun-loving husband and my loyal, huggable, strong son. Huge appreciation to Gene Flynn, Lauren Daniels, and Pamela Jeffs who helped and supported me every step of the way in this madness. Thanks to Daniele Serra who kindly donated the beautiful cover illustration.
Also to all the authors in the SWG and FB, for their enthusiasm & support; and to my many wonderful family and friends who are helping me through this difficult time.

Big thanks to Jonathan Strahan, without whose help I would not have been able to pull this crazy project into shape.
And to Ellen Datlow for her kindness and direction. And to Dirk Flinthart for his encouragement.

This anthology is likely to be my last project before I head off to Valhalla. So I'm hoping it will bring to your attention, dear reader, several new authors as well as let you relax with several old friends.

When you finish, if you enjoyed it, please leave a review on Goodreads or your ebook retailer so others can find it as well.

Contents

Washing the Plaid

By Juliet Marillier

The Bridge House is a wreck. It's been empty for years, and it's old and crumbly and falling apart. When I walk past on the way to the school bus, I can see peeling paint and cracks in the walls. The wooden porch sags and the front door is faded to a weird shade of gravestone gray. The garden's a mini-jungle of rioting weeds, half-dead in the end-of-winter cold.

So, everyone's surprised when the house finally goes up for sale, then super-surprised when it sells almost immediately. The biggest shock is when Mrs. Mac moves in. That's what people call the old lady. It's short for Mac-something.

"Why on earth would an old girl like her buy such a huge place?" my mother asks one night at dinner. "It'll cost a fortune to fix."

Mum's an accountant so everything is about budgets and money. I ignore her and flip the page of my book.

She frowns. "And Mrs. Mac must be eighty at least. Living on her own with all those dogs—that's crazy. What if she trips over one of them and breaks her leg? Or forgets she left a pot on the stove and sets the place on fire? Mr. Briggs next door won't be happy if they make a nuisance of themselves. He's always hated dogs." She points at my plate. "Rachel, close that book and finish your dinner. No reading at the table, remember?"

"If there was a fire, wouldn't the dogs bark?" I don't really want to be part of the conversation. I'm only here because Mum expects us all to sit at the table for meals. But someone should stand up for Mrs. Mac. "And we'd smell the smoke." We live directly opposite the Bridge House.

"Would've been a smart buy for a developer." Dad's off on his own train of thought as usual. "That's prime riverfront land. Demolish the old house, build a luxury two-story place, maybe a private jetty. You'd make a healthy profit. That's if you could get around the heritage guidelines. The owner should have got us to handle the sale." *Us* meaning the business he and my uncle run: Premium Property. He pauses to shove a forkful of spaghetti in his mouth, chews, and swallows. "Still, she's an old woman," he says. "I suppose it'll be up for sale again before long."

I imagine a gleaming modern house sitting there on the riverbank like some alien craft that's landed among the big old gum trees, knocking quite a few of them over. A private jetty would mean we couldn't walk along the riverbank anymore. It would block the path for other things too—wallabies, lizards, water birds, all the creatures that live in that patch of bushland. It might send them up onto the road where they'd get squished by passing traffic.

A house like that would never belong.

I finish my spaghetti in silence. Mum and Dad have changed the subject to some cocktail thing they're attending on Saturday, and they're working up to an argument. That happens a lot these days. James and I exchange a glance and take ourselves off to the kitchen. We wash and dry the dishes. In the dining room, Mum has gone quiet while Dad gives one of his lectures.

James goes up to his room, in theory to do his homework. I retreat to mine and shut the door so James can't sneak in. He loves snooping and solving pretend crimes.

I've got homework, too. More than James, since he's still at Ashburn Primary and I'm in my second year at high school. But all the talk about Mrs. Mac has given me an idea for the next part of my story and I need to write it down before it slips out of my mind. Ideas do that sometimes; like when you have a fantastic dream and then you wake up and for a moment it's still there, bright and clear, but just fades away. That's so cruel.

I write and write. I don't stop until I hear Mum coming up the stairs. My neck hurts and my fingers are all cramped and it's dark outside. I've written six hundred words without even thinking, as if something was sitting on my shoulder or, even creepier, in my head, controlling the whole thing. I like it when that happens; that's when I do my best work.

But I can't check it over now because Mum's knocking on the door. She barges in without an invitation.

I hide my story behind a French translation assignment on the screen. I've never let anyone read my work. My real work, I mean. I've written stuff for English at school and earned high grades for it. Teachers have suggested I might do creative writing at university. But Dad wants me to work for the business, and Mum thinks I should try to get into law.

Before Mum can say, *Finished your homework?* something outside catches her attention. She walks to the window and stares down into the street. There's a light out there, not the whitish streetlight but more of a gold glow, moving about.

"What's that?" she asks.

Mum's gazing in the general direction of Mrs. Mac's place. I look over her shoulder, remembering the comment about pots on the stove. My eyesight is better than hers. The warm light comes from a torch. Holding the torch is the small, shadowy figure of Mrs. Mac with a shawl around her shoulders, a woolly hat on her white hair, and trainers on her feet. Beside her pads the biggest of her dogs. Its head is nearly up to her shoulder. After she moved in, I looked up dog breeds, and that one's a Scottish deerhound. You don't see many of those being walked around Ashburn.

"Mrs. Mac," I say. "Just walking the dog, I guess." Maybe two dogs; I think I spotted a tiny one tucked into her shawl, like a baby in a sling. Perhaps that one can't walk very well.

Mrs. Mac goes in her gate with the deerhound alongside. The gold light bobs about for a bit, then cuts out as she enters the house.

"I don't know," mutters Mum. "Out walking in the dark, all on her own…" Her tone changes. "Finished your homework? It's getting late."

"Not much more to do. Half an hour, tops."

Mum looks at her watch and rolls her eyes. "Don't forget to iron your school shirt for tomorrow."

"I'll do it in the morning."

"Rachel." She uses the warning voice. I hate that. It's like a threat: *Do it or else (insert horrible thing that might happen).* I've tried to explain how important my writing is, but she just doesn't get it.

"I'll do it when I've finished the homework."

She takes the hint and leaves. I do some math problems and the French translation, all of which takes more than half an hour. Since she hasn't come back up to hassle me about having a shower and going to bed, I write some more of my story, adding a witch who looks like an eccentric old woman with dogs and turns out to be immensely powerful.

"Mess with me at your own peril," I mutter as I save and close the document. I put my school stuff in my bag for the morning, then go over to the window.

Mrs. Mac is out there again. Not on the footpath, but in her front garden, shining the torch up into the trees. Looking for owls? Hunting for a lost cat? I'm about to close the curtains when she looks straight up at me. She kindly doesn't shine the torch into my eyes. She gives me a little wave. I wave back. Then she's gone. I don't feel embarrassed to be caught watching her. I'm weirdly happy that she saw me and was nice about it.

#

When I get home from school the next day, there's mail sticking out of our box, so I take it inside, call out "Hi!" to Mum so she'll know I'm there, then check the letters to see if there's anything for me, unlikely as that is. They are all bills or junk mail, except for one. It's a longish envelope with interesting stamps on it. They're all pictures of monsters: a dragon, a weird horse with too many legs, a thing that might be a phoenix. It's from the UK, and it's addressed to Mrs. M. MacEachern at number 29, which is the Bridge House.

I wonder what the M is for—Mary? Millicent? Myrtle?

Mrs. Mac might be waiting to hear from a son or daughter, a grandchild, a dear old friend she hasn't seen for years. I should take it over to her. I should knock on the door and give it to her. That's more friendly than stuffing it in her letter box. And I might get a peek inside the house.

I'm not going to say, *Hi, Mrs. Mac.* That would be rude. But I have no idea how to pronounce MacEachern. I get out my phone and search for a pronunciation guide. YouTube gives two ways of saying it, mac-EECH-ern, and mac-EK-ern. Since the first one's the name of an American high school, I go for the second one. I practice a couple of times. I tell myself not to be nervous; she did wave to me last night.

The gate creaks as I open it, and from inside the house there's muffled barking. I picture myself in hospital, swathed in bandages from head to toe. I hear my mother and Mr Briggs saying, *I knew those dogs would cause trouble. I'm calling the council right now.*

I hesitate then swallow and lift my chin. All right, I'll do it. I won't be bookish, shy Rachel who barely talks to anyone at school. I'll be a brave and bold adventurer with head held high.

I reach the door, which has a fresh coat of paint in glossy dark blue—when did that happen?—and knock three times. There's a frenzied yipping and a scuttling sound, then claws scratching on the other side of the door.

Footsteps.

"Sybil, no!" says Mrs. Mac, and the scrabbling stops. The door opens and there she is, with the tiny dog in her arms and the huge one beside her, and a couple more bouncing up the hallway behind her. "Wait," she says over her shoulder, and they do. "Oh, you're the young woman from across the road." She gives me a close look, sizing me up. "Hello."

"Hi, Mrs. McEachern." My voice shakes. Why am I so pathetic? I hate myself sometimes. "I'm Rachel. This letter's for you—it was in our mailbox."

She's holding the dog and doesn't have a hand free to take the envelope.

"Lovely," she says, backing into the house. "Will you bring it in? And close the door behind you—Sybil is liable to bolt at the slightest opportunity."

I do as she asks. I may be breaking the family rules about stranger danger, but I can hardly do otherwise, since Sybil is thrashing around as if she's seen a demon. Mrs. Mac sets her on the floor. The little dog hurtles off down the hallway.

"I thought that small one couldn't walk," I say.

"Ah. Come through and I'll explain. Cup of tea?"

"I can't stay long." I follow her toward the back of the house and try not to gape. The place may be old and neglected, but it's still amazing. I don't know where to look first. The ceiling's a riot of plaster flowers and animals and things that might be cherubs or strange fairies. The carpet runner has a long dragon on it that would once have been brilliant red on a deep blue background. It's faded badly, but I can still see all sorts of delicate details: people in tiny boats, a bug-eyed monster guarding a tall palace, and a field of flowers with crows flying over it, and…

"That carpet has a hundred stories in it," says Mrs. Mac, looking back at me with a crooked smile. "Every person who looks at it finds new ones."

I'm speechless, because the carpet has put several new stories in my head, where they're jostling to be first in writing order. With test week coming up at school, that's not a good thing. But it feels great, like a door opening on a wider world.

I follow Mrs. Mac through to a big kitchen, where there's a long table with five chairs, none of them matching; and an old-style stove, the kind that uses wood or coal. Lots of things hang from the ceiling: herbs and garlic and stuff, but also a string of little silver bells and three pottery owls in different sizes.

At the back of the room, overlooking the river, a row of windows lets in the light. Some have stained glass; some are plain so you can see the water and the trees and probably kookaburras and magpies and spiders. On the outside there are spiderwebs in every corner.

"Live and let live," murmurs Mrs. Mac, apparently reading my mind as she puts a kettle on the stove and gets out cups and saucers. "They keep the flies out. Please, sit. Now, would you like ordinary black tea, or Earl Grey, or a herbal brew? I make my own mixtures; you might enjoy this one. Lemongrass, peppermint, marigold, a touch of this and that." She opens a squat earthenware jar and offers it for me to sniff. "What do you think?"

Awkward Rachel, who hates speaking up and getting things wrong, would ask for ordinary black tea because it's the safest. But this house calls for courage.

"That smells interesting. I'd love to try it, thanks." I perch on the very edge of a wooden chair and watch Mrs. Mac potter about the kitchen.

Sybil does a great job of getting underfoot, but Mrs. Mac doesn't step on her even once. When the tea is ready, in a pot that looks like some sort of creature but I can't tell what—a toad, maybe?—Mrs. Mac clicks her fingers and says quietly, "Dogs!"

Just like that, they're all around us; Sybil and the deerhound and the two from the hall—sturdy brindled Staffies. They sit, watching us.

"This is Finn," Mrs. Mac indicates the deerhound, "and these are Minnie and Paddy, or Minerva and Patrick if you want to be formal. One named for a goddess, the other for a saint. And Finn, of course, was a great hero. Then there's Sybil, and her brother over there."

There are dog beds all over the place, from an oversized one that must be Finn's to a tiny one with built-up sides. A head pops up from that one, round eyed and big eared. That dog's just asking to be called Yoda. When Mrs. Mac lifts him out of his bed, I see that his hind legs are deformed.

"Oh, poor thing," I say.

"Here, hold him while I pour the tea. One hand under his rear end, that's it, and one around his chest. Take a firm hold. He won't break."

"What's his name?" I'm trying to think of a god or saint or hero who couldn't walk.

"Frankie. You'd be far too young to know how that name was chosen."

I sit at the table with Frankie on my knee, wishing I could work it out. "St. Francis?"

"Good guess, but not right. You may like a spoonful of honey to sweeten that tea. Let it cool a bit before you drink."

Frankie. Francis. Or maybe just Frank? Wasn't there once an American president who used a wheelchair? Pity I didn't bring my phone with me. But she'd probably think that was cheating. I stroke Frankie's oversized ears and rub him under the chin. He relaxes against my chest. Why do I suddenly feel like crying? I hold the dog steady with one hand while I stir some honey into my tea. And the answer pops into my brain all by itself. "Franklin," I say.

Mrs. Mac grins. "Very good, Rachel. A reader, are you?"

"Lucky guess. We don't do much American history at school. And yes, I do love to read." I focus on my tea, my cheeks hot. I'm waiting for the usual jokes about how a girl my age should be into clothes and boys.

But she just smiles and says, "Frankie has some wheels. He's just getting used to the contraption, but he can scoot up and down the hall quite well."

We sit quietly drinking our tea for a bit, then Mrs. Mac asks, "Do you know anything about the history of this house? How it came to be built, and who lived in it?"

"Nothing much. Only that it's been empty for a long while."

"You might do a little research. See what you can tell me, next time you visit."

"Like homework?"

She laughs, not a polite-old-lady chuckle but a full-bellied guffaw. "Not at all. Expanding your horizons. Broadening your knowledge. Preparing for the future, and I don't mean in a *learn this or you'll never get a job* way. More tea?"

I remember suddenly that I only came over to give her the letter. "Oh—I'd better go home. My mother will freak out if she can't find me. Sorry to seem rude, I..." I get up and almost step on Sybil. "Oh, sorry!"

"There's no need to apologize for yourself, Rachel." Mrs. Mac gives me a searching look. Her voice is kind, though. "If you need to go home, go. And if you'd like to visit me again, please do. Sybil! Up!" The tiny dog executes an unlikely leap into Mrs. Mac's arms. "I'll see you out."

As we go down the hallway, I glance through a part-open door—that I'm sure was shut before—and my feet refuse to take another step. The room within is large and shadowy. The walls are lined with shelves, and the shelves are crammed with books. There are little round tables with lamps on them, and some squashy-looking old chairs. I stand there gaping. Those books can't have been here while the house was empty. They'd have been eaten up by insects or fallen apart from mold or something. When did she move them all in?

"Not completely sorted out yet," Mrs. Mac says. "Maybe you could assist me next time you visit. Let your mother know first. She'd surely approve of helping an old lady, mmm?"

I walk on, reluctantly, and say goodbye at the front door. As I cross the road, I think out what to say to Mum. *I'll be going over sometimes to help Mrs. Mac sort out her books, if that's okay. She can't reach the highest shelves on her own.* I don't like to lie, but the truth would freak Mum out.

That house is full of magic.

#

To my surprise, Mum says I can go over after school a few days later to help with the books. The night before I go, I make muffins to take with me. I'm nervous, even though Mrs. Mac was so nice. What if I interrupt her when she's busy with something, or taking a nap?

The thought of being a nuisance makes my stomach queasy. It brings back all the times I've heard other kids talking about me at school, as if it was freakish to read a book at recess or ask questions they don't understand or get so wrapped up in writing that I miss the bell to go back to class.

I can't talk to my parents about this. Their solution would be signing me up for basketball or hockey or something, on the assumption that playing team sports would suddenly make me fit in. James can tell something's not right at school. But I can't talk to him, he's only eleven. And he'd pass it straight on to Mum and Dad.

Mrs. Mac opens the door and smiles, and my stomach settles. We eat the muffins and drink tea, and I'm allowed to fasten Franklin into his little wheeled contraption so he can whizz up and down the hall with Sybil running alongside.

Then we go to the library.

This time there are reading lights on, and the curtains are open, and the big room is bright and warm and welcoming. In between the floor-to-ceiling bookshelves are quirky corners and niches holding different things: a jar full of feathers, a scowling mask, a candelabra shaped like a woman with snakes for hair. There are window seats with cushions—an invitation to curl up and lose yourself in a book. At one end of the room is a tiled hearth for an open fire. The tiles have creatures on them, a bit like the ones on those stamps.

I take a big breath and let it out slowly. My home across the road is nice enough but it's not the sort of place that brings stories bubbling to the surface.

"This house is beautiful," I say as I look at the intricate pattern of leaves and vines and birds on the curtain fabric, and the carpet square like soft grass, and the diamond-shaped windowpanes. There are so many surprises here. One of them is the desktop computer setup, with big screen and printer and ergonomic office chair. Hers? I guess it must be.

There are books on a small table, and one catches my eye. *Tracing the Cailleach: The Hag Figure in the Folklore of the Western Isles* by Dr. M. G. MacEachern. I'm about to ask if Dr. MacEachern is a relative when I turn the book over and see the author's photo on the back. It's her, but a lot younger, around my mother's age. She's standing on rocks with the sea behind and her long dark hair streaming out in the wind. She's not dressed up for a fancy author photo, but sensibly clad in a parka and jeans.

"That's a great picture. You look happy."

"I was happy. I'd finished my doctoral thesis and seen it published, and I was in one of my favorite spots in the world. You might find that book a little dry; it's heavy on scholarly references. Try this instead." She passes me a slimmer volume. The jacket illustration shows an old woman emerging from a dark wood, holding a lighted lantern and accompanied by a wolf. It's a fairy tale version of Mrs. Mac. The title is *Maiden and Crone: Tales of the Western Isles* by M. G. McEachern.

"They left the 'doctor' off your name," I say.

"That one's not a scholarly work, simply a collection of some of the tales I discovered along the way. It was a lot of fun to write."

I look through the pages. The illustrations are brilliant. One shows the witch, or maybe she's a hag, standing in a giant whirlpool and washing what looks like a tartan blanket. She's wild and powerful and completely unafraid. She's exactly the way I wish I could be.

"We can be whatever we choose," says Mrs. Mac, as if she's read my thoughts.

"A goddess? A witch? In Ashburn?"

She smiles. "You won't live your whole life in Ashburn. Not that it's so bad a place to be a witch. Often it's places like this that most need one."

"What does that word mean—Cailleach?" I point to the title of the first book. "Sorry, I'm sure that's not how you say it."

"You're doing it again. Apologizing."

"Sorry. I mean…Could you tell me how to pronounce it, please?"

Mrs. Mac demonstrates. It sounds like KY-akh. "It means Hag," she says. "Some folk imagine a hag as a hideous old woman. I see her as a force of nature. One which has been around since the time of our ancient ancestors, or longer still. But, of course, she could be both."

"She doesn't look hideous there. She looks as if nothing in the whole world could scare her."

There's a pause while Mrs. Mac pats Minnie and Paddy, who have come in quietly to sit on either side of her. "That's how we need to be, Rachel," Mrs. Mac says. "Unafraid. Unapologetic. Like the Cailleach. You'll find that story at the end. It's called 'Washing the Plaid.' Read it now, if you like."

She doesn't speak while I look the story up in the contents and find the right page. The title has a little wreath around it—half spring flowers, half snowflakes.

Then Mrs. Mac says, "She's young like you. Brigid, a springtime goddess. And she's old like me. The Hag, bringer of winter. That tale is about the way things keep changing, yet stay the same. How they renew themselves after turbulent times. How we stand strong, no matter what."

I glance across, and for a moment I see not elderly Mrs. Mac with her white hair and wrinkles, but the woman in the author photo: a traveler, an adventurer, fearless and joyful. She's young and middle-aged and old, all at the same time. Magic.

With a shiver, I bury myself in the book. It's weird reading the story right after I've had that thought, because when the Cailleach washes her plaid in the whirlpool in late autumn, the tartan colors fade to white, and winter creeps over the land. When it's time for spring a young goddess, Brigid, takes the Cailleach's place, and things warm up and start growing again.

A note at the end tells me that in some versions of the story Brigid and the Cailleach are the same person. Young and old, spring and winter. In others, they're separate goddesses. Either way, it's about changes being part of a long steady pattern. That makes me think of how Mrs. Mac came to the Bridge House. And how you can't judge things on the way they look at any given time, though lots of people do just that.

My mind fills up with ideas. I'm bursting to write about this.

\#

I write at home. I write at school, and when people make snarky comments, I ignore them. I write at the Bridge House, after school or on the weekends, while Mrs. Mac works on her computer. But although I get deep into writing, I'm not blind to what's happening around me, some of it seriously weird.

It started with the blue front door, and it keeps happening: fresh paintwork, wobbly steps fixed, broken windowpanes replaced. Inside, the house seems lighter, fresher, the curtains clean, the colors of the dragon carpet no longer faded. No cobwebs in the high corners, though there are still lots outside the kitchen windows. Mrs. Mac doesn't ask me to sort the books, but someone's doing it, because from all mixed up they've moved into library order. The jackets look brighter.

I don't ask how it's happening. I don't want to break the spell

\#

Each time I go home, I tell my parents I've been helping Mrs. Mac fix up the house. As long as I do my homework, they don't seem to mind. I'm not ready to show them my stories yet. And if I told them I want to be a writer, they'd probably say Mrs. Mac was a bad influence, and make me stop visiting the Bridge House.

Why don't I want anyone to read my stories? Because I couldn't bear to be told they're rubbish. It would be even worse if someone tried to be nice and I could tell they actually thought my stuff was terrible.

But I remember how Mrs. Mac gave me her book to read when she hardly knew me, and I think about the gazillion great story ideas I've had since visiting her, the house, and the dogs. She's a writer too, a real writer. If there's anyone I should trust to look at my stuff, she's it.

I do have one story I'm fairly proud of. It's my version of "Washing the Plaid." Will Mrs. Mac like it, though? I imagine the Cailleach standing out there in the whirlpool, strong arms wielding the plaid like a banner, and I know it's time to be brave.

I print a copy and give it to her the next time I'm at Bridge House. My hands tremble and I run home before she opens the first page.

The story starts like this:

You know me. But you don't see me. I'm the shuffling bag lady in her worn-out shoes, the muttering derelict whose disturbing smell turns your head away and speeds your footsteps. I'm the wife and mother who one day, without explanation, throws a few things in a suitcase and walks out the door forever. I'm the snowy-haired grandmother, wizened as an apple left too long in storage, who stares at you with knife-sharp eyes, daring you to call her a little old lady.

I'm a witch. I'm a wisewoman. I'm a force of nature, a power to be reckoned with. I have a thousand names. I've lived a thousand lives. I am the spark of being, the flame of courage, the danger and the choice. I'm in every woman, deep down. Sometimes blinding bright, sometimes a steady glow, sometimes the merest flicker in a cavern of uncertainty. Disregard me at your own cost.

#

The next day I'm nearly home from school when I hear the shouting. There are people on the road outside our house and cars everywhere. I see James and Mum and Mr. Briggs, our neighbor. He's the one doing the shouting.

I start to run, my schoolbag bouncing on my back. As I get close, I spot something tiny darting around on the road. Oh, God, it's Sybil.

"Wait!" I call out, gesturing wildly, but nobody's looking at me. Sybil's in a panic, zigzagging all over the place. A driver coming the other way has stopped. People behind her honk their horns. A car comes up behind me. The driver slows; I step off the curb and put a hand out. *Stop.* With a grimace, he hits the brakes.

When I turn back, Mum has moved out to face the opposite line of traffic, signaling to the drivers to wait. I dump my bag on the footpath outside our house. James is crouched beside the lead car, trying to see underneath. The driver opens her door and gets out.

"It's under here," says James.

"Stay where you are. I'll go on the other side," I tell him.

The driver moves to the front of the car and gets in position for a quick catch.

There's still an exit for Sybil—at the back. If she goes out that way, her path will lead straight under the line of vehicles with their impatient drivers. Mum stays right where she is, making sure nobody tries to drive through. Her expression startles me. *Disregard me at your own cost.*

"We need someone at the back of the car!" I call out.

In a moment, there's Finn, come from nowhere to station himself exactly where he's needed. I kneel on the road, peering under the car. Sybil's right in the middle, out of reach, hunkered down on the ground, trembling.

"We need a broom or something," says James, peering at me from the other side.

"How about I release the brake and we roll the car slowly forward?" suggests the driver, getting back in.

"Get that vicious brute off the road!" yells Mr. Briggs. "Should be muzzled and locked up!"

"Keep your opinions to yourself," Mum snaps. "Right now, we need a couple of people to push the car gently forward. Thanks," she adds as other neighbors come over to help. "Slowly. That animal must be terrified. Ready? One, two, three—now."

The car moves forward to reveal Sybil, now lying motionless on the road. Oh God, she's had a heart attack or something. But no—she raises her head. She's up on her feet, gathering herself for a sprint. Finn steps forward and places a majestic paw on her back, and she relaxes. I gather her up, holding her tight against my chest. My heart's thumping super quick and so is Sybil's. I feel dizzy, as if I might pass out.

"Thank you so much," Mum is saying to the crowd. "It looks as if the little one's fine. Thanks, everyone." She ushers Sybil, Finn, James and me onto the footpath, then signals to various drivers that they can be on their way. One or two of them toot their horns briefly before they drive off, as if to say, *Well done.*

Mum waves.

I could swear she's enjoying herself.

"I'd better take Sybil to Mrs. Mac's," I say when the traffic's cleared. I can hear Mr. Briggs muttering something with "council" in it as he shuffles off home.

"Not on your own," says Mum. "You've had a shock. We'll all go. James, take Rachel's bag inside, will you? And fetch that packet of Tim Tams from the pantry."

We wait for him at Mrs. Mac's gate, which is slightly open. There's no sign of her; I hope she's okay. James returns with the biscuits, but when we're heading up the path he hangs back.

"Mum?" He sounds unusually serious.

"What is it, James?"

"Mr. Briggs let the little dog out. He opened Mrs. Mac's gate."

We stand in silence for a few moments. Then Mum says, "How do you know?"

"I saw him. From Rachel's window."

Mum looks at me, a question in her eyes.

"Mrs. Mac wouldn't leave the gate open," I say. "And there's nowhere else Sybil could get out, even though she's so small."

"It'll be James's word against Mr. Briggs's if someone complains to the council," Mum says.

"I took a photo," says my brother, "before I ran downstairs."

I grin at James as we go up to the door. "The boy detective solves another crime!" A photo. That's pure gold.

We knock; Mrs. Mac is slow to open the door.

"So sorry, I was just wrapping up an online tutorial...Sybil! Finn! What have you been up to? Come in, please..."

Mum tells the story as we go through to the kitchen. They introduce themselves properly and I learn Mrs. Mac's first name: Morag. I hand Sybil over and make tea for everyone. James goes around patting all the dogs.

"You might get a visit from the ranger," says Mum. "Briggs is the complaining type. Though no harm was done. Your dogs are very well behaved."

"They are. I do have a council permit to keep more than the regulation two. Oh, chocolate biscuits, how thoughtful! I should be rewarding you, not the other way around."

"Any time," Mum says. "You were giving a tutorial? In what field?"

"Folklore. For the University of Aberdeen. Thanks to the wonders of modern technology, I can teach from anywhere, though I am semiretired now. What field are you in, Mrs. Gordon? Or may I call you Alison?"

"Alison, please. I'm an accountant."

Mrs. Mac nods. "And do you enjoy that?"

"It's a job," Mum says, fiddling with her cup. "Funny, thinking back. When I was Rachel's age, I wanted to be a dancer. I was offered a scholarship, but my father put his foot down. It meant going to live in France, and he thought I was too young. Maybe he was right. How often do those childhood dreams come true?"

Only when you make them come true, I think. The conversation feels somehow dangerous. I drink my tea and let the two of them talk.

Mum has surprised me today, and not only by taking control out there on the road. A dancer. Why had she never mentioned that?

"Rachel," says Mrs. Mac, "your brother might like to see Frankie's contraption in use."

We put the wheels on the little dog and take him into the hall, where he shows off his speed. Now that we're out of earshot I ask, "What were you doing in my bedroom, James? When you took that photo?"

My brother turns pink in the face. "Reading," he mumbles.

I lay my palm against the wood paneling of the wall and imagine the house is making me calm and strong. When I ask, "Reading what?" I manage not to sound angry.

"That story about the dragon that gets woven into a carpet. I read some of it yesterday before you got home and I had to finish it."

I swallow harsh words. *You know you're not allowed to go in my room without asking! Who said you could read my story?* But I did leave a printout on the desk where anyone could find it. And it sounds as if he enjoyed it.

"Sorry," my brother says. "I know you don't like people reading your stuff. That story's really good."

"Thanks." He's just a kid. And as brothers go, he's not bad. "It's just as well you did go into my room, I guess, or Sybil might have been run over. And there would be no evidence."

James flashes me a grateful smile. "Have you got any more stories I'd like?"

"Maybe. But ask first next time, okay? Some of them are too grown-up for you."

I can hear snippets of conversation from the kitchen, and I'm glad we're not there, because it's really personal stuff from Mum, and the occasional comment from Mrs. Mac.

She held onto my *Washing the Plaid* story overnight; I still don't know if she thought it was any good. Is she telling Mum about my writing? I hope not.

After a while, we take Frankie back to his bed. Mum and Mrs. Mac are still talking, but Mum looks at her watch and gets up.

"I should be making dinner. Thank you so much, Morag. It's been wonderful talking to you." She dabs her eyes with a tissue. Has she been crying?

"You're welcome to drop in any time, Alison," says Mrs. Mac. "You too, James. The dogs love a play. And thank you again, all of you. You saved Sybil's life today."

I'm considering this as Mum and James go out ahead of me. Thinking of a story in which Mrs. Mac made the whole thing happen—the gate, Sybil's escape, my family's intervention, the kindness of strangers. Wondering why.

"Wait a moment, Rachel," says Mrs. Mac.

"I'll catch up to you!" I call to the others.

Mrs. Mac waits until they're out of earshot. "I loved your story, and not only because it's about the Cailleach. It's a remarkable piece of writing. I made a few notes, not corrections, just possibilities. I'd like to read it again tonight, if you don't mind collecting it after school tomorrow. Writing is hard work, isn't it? Frustrating sometimes. But there are moments of sheer magic. Like your story."

I can't wipe the smile off my face.

"I'll find you a link to the course I teach at the University of Aberdeen. Folklore and Ethnology. A possibility for the future. It's a postgraduate degree, so you'd have a good while to convince your father that a year of overseas study wouldn't turn you into a wild creature."

And I think, down deep, I'm wild already. Trying my hand with the plaid. Freeing the dragon. Stirring the cauldron.

"You could enter that story for the Young Writers' Awards," says Mrs. Mac. "You'd need to show it to your English teacher. Think about it. Another monster to be confronted. One that might prove very helpful. Now you'd better go, your mother would probably appreciate some help in the kitchen." A pause. "I like her."

"She likes you. Bye, Mrs. MacEachern. I'm so glad Sybil is okay. And thank you for reading the story."

"It was a joy, Rachel. See you soon."

As I cross the street, I sense the presence of the Bridge House behind me. There's no sound but distant traffic and the warbling of sleepy magpies, but I feel the house sigh and settle, like someone who's done a good day's work. I glance back. The neat, white-painted walls gleam in the warm afternoon light. Freesias bloom in Mrs. Mac's garden; their sweet scent fills the air.

It's springtime.

The Names of the Drowned are These

By Angela Slatter

Every so often, there's a chance for reversal.

For a thread pulled to drag things *backwards*.

For the drowned places to rise. For the dead to walk again. To breathe air rather than water.

Sometimes, there's a chance.

Adie Kane came home last week—just as she has done once a year for a decade of searching—to visit Nessa's View. She took a room in the tidy little bed-and-breakfast at Ganymede, unpacked her suitcase, then got back in her rental and drove up to the lake (dam). She parked, and went to sit by the shore, careful to ignore the spillway and great curving concrete wall to her left. She sat on a rock (the same one, each and every time), and stared into the same black, unmoving waters—*surely, it's the same liquid, nothing flows, nothing shifts, not since that first flood settled*—and thinks about the end.

#

Michael had been on the road for hours. Everything in Tasmania, he'd discovered, took precisely forty-five minutes longer to get to than Google said it would. It was his first trip, though his grandparents had both been bred here. And the roads... shit, the roads were an eclectic mix of blacktop, washed-out gravel, and fuck-you potholes that turned into gullies, abysses, or crevasses, depending on the personal inclination of each and every bloody hole. Barely wide enough for two cars, he'd had to back up five times this morning to let someone else by, someone with a much bigger vehicle.

There was an etiquette to it, he realized, a hierarchy on which he was the bottom rung due to his shitty little hire. He might as well have painted a red mark on his forehead. He kept seeing lips move in the shape of "fucking tourists" every time someone drove past him, the gale produced by massive 4WDs with mud on their bull bars and back windows shaking his flimsy Hyundai. The really serious ones had winches and steel cables for pulling idiots like him out of ditches and lakes.

He was already regretting that he'd agreed to meet Adie here. That he'd agreed to meet her family. But the sex was good and he wasn't quite prepared to give that up yet. Not quite. Michael smiled, thought about Adie. Felt things move lower down, thought about it too much and was almost run off the road by one of the too-big mining trucks that carried ore to the ports and took the ridiculous curves and corners as if they were auditioning for a Mad Max chase. Michael pulled over, half-on, half-off the bitumen; the engine coughed itself out. Kept his hands tight on the wheel because if he let go, he'd see how hard they shook, and he wasn't sure he wanted that knowledge. He inhaled a deep breath, started the car again, took a good look around then drove gingerly back onto the road.

#

The first proper house had been the sandstone one built in the 1800s by Adie's great-great-great-great grandmother, Nessa Kane. A structure built, rather, by convict labor, all the rough men assigned to the property that would eventually grow into a town. Adie's aunt would tell tales of Nessa, though she'd never met the woman, and those stories were third-hand from her own mother. It was said Mistress Kane was far more feared than her husband or even the overseer. She would take the whip from that man's hand and use it herself on any member of the work detail not pulling his weight. She'd make sure they bled, that she could hear the patter of their blood on the ground, on the stones. Like so many from the Old Country— wherever that might happen to be—Nessa Kane knew the value of red.

She also knew that nothing stable or worthwhile came for free, and she was smart enough to make sure someone else paid the price on her behalf. Others might have called her a witch, though not to her face—her husband included—but she simply saw herself as a careful builder and protector of the family that was to come. And her husband let her have her way. He saw how she brought him a prosperity he'd not have had the will to wring from the earth. He didn't question her, in the cold hours of a moonlit night, when she left their bed in the little ironbark hut they shared while the big house was being built. He did not follow.

Nessa Kane led one of the convict men to the newly dug foundations. Younger and stronger than the others, he'd kept his shape better, not starved to string and sinew. He had good teeth, and was clean enough for her purposes.

She took him to the required place, and though he hated and feared her in full knowledge of what he'd seen her do—*felt* her do, for he'd been no more proof against the bite of her whip than any other—she was beautiful, though older. She was alluring and demanding, and he'd not had a woman in months. So, when she came to him warm and wet, half-naked with breasts dark tipped in the moonlight, smooth thighed and greedy, he did not seek a deeper reason, for most men are fools.

He did not think as he came inside her, did not think as a sharp, hot pain tore across his throat in the wake of the blade. He remained nameless, this father of Nessa Kane's first child, voiceless but for his final moan, last act, last coming. He was what she needed: a man no one would look for, who might truly have run away into the wilderness and been lost just as she would claim. Yet he stayed; not by his will but he stayed. Buried in the foundations, he formed the family's first connection to the land, paid the required tithe, gave them an anchor to the earth.

A sacrifice to the past and the future.

His blood, it was, kept Adie Kane coming back, year after year, like a leash that let her wander only so far. Kept her searching for what was needed, following a trail of relocations and feints, dying outs and changed names, as if someone was trying to hide it.

It kept her seeking until she found it.

#

Adie's hungry but she doesn't let the rumbling of her stomach distract her. She'll get something when Michael arrives. If there's time. Instead, she sits on the rock, shivers a little in her coat; no matter how thick it is, there's always that tiny piece of heart-ice to keep her chilly on the warmest of days—and this is not a warm day. The sun's watery, too often behind the gray clouds that scud across the sky. The wind is like a slap in the face that she's grown used to, can barely feel on her cheeks now.

She doesn't look down and far to her left, to where the new town sits. Instead, she stares out at the strangely still surface of the lake (dam). No waves are kicked up. It's like glass. If she concentrates long enough, Adie's convinced she might see the houses *beneath*, where Nessa's View used to be.

Ganymede.

Ganymede was on a lot of maps because its mine produced a lot of copper ore. It was on a lot of other maps because the process released arsenic into the soil, turned the water red as blood, poisoned the surrounding areas for years and years and years. Almost as if it could only protest its own birthing in the most toxic way possible. Adie hates the place, though she'd lived there much of her life. She hates how ugly it is, how it scarred the land. She hates that something so ugly had been allowed to live—encouraged to thrive—when Nessa's View had been condemned. Flooded one town, built another further downstream.

Economics.

Filthy word.

Poor excuse.

Not everyone stayed in Nessa's View. Some moved away, to Hobart or the mainland. Some moved sooner, some later. Some even moved to the nascent Ganymede, got jobs in the mine. They found new houses, though not true homes; kept dying out until there was just Adie, almost alone in her generation. Aunt Miriam and Uncle Toby brought Adie up; however, they didn't thrive. They put everything into raising her, yet she couldn't help but feel they continued living only out of duty, until she could stand on her own two feet. Toby died a few years after Adie left high school, but Miriam went on until the girl finished university, then promptly succumbed to breast cancer she'd not bothered to have treated.

Miriam taught her niece the things she needed to (Nessa's ways hadn't been lost, although not all the family approved), made sure the girl understood what she was meant to find. What she had to do. Miriam didn't consider herself up to the task; she was too weary and worn by life and the loss of a home. Her niece and the other were the required vessels; two for Eden, two-by-two, two to tango. She'd left Adie alone with a burden to carry forward. The burden of names.

#

Michael locates the bed-and-breakfast sometime after lunch. The woman at the front desk looks him up and down when he walks in, suspicious. Not the best way to encourage the tourist trade, he thinks, but feels too tired to make a point. Instead, he hitches a smile—the same one he deploys when he's occasionally unlikely to make rent because the costs of being a millennial have caught up with him—and detects only the slightest defrosting.

"Uh, hello. My girlfriend's already checked in? Adie Kane? A few hours ago?"

The woman's expression doesn't get better or worse. Michael accepts he's not going to make any friends here; his hostess's got permafrost of the personality and his charm is wasted. But she fishes about under the counter and dredges up a key, big and old-fashioned, attached to a small chunk of raw copper. She holds it out like a lure and he half expects her to tug it away when he reaches for it.

But no, there it is, hard in his hand.

"Back out the front, turn right and take the path to the rear garden. Foxglove Cottage."

"Is Adie here?"

She shakes her head, and Michael feels he's been given all he's likely to get; he beats a hasty retreat. It doesn't occur to him that the hostility might be directed mainly at Adie, and only peripherally at him. He's the center of the universe, after all.

The cottage is sweet, blue and cream walls and furnishings, a large open-plan room; toasty air burring up through vents in the floor. A sofa, TV and coffee table mark out a sitting area; in one corner, a small fridge with a kettle and assorted items on top. A brass-framed bed and a spa bath take up the other half of the space. One door leads to a cupboard (where he sees Adie's overnighter), another to a small loo, shower and handbasin (her makeup bag already on the sink). Michael unwinds his scarf—one of the ones his grandmother made compulsively in her final years, like she could knit her world back together as the memories were plucked from her day by day—dumps his backpack on the sofa, and makes for the bed.

Starfished facedown on the soft mattress, he closes his eyes and moans. Stillness for a while, no more Tasmanian roads, warmth. Food soon, Adie sooner, he hopes. His pocket buzzes and vibrates beneath him. He groans, wants to ignore it. Obeys and pulls forth the mobile.

At the dam. Bring food.

He considers ignoring this for a moment too. Thinks about filling the spa bath and soaking there until she comes back. Looks at the minibar bottle of local wine, the artisanal cookies and the cylinder of Pringles. Michael heaves himself up with a grunt.

#

The names of the drowned are these:

Rose McColl (single, fifty-seven, kept seven cats).

Agnew Foster (forty-five, widower, owned the local grocery store).

Sian Jones (eighty-nine, blind, made jam).

Abel and his brother Cain Katzenjammer (fifty-three, unmarried, twin sons of religious parents).

Scout Taylor (twenty-six, pregnant, daughter of a mother obsessed with Harper Lee; her husband did not stay).

Elizabeth and Benedict Kane (Kane on both sides, a closer blood relationship than either church or state preferred, landowners); their daughter Sarah Kane (Adie's mother; Adie's father unknown).

All those too stubborn to leave, too foolish to believe the government wouldn't flood the valley. They all bore, to some degree, the blood of Nessa Kane and her sacrifice.

These, they stayed.

These, they drowned.

In the end, the house of sandstone and polished wood sank beneath the black waters as easily as the corrugated tin shacks and small wooden abodes, the petrol station and the general store. Even the unnamed man's blood wasn't enough to keep such a flood at bay; perhaps age had weakened it. The magic had faded, paled, enfeebled.

The flooding of the valley was another kind of magic, an unintentional one but its power was enough to overwhelm what Nessa had wrought.

Not wash it entirely away, however.

A matter of potential, floating beneath the surface.

But it was there.

And it waited.

A thread that stretched back. A thread that might as easily lead forward. A thread, waiting to be pulled. A thread of blood, thicker than water.

#

"Ganymede's a shithole."

The moment the words are out of his mouth, they don't feel like a joke. They taste flat as they exit his lips and he regrets them. He sounds childish. He rustles the plastic bag from the takeaway shop as if it might cover up. It didn't take him too long to find her—the rental car (considerably bigger than his, more expensive, less likely to be run off the road) was the giveaway—but the fast food's cooling rapidly.

She doesn't answer him, just shifts over so he can sit beside her. He holds the mouth of the bag open so she reach in.

"Sausage roll. Easier to manage than a pie." He looks sideways at her: skin pale, green eyes bright, crow's feet deeper than he remembers from a week ago in Brisbane, brows dark as a raven's wingspan, lips full. He leans over and kisses them: so cold, a little chafed from the wind. How long's she been here? He touches her face: icy. Reproachful as he says, "Adie."

She takes two bites of the sausage roll before starting to chew.

"Thanks," she says around the flaky pastry. "Starved."

"Couldn't we have had lunch in town? Together? Couldn't we have met your family for lunch? Couldn't we have stayed with your family?" *Instead of staying at the Bates Motel*, he thinks. *Cheaper*, he thinks.

"We are with my family," she says, then polishes off her meal. She doesn't offer to pay him back because she never does, and she never does because she always pays for the expensive things they share (like Foxglove Cottage). Doesn't stop him from resenting it.

"Where's their place?" he asks doubtfully and hunches into his jacket, burying his nose in the scarf.

"Here."

"Adie." He doesn't know why he thinks of his grandmother and her dementia when Adie's behaving like this. She's older than him, sure, but not *that* much older. Not really. He changes tack. "Did you find what you were looking for?"

She'd arrived a few days before him on that pretext. She nods.

"Well. That's good."

"I found it before I left, really," she says, and links an arm around his. There's not much warmth coming off her; he feels like she's stealing his. "You had family down here, right?"

"Yeah. Somewhere. Didn't talk about it much." He shrugs. He never paid much attention, but remembers Granny whispering, "*Best forget*," as her fingers dug into the meat of his upper arm. "What is this place, Adie?"

"This is the drowned town." There's a catch in her voice, but no sign of emotion on her face.

"Drowned?"

"To make the dam. They keep calling it a lake like it's a natural thing, like it might make people forget what was here. But we remember. There was a place called Nessa's View."

"Don't they compensate people when that happens?" he asked and knew from the way she stiffened it was the wrong thing. Again.

"How do you compensate someone for drowning their home? Taking away everything they've ever had? The place they've bled into, onto?" She turns to look at him and he thinks for a moment she's stared so long at the lake—*dam*—that it's leached into her eyes, they've darkened so much.

"I...and they..."

"The government sent officials with offers, then threats. Most of the population took the money and ran. But not everyone wanted to go. They didn't believe it would happen. Nessa bound us here with blood, gave a promise, and her children believed they were safe."

"Nessa?"

"My ever-so-great grandmother. She made this place. The day of the flood, there was a cursory sweep of the town, but I don't think they really cared. The inhabitants had been so troublesome—sabotage, legal battles, whatever they could do—that no one really cared if they'd left or not. So the stubborn old-timers, young-timers, those with nowhere else to go remained behind their closed doors and drawn curtains, refusing to believe the morning would end in death. The waters rose and Nessa's kin finished with their faces pressed to ceilings, pushed into corners where cobwebs had waited unspoiled for years, against crown moldings that had once been the height of fashion. Gasping for a final skerrick of air. There was no point running."

"When…when was this?"

"Sixty-three?" she says it as if she's not sure, as if Aunt Miriam hadn't drilled it into her.

"You're not old enough…"

"To have seen it?" She stares at him and for a few seconds he thinks she is. She's older and older. Then she grins, a spark of humor in a taut face. "No, my aunt told me. She watched. Her mother was one of those who stayed. And mine."

"Why? Why stay?"

"They didn't want to leave so they chose to sink, to be taken." She sighs. "May as well ask why come back? Blood draws you places you don't know or understand. You're here, aren't you?"

"Coz you asked me." And he's regretting it, oh so much.

That grin again. She touches his hand. "My family's here. Yours is too. Your grandmother was a Kane."

"Nah, Teague."

"She married a Teague—after she'd married a Bowen, and a Smith. Was born a Kane. Here. Tried to hide but I found her—you."

He shakes his head. "So? Are you telling me I'm fucking my cousin?"

"Pretty distant, but yes. But that's not the point."

"By all means, let's get to the point." He can't keep the tone out of his voice. He's regretting everything about this trip, about meeting her. Everything.

"The point is they remained. They're shadows beneath the waters, the bones of the land. They were already held here by blood, choosing to die here gave their deaths meaning and power. Blood's thicker than water, and their blood's a thread that can be tugged at to create a path that might lead *back*. They're at one end, we're at the other. You and I? We're the ones all the bloodlines end in. They need us."

"Jesus fucking Christ, Adie. What are you on? Let's just go back to the BnB and you can have a rest."

She gets up and walks to the water's edge. He follows with a sigh. And Adie takes out a knife. Nothing special about it—not the knife Nessa used on her sacrifice all those years ago, no grand history to it—it's just neat and tidy, a Swiss Army knife, with that red handle and white cross.

"Adie, what are you doing?" Michael's voice wavers.

He's bigger than her but she's quicker, got an older head; she's watched him these months together and taken note. She knows what he'll do, how he'll react, so she's ready when he raises his hands, palms out as if that might protect him. He's a bit of a coward, but it's not his courage she needs. She slashes up, catches one of those vulnerable palms, leaves a deep slice there, watches with satisfaction as the blood oozes dark and rich from the furrow in his flesh. He shouts and she slashes again, this time at her own hand.

"Oh, shut up," she says matter-of-factly, although the cut *does* hurt. She grabs his injured limb and slaps their wounds together. Adie squeezes—he whimpers—so their blood mixes and drips quickly into the still liquid of the dam.

"Blood is thicker than water," she mutters as if it's a spell (and it is) then starts to recite a list of names that mean nothing to Michael, but she cycles through them, then repeats again and again.

The water nearest where they stand begins to bubble, sweeping out across the surface, turning into white horses that gallop all the way to the far side—but those horses are carried by a blood-red wave and Adie can smell a whiff of iron in the shifting air. Then the water moves like a tidal wave dragging back, back, back, and finally charges forward, toward the dam wall. Adie and Michael watch, hand in hand; the tsunami hits and the concrete bursts out in enormous chunks as if charges had been laid and detonated. And the water follows it, pouring through the breach so quickly it takes Adie's breath away. Her aunt told her what to do, but it didn't mean she believed—*truly* believed— it would happen. It takes a lot less time than she thought.

Somewhere, downstream, Ganymede is being hit by a wall of water held back for years and years. Michael thinks of the frosty woman at bed-and-breakfast, wonders if her expression will change as the flood closes over her head.

And now, in front of them—these two children in whose veins the blood has come to rest—lies Nessa's View, uncovered for the first time in years. Houses—those that are intact—are covered with the green of algae and weed, windows are dark with silt and mud. The remains of the petrol station looks like a dinosaur skeleton. Everything still, barely the flap of fish struggling in the rapidly shrinking puddles. Everything is a held breath, a frozen moment.

But then…

Oh then, the doors begin to open, with swollen wood and fractured frames, and things—green and bony, the fish-bellied dead—walk out, blinking in a sunlight they'd forgotten.

Adie stares, empty, her burden, her duty done. The names of the drowned suddenly forgotten. She's made them *saved*.

Michael, still holding her hand, says in a strangled voice, "Oh,

Adie. What the fuck have you done?"

"Time to meet the family, Michael."

The God Complex

By Jan-Andrew Henderson

In physics, the "observer effect" is the theory that the mere observation of a phenomenon inevitably changes that phenomenon. This is often the result of instruments that, by necessity, alter the state of what they measure, in some manner.

Murphy leaned around Jensen to get a better look through the smoked-glass partition. On the other side, a dumpy, middle-aged woman sat at her console. She had unusually dark hair, short and permed, with a purple butterfly clasp fastened to one side. It looked remarkably like a wig.

"We call this part of the facility The God Complex," Jensen said dryly. "That's a pun."

Murphy sighed and scratched at his wrist, where the manacles had rubbed the skin raw.

Of the pair, Jensen was taller and thinner. He had a clipboard under one arm and was wearing a white lab coat. He looked so much the typical scientist, Murphy wondered if the man had ever considered becoming anything else. Murphy, on the other hand, resembled an Irish bricklayer—short, squat and ginger—and the name didn't help.

He squinted through the window at the woman. She wore a gold badge that said "Edith" in small black letters. With a handle like that, it was no surprise she was middle-aged, Murphy thought. Edith had a small microphone on the desk in front of her and was talking into it. Two wires, one red and one white, wound from the back of her head into a bank of steel panels set in the roof. Sets of lights above her head winked on and off and the whole apparatus gave a low hum.

"It's really quite fascinating." Jensen's voice was slow and emotionless, as if he mentally read over everything before saying it. "It's almost like you…plug yourself in. You…plug yourself in, yes. Plug yourself into the computer."

"And you can see what's going on in the past?" Murphy asked.

"You see, yes. No. Yes," Jensen replied hesitantly. "You… experience. You…You…Yes, you see, in a way. Sort of."

Murphy sighed again. He had long ago given up expecting straight answers from anyone in authority. Jensen turned a dial on the panel beside him and the woman's voice suddenly became audible. She sounded like she'd been smoking since she was twelve. Continuously.

"I'm on horseback behind three medieval knights," she narrated. "They're called Bors, Percival and Galahad—I know that 'cause they have names stencilled on the back of their armor, just like the players in the soccer cup final I was watching last night. So that's handy."

Jensen visibly ground his teeth.

"It's dark. It's night. They're approaching an old ruined castle, though there's a light coming from one of the windows. Percival is eating a chicken leg and it's pissing the other two off, 'cause he keeps wiping his hands on their mounts' butts. Bors has gotten really narked and threatened to stick his mace right up Percival's culet, whatever that is..."

"Too descriptive!" Jensen snapped at the glass, though it was obvious Edith couldn't hear him.

"How does this set up work, then?" Murphy tried again.

"The computer...it's a quantum computer. It can calculate infinite possibilities. See?"

Murphy didn't see.

"Well," Jenson continued, "they say that, if you think you understand quantum physics, you don't understand quantum physics. So it's hard to explain."

"Try."

"OK. Eh...We can use the computer to break down all matter into its basic components and study their trajectories." The scientist traced the imaginary fragments with his fingers, looking a bit like the world's palest rapper. "How they move, you know? Where they go. And...once you know how something moves and where it goes, you can tell where it once...was. Our quantum computer does that, yes."

"Quite a feat."

"It's a big computer." Jensen was still watching Edith, who had begun speaking again.

"Percival is bursting for the toilet but it takes forever to unfasten all those straps. And Bors is still in a monumental huff, so Galahad is going in alone. I'm following him. There's a strong smell of sulfur. He's entering a little room and there's a really old bloke there, sitting by a fire. He looks a bit like Sean Connery and, for some reason, he's surrounded by old-fashioned goblets. A couple of them seem to be solid gold and some are crusted with jewels."

The woman pulled a wad of gum from her mouth and stuck it under the console. She suddenly sounded a lot clearer.

"He's asking Galahad to pick which relic he thinks is the Holy Grail. Holy shit! Says if he gets it wrong he'll die. That's a hell of a risk just to get a cuppa."

"This is an awful lot like the plot of Indiana Jones and the Last Crusade," Murphy said suspiciously.

"She watches a lot of TV." Jensen raised his bony shoulders in resignation. "What can you do?"

"Then, why are you using her?" Murphy picked at a smear on the pane, a motion made more difficult by his metal cuffs.

"Ah. That's the tricky part." Jenson stroked his chin. "As I said, the quantum computer analyzes the trajectories of every bit of material in the world and then projects backwards. And so...we can chart exactly where each particle was located at any given moment...right back to the dawn of time, if you like."

"That's amazing." Murphy gave a low whistle. "The possibilities must be endless."

"Actually we haven't found a useful application for it at all," Jensen admitted. "We can't even make a bomb. Ce'st la vie, I suppose. Scientists are a bit like explorers. Some find America. Some discover Lapland."

"And?"

"And what?"

"Who discovered Lapland?"

"Beats me." The scientist glanced sideways at Murphy, probably to gauge if his interest was genuine. "If you really want to know, we can find out."

He pointed into the booth.

"See, that's what Sonja there does. Builds up a complete map of the past. She can see history."

"Sonja does all that?" Murphy looked at the woman with new admiration. "So, why does her badge say Edith?"

"Sonja's the name of the computer," Jensen replied scathingly. "Edith is a religious nutter. But...if she can discover something valuable, like the final resting place of the Grail or...a bit of the True Cross? Well...that would give us the money to keep running for years."

Edith began speaking again. "Galahad is having a good look at all the different cups. He's hovering over the fancy ones. Not surprising, really. They must be worth a fortune."

"This is our real stumbling block," Jensen whispered, so as not to drown out the woman's commentary. "In order to properly monitor history, our Witnesses, as we call them, need to hook themselves directly into the quantum computer. They have a symbiotic relationship, you might call it. They link together. Yes. Fuse."

"Isn't that a bit dangerous?" Murphy looked at the wires protruding from Edith's head and gave a shudder.

"That's why we use people like her."

"You don't like women much, do you?"

"I love women," Jensen snapped. "I just don't like Edith."

"Still...this is fantastic." Murphy wasn't about to get in the middle of a personality clash. "You could learn so much about...Everything."

"That was the idea, yes," Jensen agreed. "But like every new project, it has a few...em...glitches."

"The wrinkly dude is reminding him that the Grail was used by Our Lord at the Last Supper." Edith carried on, oblivious at being the focus of attention. Murphy assumed the window only worked one way.

"Hey, you old fucker! Stop helping him out. No cheating!" She

- 49 -

snapped her fingers indignantly. "Now Galahad's studying the plain wooden ones. That seems a better bet, but I'm still not sure it's right."

"See, it's like she's actually there," Jensen hissed behind his hand.

"Glitches?" Murphy asked.

"Sort of." Jensen grimaced. "According to Edith, when Judas kissed Jesus in the Garden of Gethsemane, Christ punched him in the mouth." He rolled his eyes. "How do you think a revelation like that would go down with the Christian community?"

"No shit!" Murphy gave a gasp. "That really happened?"

"But Galahad's no dummy." Edith chuckled. "He's put the wooden goblet down and is still considering. That's it. Left a bit. Warmer. Warmer. Red hot!" She gave a smug smile and punched the air. "Yes! He's gone for the ceramic mug with 'What Would Jesus Do?' written on it."

Her face took on a faraway expression. "Isn't that funny? I've got one just like it at home."

"Who knows?" Jensen scowled at the woman. "That's problem number two. The Witness becomes…eh… part of any given scene they observe. Their emotional state and desires influence their…interpretation, if you like."

He gave a stoic shrug. "Now we have to employ a team of psychologists to separate what really happened from what the Witness wants to happen. It's costing us a fortune."

"So, where do I come in?" Murphy had a cold feeling in the pit of his stomach.

"You kidding?" Jensen opened the clipboard and began to read the contents. "Billy Wayne Murphy. Life imprisonment for the murder of two eleven-year-old girls. Psychologists say you've never shown remorse. Have no emotional involvement with what you've done. In any capacity, whatsoever."

He raised an inquisitive eyebrow. "I can't imagine how that must feel. Which is the whole point, really."

"It doesn't feel like anything at all," Murphy said coldly.

"Of course. Of course." The scientist shut the clipboard with a snap. "Of course, of course, of course."

"Because I'm innocent, you idiot," Murphy fumed. "I was framed."

"A man without emotions." Jensen was still lost in his own musings. "Absolutely perfect. You'll be able to trawl through history in an objective manner. Aha. See things exactly as they are. You're just what we need to save the project."

"I am not a psychopath," Murphy repeated. "I was fixing my toilet at the time."

Then an incredible thought struck him.

"Listen!" he said. "We could use your machine to prove my innocence! Go back and find who actually killed those girls!"

He tried to grab the scientist's arm but both hands were shackled to his legs by chains.

"We already did." Jensen glared at him and pulled away. "It was definitely you."

"Wait a bloody minute!" Murphy exploded. "You just said, if the observer expects me to be the killer, or wants it to be me, then that's exactly what they'll see. Right?"

"Correct." Jensen nodded.

"So who was the sodding Witness?"

"Me."

"You bastard!" Murphy tried to lunge at the scientist but his chains snapped tight and he fell flat on his face.

"You're hardly going to be impartial yourself, eh?" Jensen hauled Murphy to his feet. "At least helping us gets you out of prison."

Murphy thought for a while. Then grinned.

"When you plug me into Sonja, I could see who really committed the crime." He brightened. "Once we know, we might be able to find physical evidence to back that up."

"Ehm…" Jensen looked sheepish. "Not anymore,"

"S'cuse me?"

"It's a quantum thing. Schrödinger's cat and all that stuff." The scientist pursed his lips. "Once a past event has been observed on a quantum level, it kind of…becomes history. To all intents and purposes."

Murphy frowned.

"Take your case, for instance," Jensen continued. "Did you kill those kids? There are only two possibilities: yes or no. But…ehhh…now that I've looked at it, there's only one. You definitely did it." He spread his hands generously. "Therefore, you may as well assist us. Get off death row, eh?"

"I'm not a psychopath," Murphy shouted. "I have emotions. My view of history won't be worth a crap."

"Shhh! Nobody has to know that." Jensen put an urgent finger to his lips. "We need you on board to keep up corporate funding. The chairman's patience is running out."

"Oh. I see. Right." Murphy gritted his teeth. "Well, since the morality of this project also seems to be a thing of the past, why don't you just pretend Sonja found some terrible scandal in this…chairman's past and blackmail him into keeping it going?"

"Because we needed a totally credible Witness to take on someone that powerful." Jensen smirked. "Which is where you come in."

"And people call me criminally insane," Murphy snarled.

"Yes. Well. You don't have to be mad to work here, but it helps."

Jensen's smile widened into a manic grin. "Ha hah. Hahahahahah ahahahahahahahaha. Sorry."

He pointed to a door behind them.

"The guards will take you for briefing and induction now. We'll expect you online in a couple of days."

Murphy's shoulders drooped and the chains clinked sadly.

"Maybe you're right," he said finally.

"Good man." Jensen patted him gingerly on the shoulder.

"I mean, you've proved I'm a stone-cold killer, then double-crossed me, eh?" Murphy gave a warped grin. "So, your days are most definitely numbered."

Jensen blanched. "Statements like that aren't going to go down well with your parole officer."

"Just watch your back, that's all." Murphy turned and shuffled out the door, the scientist following a safe distance behind.

Edith pressed a few buttons and the men slowly faded away. She checked that the time stamp read seven days ago, inserted an earpiece and began to talk into the microphone again.

"Chairman? It's me. Just went back and looked a week into the past, as ordered. Your suspicions are confirmed. Professor Jensen was obsessed with the impending failure of his project and intended to blackmail you for some fabricated indiscretion, to keep his funding coming."

She adjusted her wig.

"He enlisted a psychopathic convict called Murphy to facilitate his scheme, but the potential Witness threatened to kill him. Since the professor was found dead a few days later, I assume Murphy found a way to make good his promise."

She coughed politely.

"If you like, I can look at the day Professor Jensen died, just to be sure. No? Oh. You've already done that. I understand…And Murphy's back on death row? Excellent."

She nodded sagely.

"Let sleeping dogs lie, eh?" She glanced at her watch. "In that case, I've a couple of hours before lunch."

Edith switched off the microphone. She retrieved her gum from under the console, popped it back in her mouth and sat back contentedly.

"Just enough time to find out what happened to a certain thirty pieces of silver."

A Malediction on the Village

By Garth Nix

It was the end of winter and a witch on her broom flew with one of the south-bound scattered skeins of pink-footed geese, enjoying their sidelong glances and high-pitched honking, before she sheared off to her destination.

Mari Garridge had carefully studied her course in *Flight Directions for the Sunken Eastern Lands of Anglia*, but it was still quite difficult to fix her location and thus, her destination. The ground spread out flat beneath her in all directions, and was crisscrossed with a mystifying number of cuts, canalized rivers, dykes, and flood-mitigation workings leading up to and surrounding the many, muddy branches of a big estuary with several smaller inlets. Beyond the estuary lay the vast swathe of the sea.

Every small patch of relatively high ground held a church, and a village around the church, often sprawling into areas that surely must flood with great regularity. They all looked much the same from the air.

But only one village in roughly the right place had a large and shining, official-looking car parked by the green, and what might be described as a small throng milling about: clearly the welcoming party Mari had been told to expect. She angled her broomstick down towards them, once again thanking the unknown genius who had worked out how to affix a padded bicycle seat to the ancient stick of yew. The witches of yore had ridden sidesaddle on the barest padding of sackcloth and leather, a position Mari thought must have led to many falls on long air journeys.

As always, even with the bicycle seat, she dreamed of having a flying chair or chaise longue of her own. The broom, a borrowed mount which had served the fellows of Ermine College far longer than Mari had been alive, bucked, possibly in response to this thought. She hastily stopped thinking about comfortable cushions and actually sleeping while in flight, and patted the broomstick.

"Thank you, good broom," she said, "for all your service."

The people below were waving now, so it had to be the right place. Mari came in for a perfect landing on the road by the green, only having to run on three or four yards before she could stop. She stepped off, unstrapped her valise and set it and the broom down before turning to face the welcoming committee who had gathered in front of the war memorial, a plinth of three steps surmounted by the usual figure. This had supposedly been designed so that from different directions, it could be seen as either man, woman or child, and uniformed as being a civilian or a member of any of the four services; but in practice it mostly didn't look like anything in particular.

It was easy enough for Mari to identify the chief constable, a hawk-nosed lady of least sixty, because she wore full dress blues, her epaulettes sporting shiny, silver crossed batons. Dame Keble was accompanied by a short male sergeant and a tall woman constable, both in far less well-cut and resplendent uniforms.

Behind the police presence stood the vicar, also distinctive in a typical green skirt and blouse with the tawny shawl of the Goddess over her shoulders. The man in the bespoke, but now rather faded, gray suit at her side was probably her husband, particularly as he was holding up a plate of raisin-studded rock cakes. Behind him, the woman in overalls holding the Gladstone bag was probably the local doctor but might be the vet.

The final two members of this ad hoc welcoming party were less immediately identifiable: a man and woman of similar middle age, both countrified professionals of some sort, or so their well-cut, subdued tweeds declared.

Behind them all, lounging on the upper step of the war memorial, a russet Labrador with intelligent brown eyes and muddy paws watched the new arrival with interest. Or perhaps she was looking at the rock cakes.

"Who are you?" bellowed Dame Keble, as if Mari was a county over, and not standing in front of her.

"I'm the district witch," replied Mari. She undid her chin strap, took off her pointy hat, and flying goggles. Her hair was short, but not cut in a fashionable bob. She ran her fingers through it in a vain effort to make it sit down on top. "Aren't you expecting me?"

"You are not the district witch," declared Keble. "Mother Hartpool is, and she's due any moment, so you'd better shove off. We don't need any unlicensed witches here today."

"I really am the district witch," replied Mari, with a sigh. Mother Hartpool had warned her that Dame Keble was rather stupid, the beneficiary of tradition rather than any policing expertise. She caught the vicar's eye behind the chief constable, noted her apologetic expression, and continued. "That is, I am a locum, standing in for Mother Hartpool. Didn't you hear she's been called away to her daughter's? A new grandchild, I believe."

"You're too young," said Keble, her eyebrows gathering together above her nose in what was either disbelief or anger. "We need someone qualified!"

Mari sighed, collapsed her hat and tucked it into her shoulder bag before rummaging around to retrieve her card case. Flicking it open, she took out one of her still new visiting cards and offered it to the chief constable. The worthy received the rectangular pasteboard gingerly, as if it might be cursed, and held it up so she could peer down at it through the lower part of her gold-rimmed spectacles. The sergeant stretched up to read it as well. He was very short, though broad across the shoulders.

Dr. Mari Garridge BWch MSorc MagD
Junior Fellow
Ermine College
University of Hallowsbridge

"Hmmm," muttered Dame Keble. She still sounded suspicious. "Ermine College. Why would a Hallowsbridge scholar take on a locum here? And you're still too young."

"I have only recently taken my doctorate," replied Mari diplomatically. "I've been in Morcoln for several weeks, doing some research into...well...naturally I had called upon Mother Hartpool when I first arrived, so when she got your telegram, she came around to ask if I might stand in, given her imminent departure to her daughter in Stondbury. I agreed, so here I am."

"You can't just become a district witch," complained Keble. "Ermine College or not. There are necessary procedures, forms to be completed—"

"I hold a warrant as a provost of the university," interrupted Mari. "So, *ipso facto*, I may be commissioned as a district witch at any time or in any county by the Board of Black Velvet. This was in fact done by telephone earlier today, and I have a letter from Mother Hartpool confirming I act in her place. Do you want to read it?"

"Oh, that's not necessary," said Dame Keble, suddenly hearty. Mention of the far-off but potent bureaucratic power of the Board of Black Velvet in Londinium had her backpedaling as fast as she could. "Please pardon my initial...er...remarks, Dr. Garridge. My natural concern over the situation here has made me...worried. Very worried indeed."

"Exactly what is the situation?" asked Mari. "Your telegram didn't say. Other than it was urgent business for the district witch or wizard. Sir Henry sends his regrets by the way. The press of other duties, or he would have come too."

Or, to be more accurate, Mari thought, but did not say, Sir Henry Brodlington had snaffled the more interesting problem of an ancient oak that had inexplicably relocated itself to a point three miles from where it had stood for a thousand years, its new rooting place unfortunately being in the middle of a significant crossroads.

"No one else is coming?" asked Keble. She looked up and down the road, as if some sort of convoy should be approaching. "I mean, you're not expecting anyone?"

"No," replied Mari. "I'm sure I can assist you with whatever the problem is. What is the problem?"

"Well, now you're here, perhaps I should leave it to Sergeant Breckon to explain," said Keble. "It is a local matter and he has all the details. Good luck. Come, Entwhistle."

Mari was unable to hide her surprise as Dame Keble hurried over to her car, dove into the back and slammed the door behind her. The tall constable took a deep breath, strode stolidly to the front of the car to turn the crank several times before assuming the driver's seat and pressing the ignition. The car started with a series of loud bangs. The constable engaged first gear and exchanged an indecipherable look with the sergeant, before the car departed in a cloud of blue smoke.

"Mother Hartpool is often followed about by the *Morcoln Messenger* and sometimes even reporters and photographers from the metropolitan newspapers," said the vicar, stepping forward to join Mari, who was staring incredulously after the departing vehicle. "I am sure that's the only reason Dame Keble came today. Since you have arrived without the folk of the Third Estate, we have become surplus to her diary. I do apologize for the poor welcome to Nether Warnstow, Dr. Garridge. I am Kathleen Evenholme, the vicar here, as no doubt you have deduced. My husband, Lawrence; the good Sergeant Breckon who represents the law in both Upper and Nether Warnstow and two other villages besides; Dr. Ware, who has the local general practice; Lady Lovatt's steward, Arthur Robe, and her ladyship's solicitor, Jane Rawson. Ah, I should say Lady Lovatt is our squire, but she is well past ninety now, and does not leave the manor."

"Would you like a rock cake?" asked Lawrence Evenholme, proffering the plate.

"Not right now, thank you," replied Mari. "But what exactly is happening here? Why do you need my help?"

Everyone suddenly spoke at once, a cacophony which Mari could not follow, though she was disturbed by the use of one word they all employed.

Malediction.

Mari held up her hand. "Quiet please! I cannot listen to you all at once."

They stopped talking. The police sergeant and the vicar both tried to start again, but the vicar's glare and sniff put paid to the sergeant's effort and he closed his mouth with a thwarted huff.

"As I was saying," said Kathleen Evenholme. "There appears to be a curse on the village. Some malediction has been laid, and we need it found and lifted."

"I see," replied Mari, though she didn't. There was no evidence of a curse or malediction. Usually it would be all too apparent. Dying trees, browned grass, sickened livestock, dead birds, streams and ponds turned to blood, bloated toads burst upon the road…there was none of that, or any of the other portents. The people of Nether Warnstow also looked perfectly healthy. "How has this curse manifested?"

The vicar held out her thumb, followed a moment later by the others all doing likewise, save the solicitor, Rawson. Mari obligingly stepped forward to peer at the vicar's offered digit. It was rather red, more so than Evenholme's other fingers. But only as if she had been washing dishes and her thumb had somehow soaked in the suds longer than the rest of her hand. The others all had similar, somewhat reddish, perhaps slightly chafed, left thumbs.

"The curse has made your thumbs a little red?" Mari asked. She knew a faint smile was spreading on her face and tried to pull her mouth back into a stern, professional line.

"Rather more than that!" protested the vicar. "Something tried to pull it off!"

"Something?" asked Mari.

"An unseen presence," said the vicar, pulling her priestly shawl more tightly around her shoulders. "I was working on a sermon last night in my study when it came in. I heard the door slam open, the lamp at my desk suddenly blew out, and the next thing I knew a creature of darkness had my thumb in an icy grip and was pulling me across the room! If I hadn't struck at it with my pen who knows what might have happened."

Mari blinked. A creature of darkness that could be sent off by stabbing it with a fountain pen did not sound very likely. Anything summoned or released by a real malediction would have had the vicar's thumb entirely off in a second, and her head a moment later.

"A creature of darkness? Did you feel the Goddess react to this, or sense Her presence?"

"No..." replied the vicar. "One doesn't, most of the time."

The central tenet of the Church was that the Goddess was asleep, and Her few interactions with the living world came about from the deity's occasional dreams. As this also applied to Her Antagonist, it was considered in the world's best interests if the sleeping continued and the dreams were sparse. This could be assured, the First and Second Testament said, by doing good works, which kept the Goddess happily slumbering, and refraining from doing bad things, which might wake the Antagonist.

Despite her somnolent state, the Goddess *was* known to make Her presence felt if real evil intruded upon her consecrated servants, even though She rarely did anything useful about it. Her lack of interest tended to suggest that whatever had gripped the vicar's thumb was not a truly *malignant* creature of darkness.

"You did not see anything, or perhaps feel the shape of the intruder?"

"No. Only it was cold. Like ice water."

"Did it feel like a hand gripping your thumb? Could you feel individual fingers?"

The vicar shook her head slowly. "It was so cold..."

Mari looked at the others. "You all had a similar experience?"

Everyone started to talk at once. Mari quietened them again, and listened carefully to their stories. They were much the same as the vicar's. Each had been 'attacked' in the night, their left thumbs gripped and held up, but it was clear to Mari that the otherworldly assailant had not actually tried to pull the thumbs off. Nor had it been driven away by poking with a fountain pen, an uppercut from the sergeant—like punching a snow drift, he said—or any of the other defensive reactions. The reason that Rawson's thumb had *not* been pulled was also clear: she lived in another village, several miles away.

"I do not think this has been caused by a malediction," said Mari. "It has the classic signs of a shade of some sort seeking a part of its body that has been removed, in this case the thumb bone. Have you had any recent burials? No? Your graveyard is by the church? Perhaps I might have a look?"

"Certainly," replied the vicar. "But there has been no disturbance. The most recent burial was old Jaggers, and that's six months—"

"Eight months ago," interrupted her husband. He was still carrying the plate, but the pile of rock cakes had diminished and every shirt but Mari's and the vicar's was adorned with crumbs. The russet Labrador had left the war memorial steps and was following along to collect the fallen remnants and the odd sultana with judicious licks of her tongue.

"Eight months ago," continued the vicar smoothly. She pointed to the lych-gate in the low wall on the far side of the green, next to the church.

"I think we can let these good folk go about their business," said Mari, as it seemed clear the full entourage hoped to dog her steps. "Perhaps we can meet later to discuss whatever I have found. Oh, could someone put my broom and valise somewhere safe?"

"I'll take it to my police house, Dr. Garridge," said Sergeant Breckon quickly, for once, getting in before the vicar. "Sixth house down the street. The blue lamp is outside, but hard to see; it's a little overgrown with the passionfruit."

"You can grow passionfruit here?" asked Mari with interest. "Through the winter and all?"

"Year-round. It's the only passionfruit for two hundred miles," replied the sergeant proudly. "It is said a Roman wizard planted it, in ancient times, when they first drained the fens. That's why we never cut it back."

"I must take a look at it," said Mari.

"You don't think it has something to—" the sergeant began, a look of absolute horror forming on his face.

"No! No," Mari hastily reassured him. "I am sure it doesn't. I'm curious, that's all. And I like passionfruit."

"Oh, good," said the sergeant. "I'll take your broom and bag, Miss. I mean, Doctor."

He did a smart about-face, almost ruined by the others not getting out of his way, and marched off. After a few moments of hesitation, Dr. Ware, the steward Robe, and the solicitor Rawson muttered largely inaudible pleasantries and followed him.

Only the dog remained, eyeing the single remaining rock cake.

"Go home, Bella," said Lawrence, pointing to the imposing vicarage that could be glimpsed behind the church. The dog looked at him and set off across the green in the opposite direction. Lawrence sighed and shook his head.

"Oh, do come on, Lawrence," urged the vicar, though her husband was already moving towards her. "I have a great deal to get through today, after all this disturbance."

The graveyard did not provide Mari with any clues. It was undisturbed, and there was no sign any of the inhabitants had been roaming. In fact, it was quite peaceful, and when Mari leaned her hand against one of the hawthorns that lined the southern side of the cemetery, the tree confirmed that nothing untoward had occurred in all its long life, extending back a century or more.

"Have any of the other villages nearby reported any…er…thumb attacks or anything similar?" asked Mari.

"No," replied the vicar. "Not even Upper Warnstow. Are you sure it's not a curse, centered in the village?"

"I am confident it is not," said Mari. She thought for a moment. "It *must* be a shade seeking a missing bone. But that means a recently disturbed grave, or a death, somewhere close to the village."

"I don't think there's been anything like that," said the vicar, her husband nodding confirmation.

"I should have asked Sergeant Breckon if there are any current missing persons," said Mari. "Or a tramp perhaps, dying somewhere nearby."

"Neither one," said the vicar firmly. "It would have come up in the meeting of the parish council this morning, when we decided we needed your assistance."

Mari thought for a moment. A thumb bone separated from a skeleton had to come from somewhere…

"Do you have a local museum?"

The vicar and Lawrence shook their heads.

"What about archaeological excavations? Are there any taking place nearby?"

"No," replied the vicar, but as she spoke, her husband cleared his throat. She looked at him crossly, as if he had interrupted her.

"Not nearby, as such," said Lawrence, with an apologetic glance at his wife. "But I believe there is a dig going on at the upper end of the northernmost arm of Castwell Creek."

"Is there really?" asked the vicar, as Mari said, "How far away is that?"

"A good seven miles as the crow—you might fly," replied Lawrence. "But at least nine miles by road, because you have to go along the New Cut for such a way before the crossing at Bridge. Would you like a rock cake? There is only one left."

Mari took the cake and ate it slowly. It lived up to its name, being very hard indeed. Seven miles was a long way for a shade to go, but it was not impossible. So far, the spirit was not malevolent. But it might become more urgent in its searching, and serious thumb injuries could result. Or become annoyed and take even more drastic action.

One puzzling aspect was that the shade should already have found the thumb bone and taken it back. It ought to be able to sense where it was, unless there was interference of some kind, or it was being moved about. The testing of people's thumbs was also curious, as if the shade hoped to find its own member attached to a living person.

She wondered if she should try to find the thumb bone herself, by divination or augury. But the fact the shade itself was having difficulty suggested this would not be easy. Locating the skeleton the thumb came from should be more straightforward.

"I had better go and have a look at this archaeological dig," she said when the last crumbs of rock cake had cleared her throat. "Though I'd rather not fly. My broom is rather old and needs a rest. Does Sergeant Breckon have a car?"

"He does not," replied the vicar. "But I do. Lawrence shall drive you over immediately."

"Oh yes," said Lawrence mechanically. "Delighted."

The vicar's car turned out to be a well-used but apparently entirely unsprung two-seat roadster of considerable vintage. It was even more uncomfortable than Mari's broom. The rock cake also sat uncomfortably in her stomach, and several times threatened to rise as they hit a pothole or bounced over a flurry of flood-scoured ridges in the road.

It seemed considerably further than nine miles, much of it beetling along the raised road alongside the New Cut before crossing the iron bridge at Bridge, only to go back up the Cut on the other side. From there they took a road between two long, thin arms of the estuary, the narrow strip of bitumen often lower than the water on either side, protected from inundation only by turfed-over banks that did not seem sufficiently high or thick.

The dig itself turned out to be in a creek that joined the left-hand arm of the estuary. Several cars, a motorcycle and a lorry were drawn up on a hummock of raised ground at this conjunction of the waters.

When Lawrence parked the two-seater, Mari stood up on her seat and saw that the tidal creek was dry, the sea kept back by a coffer dam made of sandbags and heavy beams of timber. Behind the dam, silt and mud had been carefully dug away down at least a dozen feet to reveal a buried longboat, its timbers still solid but dark as pitch from their long submergence.

Several people were digging in various corners of the boat, all of them quite young. Undergraduate archaeologists. Mari was familiar with the breed.

More importantly, from Mari's point of view, were the tall, rune-carved willow wands topped with silver lamps that surrounded the lip of the excavation, one every seven paces, in the orthodox pattern. These were ghost-wards, deployed to prevent any shade or revenant from rising from the burial ship—as this had to be—to terrorize the surrounding countryside.

The willow wands were twinned with shorter rods of spell-engraved iron, thief-wards designed to keep people out, save for those mentioned by name in the warding spells.

Mari nodded to herself and climbed out of the car, pausing to push out and don her pointy hat. Lawrence followed, falling a few steps behind, his accustomed spot behind his wife, the vicar.

They had just reached the creek-side when one of the archaeologists in the boat saw them and called out.

"Hello! Stop there, please! The wards won't let you past. I'll come up."

He was older than the others. Although he wore the same colorful cravat, untidy shirt, loose bags and tennis shoes as the students, male and female, he also wore an iron necklace tucked under the cravat, plus a tweed coat with heavily overloaded pockets, a symbol of authority and absentmindedness. Mari knew he would be roughly her equivalent, a junior fellow or something similar, recently awarded his doctorate, and here in charge for the first time on his own dig.

"Hello, hello," he called again as he nimbly made his way up a ladder to the creek bed and then scrambled up the bank. "What brings a witch and...er...here?"

"I'm temporarily the district witch," replied Mari. She liked this man for his cheerful countenance and greeting. "Dr. Mari Garridge, usually a junior fellow of Ermine College, Hallowsbridge. This is Mr. Lawrence Evenholme, the husband of the vicar at Nether Warnstow, who kindly drove me here."

"Oh yes," replied the man. He offered his hand, apologized for its filthy state, and quickly withdrew it. "I'm Dr. Robert Jacoby. Bob. Or Jac to some folks, take your pick. I'm a treasure-vigile from the museum. Friend's College, originally, though I expect I was up at Hallowsbridge somewhat before your time, Dr. Garridge...

Garridge…um, are you here on official business?"

"I'm afraid so," replied Mari. She paused and tried to frame what she had to say as kindly as possible. A treasure-vigile was a kind of archaeologist who was also something of a wizard, which might mean not much of one at all or the full magic, so this cheerful chap had probably placed the ghost-wards himself. And there was a problem with them.

"Last night a shade haunted Nether Warnstow, I think trying to find its missing thumb bone. I suspect the shade's skeleton is here."

"But…but that's not possible!" exclaimed Jac. He turned and gestured to the willow wands. "I placed the wards before we even started the dig."

"Yes, I see," said Mari. "But I'm afraid you haven't taken something into account."

Jac stared at her, an expression of intense puzzlement screwing up his plain but quite appealing face.

Mari pointed at the coffer dam. The tide was on the ebb, but the muddy, roiling water still came more than halfway up the dam. At the flood tide, it would be only a few feet from the crest—putting the water well above the height of the wands.

It took Jac a long, epiphany-dawning moment to work out what she meant.

"Oh Goddess," he groaned. "Proximity of salt and the action of the sea! How high should I have made the wands?"

"At six-yards distance, one and three quarter times the height of highest water," recited Mari from memory.

"Garridge," said Jac and he groaned again. "You're the sizar who saved Ermine and re-established the bounds…I feel so stupid."

"Wards and binding are my specific area of research," said Mari. "I am sure wizardry is only an adjunct to your archaeological expertise. Can you let us in to take a look at your skeleton?"

"If I've stuffed up the wards, you don't need—"

"Only the ghost-wards are ineffective, the thief-wards are active. Iron-based wards are more resistant to the action of the sea," said Mari. "And…I hate to rub salt in the wound, but you've erred in the opposite direction there, they're almost double the size required, particularly since you've used wrought iron when most people these days use cast, which lessens the efficacy of the spell."

Jac nodded ruefully and ran down the bank to the closest iron thief-ward. Bending over the iron rod he whispered the spell and the visitors' names, and beckoned them to follow him.

The skeleton, when it was finally revealed from under several layers of tarpaulin, was a surprise to Mari, and not a welcome one. The presence of Jac as a treasure-vigile was immediately explained by the great weight of gold and silver and amber and ivory that adorned the skeleton. There was even a jeweled crown upon the skull. The only item that wasn't loaded with gemstones was the axe by the skeleton's side. It looked completely utilitarian.

The quantity of treasure was surprising, but not as much as the fact that the skeleton possessed all its appendages.

"It's got both thumbs," said Lawrence, unnecessarily.

"She," said Jac quickly. "She's a Norse warrior princess. Possibly Inga the Head-Gatherer."

Mari stared down at the skeleton, thinking hard. Her working hypothesis that the thumb bone had to come from this site was shaken, particularly since she also had a strong suspicion of how it had got to Nether Warnstow.

Could there be some other explanation? If the shade wasn't looking for its finger bone, could it be searching for something else?

She knelt down, drew her athame and held it horizontally over the skeleton's hands, concentrating her witchy senses. Some of the skeleton's treasures had once contained mighty magics, but there were only echoes and whispers now. Yet there *had* been something else present, something stronger, she could feel its absence.

"Jac," she said, standing up and sheathing her knife. "May I call you Jac? Princess Inga has rings on each finger, except her left thumb. Was there something there when you first dug her...when you first excavated the skeleton?"

"Gosh," said Jac. "Yes."

He stared at the princess. His four students crept closer and gazed down. One muffled a worried cough, her neighbor looked like he was about to cry, and the other two simultaneously took out their notebooks. Jac produced his notebook as well and frantically searched through it.

"I'll be defrocked," he moaned as he turned the pages. "Losing a relic is practically a capital crime for a treasure-vigile."

"Defrocked?" asked Mari.

"We have a ceremonial uniform," replied Jac despairingly. "They cut your buttons off and break your trowel in a defrocking." He jabbed a finger at his notebook, leaving a dirt smudge on the paper. "Here it is. Left thumb. A relic ring of red dragon bone, one-quarter-inch width, three-quarter-inch diameter, one sixteenth thick, carved with a depiction of serpents entwined...er...possibly mating. Here's a drawing."

He held up his notebook to Mari.

"I suppose one of my team must have taken it," he said gloomily, turning so his back was to his young students. "Or you think I stole it?"

"No, I don't think so," replied Mari encouragingly.

There was a general lessening of anxiety and a couple of sighs of relief, but also general signs of bafflement, particularly from Jac.

"But you said yourself the thief-wards are working," he said. "Loathe as I am to say it, it has to be one of us."

"Then why would the shade be looking for it in Nether Warnstow?" asked Mari. "It is certainly searching for the ring. I think I know where it might be, and how it got there, despite the thief-wards. We'll have to work fast to get it back to the princess before nightfall though. Can you take me back to the village, Lawrence?"

"Certainly," replied the vicar's husband. "This is all terribly interesting."

"Can I come too?" asked Jac. "It is my responsibility."

"You'll have to sit behind on the dicky seat," warned Lawrence. "It won't be comfortable."

"I could follow in my car...no, I suppose not," said Jac. "Even if I promise I won't hare off to catch the Druppe ferry?"

"I really don't think you've stolen the ring," said Mari. "But it probably is better if you come with us."

Mari did not mention the dicky seat would be no more uncomfortable than anywhere else in Lawrence's car. There was also a chance she was wrong and the ring had been stolen by Jac or one of his students. To guard against that possibility, she delivered a witch's glare from under the brim of her hat, encompassing all the students. If she needed to find any of them in the next few days, they would not be able to hide. A few of them winced as her eyes briefly flashed with green fire, but they did not protest.

The drive back passed largely in silence. Jac did not complain about the discomfort of the dicky seat, but he did keep moving, as if there was some chance of achieving a better position.

"Where to, exactly?" asked Lawrence, as they neared the village.

"Do you have a butcher's? Or a general store?"

"Neither one," replied Lawrence proudly. "But Mrs. Hobspawn at The Lamprey can usually spare a few chops or some sausages if anyone's missed a delivery from Hawsey's Meat or the Everything Stores."

"The Lamprey to begin with, then to the village green," said Mari.

#

"Do you really know where the relic ring's got to?" asked Jac plaintively, as Mari emerged from the tempting interior of The Lamprey, bearing a brown-paper-wrapped parcel that was already stained with leaking blood.

She had taken longer than she'd hoped, having to several times decline Mrs. Hobspawn's offer of "one for the road, witches drink on the house." It had been much harder to decline a cup of tea and a massive ham sandwich. She hadn't had lunch and her stomach hadn't recognized the rock cake as food, but as an imposition.

"You'll see," replied Mari. She hoped she sounded more confident than she felt. Her certainty had diminished a little now it was to be put to the test.

Her return to the village had been marked, and the stop at The Lamprey had allowed time for her original welcoming party to gather back at the green, with reinforcement by various other inhabitants of Nether Warnstow. Sergeant Breckon was making himself useful by ushering people back from the road, allowing Lawrence plenty of room to pull up. But they all rushed over again as soon as he turned the engine off.

"Now, now, make way, make way for the district witch!" roared the sergeant.

The crowd parted as Mari walked over to the war memorial, unwrapped her parcel and laid a nice chop on the bottom step. Turning around, she asked Lawrence, "Is your dog's name just Bella?"

"In full it's Isabella Bird, because she's always off exploring the world," said Lawrence, rather surprised. "Oh, her full pedigree name is Isabella Bird Dawn Fire Russet-Russet. Why?"

"You'll see in a minute or two, I hope," replied Mari. "And she'll be fine. Don't worry."

"What—"

Mari drew a slim ivory and silver wand from her sleeve.

Lawrence swallowed his question and there was a general shuffling backward, away from the wand.

She tapped the chop with it, speaking a spell that fell from her lips with a noise like branches scraping across a window, a sound that was either comforting or unsettling depending on what you were expecting. At the end of this strange vocalization, the name "Isabella Bird Dawn Fire Russet-Russet" rang out.

A hushed silence fell. Mari took off her hat, wiped her brow, and put the hat firmly back on again.

There was an "ooh" from the crowd as Bella the russet Labrador ambled across the green, as muddy pawed as ever. Catching sight or scent of the chop, she accelerated, rushed to the step and ate the meat down in several gulps before anyone could think to stop her. Finished, Bella lay down on the step and pretended it hadn't happened.

Mari tapped her on the head with the wand. Surprised, but not upset, Bella sat up on her haunches. A moment later, a slightly rueful expression came over the dog. Her big brown eyes widened, her jaw reluctantly opened and some nasty gagging sounds emanated.

Mari stepped back. Bella lowered her head and vomited profusely on the grass below the step. Chunks of barely chewed chop came out first, followed by more indistinguishable and longer digested mush, and then with another but much louder "ooh" from the crowd, out came a bright red ring of dragon bone, big enough to fit a thumb.

"Thief-wards don't stop *dogs*," explained Mari.

Bella lunged forward to swallow the ring again, but Mari grabbed the dog's collar and hauled her back.

"I'll give that a wash in the pond, shall I?" asked Lawrence. Clearly, as Bella's owner, he felt he was expected to retrieve the ring from the vomit.

"No!" shouted Mari and Jac, but Lawrence had already picked out the ring from the noisome pool. He gripped it gingerly with the tips of his thumb and forefinger, but somehow the ring slid fully on to his thumb.

He gasped, made a choking sound and fell to his knees. Scales began to form on his throat. Shining thumbnail-sized scales of gold-edged scarlet. His back rippled alarmingly with the hint of wings beginning to form. His eyes turned entirely red. The awful dark red that was almost black, like the crusted blood of an old wound.

Mari pointed her wand and began to speak Brythonic words of power. A brute-force attempt to stop the draconic identity subverting any more of poor Lawrence's body before she compelled it to return to the ring.

If she could.

Even after so long immured under the earth, the dragon contained within the ring was powerful. Princess Inga would have known its name and the words to compel its service, but Mari did not. She could only set her strength against the worm.

Power against power, with no finesse.

Even if she won, it would be fatal for Lawrence. His body would be destroyed, either by the dragon's emergence or by the magic Mari must employ to prevent it.

But it had to be done, or the dragon would fully manifest and all the villagers present would die, and many more soon after. Nether

Warnstow and all the villages from the sea to Morcoln would burn, before Sir Henry or some other powerful wizard or witch could intervene.

Mari reached deep inside herself for a word of power that she had learned but never used. But before she could bring it, sharp and terrible, into the world, Jac pushed in front of her. He raised a small, heavily engraved bronze box, with the lid open. It was impossible to see what was inside. Indeed, it didn't seem to have an inside, only an absence of one.

He spoke a simple spell; one Mari did not know and afterwards could not recall.

Next came a painful, metallic ringing, like a cymbal crash-struck too close to Mari's ear. She flinched. Lawrence screamed and roared at the sky, flames bursting from his mouth. A moment later the ring flew from his thumb to the box. Jac slammed the lid shut and locked it with a golden key he wore on the chain of black iron around his neck.

Lawrence fell to the ground. The scales faded from his neck, his clawing hands relaxed, no fire came with his panting breath, his eyes became human once again. Dr. Ware rushed to his side and felt the pulse at his neck.

Mari looked at the box Jac was tucking away inside his coat pocket.

"I might not be good with wards, but I do know a thing or two about powerful ancient relics," he said. "We always have to be ready for little antics like that."

"I'm glad you were," said Mari sincerely. "I think I might have mastered the dragon, but poor Mr. Evenholme would not have survived. As it is, he seems to have escaped the worst. It wasn't in him for long."

Lawrence had managed to sit up. Dr. Ware checked his throat, but not in an urgent, worried way. Most of the other villagers crowded around, asking questions that presaged the likely transformation of this event into years or even decades worth of anecdotes to come.

Mari let Bella go. The dog rushed to her master and began to lick his face. Her vomit-laden breath prompted Lawrence to leap to his feet without assistance, indicating he was recovering very well indeed.

"Lawrence! What are you doing? Why is everyone fussing over you, and what has that dog of yours done now?" The vicar's shrill cries grew louder as she hurried over from the church.

"I think a speedy exit is called for," said Mari.

"Yes," replied Jac, but he made no motion to leave.

"Would you like to have lunch, Dr. Jacoby?" asked Mari. "The food looked rather good at The Lamprey and..." she glanced at the pool of dog vomit nearby and wrinkled her nose "...despite the circumstances, I am absolutely starving."

"I would be delighted, Dr. Garridge," said Jac.

Of course, by the time they'd idled their way to The Lamprey, talking six to the dozen about Norse princesses, capture boxes, the differences in wards of wood and bone and metal, and much else, the lunch hour service was finished, and Bella had somehow got ahead of them and vomited again on the pub's doorstep.

But that is another story.

In Opposition to the Foe

By Pamela Jeffs

The rainforest whispers in a language all its own. Its voice is the drip-drop patter of water to the leaf-littered earth and the cackle of bright-breasted parrots in the canopy. But danger covets the cloak of the forest's dense skirts. It lurks hidden, concealing the wicked teeth and misshapen bodies of those human mutations created in the buru labs but deemed not worthy.

The aliens sent their abominations into the wilderness to die. But humans are strong. Even corrupted, they proved stronger than their creators gave them credit for.

Now, they roam.

They hunt.

And they should be feared, but I'll brave them today. For word runs hot over the buru comms channels. The aliens are planning a search. Unguarded tech rests out here somewhere.

Whispers of a wreck.

A ship I can, maybe, use against the invaders.

I push open the access hatch leading out from the ancient World War II bunker. The wild ginger clump concealing the entrance parts as the door swings on well-oiled hinges. I step clear.

The light is filtered green and the air smells clean outside. Not like the damp, musty corridors below; corridors filled with everything I own—supplies and munitions. I glance back. It's not much, but it keeps me safe and it's a place to call home.

Home.

More like just walls and a roof built from the ruins of our invaded civilisation. But it's all I have left.

No, not quite all.

I glance up. Soleil is where she always is, sleeping in the branches of the tallest tree. As much as I've tried, she refuses to join me below ground. Her eagle head is tucked tight beneath a shining wing and her lion body disappears into the shadows of dense leaves behind. She looks every part a griffin from legend. My heart clenches. As always, I can't help but remember all she was, and that which she no longer is.

If only I had been braver. If only I'd left my hiding place when she had screamed for me.

Her true voice still rings in my mind—

Aster! Help me!

What I wouldn't give to change the past. But I can only influence the future. Only protect her as best I can.

I whistle low. Soleil responds, head emerging and bright eagle eyes blinking. She tips off her branch and glides to the ground. I rest a hand on her beak. She keens quietly in greeting.

"Ready to hunt?" I ask, knowing she understands me but cannot answer.

She tilts her head and her golden eye swivels to mine—an eye weighted with the wisdom only a human soul can own; a human soul tied to a mutated form. I sense her eagerness.

I holster the pump-action shotgun across my back and check my ammo belt. On one hip hangs my grandfather's *xiphos*. The old man gifted the ancient Greek blade to me when we brought Soleil home. Both are my responsibility now.

"Let's go then."

#

The forest never welcomes. It despises our presence here, holding its secrets close. I press forward into the sombre wall of green and black. The vegetation parts reluctantly around me. Spikes pluck at my shirt and the rotten stench of carrion flowers fills my nostrils. I flick away a fly and shoulder my way past a dense curtain of broad-leafed vines. Soleil follows, her cat-like reflexes gifting her silence as she moves through the undergrowth.

A branch creaks.

No sounds are accidental in this place. I ease my loaded shotgun free from the gun slip. The xiphos remains in its scabbard. That's for close fighting and I'm hoping it won't come to that.

Another creak.

My gaze snaps up.

The forest canopy falls silent.

I stretch an arm wide across Soleil's chest. Her wings flare as she shoves her feathered breast against me. Then she stops also, her neck arched back.

We both sense it.

Something approaches.

I lick my lips. A beat of sweat slides down my neck and a mosquito whines by my ear. I glance at Soleil. Her gaze is fixed on the trees.

Snap.

Crack.

The forest erupts.

I squeeze the trigger and the shotgun roars, recoiling through my shoulder. The stench of gunfire chokes the air. The shot hits its mark. A peacock-scaled, half-serpent, half-human female falls from a tree, screaming. Her sibilant cry, slithering from a fanged mouth, burbles away, drowned in the blood-soaked ruin of her lungs. She lands with a muted *thump*, curled auburn hair a shock of color splayed like a carrion flower across the undergrowth. Her viper tail thrashes, scattering leaf litter and gore.

Two more creatures follow. First, a male with muscled forearms and the wicked glare of a deranged psychotic. He aims for Soleil. Her battle cry cuts the air in a shriek that speaks of high places and quick kills. She launches, wings raised and talons extended.

The last creature is mine. I fire. And again. The trigger clicks. *Damn.* Gun's jammed. But my attacker's been hit—left arm bleeding. He snarls, venom on his lips. He isn't ready to end this fight yet. I toss the firearm aside. I'll get it back later. The xiphos rings clear of its scabbard.

But the mutant has already crossed the distance. No room for me to swing. He lunges and the flat of my double-edged blade slaps against his chest. He drives me down, coiling his sleek tail to pin my legs. This close, his hot breath smells of rot and sulphurous venom. Clawed fingers find my throat and squeeze. A grip like iron.

My gritted teeth slip and cut my tongue and I taste blood. My lungs burn. I buck and push harder on the blade, trying to twist it, trying to cut the scaled chest pressing down on me. The viper-man's mouth widens, fangs just a handspan from my shoulder.

This is a stupid way to die.

A stupid place to die.

The soundtrack of Soleil's battle plays somewhere behind me. Hisses versus eagle cry.

"Hih! Hih!" A stranger's voice.

The pressure on my neck eases. A trickle of air rakes its way into my lungs. I cough. The mutant looks up and away. His features change—a predator suddenly made prey.

He slithers off me. With a flick of his tail he retreats, scaling the nearest tree and disappearing into the canopy. Nearby, the rustle of leaves betrays the departure of Soleil's opponent. I lie on the rich-smelling ground, exhausted. Soleil, breathing heavily, moves to stand over me, her stance tense. She cries out a challenge.

I sit up. Everything hurts.

And I see him.

In the clearing with a worn blaster held in one hand and my shotgun in the other.

A buru.

Shit.

#

The buru points both weapons down and away. A sign of peace? Impossible. His kind doesn't collaborate. They care only for the conquering of planets and the mutation of any native species. Universal domination is their aim.

I keep my blade raised.

The alien moves forward with languid grace—long-limbed and lithe with blue dreadlocks coiling past his gold-skinned cheeks and over his shoulders. His eyes are the cruel doorways to his soul, solid orbs of scarlet.

He points to Soleil. "How did you tame that griffinous?"

I've never heard a buru speak before. Heavily accented, he sounds something almost between a Greek and French person trying to speak English.

"She's got a name. Soleil."

His chin tilts. "Soleil. How is it she is so quiet?"

I can't tell him even if I wanted to. She has always been that way around me, like I tether her to reality or the past, somehow. "She's special."

He moves closer still, a cautious step—the type you take when approaching a wild animal. His black metal armor seems to soak up the light.

"Were either of you bitten?" he asks. "I can help you, if you will let me."

My hand tightens around the hilt of my blade. "You help us, buru?"

The alien's thin lips quirk up. "I have a name, also. Dinuth."

"I don't care."

"Perhaps you should. Some say I am special too."

I get to my knees. "I don't believe you."

But before Dinuth answers, Soleil stumbles. Her legs crumble and her head collides with the ground.

"No!" I cry, scrabbling to her. Froth bubbles from her beak, her gaze roams wildly, following shadows that I can't see. The buru appears by her head. He runs a long-fingered hand over her beak and down her neck. His blood-colored eyes flick to mine.

"She's been bitten. Viperion venom will kill her within the hour unless you let me help her."

Viperions. So that's what his kind calls those human-snake hybrids.

"You bastards made those things."

"Yes. But I can save her from them, too."

I glare at him then look back at Soleil.

I can't help her.

But maybe he can.

"She dies and I'll kill you. You hand us over to other buru to experiment on and I kill you."

Dinuth moves to my side and hands my shotgun over. "We are without issue then, for I have no desire to depart this life, I assure you."

#

Dinuth leads me, deeper than I have ever gone, into the forest. At over seven feet tall, he is plenty strong enough to carry Soleil. Still unconscious, she hangs draped over his shoulder, her avian head bumping gently against his back. I'm reminded of a chicken I saw as a child—a bird with a broken neck strung up on a line and swaying in the wind.

The forest floor gives way to bog, and the trees here show signs of dying—withered leaves on finger-like twigs and bark peeling away to reveal silvered heartwood. The stink of decaying vegetation rises around me, a miasma that clings like a damp, mouldy shirt. My boots mire in black mud, but it doesn't slow Dinuth. Head down, he's on a mission and it's my problem to keep up. My bruised throat aches as I suck in urgent breaths.

The tree trunks grow blacker. The smell grows worse and then the forest parts.

The buru pauses at the edge of a dark lake. An errant breeze ruffles from across the water to kiss my brow, carrying with it the scent of stagnant salt. Dead trees circle the bank—white, skeletal limbs frozen in the rictus of death. But the black and white landscape pales in comparison to that which lies half-submerged in the lake.

A wreck, ten stories tall.

It's all that remains of a buru scientific cruiser.

I've seen what they do in those transports…and it's the same type of cruiser I saved Soleil from.

A chill crawls up my spine.

Nothing about this is good.

The visible portion of the ship's hull towers over water that reflects like a mirror. A rusted metal skin, pitted with corrosion, rolls over the ship's hollow bones. Ragged holes, bitter eyes of darkness, mar the structure just above the waterline.

"There is no way we are going in there."

Dinuth turns. His brow furrows. "My workshop is inside. What we need to save her is there."

"This is a buru science facility."

"Once perhaps. Not now."

I rest a hand on the pommel of my xiphos. "I'm not an idiot. Soleil and I go in there, we don't come out the same."

The alien's gaze flicks to my hand then back. He shakes his head. "This facility was destroyed by a storm many years ago. The other buru have since dismissed it. You are safe here."

"No, we are not. I heard them on the comms. They're looking for this place."

Again, Dinuth shakes his head. "No. They seek a different fallen ship. One that malfunctioned two days ago and fell closer to the ocean."

So, this isn't the wreck I was chasing.

"Please," says Dinuth, voice anxious. "This delay may cost your friend her life."

I glare at him. "She isn't my friend. She's my sister—or what your people left of her."

The lines of Dinuth's face deepen. His eyes lower a moment, long black lashes brushing his cheek. He clears his throat.

"A sibling, you say? And one with close-matching DNA, I'd hazard."

"We are—were—twins," I admit.

"Rare," says Dinuth. "An important discovery. Interesting, though, that you were kept human and they changed her."

"They didn't do it on purpose. I was never captured. Soleil was."

Dinuth frowns, eyes full of pity I don't need from the likes of him.

"I see," he says. "Still, fascinating that your familial connection was enough to keep her tame. Most others…" he glances at the forest "…turn to madness. She is a perfect specimen."

"Specimen?" I spit. "She was a perfect human being!"

Dinuth's lips press thin. "And perhaps she can be again. Come. Let me show you."

I clench my teeth and consider pulling my blade as he presses two fingers to his lips. A long, low whistle echoes across the lake.

"Look," he whispers, pointing to the wrecked ship.

A small, white face appears at the lower edge of the largest hole in the ship's hull. The child waves a hand and then disappears.

An undeniably human hand.

An unbound human on a buru ship?

My curiosity is piqued. Humans are never allowed to roam free around buru. I'd raided enough ships in my search to find Soleil to know. I've seen terrible things. Humans chained and experimented on; the savageness of the resulting abominations—creatures I have no names for.

"Will you trust me or let your sister die?" asks Dinuth.

Soleil stirs on his shoulder and falls limp again.

I have no choice. "Trust? Never. But for my sister's sake, I'll come."

"Good."

Dinuth presses a button on the inside of his armored wrist. The edge of the lake boils in response. Black, stinking sediment rises, coiling just beneath the surface of the water. Then a small platform breaks clear. It stops, dripping mud, and hovers just above the lake's surface. The buru leaps onto it and beckons. Against my better judgement, I follow.

#

The facility looks even more decrepit up close. The traveling platform halts outside the largest hole. The small, white, human face resolves into that of a young girl—well almost. She looks human except for yellow eyes and a dusting of rainbow-colored feathers where her eyebrows should have been.

"Dinuth!" cries the girl and launches herself to embrace the alien's leg.

The buru places a large hand on her golden hair. "Well met, Jane. But we have guests who are injured. Run. Tell the others to prepare the vaccine chamber."

Jane peeks around the alien's muscled leg. "You're lucky he found you, you know." Then she smiles. "Don't look so afraid. You're safe here."

#

The vaccine chamber is the one place so far on the ship that looks cared for. Rusted gantries and ruined quarters lined the journey to this room, but here the metal surfaces look newly made, gleaming like ice under the glare of acid white lights.

Dinuth places Soleil on a steel bench. He adjusts her wings and legs to rest comfortably and then reaches for a tube tied to a frame above. He inserts its needle end into her foreleg. My sister doesn't move. I fear she is already dead.

He presses a button on a panel below the bench. Thick purple liquid courses down the clear tube and into my sister's leg. She takes a deep breath and then settles back. The alien's shoulders slump and his head bows for a moment.

"We made it. Your sister will live." He sounds weary.

"What are you putting in her?"

Dinuth looks up. "Viperion vaccine." He straightens. "I am a chemist. I have developed vaccines for most venoms from reptile-human mutations."

"Why would you do that?"

"I developed them while trying to perfect the process for my other work."

Uneasy, I swallow. "What other work?"

"I can show you."

I glance at Soleil.

"Your sister will remain asleep for a short while. We will return before she wakes."

I don't want to leave her, but the need to have questions answered presses more urgently. I nod and Dinuth heads for the door.

Dim light filters down through the ragged holes in the hull to light the gantries. They crisscross the vaulted, cavernous space within the ship like tendons through a body. As we move deeper, the structures seem to be in better repair. But the stink of the lake lingers, a pervasive stench.

Dinuth's boots clang against the metal grates. The light grows dimmer still as we move down another level. The black, oily looking lake ripples far below. Gently swelling, its surface catches light in places it shouldn't. I'll bet death lingers in that water. This ship is as good as a tomb.

The gantry ends at an access hatch. The use of many hands has worn rust off the handle. Dinuth pushes on it and the door creaks open. Inside is a balcony and staircase that looks over a room filled with white electric light and laughter.

Dinuth moves to one side as I step across the threshold. I stare in wonder at the group of human children clustered around a table. They are eating food I haven't seen in many long years. The scents of garlic and warm bread make my mouth water—roasted mushrooms and lemon juice over warm, steaming fish.

How can there be humans here? I count at least ten in all. I glance back at Dinuth, lost for words. His lip quirks up, his blood-red eyes suddenly don't seem so terrifying.

He holds a hand out over the scene. "My work," he says. "A cure for mutation."

My sister's face flashes before me.

"You can change mutants back?" I whisper the words, afraid their truth is so fragile as to fade away.

"Well, almost," says Dinuth. "The process has not been perfected. I am as yet unable to split away all the genetic modifications, but they are as close to human as they can get."

I spot Jane at a far table. Her feathered brow glistens in the light. She seems human enough for the small addition not to matter.

"Why?" I ask. "Why would you mutate us if you mean to change us back?"

"I do not represent buru interests," says Dinuth. "In their opinion, I would be considered a traitor."

My eyes narrow. I consider his admission—try to work his angle. Why would he want these human children? Why would he collect them here? Is he trying to create a child army to draw out the last vestiges of humanity still resisting his kind?

Dinuth must sense my hesitation. "These children are here because it is not safe for them to reside outside. They would be captured again and the other buru would discover my work. They would come for me and destroy everything."

"Why do you care about humans?"

Dinuth tilts his chin. "I was not always buru," he says. "I came from another place—a peaceful world—also invaded by them. All my people were mutated into hybrid creatures—made into mindless warriors. I alone was permitted to keep my free mind because of my knowledge of chemical compounds. I could help the buru create new crossbreed species—make stronger soldiers for their armies. But to control me, they changed me—mutated me into their image."

He grabs his own chin. "This is not the face I was born with. I know what it is to lose yourself, to have your essence corrupted." His gaze grows distant. "So, I learned their methods. I perfected the science. And then I escaped. Now I work to at least give your kind back their identity. I wish to save humanity."

And I believe him. I'm not sure why, but I do. I've killed a hundred buru in my quest to save my sister. Looked into those hundred pairs of eyes as the light faded from them. Never once have I seen the torment I now see in Dinuth's gaze.

I glance back at the groups of children laughing below. "And you can do this for my sister? You can change her back."

Dinuth nods. "I already have. I added the modifier to the vaccine. Your sister will be herself when you return."

My chest squeezes and my eyes burn with tears I have held back for ten years. My sister. I'll finally be able to tell her that I am sorry.

#

An explosion rocks the ruined vessel. The hull groans and a rain of rust, debris, and embers falls from the tattered hull. We collapse to the gantry, choking on the filthy air.

I cough. "What the hell was that?"

"Buru weaponry," says Dinuth. "Missile by the sound of it. How did they find me?"

"I told you they were coming!"

The muscles in the alien's cheeks bunch. He knows as well as I do that it doesn't matter how they got here. We just need to get out.

Dinuth stands. "They'll send in their mutants next. We need to get to the weapons store."

"How far away is that?"

He points to the roof. "Maybe too far."

I look up. Dusk's red glow filters through the holes in the hull. Then the light disappears as a wave of shadows flood across. Shapes shift and blur. A horde of mutated bodies—an army—coming to snuff out the spark of hope that Dinuth has built here.

He places an urgent hand on my shoulder and squeezes. "Please. Go back and protect the children. I'll get your sister and additional weapons. We will make our stand in the common room."

I hesitate, unsure. Do I get my sister and run or stand and fight with this buru traitor?

"Surely you trust me by now?" asks Dinuth.

"Okay." I pull out my xiphos and hand it to him. He takes it, wide-eyed.

"I'll give you five minutes," I say, "then I'm coming to get my blade back from you."

Dinuth's smile is grim. He nods and turns, gone before I even know he's left.

#

The children are huddled under tables pulled together in a type of fort. The younger ones are crying, tears falling down their smooth, pink cheeks. The older children stand ready with makeshift weapons—pots and kitchen knives. They tense as I enter.

"I'm here to help." I move forward, but the children are wary.

"Who are you?" calls an older boy with slit-pupiled eyes like a lizard's.

Jane crawls out from under a table. Her hair has fallen free of its ponytail. "She's with Dinuth," she says to the boy. "She's got a sister here being changed back. We can trust her."

The boy's eyes narrow but then he nods. He hands me his kitchen knife.

I reach back and pull my shotgun free. I tap my belt and the eighteen cartridges stored there.

"Thanks, but I've got my own weapon."

The younger children grow quiet, and the room falls silent but for the sound of breathing. Outside, mutants roam, claws clicking over metal and raucous voices screaming in languages that have nothing to do with being human.

The seconds pass. One minute turns to four. The tearing of metal screeches out closer than before; sounds like the hull is being sheared open.

Five minutes. Still no Dinuth.

I wrack my mind, trying to recall other buru ships I infiltrated in the past. My gaze slews to the far workbenches that serve here as the kitchen. The eyehooks welded into the surfaces are something I have seen before—this was a human bonding room.

There are large drainage ducts below those benches.

"Quickly, children," I whisper as the noises outside the room grow louder. "To the benches." I sprint the fifteen meters and drop to the ground. I take the knife off the boy and wedge the tip into the metal plate flooring. A grated panel slides free to reveal a dark passage below.

"Get in here," I say to the huddled children. "These ducts will conceal you while I go to find Dinuth. Crawl down as far as you can." I hand the knife back to the boy. "When you reach water, start prying at the side panels. They'll open to the hull's skin. Swim for the forest."

"But there are monsters there," whimpers Jane.

"There are more monsters here," I say. "You have a better chance of survival hidden in the trees."

I look to the older boy. "Get them across the lake and into the forest. Head north until you find the corpse of a female snake mutant. Go about sixty meters further on into the undergrowth. Behind the wild ginger clump there's a hatch to underground bunker—my home. Hide there and we will come for you."

The boy nods and disappears into the duct. The others follow.

Only Jane hesitates. "Promise you will come for us?"

A smile is all I have to comfort her. "I promise."

She disappears into the hole. I replace the plate and stand. Time to find Dinuth and my sister.

#

The ruined ship crawls with mutants. Viperions, griffinous, and others I cannot name, but all equally as terrifying. I cling to the shadows easing my way along the gantry towards Soleil's room. My gun is loaded and ready to fire.

Ahead, a commotion. A group of humanoid insects, by the look of their diaphanous wings, faceted eyes and black exoskeletons. They batter at a door with a rusty beam, chittering and cackling as the door shudders with each hit. Something in there has drawn their attention. It can only be one thing.

I aim and fire. The first shots plow into the mutants. Some fall and others flit away to hover in the darkness. I reload, the pump action sliding smoothly. I fire again, surging ahead. My back meets the damaged door. I yell out.

"It's me. Let me in!"

The door creaks open and Dinuth pulls me through. The metal panel slams shut and the hatch is sealed.

"Where are the children?" he snarls. His armor is scratched and mired with blood. The fight to this room doesn't seem to have been easy.

"Getting off this ship."

"You have as good as murdered them!"

"No," I growl back. "I gave them a chance to live. We'll die if we stay here."

Dinuth scowls but what can he do? He swings away. A vial of vaccine glistens purple at his belt.

The battering outside starts again.

He turns back, face resolute, and steps to one side.

But I barely see him.

Because *she* is standing just behind him, dressed in buru armor and with my xiphos held tightly in her right hand.

Soleil.

Tall, blonde, and eyes like a summer sky.

My sister is human again.

Almost.

At her throat, she wears a collar of pure white feathers.

"Aster?" Her voice is a whisper, as if she has forgotten how to speak our language.

"Oh god," I sob. Tears brim over and my throat feels dry. So many things to say but the hammering outside grows more insistent.

Not nearly enough time to say it all.

So, I holster my gun and run to her.

She feels bird-like and featherlight in the circle of my arms.

"It's okay," she whispers into my ear. "I know and I love you, too."

But no time to linger. I pull back and smile at her. "Ready to hunt?"

She nods, grinning, and together, we turn to face the door.

Soleil wields the blade. I hold the shotgun. Dinuth, unable to secure other weapons, has only his blaster but, old as it is, I doubt it's worth the metal it's made from.

The door buckles. Another hit and it skews sideways, ragged lock left hanging. The insects outside see us through the gap. They grow agitated. Claws rake at the opening, wings clatter and batter like panels of fragile plastic against the door pillar.

"Hold steady," whispers Dinuth.

I can almost taste his fear—it has the same flavour as my own. Beside me, Soleil shifts and gulps. She has never fought anyone while in human form. But her jaw hardens and her grip on the weapon is steady.

The door falls inwards and the mutants heave forward. Black carapaces glint in the light and razor claws scrabble across the panelled metal floor. The room fills with their inhuman voices and the stench of their carrion-laced breaths.

Dinuth moves first. His blaster sizzles a bolt of energy into the foremost insectoid. It falls into a pile of smoking ash. The others crawl over it—uncaring. Dinuth fires again, but this time the blaster fails, the old tech ruined by neglect.

I step into the breach. The shotgun roars and more mutants fall, their gore splattering the floor. But it's not enough. Soleil dances into the fight, light-footed and quick. Wielding the xiphos in one hand, she carves it into the wall of thick, brittle chitin. The blade glimmers, an arc of polished steel. Wing fragments fly, floating like pearlescent glitter. Black blood follows, splattering her face and the wall and the floor.

Dinuth uses the blaster like a club. A mutant ducks past his defenses and plunges its razor-tipped claws through a gap in his armor. Between the hip and the abdomen. Dinuth grunts and punches the creature in the face. It falls backwards, and so does he.

Overwhelmed by the numbers, I fire round after round. The chamber clicks empty. My last nine rounds are loaded. My empty ammo belt feels too light for comfort. I shoot again.

The gun jams.

"Shit, not again," I snarl, working to clear the breach. It frees. I snap the gun back to my shoulder and squeeze the trigger. The recoil is a bitch when this time it fires.

Bodies pile up against the opening. One shot. Two. More shots. Then nothing moves in the doorway. It's blocked. The other mutants can't get through. I glance down. Still got two bullets left.

Soleil, splattered with black blood and xiphos in hand, stands breathless by the door.

"Is he okay?" she asks, eyes on Dinuth.

I kneel by the buru. His hand flutters by his belt. The vial. But it lies shattered at his side, purple liquid scattered across the ground.

His fingers touch the fluid and his breath catches. His eyes close. "It's gone," he says. "Everything I worked for. Lost. The buru have won."

But I'm not willing to let these goddamned aliens win.

"Not yet they haven't." I tear a strip of fabric from the hem of my shirt and plug his wound. "Here hold this," I say.

Dinuth presses his palm to the wad. "What are you doing?"

"Getting us the hell out of here."

"But the formula is gone."

I lean in close to his face. "But you aren't. You created it before and you can do it again. And maybe, just maybe, you can perfect it with the help of me and Soleil. Maybe our DNA is the answer. One was mutated, one not. That's what you need, isn't it? A comparison?"

Dinuth's eyes widen.

"Now, I'm going to get us all out of here," I say. "We get the kids and we set up a new lab in my bunker."

"And get back to work," whispers Dinuth.

"Exactly. We have aliens to destroy and humanity to save."

I turn to my sister. "Hand me that blade."

She nods and takes my shotgun. Her gaze catches mine. She smiles. My heart squeezes again. It's so good to have her back.

Then I press the tip of the xiphos to the metal plate in the floor.

It lifts.

The darkness of the duct beneath beckons.

The Echo of Love

By Marianne de Pierres

Professor Kyne? The stationmaster would like to see you.

Kyne paused his case book and replayed the message from his Mind-Aide to confirm that he'd heard correctly. With a speech to write, and at least a hundred case files left to review before the official opening of Leto Station's new science wing, it was both a surprising and unwelcome interruption.

But not one he could ignore. The message had not only cut into his direct private audio feed but was blinking with a priority alert on his virtual eyewall *and* all his external screens as well.

"In reference to…?" he asked his M-A.

A topic has not been flagged, Professor. But the priority is red.

Kyne pulled the patch from his ears in exasperation. What could Floraboden possibly want with him? The stationmaster usually only deigned to give his time to the physicists and the astromeins. No one ever took an interest in Kyne's work. Psycho-realism was seen as the poorest relative of psychiatry and the hard sciences. Fools!

He stood, stretched, and waved his fingers in a practiced pattern. The nano-receptors around his workstation fed the gestures into a decoder, which set the station to lock. The screen, his case books, and documents all turned blank.

He locked his office as he left—even though no one came to Floor 773 unless they were lost—and stalked to the airvator shaft without passing a single person. He knew every ripple in the insulation and every ding on the exposed piping that ran along the ceiling, but today he didn't pay them mind.

Even when the air-cushioned tube lift opened, he remained deep in contemplation of his research. Maybe this was his opportunity to ask Floraboden for a research grant. Two years into his study, his sample group remained frustratingly limited to station personnel and employees from the Leto–Bellatrix service shuttles. He needed a wider sample to gain credibility.

"Floor 550 on priority," he told his M-A. It sent his request to station logistics, who rerouted the airvator into an express channel. At least he wouldn't have to travel with the public.

Ten minutes later, Kyne stepped out.

The lights in the corridors were brighter up here, the smell cleaner. It seemed that the lower in the station you worked or lived, the more the sweet stench of carbon tetrachloride tainted your life.

Kyne waited in front of the security scanner. The stationmaster's Lostolian valet came out to greet him and ushered him into the screening parlor.

He took care not to touch the creature. Lostolians' personalities— along with their skin—were too tightly stretched and easily torn. Arrogance seemed to be their species' default. They made great bureaucrats, always fussing over something.

Not that Space Station Leto was a place for species prejudice. Three hundred and fifty-four different types of sentients resided here. Tolerance was another key parameter for selection, and Kyne had rated highly on the species-empathy scale. He knew how to fudge a test. He'd designed enough of them.

"The stationmaster is waiting for you," said the valet.

Kyne resisted apologizing. He'd come as quickly as he could. Instead, he walked straight-backed into the chilled inner sanctum.

Stationmaster Floraboden stood in between two nano-generators with his eyes closed. Kyne could see their little winking lights at work.

Other than that, the room was sparse: two kneeling chairs facing each other, a food dispenser, and a multidimensional picture of a cobalt-blue planet.

Please wait while Stationmaster Floraboden disengages from virtual, Kyne's M-A told him.

Kyne sank onto the cushioned pad of one of the two kneel chairs. A trifle confrontational. Not all the species on this station would be able to fit on, or be appreciative of, the proximity of these chairs. Clearly the ergonomic designers hadn't consulted a behaviorist.

"Welcome, Professor," said Floraboden joining him on the opposite chair. "I know you don't like to be disturbed when you're working, but I have a unique situation and…an opportunity for you. However, this requires the highest security clearance. I would need certain assurances on your part."

Kyne experienced an unsettling sensation in his stomach. "Is it dangerous?"

"Not inherently," said Floraboden evasively.

Kyne observed the man's movements and replayed the tone of his voice in his mind. The stationmaster was hiding something. "Why would you require *me* for this high security…situation?"

"Your research and your talent for interpreting voice are uniquely suited to the task."

"Indeed?" Kyne's curiosity was piqued, and he relaxed. He'd never had someone of the stationmaster's status give kudos to his work before. Perhaps an opportunity had finally come his way.

"What's required for me to gain clearance?" Kyne asked.

"Just a signatory assurance that you'll abide by our protocols, and of course, a prosecutable declaration you won't discuss your involvement with anyone."

"And my recompense for such a commitment?"

Floraboden's smile crinkled his face all the way to his ears. "I thought you might have some ideas on that. What would you like, Professor Kyne? What would be suitable reparation for assisting us to maintain the safety and wellbeing of your home?"

The stationmaster delivered the veiled rebuke with perfect good humor, as though it wasn't really one at all.

But Kyne knew exactly what he wanted. "I should like to be moved to an office in the new science wing, next door to Dr. Dente Freeburg."

Floraboden's eyebrows shot upward. "Professor Freeburg is our leading physicist and astronomein. The new wing is for the hard sciences."

"A profoundly ignorant decision, if I may say," said Kyne.

"Aaah," said Floraboden nodding his head. "You're an activist in the war of the sciences?"

"I decry the physicists and astronomeins hegemony's stranglehold on public perception. Yes."

"Quite," said Floraboden. "Well, let me see what's available."

He lifted a hand and wove a quick, new pattern with his fingers.

His eyes glazed but remained open. The receptor implants across his forehead and down the left side of his face winked in a mesmerizing light pattern.

Most station operators could manage a decent load of procedures from anywhere on the station while still engaged in the real world. Floraboden, however, was renowned for his ability to compartmentalize and endlessly multitask. It was a stationmaster's lot.

"I can agree to your request," said Floraboden eventually.

"It must have an external view," added Kyne. "I want to see outside."

Floraboden scowled and twitched his fingers. Then he rose and returned to his command field.

The door opened behind Kyne, and Floraboden's valet entered.

"Your request has been approved. Please follow me to give your signatory," said the Lostolian.

Kyne glanced back at Floraboden, but the stationmaster had already resubmerged into station space, his eyes shut, and both hands conducting with fervor.

How annoying that the only person Kyne had spoken to in the last month didn't have the courtesy to say goodbye.

#

It was a full day before Kyne found out what he'd signed up for. The guard escorts who came for him the following morning wore station insignia and armed-combat suits.

His stomach tightened. "Am I in danger?"

None of them saw fit to reply, other than to insist—with gestures only—that he should don a privacy helmet, so he remained blind in transit.

To allay his jitters, Kyne imagineered himself in his new office with his name plate outside on the wall next to Freeburg's. He concentrated on picturing the physicists' faces when a psycho-realist moved in among them. *Sometimes, you have to fabricate your own success.* Being in the hard-science wing would give his work some solid exposure. For one thing, it meant an automatic invite to the Scientists' Union tri-cyclic symposium.

The very idea broke a fine sweat on his skin.

So deep were his contemplations that Kyne lost track of direction and time. He only roused from them when a guard tapped his shoulder and removed his helmet.

They'd brought him to a small room, even by station standards, which comprised an armchair, three gray titanium walls, and an interactive screen as the fourth wall. The screen was inactive.

The guard proffered him a tube of water. When Kyne accepted it, the guard left the room. The door shut after him with discernible finality.

Kyne stood, holding the tube. What next?

"Please be seated, Professor Kyne," said Floraboden's voice.

The screen flickered alive and the stationmaster's head and shoulders appeared in sharp definition. The ridge of flesh along his hairline was stained from medical scans from the implants. Stationmasters were prone to cranial bleeds.

"On the other side of this screen we are detaining an A-Class alien. We would like you to begin some preliminary discourse with the creature. As your specialty is psychic interior realism, we believe that you can bring us some insight into the true nature of this creature."

"That's it? You want me to just talk to an A-Class?"

"Yes."

"But I haven't prepared. I need a profile tracker."

"We'd prefer you did this on instinct and gave a spontaneous verbal report after every meeting."

Kyne shook his head. This was most inappropriate. Most *unscientific*. "What can you tell me about the A-Class?"

"Our forward scout found...her—I use the gender tag in a qualified manner, for ease of discussion—in the brig of a JetShift trader. The humanesque crew were all dead. She seems to be able to communicate in our language and has chosen to be known as Sarin."

"Sarin is the fourth brightest star in the Hercules constellation."

"Indeed, Professor."

"What does *she* look like?" asked Kyne, stepping closer to the screen.

"It's unclear. Sarin is encased in an opaque crystalline structure. "She has described it as her cocoon. She chose that description, she said, so that we could conceptualize it."

"Fascinating," said Kyne. "Did the JetShift logs explain more?"

"No. You'll spend an hour with Sarin today, and every day hereafter, until we know enough. The guards will collect you from your rooms every morning and return you afterwards."

"What if I should like to stay longer with Sarin?"

"That will not be permitted."

Kyne sucked in a breath. He was not used to such confining parameters when working with test subjects. Still, this could look good on his resume. "Floraboden, is this blindfold nonsense truly necessary?"

"Good luck, Professor," said the stationmaster, ignoring his question. The image faded out.

The texture and color of the screen changed, and Kyne saw the outline of a sarcophagus-like structure in an otherwise empty space. He seated himself and leaned forward and studied the dimensions. It appeared—if the scale was true—to be a little longer and wider than the dimensions of an average female humanesque.

"Hello, Sarin," he said, not sure what else to do.

"Hello, Professor Kyne. Stationmaster Floraboden told me to expect you."

Her tone, though a little husky, was a perfect replication of the Mintakan accent. Humanesques in this sector of Orion clipped the end of their words. It was quite attractive to a Procyonite like Kyne who was used to the sound of his language bubbling like air in a water pipe.

"Are you comfortable with being called Sarin?"

There was a long pause, then she replied, "It's my name."

Kyne nodded, even though she couldn't see him. He felt the mantle of his professional persona slip across him. "You may call me Professor or just Kyne."

"Just Kyne. That is an unusual name even for your kind."

That made him smile. "It's not my name, Sarin. It's semantics. Calling me Kyne will be sufficient. Our scout found you on board a damaged ship. Do you know what happened to the crew?"

"Interrogatives are not appropriate among my kind until a couple knows each other well."

Kyne raised his eyebrows at the crystalline structure. "Are we a couple, Sarin?"

The A-Class was silent for a moment. "That was clever of you, Just Kyne. Creating intimacy from nothing."

Kyne took a moment to consider her response then said, "I apologize if questions make you uncomfortable. It's an accepted form of communication among humanesques. If you tolerate my lapses, I will attempt to reframe my speech, until we know each other better."

"Your response is appropriate."

"Good. Now...you were alone on a deserted JetShift."

"It was not my choice."

"Did they capture you? I'm sorry, let me try that again...According to what we could tell, the JetShift had been occupied by pirates." Kyne made that up. But it seemed a reasonable assumption. Traders and pirates were interchangeable in this sector.

"I appreciate your attempted sensitivity with interrogatives, Just Kyne. However, I am not sure what a pirate is."

"A vagabond. A scavenger. Pirates operate outside constellation laws."

"I heard my captives speak of Orion. I believed it to be the name they give this area of space."

"Place names are only useful if everyone knows their locations."

"I would agree. Our cluster-space ☐ ☐☐ will not be familiar to you." The sound she made was utterly strange and discordant.

"Or, it may be familiar, but not as that," he said.

"Of course."

"Perhaps I will bring a celestial map on my next visit. We could exchange neighborhoods."

"You sound coy, Just Kyne."

"*Coy* is a very advanced linguistic concept, Sarin. I'm impressed by your command of our language."

"I have also learned that humanesques use flattery as deception."

"I had not intended deception. I only seek veracity."

"My apologies. *They* used a similar tone to yours. It was followed by either falsehood or demands. It is reasonable that I assume you would do the same."

A little surge of excitement prickled across his skin. He felt intrigued and unexpectedly aroused. It was a long time since he'd had an interesting and challenging conversation with a female...

A-Class alien female. He frowned. Inside that casing, she could be the shape of a jellypod.

"On my next visit, I'll bring you some music to listen to," he said. "I find it soothing and uplifting. Perhaps it will have the same effect on you, Sarin. It also speaks to the nature of our species."

She didn't reply immediately, but Kyne noticed the sarcophagus infusing with a rosy color.

"You've changed color," he said, delighted. "I find that hue warm and pleasant. I shall assume that it's a sign of your approval."

The color deepened.

Kyne spontaneously reached out to touch the screen between them, but as his fingers contacted the surface it went blank. "Sarin?"

The door in the side wall slid open and one of the guards burst in. He lifted Kyne from his chair and roughly bundled him into the corridor.

"What is this? My hour with the A-Class isn't finished! And your manner is unacceptable!" protested Kyne. "I'm an esteemed member of the station scientific community. You c-cannot treat me this way!"

He would've said a lot more, but a four-guard escort formed around him and began to move. He had to lift his knees and jog to keep from being trampled by them.

The guards maintained a silent and threatening manner on the trip back to his rooms.

Kyne squirmed in their grip. But they held fast, implacable, and unyielding.

Ridiculous! Excessive! He tried to send a complaint to the stationmaster as soon as he was alone again.

Stationmaster Floraboden is engaged in a Level Five scan and unable to be disturbed. His M-A sounded annoyingly prim.

Kyne swore and poured himself a double measure of Mintakan port. The sweet, thick wine coated the raw anger burning his throat, and soon he settled at his desk to select music for Sarin.

His visits to her followed a pattern after that: somber and silent guard escorts, time in the little interview room communing with Sarin, then a somber and silent return. Kyne was careful not to touch the screen in the interview room again, and the guards did not treat him roughly.

Soon he looked forward to the daily visits, and he learned much about Sarin on the strength of his own conversational skill and linguistic savvy. Kyne knew he was doing a good job.

Sarin also seemed to take pleasure in speaking to him, often showing her emotions by changing colors.

He compiled daily verbal reports for Floraboden, pleased that he'd identified that she was from Pleaides, specifically a 4.17-magnitude star she called □□!□□, which Kyne believed to be the star they knew as Merope.

The crew of the Jetshift had found her crystalline casing floating in a rocky belt orbiting a one of Alderberan's planets and thought it might be valuable. They'd held her captive for over a ship year, despite her request to be set free. (He was estimating the length of time based on Sarin's description of overheard conversations.) How Sarin got to be floating free on the edge of Orion's boundaries was still not clear.

Kyne needed more time with her, and more music. Sarin appeared to enjoy Reikebord, Isikayao-Wha, and Piaf. Her favorite though, was Vangelis, an old, old song called *Damask Rose*. Kyne had taken to playing it at night in his rooms while he thought about Sarin and their conversations.

Her wit and her fine tastes suggested a rare kind of woman. What was she like inside her shell? If only he could catch a glimpse of her. Perhaps she possessed beauty of kind to which he could become accustomed? And her to him. They were in every other way in tune.

On his next visit though, Kyne became concerned. As the strains of a Vivaldi concerto faded, Sarin uttered a sound that could have been a sigh.

"You seem sad," he said, taking care to frame it as a statement.

"I miss ☐ ☐ ☐."

Kyne took a moment to consider that. "Your language is quite beautiful. And should I try and guess, I would say that the reason you were found by the pirates so far from your home is because you were on a quest of some kind, perhaps a rite of passage. It's common among far-traveling species that the young are sent out to find maturity through discovery. I believe your sense of longing is for lost opportunity to return home with some kind of prize."

Sarin's crystalline sarcophagus took on the rosy hue he'd grown to understand meant agreement.

"Your insightfulness is outstanding, Just Kyne. You must be from a superior subgroup of your species," she said.

Kyne's cheeks warmed. "I am trained in a specific area of social behavior. Internal realities are my special interest area. Understanding external cues allows me to make intuitive conclusions about how humanesques think."

"But I am not a humanesque," said Sarin.

"And yet it appears that I understand you. I could share more of my theories with you, Sarin. We could see how closely the architecture of our minds is aligned."

"I look forward to that, Just Kyne. I look forward to you. Will you come again soon?"

Kyne's heart tapped a little faster in his chest. The idea that she wanted him brought him unexpected joy.

Later, in his rooms, he lay on his bed thinking about Sarin. Her last words to him had been in the form of an interrogative. Did that signal a shift in their relationship?

His body throbbed in answer and the arousal surprised him. How long since he'd felt so stirred? And how absurd that he'd found intimacy in this situation!

Yet his feelings were as tangible as the bedsheet rubbing against his foreskin. Regardless of how hideous or repulsive Sarin's real form was, he knew he was losing his heart.

He fell asleep dreaming of her but was woken a few hours later by his M-A.

Professor Kyne, you have a call from Stationmaster Floraboden, it informed him.

He jolted upright. "Yes, Stationmaster?"

"I apologize for interrupting your rest, Professor. Your interviews with the A-Class have been terminated. Thank you for your service," said Floraboden without preamble.

"What?" exclaimed Kyne. "But I haven't finished. Sir, you must—!"

"The A-Class has been declared a hostile and is no longer available for study. Please send your final report through in the morning. Good night, Professor. Thank you for your work."

Thank you for your work?! Kyne sat on the end of his bed, his outrage growing. How dare Floraboden terminate his study!

He paced, fuming over it.

Until, slowly, fear began to replace anger. What had suddenly changed? If Sarin been declared hostile, what was Floraboden planning to do to her?

Kyne knew the regular security protocols. Declared hostiles were ejected from the station into the black.

His stomach lurched. *No!* He couldn't let that happen.

He sprang up, hurried into his office, and opened his specimen fridge. On the shelf above the preserved samples lay containers of formalin. He retrieved a couple and two hypodermics patches from his equipment cube.

Sarin, I'm coming!

#

Wild thoughts swirled in his mind as he ran along the passages to the airvator. He must find her. He must change Floraboden's mind. She was...they couldn't...this had to be stopped!

He entered the shaft, panting and trembling, and closed his eyes, taking a moment to recall the sequence. He'd made this trip so many times that he knew exactly how long it took. If he counted, he should be able to locate the correct floor.

Ready...now...771...659...578...430...335... 242...191...stop!

Kyne placed his finger on the emergency tab and the airvator stopped so quickly that he stumbled. He opened his eyes and with shaking hands, loaded the vials into the hypo patches. He had to be quick. *Forceful if needed.*

"Open," he told the concierge when he was done.

He walked quietly down the cool, familiar corridor to the interrogation cells, expecting at any moment to be stopped. To his surprise, he found no one guarding them.

Suddenly panicked again, he burst into the interview room. "Sarin! Where are you?"

But the room was also empty, and the viewing window was inactive.

He went over and hammered on it. "Sarin! Sarin! You're in danger!"

But the window didn't change, nor did she reply.

The agitation inside him coalesced into something monstrously aggrieved. Where was she? His love…what had they done to her? The pressure in his chest made it hard to breathe. How dare they interfere with his work. His life—

"Professor Kyne," said a clipped voice from the doorway. "The A-Class is no longer available to you."

He turned and glared at the soldier. Vaguely, maybe, he recognized him. One who'd been pushy with him in the past.

"Where is she?" Kyne demanded.

The soldier ignored his question. "Place the hypos on the floor in front of you. NOW!" He closed the visor of his helmet and lifted his weapon.

A haze of emotions blinded him. Frightened, he launched at the man, and thrust the hypo against the soft skin under his helmet strap.

A soft gasp escaped the guard's lips.

They were locked together, for an instant, struggling in a tight circle. Something whirred. The guard's weapon had activated.

He tried to wrench it away. As he twisted, it discharged a pulse of heat that burned deep into Kyne's chest. He staggered back, his vision clearing for a moment.

Movement flickered on the viewing window. As if she was watching.

"Sarin!" he choked out and fell.

#

Floraboden welcomed everyone to the virt-meet; sector stationmasters were present, as were senior members of the Orion League of Sentient Species—OLOSS. He had to play this right. The meet would remain on record for analysis.

"Proceed with your evaluation, Stationmaster Floraboden," said the OLOSS facilitator's avatar opposite him.

"We captured an A-Class alien on a JetShift trader close to Bellatrix. It took the form of a crystalline sarcophagus, which protected the actual entity inside."

"And the traders handed the A-Class over to you without quibble? I'd like to have seen that!" said one of the other stationmasters who favored an avatar with a thick fringe and large ears.

Floraboden glanced at the speaker's name: Cobb from Cobb-Vermont Station out near Saiph. They were rivals with Leto for the next round of OLOSS maintenance grants. It would suit Cobb well for Floraboden to look bad in this.

"The traders were all dead, S-M Cobb. By murder and suicide, we determined," he said.

Cobb grunted. "Mutiny then?"

"Of a kind. Yes. We verified the A-Class as a threat, based on the situation we found."

"Which was?"

"The bodies were within the proximity of the crystal casing. It had shot out crystalline threads to attach to them."

"Feeding off them?"

"There was evidence to suggest it had absorbed amino acids from the corpses. So, yes."

"And your response?"

"We employed one of our *psycholgeestes* to study it. If you have read the report uploaded to your M-As, you will find events logged in chronological order?"

Nods from those who had read it were vehement. Cobb clearly had not and shrugged.

"Just prior to Professor Kyne's unfortunate psychotic episode, we were able to breach the sarcophagus and identify the true nature of the A-Class," added Floraboden.

"Breaching an A-Class? That is outside protocol boundaries, Floraboden. Not to say, risky," said one of the OLOSS members.

"I understand that, Pre-Eminence. But we feared an outcome like the one we found on the JestShift. I decided that we should act in the interest of station security."

He watched the mixture of reactions. At least half of them approved—better than he'd hoped.

"So, what did you learn? And why was it not included in your report?" asked the Pre-Eminence.

"I thought it better you heard it from me, so there was no misunderstanding. You see…we found nothing," said Floraboden.

"Explain!" demanded the OLOSS contingent in a synchronous chorus.

"The sarcophagus held only a tiny, tiny creature. Or at least, a part of a creature that we believe to be its detachable projection organism. I oversaw the opening myself."

"You mean the A-Class had left an *echo* behind in its shell?" asked Cobb.

"Yes. Years ago, we believe. The projection organism that Kyne interacted with was merely as you say, an *echo*, left as a guardian against scavengers, in case the A-Class needed to return to use the casing again."

"You're saying that your *psychologeeste* developed a relationship with the echo of the original inhabitant?" asked Cobb, seemingly amused.

Annoying fellow. Floraboden pressed his lips tight. *Restating the obvious and asking questions he should already know the answers to.* In real time, Floraboden rubbed his throbbing temples, but didn't allow his avatar to copy the gesture. "So, it seems."

"And the crew of the JetShift?"

"The same fate, I imagine. After they were dead the sarcophagus harvested the amino acids from the bodies to boost its energy signal—like a location finder."

"So, you sacrificed one of your own to learn what the A-Class was up to?" Cobb, was openly sticking the needles in now, insinuating that Floraboden had mishandled it.

"Professor Kyne was appraised of the risks and chose to serve his community. By observing his interactions with the echo artifact inside, we were able to deduce how it worked. It is adaptive and responds differently to varying stimuli," said Floraboden, stiffly.

"So, with your Professor…err…Kyne, it chose seduction."

"Yes. We think it reacted to his…umm…well…Kyne kept to himself. He was perhaps more vulnerable than we realized. It used his loneliness to form an attachment. Then Kyne became irrational and attacked a guard. Both died during the incident. We believe a similar situation may have occurred on the JetShift. The creature's echo seems to be able use human emotions as a weapon against us."

"Ingenious," said Cobb.

It was not the word Floraboden would have chosen.

"We'd better keep this one under wraps. Wouldn't want our enemies to know things are so loosey-goosey over Leto way," Cobb added.

Floraboden enjoyed a momentary image of strangling the man before his M-A registered his spiking blood pressure and flooded his body with a light sedative. "The situation was handled perfectly professionally, S-M Cobb. We suffered no loss of life and followed the OLOSS protocols once we established the A-Class was potentially hostile. The casing is on a trajectory with the Mintakan calcium cloud."

It was only a half lie. There was no way he was reporting in front of Cobb that they'd found a second guard dead with his hand adhered to the observer's window. Floraboden would back channel that information later and blame it on an accidental station death.

Eventually, the OLOSS chorus spoke. "Thank you, Stationmaster. We'll retire to consider the implications of this. Meanwhile, please award Professor Kyne a memorial plaque for services to humanesquekind."

The meeting adjourned and Floraboden was left alone in his rooms. He let his valet know he was ready for a glass of grape juice and settled himself on one of the kneeling stools to think about Kyne. He recalled the terms of their agreement.

Mount a plaque to honor Professor Kyne in the corridor near Professor Freeburg's office, he said to his M-A.

At the mention of the dead man's name, he noticed the normally white lights along his array turn a rosy hue. An anomaly. But after a quick system check, he could determine no issues. Maybe he'd been awake too long and was hallucinating again. He logged a check-up with the station medic and went back to his maintenance schedules.

16 Minutes

By Jasper Fforde

The technical term was 'Closed-Loop Temporal Field Containment' but to everyone who had been so incarcerated, it was known as Looping. You were a looper, you had been looped. The period of time in which you found yourself was a loop. The company that managed the system on behalf of the Chronoguard was named Loop Inc.

Loop, loop, loop.

Which is what you do these days: same sixteen minutes of time, exact same place, exact same people. You can explain to others what's happened to you, but success is short lived. Even if someone does believe you, it will never be for very long. Inside the loop those sixteen minutes are all you have; outside the loop those sixteen are simply an empty block of time that, to most people, is utterly unremarkable and has now long receded into the dim forgotten past.

Cruel and unusual? Sure. Effective? Youbetcha.

"Will sir be having a dessert today?" asks the waitress, taking away your plates. She is young and pretty and has a kindly face. She has served you nearly twenty-five thousand times. You've told her your name every single time. She hasn't remembered once. She can't remember. There are any number of her, but only one of you.

Anything you have with you, stays with you; anything you put down is lost into the Chronoclastic ether next time the loop was reset. You change clothes, washed, ate, drank, disposed of waste— everything is supplied accessible within the temporal window they gave you. That's why loops are generally centered around shopping malls with a food court and public restrooms. It wouldn't take you long to starve, stuck inside sixteen minutes, in say, the middle of the Atlas Mountains.

When you arrive at Loop 1, you first find a notebook and pen to log the number of Loops, the equivalent of chalk marks on the wall of the cell. You have no money, but you can steal what you want, because your punishment for a world in which there are consequences is to be banished to a world where there are none. The irony and perversity are not wasted on you.

You try using the phone, but there's no one to call that can help you, nor believe you. The people you call think you're a crank or a hoax caller, and you're reset every sixteen minutes, so it's like it never happened. You even try calling your past self to figure out a work-around, but your past self is only eleven.

Whatever happens in the Loop, stays in the Loop.

You shout and cry and carry on until Loop 20, and then you calm down. You start to explore, and by Loop 450, you have a general understanding of the parameters of your prison. The date, the time, where to find food, nearest toilets, bookshop, that kind of thing.

By Loop 1000, you will have extended that particular knowledge to reflect your own particular needs more usefully. Who will be kind, who will not, who you can talk to, who can be relied upon to perform a physical act at short notice on credit.

At Loop 2500, you have your first visit. Your caseworker, wanting to know how you're settling in. They don't know because you're not observed. Even if they could, there's no need. What you are doing, you're doing in the distant past. If there was a ripple in the Standard History Eventline they'd know about it, but there is nothing. In these sixteen marooning minutes, fixed somewhere in a backwater of the 1990s, you're temporally insignificant. A very small pebble in a pond with much larger, more recent and more relevant ripples.

Your caseworker doesn't stay for long; just to tick a few boxes and move on to the next parcel of time. You ask him for outside news.

"There's no news," he says. "This is 1996. Everything you ever did, all the wrong you've ever done, all the happiness you've ever had—it hasn't happened yet."

"Then I haven't actually committed a crime either."

"Not yet," he agrees cheerfully, "but you will, and with a hundred percent certainty. If it's in the Standard History Eventline—which it is—it will happen, it did happen, it has happened. The fact that you're here proves it."

The logic isn't totally sound, but then in the time industry, very little is.

"Has my lawyer lodged an appeal?"

The caseworker points to a pram the other side of the food court.

"That's your lawyer. She doesn't even know she's going to be a lawyer. Take it up with her."

He was bluffing. The toddler's name is Charlotte. Her mother is Keilly, waiting for an old friend from school who is having a hard time. Good person on the whole, doing the best she can. You know, because you've chatted. Twelve times.

By Loop 5000, you've pushed the geographical boundaries of your prison, and discovered just how far you can get in your minutes.

You can catch a bus or a train or even a cab—but the furthest you can get, furthest you ever got, is on a stolen motorcycle. Not the most powerful you could find but the fastest within the shortest time frame. You get almost twelve miles out of town to the south, but your time runs out within sight of the cast-iron road bridge. And no matter what you do, you can't change that. You challenge yourself, you practice endlessly, you push too hard and you die in the attempt. It's painful, but you come back, right as rain, just with a scuffed coat. No matter what you try, you never cross the bridge; it is the limit of your time and space. It's the horizon you won't ever cross.

By Loop 10,000, you're starting to get weird, and angry, and desperate. You stop logging how many loops you've been in, and you kill yourself for the first time, then, when that doesn't satisfy, you kill someone else. Someone you didn't like to begin with, then just random people. But you don't actually kill anyone or at least, not for very long. You may go on an orgy of violence just then, and work through your fury in a hundred or so loops until you calm down and start to log your loops again.

By Loop 20,000, you'll have been Looped for over six months, and pretty much every sound, movement and scent will be familiar to you. You can predict what people will say, what people will do. You start to relax, read books, sketch, learn a musical instrument.

You start to count how many loops to go, rather than how many have been. Eight hundred and twenty-two thousand, six hundred and fifty-four, or thereabouts: about twenty-two years in sixteen-minute hexitemporal segments. A couple of days later, when the subtracted Loops don't seem to be making much of a dent from your tally, you go back to counting up again, and life gets back to normal.

You start talking about yourself in the second person. You're not sure why.

You eat, you sleep, you shit, you wash, you exercise.

You are Looped. You are relooped, you are relooped again. Again, and again, and again.

"Will sir be having a dessert today?" asks the same waitress, taking away your plates and smiling in a friendly yet mechanical manner. You usually eat here and always the same—a ready-made burger that you divert to your table using some pretext or other. You've become connected to the waitress, but she doesn't know it. You know her name, and what her mother thinks of her new boyfriend. Little by little you get to know everything about her, but she knows nothing of you. To her, you are just one more faceless customer on an unremarkable Wednesday late in the summer of 1996. You don't know how her life turns out.

"Time is short," you say, "but thanks anyway."

"I'll get the check."

She doesn't have time to get the check but you knew she wouldn't. The world resets to the beginning of the loop. You are back outside in the parking lot, the place and time where your loop always begins. You have a generic car key in your pocket but the parking lot is large. Every tenth loop, you search for the car you arrived in, but you have yet to have any luck. It wasn't in the multi-story, nor any of the open-air lots. You are slowly working your way through all the parked cars, but it will take some time. Hereford is a big place.

That's when Quinn arrives. You haven't seen him since your trial. He won, you didn't.

"Hello, Algy."

Anything remotely new in the sixteen is so utterly alien that it leaps out at you like a chainsaw on full power. You jump.

"Sorry," says Quinn, looking around. "Want to talk?"

You know it's a dumb question. Of course you want to talk. You go to a cafe. You order coffee, he orders nothing. The rule is never take anything out of the loop - not even liquid.

He asks how it's going.

"It's kind of samey," you reply, trying to be sarcastic.

He asks if you're past the berserker stage and you say that you are.

"How many did you kill?"

"One day it was eighteen, I think. I wasn't really counting."

"It gets tiresome, doesn't it?"

"Yes," you say, "and messy, and pointless. What do you want?"

"We want to know who was responsible. Who gave you the access codes, whose bright idea it was to go trolling around the Middle Ages. Most of all, how you all got past the 1720 pinch point without setting off every trembler at head office. That could be real useful to us."

You tell him you flashed through during the monthly telemetry squirt from the Renaissance, but you know he knows this. What he actually wants is the gold. Taking that much historical gold destabilized the monetary supply in the early history of banking. And banking doesn't like to have its history pissed around with. The ripples cause crashes. Our heist has already been blamed for two depressions, the crash of 2008, and some inexplicable currency variations. Historical gold is a good moderator. You want financial stability? Flood the past with gold. Lots of it.

You tell him it's in the Holocene.

"The Holocene is a big place," he says. "You need to be more specific."

You tell him you never knew where the gold went. That only Kitty knew.

"Kitty says that you know."

"Kitty's lying."

"One of you is."

"I was only a small cog," you tell him, "blinded by cash and the misplaced hubris of down-streaming. I'd never done the Middle Ages before. Kitty asked me to join her. I was...flattered."

Quinn takes a deep breath. Your sixteen minutes were up long ago and you haven't reset. That's what happens when they drop someone into your loop. You hear new stuff, see things that hadn't happened, like you're watching a sequel to a film you're very familiar with.

"Last word?" asked Quinn.

"Last word."

And you are back at the multi-story, Loop 42,001. All the players have reset themselves to their start positions. The kid on the bicycle, the balloon seller, the harassed father with the two unruly kids, the busker with the accordion. The same sixteen-minute section all over again. You look for your car, and you don't find it. You give up at Loop 61,200, and never look again.

You're hungry again and go and find the waitress. The burger tastes the same. It should do; it's the same one. You try out a joke you found in a book in Waterstone's. You think she will laugh, and she does. You know her sense of humor. You know her.

At Loop 150,000, you have an intimate knowledge of the town and everyone in it. Even so, you systematically search out and take fascination in anything that is new or unfamiliar. You find a new street, or knock on a door you've never knocked on before, or find your way to a room you never knew existed, with a person you've never seen, a closet space you've never explored before. You visit the same place for the next ten loops, learn everything to be learned, then move on. Everything that happened within that sixteen minutes, you are an expert upon. It is an expertise of the narrowest of fields.

At Loop 200,000, Quinn visits again. You expect he will because two hundred thousand is a nice round multiple of sixteen, and the Time Engines work on hexadecimal architecture.

"Back so soon?" you ask, still being sarcastic. Quinn doesn't do sarcasm, you realize.

"We need you to turn Kitty," he says, and shows you an agreement from the Temporal Attorney. If you could find out where and when in the Holocene the gold is hidden, you could expect to be out a hundred thousand loops earlier. You hold out for two hundred thousand, and get it.

You sign the agreement, and ask where she is.

"Where she's always been, ten minutes north."

You know this is unusual. Loops were designed never to overlap geographically or temporally. Intersections gave convicts potential areas of conflict with other prisoners. Quinn tells you to make it look like a chance meeting.

You drive out north on the same motorcycle you used to try and reach the bridge. It takes you until Loop 200,032 before you spot her, and she you. It's not hard. Anything that is at variance to the rigidity of the timeline stands out like a flashing beacon. You drive past one another on the road, you both stamp on the brakes and then back up.

"Algy?" she says.

You say hello. She doesn't look very happy. The gold heist was her gig, after all. You were just the muscle.

You find that the maximum amount of time you can spend together is one minute and nine seconds before you both get reset to the head of your loops. You tell her about Quinn's deal straight away. She is not surprised.

"He asked to find out the same from you."

She says she doesn't know where the gold is but you know that, because you've known where the gold was all along. All seventeen tons of it, lying in the open on the edge of a bay that fifteen thousand years later, will be in the Derry peninsula. It's still there, in the back garden of Mr. and Mrs. Tyrone, under eight feet of accreted soil and peat. They have barbecues over it, with their friends.

Over the next three hundred loops, you try and rebuild your relationship with Kitty, but all she wants to know is about the gold. You come to realize there was never a relationship. You think you might tell her, but you don't. There's nothing to be gained from it.

"You're not going to tell me, are you?" she says finally.

"No."

You don't meet her again. You turn back to the waitress in the burger joint. She has a delightful gurgle of a laugh. You find yourself in love.

Quinn returns at Loop 260,000. You tell him Kitty doesn't know where the gold is, or if she does, she's not telling.

"You're both a bunch of time wasters," says Quinn, apparently not realizing the irony of his words. "Enjoy your time."

You go back to your sixteen-minutes loops, over and over again. Another year's worth of sixteens go by. It's never the time, it's the *repetition*. There is not a book you haven't read, not a person you haven't spoken to. You've been served by the waitress over a hundred thousand times, and when Quinn reappears at Loop 320,000, you do the deal, but for a full pardon. You are one third of the way through your sentence. To be the eighteenth richest person on the planet, you thought you could last out.

"Everyone comes to their senses eventually," says Quinn. "If the gold is where you say it is, it'll be time served."

It is your final loop, the only one that will have any lasting consequence upon the townsfolk around you. Pointlessly, you say your goodbyes to people who have met you only a few minutes before.

To them it's just plain weird, but to you it means more than you know how to express. The man in the corner store who was always cheery, the busker who played the accordion in the main square. Most of all, the waitress. You feel emotional speaking to her. You make her laugh again and hand her your address on a scrap of paper.

"O-kay," she says, somewhat uneasily.

You have a speech, and it's a good one because you've had ten years to write it. She stares at you as you speak and raises an eyebrow. You know that no one has ever understood her so well, no one has ever encapsulated what she needs in words of such poetry and power. You know she'll remember you.

But it's not to meet in the 1990s. It's to meet you back here in twelve years, if she wants. It's a long shot, but she finds you intriguing rather than creepy, which is a good sign.

And that's where you are now, in a much-changed market town, the shop fronts modernized, the clothes different, shoppers clutching smart phones, going about their business. You've been out for a couple of days. You don't have a job and you don't have much money. But you have liberty, and the sixteen minutes you've just witnessed has faded without ceremony into the past.

There have been 8,356 different sixteen minutes since your release. It's a hard habit to break. You'll be counting your sixteens for at least another six months. You glance at your watch and wonder if she will turn up, always supposing things didn't work out for her. You hope they did, of course, because she was a good person, and deserves a good life.

You're still waiting.

American Changeling

By Mary Robinette Kowal

Half-consciously, Kim put a hand up to cover her new nose ring. It pissed her parents off no end that she could tolerate touching cold iron and they couldn't.

Iron still made her break out sometimes, but didn't burn her. It had taken forever to find someone to make an iron nose ring, but the effort would be totally worth it.

"Kimberly Anne Smith." Mom's voice caught her in the foyer as surely as if she'd been called by her true name. "I've been worried sick. Do you know what time it is?"

"11:49." Kim dropped her hand and turned to face Mom, her Doc Martens making a satisfactory clomping on the hardwood floor. "I'm here. Home before midnight. No one with me." Sometimes she thought about bringing friends home to show them what her parents *really* looked like after their glamour dropped.

Everyone thought Mom was so pretty, so Betty Crocker, and Dad was all Jimmy Stewart. Whatever. Maybe if people saw that her parents were freaks like her they wouldn't look at her with such pity.

"I specifically asked you to come home straight after school, young lady. I tried calling your cell, I don't know how many times. You have no idea how worried I've been."

"I was hanging out with Julia and Eve on Hawthorne."

Mom took a step closer, wearing pearls, even at home. "What's that in your nose?"

Kim blew her dyed-pink hair out of her face. "It's called a nose ring." Having people stare at her for the piercings and hair and leather was way better than having them stare at her because she looked prematurely old, like a progeria victim.

From the den, her father called, "Is she home?" A piece of ice clinked against glass. She so did not want to deal with Dad if he'd been drinking. He got maudlin about the old country and if she had to hear one more story about how life was so much better in Faerie, she'd scream.

"Yes!" Kim shouted. "I'm home and I'm going to bed so I don't have to look at myself."

She ran up the stairs two at a time, Utilikilt swinging against her legs. Mom hollered up the stairs at her, but Kim didn't care. She hopped over the salt line on her threshold, slammed the door to her room and threw herself on the bed without even bothering to turn on the lights. What was the point?

The mantel clock downstairs chimed midnight.

Kim's mom knocked on her door. "Kim? Come out, honey, your father and I need to talk to you."

"Why don't you come in?"

"If you'll sweep the salt aside."

Rolling her eyes, Kim dragged herself off the bed and opened the door. With midnight, the glamour masking her mother's appearance had dropped. Mom had shrunk and twisted, aging one hundred years in the stroke of the clock. Gone was her carefully coiffed platinum hairdo in exchange for sparse, dry hair. The hall light gleamed off her scalp. Her nose nearly touched her chin, where a wart sported more hair than was on the rest of her head.

The thing that burned Kim like cold iron was that, aside from her dyed hair, she knew she looked just like her mother. All changelings were born looking old. That might be fine if you lived in Faerie with other people of your species, but here, Kim was just a freak. "What."

Mom smiled, showing her scraggly teeth, but her chin trembled and her eyes were moist. "We've had a message. From the old country. Come downstairs so we can talk about it."

Despite herself, Kim stepped over the salt line, into the hall. The only time she could remember Mom crying was when their dog had died. She'd held Buffy's head and wept like her heart had broken. Dad had said the golden retriever had been the first mortal thing Mom had ever loved. Death wasn't common in Faerie.

Seeing her on the verge of tears now freaked Kim out. She followed Mom downstairs without speaking.

Dad sat in his easy chair, holding a glass of whiskey loosely in his left hand. The reading lamp lit his arm and lap, but left his face in shadow. On the walnut end table beside him lay a piece of parchment at odds with the magazine-perfect living room.

The cream Berber carpet and the cranberry French toile curtains and the tan leather couch all seemed dirty and smudged by the introduction of this one thing from Faerie. It forced itself into her vision with a crisper focus than anything of mortal origins.

Her father set his drink down and leaned forward into the light.

Like her mother, he looked scary ancient. His gray wool sweater hung from his shoulders as if he were a first grader playing dress up. His broad, pitted nose was bright red. Dad wiped his hand across his face and covered his eyes for a moment.

He inhaled deeply and dropped his hand. "This is difficult." Dad picked up the parchment. "We knew it was coming, but...Do you want to sit down?"

"No, sir." Kim bit the inside of her cheek, uncertain about what was going to come next.

Even though her parents had always told her they'd come to the mortal world for the sole purpose of conceiving her, even though her childhood had been filled with fairy tales in which she was the chosen one, even seeing their glamour, Kim had never fully believed them. Because the truth, that she was the first faerie born into the mortal world since the gate closed, was crazy. She gestured at the parchment. "Can I see it?"

Dad handed it to her and took another sip of his whiskey while Mom dabbed at her eyes with a tissue.

To Mossblossom, daughter of Fernbrooke and Woodapple
Right trustie and welbeloved, wee greete you well.
Grat is the task which wee must aske of you, but wee know you will
fulfill it in such a way as may not onely nourish and continue our
love and good will towards you, but also encrease the same. Our
good and most loving Subjects, your worthy parents, have striven to
raise you out of the sight of certaine devilish and wicked minded
enemies of ours. These enemies who style themselves the Unseelie
Court, have most wickedly and unnaturally conspired to have stirred
up (as much as in them lay) a generall rebellion throughout our
whole Realme. It pleases us to...

"I don't get this." Kim lowered the parchment. "I mean, she can't even spell."

Her mother winced and took the parchment out of her hands. "The Faerie Queen is using the high court language from before the gate closed during Bloody Mary's reign. Your father and I had to learn modern English as a second language, of course we were both very young, but—"

"Fern, we need to get moving." Dad nodded at the brass and mahogany mantel clock. "She wanted us at St. Andrew's after mass."

"What?" Kim scanned the parchment again, but the spelling was so poor she had trouble making any sense of it. The cathedral was five blocks from their house, and though she knew it held the Key, they weren't supposed to open the gate until her sixteenth birthday which was still months away. "But it's after midnight."

Her mother sniffed. "If you'd come home when I asked this wouldn't be a problem."

"Yeah, well, you didn't tell me why."

"I didn't want to distract you at school. Your grades have already been slipping and—"

"Oh, as if that matters. What? My SAT scores will get me into the best schools in Faerie?"

"Stop it." Draining his whiskey, Dad stood and pulled the letter from her hands. "The Unseelie Court know about you."

That cut her retort off. The rebel faeries who formed the Unseelie Court had nearly torn the realm apart three hundred years ago when they closed the gate. The only people through since then had been a handful of changelings, like her parents, who'd worked a complicated magic to change places with mortals. "When you say 'know'...?"

He snapped the parchment at her. "There's a traitor in the Queen's

Court. She knows not who it is, but it is clear that they have found out about you and the plans to reopen the gate. If we give them any time at all, they will send a changeling and kill you rather than let that happen."

"Woody, you're frightening her."

"What would you have? A child not frightened, but without the information to make good decisions? Fern. We can't go into the church with her. She has to know that the Unseelie have likely alerted the Catholics and that someone might be there."

"Let's just go and get it over with." Kim flipped the hood of her sweatshirt up to give herself at least a semblance of privacy. Underneath everything, a film of sweat coated her body. Her joints ached with anticipation. "Opening the gate is what I'm here for, isn't it?"

Even though it was only five blocks to the church, her parents drove in case they needed to make a quick getaway. They stopped the Prius across the street from St. Andrew's and got out with her. Farther down the block, the laughter of late-night hipsters drifted down Alberta Street. Mom put her hands on Kim's shoulders and kissed her forehead. "I want you to know that your father and I are very proud of you, no matter what happens."

Kim's heartbeat rattled through every bone of her body. She knew their allergies meant that her parents couldn't go into the church with her, but for a second, she wished they could. "Any last words of advice?"

Her dad leaned in close enough that she could smell the whiskey on his breath. "Just be safe. You see a priest, you hightail it out of there. We'll figure out some other plan."

"Right ..." It had only taken the Faerie Queen five hundred years to cook this one up. Before she could chicken out, Kim got out of the car and crossed the street to the cathedral. She'd read everything her parents could find about the place, knew all about its French Gothic style of architecture, had studied the floor plan until it was printed on the inside of her eyelids, but she had never set foot on the property before.

Once, when she was six, she'd run the five blocks from their house to the cathedral. Her mom caught her just before she got there. Kim had wanted to work the magic so she could get the Key out of the altar. She'd thought her reward would be to get wings like the fairies on TV. Mom had set her straight, explaining that there might be alarms set if any of Faerie blood approached. Since then, she'd always walked down the other side of the street rather than chance it.

Not tonight though. Tonight, she walked straight up the marble steps and pulled out the keys Dad had gotten hold of years ago. It would suck if they'd changed the locks. She put the keys in the lock, braced for something to scream or an alarm to go off.

The door wasn't even locked. All Dad's effort to get the keys and she didn't even need them. Kim hauled open the heavy door and slipped into the nave. She had been to the church's website dozens of times, but the photo galleries had not conveyed the arcing height of the ceiling. Despite the simple beauty of the oak carvings which adorned the plaster walls, her pulse ratcheted up to quad-espresso rate.

Her parents had refused to teach Kim any spells but those she needed to open the gate, because glamour would interfere with her ability to handle iron. Well, after tonight, baby, that restriction would be lifted and she'd be working it like any good Fae.

Kim sauntered down the middle of the church. Beyond a few guttering candles visible in the side chapel, the building was still and empty. At the altar, Kim put her hand on the cold marble.

All around her, wood splintered as the oak carvings forced their mouths open and shrieked.

Panicked, Kim lifted her hand off the altar, ready to run out of the church—but if she did, her chance to get the Key out of the altar was blown. Whoever had set the alarm already knew she was here.

She pressed her hand back on the altar, crooked her little finger into a fishhook and shouted the words she'd learned as a nursery rhyme:

"Stone, stone, earth's bone,

Once hid, now shown!"

Under her hand, the center of the stone burst. Its halves tilted and thudded to the ground. In the exposed middle, was a small, ornate iron casket, no larger than a paperback. Above her, the carvings still screamed bloody murder.

A door on the side of the church slammed open and a priest, tousled white hair sticking out like a halo, ran into the sanctuary.

Kim grabbed the casket, leaped over the broken altar, and sprinted down the aisle with the reliquary tucked under her arm like a football.

She hauled open the church door. Yelling incoherently about thieves and sacrilege, the priest chased her. Kim vaulted down the front steps of the cathedral, momentum dropping her forward on her knees. The pavement tore through her striped stockings.

Before Kim could rise, the priest grabbed her. "What did you do?"

Kim tried to shrug free, but the priest had a grip like a bulldog. "Let me go!"

"Stealing is a sin and what you've done to the altar ..." His other hand grabbed for the iron reliquary.

Kim kicked and twisted to keep him from taking the Key.

Out of nowhere, her father punched the priest in the nose. The priest staggered, blood streaming down his face.

Dad yelled, "Get in the car!"

Kim tore down the sidewalk. Hipsters and neighbors gawked in the street.

Dashing into the road, Kim headed for her parents' car. When she stepped off church property, the carvings went silent. The cessation of noise rang like tinnitus.

Their Prius pulled away from the curb. Her mom leaned out the window. "Hurry!"

Kim opened the back door and scrambled into the seat. Dad half fell in after her. As people ran for the car, Mom peeled out, which Kim didn't even think a hybrid could do.

Mom dodged the onlookers and drove down Alberta to the I-5 onramp. Kim stared out the rear window at the crowd milling around.

"Do you have it?" her mother asked.

Kim turned around to face the front. "Yeah. It's what I was born to do."

"Don't get cocky." On the seat beside her, Dad had his head down, trying to catch his breath.

Mom peered at her in the rearview mirror. Seeing only her eyes, it was easy to forget how old she looked right now. "We still have to get to Stonehenge to open the gate."

Kim leaned forward. "I didn't bring my passport with me."

"No, no, dear. The replica at Maryhill. We should be able to use it as a mirror with the real one."

"Oh." That was a change from the original plan. Kim had been looking forward to going to England, but she'd practiced the ritual every summer at the replica.

"Dammit." Dad leaned against the seat, still gasping for breath. His face was swollen and puffy.

"Dad?"

He tried to smile, but his breath wheezed in his throat. "Allergies. It'll pass."

It sounded like he could barely breathe. His left hand had swollen to water-balloon tightness. "Mom ...?"

Dad put his hand on her knee. "Don't, you'll worry her for no reason."

"What is it, dear?"

Kim bit the inside of her cheek. "How much farther is it?"

"Mmm ... an hour and a half, I think. Why don't you take a nap, hm? It's been a long day for you and not over yet."

As if napping were an option. "You should have seen me. It was ten types of awesome. The rhyme worked like you said and boom!" Kim leaned forward and rested her chin on the seat. "How did they make the carvings scream? I mean, this church was built way after the wall went up, right?"

Kim's mother tapped the steering wheel. "Well ... you know how, according to the rules, things may only cross between if there's a one-to-one exchange. The carvings could be like that. They could be something someone prepared in Faerie and exchanged for the ones here. Or, I suppose there could be an Unseelie agent sent as a changeling. Or it might have been Catholic magic of some sort. We've never been able to really study the spells built into their rituals."

Dad's breath was more labored now. His face lolled against the window.

"Dad?" Kim whispered.

In the passing light from a truck, his skin had a distinct blue pallor. Kim put her hand on his shoulder. "Dad?"

Nothing.

"Mom?" Kim kept her hand on his shoulder, as if she could hold him here. "Something's wrong with Dad."

Mom didn't answer, and Kim thought for a moment that her mother had not heard her, but the Prius slowed and pulled to the side of the interstate.

Still silent, her mother grabbed her purse and got out of the car. Kim could not swallow or breathe or do anything except keep her hand on her dad's shoulder.

Mom pulled the back door open, her face impassive. As the door opened, Dad started to slump out. Kim tightened her hand on his sweater and hauled him back.

"Fool. Foolish, foolish man." Mom's hand trembled as she touched his face. Her breath hitched visibly.

Kim stared at Dad, whose face had all the wrinkles puffed out of it. She did not recognize this moon-faced man in her arms. "What is it? Is he under a spell or what?"

"No. His allergies ..."

A hard laugh escaped Kim. "Allergies? I've seen your allergies before; he's not sneezing, Mom. He can't even breathe."

Her mother didn't answer but rummaged in her purse and pulled out a vial and a pack of Handi Wipes. "He hit the priest, didn't he?"

"Yeah, but ... What? Holy blood is dangerous?" She hated the scorn coming out of her, but the anger was easier to manage than fear.

"Perhaps. Wipe the blood off his hand." Mom ripped the Handi Wipes pack open and handed it to Kim. "We don't fully understand the way Catholic magic and Faerie magic interact. I don't know what spells their priests are under, but I do know this is the sort of protective spell one would lay." She lifted Dad's head and held the vial to his lips.

Kim stared, fascinated, as Mom tried to get some of the amber liquid past his swollen lips.

Her mother said, "Kim, I asked you to do something for me and I need you to do it."

"Sorry." When she touched her dad's hand, Kim flinched. The flesh was turgid with pressure but gave slightly under her hands, like a rotting pumpkin.

"How come this didn't happen to me? I mean, I cast a spell and, you know, desecrated an altar." She couldn't tell if the blood was the priest's or Dad's from where the skin had broken on his knuckles. "Oh, and stole."

"You didn't steal. Fae don't steal things. The Key belongs to us."

"Still." Kim passed the Handi Wipe between her father's fingers. "Why Dad and not me?"

Mom capped the bottle of whatever and tucked it into her purse. "We had you baptized."

"What?"

"Think of it as an inoculation against allergies." Mom slid out of the car. "Ride up front with me."

"What about Dad?"

Mom stood by the side of the car, her skirt flaring every time a car passed them. She bent down so Kim could see her face. "If we get the gate open fast enough, the Faerie Queen will heal him. He doesn't have much time. I need you to start thinking."

Kim swallowed. "Yes, ma'am." She got out on the passenger side and closed the door as gently as possible to keep from jarring Dad.

Sitting in the front seat, as her mother drove, Kim replayed the events in St. Andrew's. It wasn't her fault touching the altar set off an alarm. And Dad should have known better than to hit that priest. Right?

She prodded her scraped knee. He shouldn't have tried to protect her. And now he might die. The pain did nothing to distract her. Dad had to get better. Kim dug her nails into the raw flesh. The Faerie

Queen had to fix him.

#

On a bluff overlooking the Columbia Gorge, the monument loomed out of the dark, silhouetted by moonlight. The water below caught the moon and tossed its silver light like a ball on the surface of the river. This replica of Stonehenge had been built as a World War I memorial by a railroad industrialist. He'd built it out of "modern" materials, concrete and rebar, but made it look like Stonehenge had when new. The monoliths ringed the center, none fallen on their sides. Even so, it had an air of being decrepit beyond its years. The concrete had its share of graffiti and had crumbled in places.

They'd left Kim's father in the car because Kim's mother was worried the spell would think he was an offering in addition to the Key.

Kim huddled against the side of a monolith and tried to stay out of the wind. She ran her fingers across the sculpted surface of the reliquary as if she could read its history in braille. The heavy cross embossed on its surface bumped under her fingers in a constant reminder of what Kim had to undo.

In the middle of the monument, her mother did something on the flat altar. Kim wanted to yell at Mom to hurry and, at the same time, tell her to slow down. As soon as Mom finished prepping the altar, it would be Kim's turn. What if she didn't get it right? Dad could die. She clutched the reliquary.

Mom gestured frantically. "Kim, quickly now."

She joined her mother at the altar stone and put the reliquary in the middle of it. How many times had she pretended to do this while playing in her backyard? She felt split into two halves, the one which knew exactly what to do and the one which was sure she'd screw up. Inhaling to steady herself, Kim pressed her thumb against the catch holding the reliquary shut and let it prick her finger. She bit the inside of her lower lip as the blood welled up on her thumb.

This had been Bloody Mary's genius; the reliquary would only open to one of pure Faerie blood, but it was made of iron and would burn all Fae who touched it. She had collaborated with the Unseelie Court to close the gate in order to prevent the Faerie Queen from aiding her enemies during the Wyatt Uprising. The Unseelie stooped to her aid, ironically, to keep mortals and their taint out of Faerie. The reliquary was a perfect blend of Catholic and Faerie magics.

Carefully, Kim slid the catch aside, exhaling in a rush of relief as the lock opened. Her thumb stung where the iron had cut her, but no more than with a sunburn. Kim could feel her mother, more than see her, shifting with impatience at her side.

Digging her fingernails into the crack between the covers, Kim pried the reliquary open.

She had expected a flash of magic like in the *Lord of the Rings* movies, but nothing even glowed. Inside the reliquary lay a mat of dried leaves. Kim held her breath for fear of disturbing the thing lying on them.

Curled in a fetal ball lay the tiniest skeleton Kim had ever seen. All her life she had heard of the other breeds of Fae but had never seen anyone besides her parents. With birdlike bones, this skeleton could only belong to a pixie, the most delicate of the Fae.

Kim slid her hand under the leaves and they disintegrated. Shaking, she picked up the pixie's skull. Dried to almost nothing, it felt like *papier-mâché* and was no bigger than her thumb. She set the skeleton on the altar piece by careful piece. Most of the bones were still attached with mummified tendons and leathery skin. She did not like to think about how hard it would have been if she'd had to piece the hands together.

"Don't miss a single bone." Mom leaned forward, as if she could stick her own hand in the reliquary and fish around.

"I know." Kim scowled. They'd spent enough time telling her bedtime tales about little changelings who didn't follow the rules. Kim sifted the ashy remains of the leaves until she was confident she had all the bones.

Bowing her head over the remains, Kim held her hands over them in benediction and said the words she had been taught.

"Child of Faerie, blessed are ye in your innocence. Return ye to the state from which our ancestors preserved us, free from the knowledge of the tree of good and evil. I release ye from your bonds to the mortal world. Go in peace."

Light, golden as sunset, bloomed out of the arch behind and cast her shadow across the altar. Now this was more like it. This was magic.

Her mother hissed, "Bow. The Faerie Queen is coming."

Kim's mother lowered herself into a deep curtsy. Kim tried to follow suit, but her legs gave way and dropped her on the ground. Her scraped knee sent a bright flash of pain up into her forebrain and snapped her attention to the fact that this was happening. She was about to meet the freakin' Faerie Queen.

For the first time in five hundred years, faeries set foot on mortal soil without needing to take a human in exchange. A retinue of faerie men and women stepped through the gate. Kim's heart sank as she looked from beautiful Fae to Fae. This was worse than high school; the disdain was apparent even on their inhumanly beautiful faces. Every one of them was beautiful and she... She looked like ass.

Her mother even looked panicky at the sight of these beautiful Fae.

The light frothed over, spreading to all the arches of the

monument. The interior lit up like Kim was standing center stage in the auditorium at school. Trumpets sounded. If silver were a sound, then it bugled out of the arch. The light boiled within the confines of the stone.

The radiance in all the other arches coalesced into a horde of other Fae. They sent up a cheer as they streamed through into the mortal world.

None of her parents' stories had prepared Kim for the full diversity of faeries. She'd known about the different species of Fae, but did not realize they came in every shade of skin known to humanity and then some. Brown, black, green, blue and red—some with tall pointing ears, others with noses drooping to their chins. The sight of a scattered few who were as ancient in appearance as she was, relieved her somewhat. She wouldn't stand out like a freak in Faerie after all.

Amidst the horde stampeding into the space, strode a woman who made every model ever born look dull and ordinary. She was made of beautiful.

Kim's mother turned from the group of Fae who had come through the first arch and gasped. "Majesty!"

This was the Faerie Queen? Then who were these other guys? The Queen saw them and her perfect face blanched in horror. Kim's mind caught up. The Unseelie Court had found them.

A tall elven man with fox-red hair drew his sword and stepped between the Queen and the Unseelie. "Majesty, we are ambushed."

Only then did Kim realize that each of the first group of Fae carried a weapon and wore a red band on their sleeves. Before she had time to register more than that, the Unseelie Court fell upon the Queen and her retinue. Metal clashed against metal and sparks flew.

Her mother shrieked and scrambled toward the Queen. Kim

turned to follow her, but an Unseelie man with leaf-green hair stopped her with a sword to her chest.

Kim bent back across the altar to get away. One of her hands landed on the reliquary. Desperate for a weapon, Kim swung it up and swiped at him. The corner nicked his cheek.

His skin sizzled and peeled as if she had hit him with a flaming poker. Holy shit. Iron raised welts on her parents' skin, but nothing like this. Kim didn't waste time wondering *why*, she just started laying into the Unseelie faeries attacking her.

Kim wielded the reliquary as if it were a book in a room full of jocks. At first the Unseelie retreated from the cold iron but the reliquary gave her a shorter reach than their swords and daggers.

Another beautiful, lean Unseelie man, with eyes like ice, nearly took her arm off but a gnome stopped his blow with a shovel. Kim retreated, dodging blows that pushed her farther from the Faerie Queen. The Unseelie man drove the point of his sword over the gnome's shovel and into his chest. Wrenching it free, he stepped toward Kim.

Kim staggered and fetched up against the hard surface of one of the monoliths. He had the sword leveled at her before she had time to draw breath. As he thrust it at her, she raised the reliquary to block. The shock of impact sent tremors through the bones of her hands.

She tried to swipe at him, but he twisted the sword under the reliquary and flicked it out of Kim's hands.

A squeak of horror escaped her throat as the piece of iron flew out of her grasp.

The Unseelie smiled the coldest smile Kim had ever seen. "What now, changeling child?"

He pressed the sword against her chest lightly but with enough force to pin her against the concrete block. "By the powers, you reek like a mortal. If the Unseelie Court didn't have use for you, I'd gut you like the spelless outcast you are."

Kim tried to twist away from the sword but he pressed it forward, cutting through her shirt and into her breastbone. She grunted at the sudden pain.

And then she got pissed. "I'm not spelless, you bastard."

Kim pressed her hand flat against the concrete behind her.

"Stone, stone, earth's bone,

Once hid, now shown!"

The concrete exploded. Chunks spun through the air, slamming into the mob. The blast knocked Kim flat, forcing the air from her lungs. She rolled frantically to get away from the falling concrete and rebar.

Her chest burned, screaming for air, but she could not draw a breath. Kim pawed at her throat as if she could open it by hand.

Howling, the Unseelie man pushed a block off his chest. A host of other Unseelie, bloodied and furious, turned toward where Kim lay. She dragged air in with a terrified wheeze. A part of her brain wondered if this was what her dad felt like.

Her anger rekindled. Her dad was dying because of these traitors.

Kim grabbed the first thing she laid her hand on—a twisted length of rebar torn from the stone. Her hand stung from its rough surface, but Kim didn't care. She rose to her feet and ran at the Unseelie as he was dragging his sword from under another chunk of cement.

Double-handed, Kim brought the rebar down on his wrist. The rod passed through his arm in a crackle of flesh. He screamed and fell, leaving his hand still clutching the hilt of his sword.

No blood dripped from the wound. The blackened skin had cauterized as the rebar had passed through. Kim stared at the rod in disbelief. Of course...it was iron. She had, like, a freakin' lightsaber against these guys. And since she'd grown up here, it only stung her a little.

Kim dove forward, hacking with the rebar. Even a glancing nick with the iron made their skin bubble and peel. The Unseelie retreated before her.

This was the best weapon, ever.

Gnomes, changelings and other of the Queen's Fae came to her side and formed a phalanx, cutting through the host of Unseelie. Kim fought without grace, but the terror that her weapon brought turned the tide quickly to the Queen's favor.

Time lost its meaning until Kim found herself standing, rebar in hand, next to her mother.

And the Faerie Queen.

"Bravely done, good Mossblossom."

For a moment, Kim wondered who she was talking to, and then remembered her Faerie name. "I—thank you, your Majesty." There was probably something else she should say, but Dad didn't have time for formalities. She pushed away the possibility that he was already dead. "So, could you—"

The fox-haired Fae stepped in front of her. "I am Oreyn, the Queen's champion and I, too, thank you for your service, but I must ask you to release your weapon near the Queen."

"Oh." Kim looked at the length of iron stupidly and let it drop to the ground. "Okay. But listen, my dad needs help."

Oreyn shied as the rebar rolled toward his toe. "Of course." He stepped past it and put his hand on Kim's shoulder.

She had never been this close to anyone like him. He smelled of honeysuckle and salt. His cheeks bore no trace of fuzz and had the poreless perfection of porcelain. He lifted his left hand and put a knife to her throat.

"Oreyn! What means this?" The Faerie Queen's shout came at the same moment as a wordless cry from Kim's mother.

Oreyn spoke three quick words in some language Kim did not recognize.

The world inverted, spun and sharpened into a painful clarity. The replica of Stonehenge had vanished, replaced by crisp trees and a stark blue sky.

The iron ring in Kim's nose burned. As it seared her flesh, she screamed.

Kim didn't care about the knife at her throat. The thing burning her had to stop. She grabbed it. Her fingers flared with pain.

She jerked them away.

Oreyn laughed and let his knife fall. "The touch of iron is worse here, is it not?"

Sick, twisted traitor. *He* was the one who had told the Unseelie Court about her. *He* was why her dad was dying.

Tears filling her eyes, Kim let the sleeve of her shirt fall over her fingers. With that slight protection, she yanked the ring out of her nose. The skin tore, but the pain was nothing to what she had felt.

Kim drove the point of the tiny piece of iron into Oreyn's throat. Flame curdled the skin around it.

He shrieked.

As he tried snatching it, the fire leaped from his throat to his hands and then to his sleeves. His screams turned to hoarse wheezes. Arms outstretched, he staggered toward Kim.

She dodged, then turned and fled deeper into Faerie's perfect woods. Careening through the trees, Kim ran until her legs collapsed under her. With her arms wrapped around her head, Kim lay on the ground and sobbed.

#

She woke in an unfamiliar bed. Every thread in the silk sheets chafed, as if her skin were too sensitive from a fever. Light filtered through carved filigree windows and caressed rich tapestries. Kim squinted to hold out as much of the too-crisp vision as possible. Her head ached from all the intricate detail.

"Kim, honey?" Her mother's voice drew her gaze to the side.

She had thought Mom seemed old before, but worry had added new lines to her forehead. Or maybe she could see more in Faerie. "Dad?" Her voice cracked on that one syllable.

"Right here." From her other side, Dad took her hand and held it firmly. "How do you feel, little girl?"

She whispered, "I want to go home."

Her dad froze. "You are home, sweetie."

"Hush, Woody." Mom patted her hand. "Let's go."

They helped her stand. Then Kim's mother spoke in the same language Oreyn had used. The world twisted, spun, and Kim staggered into her living room.

The soft toile fabric and Berber carpet looked as they had left it. The clock on the mantel said it was just after seven. Outside the window, dawn was beginning to light in their yard.

Her mother said, "Why don't you run on up to bed?"

Without words to even think about everything that had happened, Kim nodded. Later there would be time to talk, but she felt too battered for thought. Kim hugged her parents for a long time and dragged herself up the stairs to her room.

She hopped over the line of salt, then turned. Squatting, she brushed the barrier aside.

Kim turned out the lights and crawled into bed.

She left the door open.

Pattern on Stone

By James SA Corey

Excerpt of remarks by Yva Alenea Brooks delivered to the Umarra
Institute, Bercale-3, August 15 2751 (relative standard)

*The purpose of our mission was to examine the Carrath artifact
discovered on Ouroboros-4 seven standard years ago. As with
previous relics of its kind, this took the form of metamorphic rock,
apparently of local origin, with a complex of channels and
penetrations that either create or contain an energetic field effect. The
effect has been compared to neural activity, but the gross similarities
between the Carrath patterns and signaling systems of either Earth-
or Eunollia-based life-trees breaks down quickly at a finer level of
analysis. The signature peculiarity of the field effect is its vulnerability*

to slipdrive transport. The first four Carrath artifacts were effectively erased in the attempts to take them for analysis on Earth, Tanabea, and Kors. It is this property that makes them as enigmatic and troubling as they are.

While there is little doubt that the analytic powers of our great institutions would reveal a great deal more than we presently understand about the stonemakers, what exactly they were, and the purpose and structure of the artifacts they left behind, it is for practical reasons impossible. We have the object. We have the means to decode it. But we can't put the two together. Someday we may discover a Carrath stone already on a well-settled and civilized planet. Or we may invest in building up a solar system in which a Carrath stone exists. Until that day, however, research teams such as my own are the best hope for understanding the mysteries that these objects represent. The stones are fascinating to me and have been the center of my own research for eighty years standard, in part because I became focused on—and to a degree seduced by—the idea of something so tantalizingly strange and also so uniquely and intimately out of reach.

#

Slipdrive pilot Peros Danari Williamson woke in his old bed and his new body. This regeneration had darker skin than he'd had before, with thick, black hair on his chest and arms, and, he suspected, the potential of a fairly epic mustache. He'd spent the last fifty years clean-shaven, and the prospect of getting a little facial hair back pleased him more than he let on. He stretched, enjoying the younger muscles and ligaments, the pain-free joints.

The smell of tea wafted in from the little kitchenette. Nadima making her usual breakfast. His sense of smell once again undimmed by age, he let the memories of the same scent of tea carry him back to the common house on Molos, the little flat in London back on Earth, and even the mud-and-bamboo hut on Lopporo that had been their first home after they'd married, two hundred years before. In all the places they had lived their shared life, Nadima has always liked the same smoky tea in the morning.

He dressed himself in a pair of canvas trousers and a casual tunic. The flooring was textured stone, and cool under his bare feet. In the kitchenette, Nadima sat on a tall stool. Her hair was white with just a hint of yellow that made her look always a little unwashed. She wore a suit jacket and a broad, dark skirt with laced boots that said she was ready to travel. Peros didn't hide his pleasure at that.

"Good," he said.

She turned to him as if just noticing he was there. "What is?"

He gestured at her—index and middle fingers together sweeping up and down her body as he walked to the coffee maker. "You're ready for the clinic. You put off the regen too long. You won't be recovered all the way before we have to go."

"Go," she echoed as if the word meant something different to her.

"No clinics on Ourborous-4. You'll be stuck like that until we get back." He didn't say *Or die that way*. Nadima had never liked the regen process. He had to cajole and bully her every time. The threat of her body wearing out and failing was a stage in the traditional argument, but it came later if he needed it.

"Yes, of course," she said, and he stopped, coffee cup in hand but still cool and empty. Her gaze floated for a moment, then found his and stayed there.

"What is it?" he asked.

"I cancelled the appointment. I'm not ready for it. Not yet."

"We'll look ridiculous. I'll seem like I'm married to my

grandmother." While he said it lightly, there was a buzz of annoyance in it. If anyone in the thousands of worlds would hear it, it would be her. She softened, which was odd. They were very practiced at how to fight with each other and how to reconcile after. The expression in her eyes and the corners of her mouth wasn't the one that two centuries had led him to expect. He put the coffee mug into the machine with a feeling like he'd slipped on ice he hadn't known was there.

"Come, you," she said gently. "Sit."

"My coffee is—"

"Come sit."

Peros felt a rush of annoyance almost anger—that even as it warmed his blood, he recognized as a mask for some other emotion. "Nadi—"

"Please," she said without a hint of pleading in her voice. As if against his will, he abandoned his cup and came to the stool beside hers.

She took his right hand in both of hers. Her skin felt thin and papery against his own. "I think we're done," she said. "You can have the tea."

She squeezed his hand, let it go, and stood with a gentle sigh.

"I have coffee," he said, gesturing back toward his still-empty mug, but she wasn't listening to him. She walked to the door of their flat and stepped out as if she were going somewhere. Peros laughed once, not in mirth but confusion, and looked at the teacup. It was perfectly full with deep brown tea, aromatic steam curling up from its surface. She hadn't had a sip of it. He took a mouthful. It didn't taste strange. The day tasted strange around it.

Even so, it was almost an hour before he thought to check Nadima's public social profile and see that, after two centuries and with no other warning, he had been divorced.

The Carrath stones themselves vary in size, but maintain a common ratio of 1 to 1.7 to 4. The channels carved in them show markings consistent with a drill, and flakes of steel suggest that this carving was done with something not dissimilar from our own technology. Some people have posited that the stonemakers are a separate branch of humanity, somehow displaced from Earth before the diaspora, and following a parallel track of technological development. It is an intriguing thought, but unfalsifiable. Florid speculation follows the stones, and I have had some flights of fancy myself. It's a hazard of the occupation.

Whether the stones were created in situ or brought to the sites in which we found them is another mystery. The first stone, discovered on Carrath-3, gave the stones their name, but analysis shows that it was not the oldest of the artifacts. It was only the first we happened upon. If the stonemakers were present in these disparate systems, why do we find no other artifacts or structures in common among these sites? If the patterns or their field effects have an origin outside the systems, how did they arrive there if not by slipdrive? And why does the stone appear to be local to the systems? What carved them, and where did the carvers go?

We have only the artifacts themselves to guide us. Which brings me to the central problem of my research, and with all research into them.

Context.

The *Forger into Darkness* was a rated ship with room on board for seventy people, a small warehouse for their supplies, the slipdrive chamber and housing, and an interior design of cream, pale blue, and an orange that should have been hideous, but somehow managed to seem cheerful. The ship sat in its gate high above the atmosphere, waiting for the last of its passengers to arrive.

Peros paced the pilot's quarters. By regulation, he could have been downgraded to a single now that he was unaccompanied by a spouse or spouses, but Nadima had left with so little time before the departure that the change would have been more trouble than it was worth. Instead, the other sink in the bathroom went unused. The other half of the bed stood witness by its emptiness. The other closet held nothing but the place where her dresses and gowns, tunics and trousers and undergarments would have been.

Sitting on the desk was the homunculus of Mohommed, their first son. The boy himself—a man almost a hundred and seventy years old, but still in Peros's mind a boy—was on a habitable moon of Ergregos-7. They were a hundred lightyears apart, but the slip made it as if his son were in the room.

"Did she speak to you?"

"Yes," Mohommed said.

"Were you able to talk sense into her?"

The homunculus lifted its hands in a gesture Peros recognized. Nadima had made it when she was exasperated, and little Mohommed had learned it and kept it in the patterns of his brain for the fifteen decades since he had left their home to start his own life. The boy likely didn't know the motion wasn't his own or where he'd learned it.

"She seems happy," Mohommed said.

Peros didn't curse, but his growl made if feel as if he had. "Is she with another man?"

The homunculus leaned forward. "She is on a walking tour of Kellar Complex on Rasia-3 with Fatima Delgado and Abby Haal. I don't think she has some secret lover, Papa."

"Then why?" Peros snapped.

The homunculus shrugged. When Mohommed spoke, his voice was weary. "I haven't lived with her in a century and a half. You woke up beside her every day. You know her better than I do."

An alert chimed. Peros was expected at the captain's table for dinner with the VIPs for the expedition. The image of Nadima's empty chair beside him intruded into his mind, a wave of black dread flowing behind it.

"I have to go," he said. "Keep at her. Find out what you can."

"Papa, this isn't going to help."

"I just want to understand."

"Well, you sound angry."

"I am angry. I can be angry and understand. I can do both."

"If you say so. Be well."

The homunculus went still and lost Mohommed's shape and features. Peros let himself curse, now that he was alone, and threw himself into his dress uniform with a banked violence. The man who looked back out at him from the mirror looked young and fierce. Not at all like a man with a wound in his heart. It didn't look like him at all.

The table was round with room for a full dozen settings. The centerpiece was a kinetic sculpture of wirework and thin membrane that remade itself in iridescent dragonfly-wing patterns every few seconds. The captain, a hard-faced woman from Gellia-3, was one he had worked with before and liked well enough. She didn't ask after Nadima, so he assumed she knew. The chair that would have been his wife's if he still had one was occupied by a pleasant, slightly horse-faced woman.

"New regen?" she said as she passed the olive oil.

It took Peros a moment to understand what she'd said, as lost as he was in himself. His smile was, he hoped, polite.

"Yes. Just before I came here."

"The first few weeks after a regen, I feel like I'm eighteen again. Terribly distracting. Mine's three years in, and I still feel like I'm getting used to it some days." She held out her hand. "Yva Brooks. I'm research lead."

"Peros Williamson. Pilot," he said. He meant to shake her hand, but she didn't move when his fingers clasped hers, so they only sat there, hand in motionless hand, until she let him go.

"I understand I was a last-moment fill-in. I hope your wife isn't ill?"

"I wouldn't know. She's divorced me," he said, and realized it was the first time he'd said the word aloud. The first time he'd confessed his new status as if it were truly done, and not merely a moment's aberration on Nadima's part.

"Ah, I'm very sorry," Yva said. "Was it a long marriage?"

"Almost two centuries," Peros said, astonished by how conversationally it came out.

"That's an impressive run," Yva said, and took a sip from her water glass. "I've never been much for long-term relationships. The alternative can get lonely, that's true, but I've always found ways to cope."

She smiled at him in a way that didn't mean anything, unless he wanted it to. But if he wanted it to, it did. Peros' heart was suddenly racing, and he felt a blush rising under his newly darkened skin. And rage. He was single. Nadima had left him. She had no grounds to object to his behavior, whatever it was.

"I would be grateful," he said carefully, "for any advice you can share."

\#

Imagine for a moment that you are in a pub with a group of people who know each other well. People who have been interacting with each other for a very long time. Imagine one of them makes a reference to some event that they shared, but that you did not. Will that be comprehensible to you? Will it not? The difference is the context. If they say "Remember the night when Toby got so drunk he tried to go home with Mira?" and you know both Toby and Mira and why they would be a poor sexual match—close consanguinity, for example—you will be in a position to understand the scenario despite not having shared the experience. If you do not, you still have enough shared context of what it is to be in a pub, what it is to be drunk, and what sorts of things inspire hilarity in one's friends after the fact to understand that the pairing was somehow inappropriate.

But what if the reference were smaller? Less complete? Imagine that the night Toby asked Mira home with him, it was because he'd underestimated the power of a new drink. Call it Ambler's Ale. Your friends might say, "Remember the night Toby drank Ambler's?" Now you are more at a loss. Your context is less useful. You might guess that Toby overindulged, but the details beyond that, shared though they are by the group, are lost to you. Or you might think he'd disliked the drink in some way that caused him distress and the others amusement. Or that it had been someone else's drink, picked up and consumed in error. Or any of a thousand other possibilities. Without more information, there is no way to choose one interpretation over another. Now imagine they only said "Tony and the Ambler's." Or just "The Ambler's night."

The meaning of all these references is identical to those who carry the context with them, but for the naïve listener, hope of understanding retreats quickly.

In this metaphor, the Carrath stonemakers are the friends, and the artifacts are the references to Toby's indiscretion. And we are— or specifically I am—the new girl in the pub, trying to make sense of what's going on around her.

My example sounds light-hearted, I know, but I chose it carefully. Because I believe the great majority of you listening to me know have had an experience like that. A moment of feeling excluded by those around you. Of knowing that there is something there that you are outside of. It is distressing—even painful—to know that there is an answer to your question, but that you cannot access it.

And because you and I share that context, I can give you a sense of the frustration of working with the Carrath stones.

#

It was strange to have a lover who was not Nadima. Sexually, he was awkward at first. Yva was forthright in what she wanted and guided him clearly to her own satisfaction. Peros was surprised to find that, outside the bedroom, he didn't know what he wanted from her or else did not have a vocabulary to ask for it.

The journey to Ouroboros was uneventful, though the sense of displacement and disorientation that came with the slip was perhaps a bit more pronounced for Peros than usual. Touchdown on the fourth planet was on a calm day, atmospherically speaking, and crew and passengers alike walked into the local sunlight with the air of going to a new park on a picnic. The *Forger into Darkness* ceased for a time to be a ship and became instead a village. For the months of the expedition, it would act as base camp for the scientists, and then become a ship again, riding the slip to Bercale-3. And, Yva made gently clear, after that she and he would not know each other.

"You should stay here," he said one evening after they had fucked and eaten dinner. "It's not good to be alone so much."

"I'm not alone," she said. "My work is very good company."

"Maybe I wasn't talking about you."

If she had been Nadima, she would have heard the hurt in his voice. She would have bent a little. If not enough to change her plan, at least enough to offer him some little reassurance. Yva laughed.

"You should come to the site."

"I'm a pilot. What would I do there?"

"See it. Look. We came all this way. Seems like a shame not to take in the sights."

"I will if you want me to."

She laughed again and shook her head. "Oh, bunny." Bunny was not her pet name for him. It was what she called anyone she liked but was presently annoyed by. He had come to understand her that well, at least.

The site was a series of sandstone caves at the side of a wide, green-gray sea. Yva drove a cart there with two of the other science team members and Peros. They talked about superimposed magnetostatic potentials and diagrammatic quantum analysis. He watched the local sun setting over the water, the clouds going pink and gold as the sky slid to indigo.

In the caves, a truckback reactor fed electricity through a snakepit of conduit and wires to assaying equipment and sensor arrays, work lights and climate-controlled habs. A dozen or more people worked there at any given time in rolling ten-hour shifts like they were running a ship. Peros walked through the place with his hands in his pockets. The smell of saltwater and local algae equivalents was rich and pungent.

Yva took his hand, pulling him toward the central chamber. "Come on. Big show is this way." He pretended to be reluctant, but in truth his curiosity was piqued.

The stone was as tall as a man, striped gray and white with tiny flecks of red unlike the sandstone walls around it. The surface was covered in complex lines that reminded him equally of wiring diagrams and calligraphy. The lines glowed, and though they were silent, he had the sense of hearing someone speaking too softly to make out the words. Yva stood before it, her hand in his. Her eyes had hunger and excitement in them, and for a moment she reminded him of a cat he and Nadima had kept in the common house on Molos, the way the little beast would stare at a mouse hole.

"This is impressive," he said, knowing the words were too small.

"It is," Yva said, and then the shared moment was over.

He stayed for an hour, watching and staying out of the way. When he told Yva he was going back to the ship, she answered with a grunt, not looking up from the screens. As he rode back to the ship, the stars had come out. The galactic disk glowed, its contours slightly different as they were on every world. Peros felt a thickness in his throat and chest and wondered if he might be growing ill or having some allergic reaction to the local air.

When he got back to the ship, he took a long shower which did not relax him, drank a glass of wine that the ship generated, and put in a connection request to Nadima, expecting it to go unanswered as his previous attempts had done. This time, however, the homunculus shifted and changed. Between one moment and the next, it developed long white hair with just a bit of yellow to it as if it had once been blonde, though it had not. Her face, tiny now to fit the homunculus's thumb-sized skull, was pale, deeply lined, and serene. She wore a dress of purple tapestry, wrapped around her shoulders, and a necklace of silver set with huge turquoise stones. Nadima had still not gone for regeneration, and the annoyance he felt at that was like hearing the name of an old friend he had almost forgotten.

She didn't speak, and—caught between *What were you thinking to do this to us?* and *I have taken a new lover* and *I miss you*—he didn't either. The homunculus tilted her head. The tiny smile seemed amused by him.

"I didn't think you would answer," he said.

"I almost didn't. But you keep trying, and I thought maybe if I did this once, it would help you be free."

"I don't want to be free. What were you thinking, Nadi? Why are you doing this?"

She shook her head. "I had my time with you. It was good, when it was good. It was less good when it was bad. And then I was finished."

"Oh, please. Marriage isn't a meal. You don't take your fill and then push your plate away. You and I are two parts of the same thing. We belong together."

"We did," she agreed. "But the woman you're thinking of doesn't exist anymore. She hasn't for years, really. There's only me now, and I don't fit the same way that she did."

He leaned over his desk, towering over the homunculus, scowling at it. "This is ridiculous. You're not talking sense. You are going to come home when I am finished with this contract. You and I are going to counseling or something. We'll work this out."

Her sigh was soft and gentle, and it made him realize that wherever she was, she was not being towered over. For her, there was a homunculus that looked like him, only tiny, on her own desk. It made him feel small here as well.

"You can call back if you like," she said. "I don't believe I will answer, but I didn't think I would answer this time either. Maybe I'll surprise us both."

Her image dissolved as he snapped "I'm seeing another woman."

He didn't think she'd heard him. When he tried the connection again, it failed. He sat alone for a time, growing more aware of the depths to which he had just humiliated himself. He didn't weep, but he permitted himself to feel the sadness that had been his silent companion since the day she'd left.

Later, he made a cup of smoky tea, and set it across the table from him, watching the steam rise from it as if it might tell him something.

#

A mystery that cannot be solved and one that simply hasn't been solved yet are difficult, if not impossible, to tell apart. We have learned a great deal from the Carrath stones, and this new one has yielded another dataset that may hold the key to deciphering all of them. Or it may not. If not, the next one—assuming there is another one found—may. Or there may be no key. The secret of the stones and their creation may require contextual knowledge we don't have and never will.

It is possible that I have spent decades of my life on a problem I lack the ability to resolve. Even if I remain dedicated to this study—and I expect I will—I may die with a deep knowledge of trivia about the Carrath stones and no insight into the issues that brought me here. Or, maybe next time it will all line up, we will find the thing that puts all the unknowns into a formula, and I will be able to write an equation that lays bare the mysteries. Maybe I already have the information, but haven't developed the wisdom yet to see the critical connection.

For me, for now, the Carrath stones and the alien civilization that fashioned them are a paradox. They remind me that, as we explore and travel this vast, glorious, tragic universe, we are not alone.

And also that we are.

The Wreck of the Tartarus

By Lee Murray

October 2033

Strapped in her seat, Captain Kennedy R. Jones clutched the console as the submarine rolled on the Atlantic seabed. Seaman McNaught wasn't so lucky; flung across the control room, his skull smashed against the interior wall. The young man's face registered an instant of surprise before it slackened and collapsed. Then Kennedy lost sight of him, the submarine still toppling, rocks and debris from the volcano battering the *Tartarus*'s graphene laminate exterior. The sub groaned, and Kennedy caught a whiff of burning rubber—electrical circuits—tasted blood, fear.

Orange warning lights flickered.

The hull shrieked, grinding, sliding on rock.

Behind Kennedy, someone screamed.

The vessel spun 180 degrees to starboard. Kennedy gasped. Her grip broke. She snatched at the arms of her chair as the sub twisted, tumbled, then tumbled again. The pride of the US Navy tossed like litter scattered carelessly on the wind.

Would it never stop? And would the *Tartarus* survive? Kennedy prayed the ship's designers knew their business.

For a moment, she thought of Cole and their girls, Carlotta and Marie, at home. Right now, it was fall in Wisconsin. At Devil's Lake State Park, the trees would be glorious, all gold and red and green; nature's fireworks reflected and amplified on the water's surface. Kennedy swallowed as the vessel jolted again. Why had she forsaken that majestic landscape for the darkest vaults of the ocean?

Her head whiplashed, a stab jolting her spine. Was the roll slowing? She clung on. The wait was excruciating, interminable.

Eventually, the sub ground to a stop. Upright, thank God. There were only a handful of her crew members in the control room, yet Kennedy could swear she heard a collective exhale. Then, just as they dared to breathe, there was a tearing, followed by an inexorable thrumming on the hull. Once more, they waited.

Minutes passed.

At last, everything fell quiet.

Kennedy unsnapped her seat belt, ignoring the nausea that welled in her throat, and took two steps to portside to check on McNaught. She touched her fingers to his neck, but he was dead—poor man. Hardly surprising, given that the back of his skull was dented cruelly inwards. Had he lived, his seafaring days would likely have been over; his right knee was shattered, the lower limb twisted unnaturally back on itself. Kennedy winced. He'd been spared that pain at least.

Fighting dizziness, she reached for a handhold, instead her fingers touched her executive officer, Cohen, slumped against the wall. Glassy eyes stared up at her. His mouth agape in a silent scream, his still-warm skin already leaching color. Kennedy's heart clenched. The *Tartarus* assignment was their first together, so she hadn't known him well, but he'd impressed her as competent and dependable. Solid. The son of a single mother, he wasn't—hadn't been—ruffled by a female commanding officer, rare even in these progressive times. She closed Cohen's eyes with her fingertips.

Where was everyone? Kennedy's pulse thrummed. Her scalp tightened. Was she the only one still alive? She stifled panic, an odd pang of loneliness already stealing over her. No, she mustn't panic. There were fifty crew members on the *Tartarus*, and she was responsible for them all. She needed to get her head together, assess the damage, see to the wounded, and make a plan to get back on course.

Steadying herself against the wall, Kennedy got to her feet.

"Captain Jones."

She started at the voice close behind. It was Chief Petty Officer Masterton. A quietly spoken man out of Ohio, he was a meat-and-potatoes sort. The type you'd expect to find behind the counter of a hardware store. A large bruise was blooming on the man's cheekbone. His eyes drifted to the side.

"Executive Officer Cohen?" he asked, squinting.

"Deceased. McNaught, too."

"Shit." Masterton shook his head. "Begging your pardon, ma'am. What do you need me to do?"

A console burst into flame on the wall behind McNaught.

The fire siren wailed.

Fuck! Extinguisher. Where is it? It'd come adrift from its bracket. *Rolled somewhere. Where?* Kennedy whirled, caught the flash of red, lunged for it. *God, that's heavy.* Pulling the pin as she clambered over McNaught, she aimed the nozzle at the base of the flame, pressed the trigger, and let the foam fly.

Speckles of foam landed on McNaught; Kennedy kept spraying. The fire sputtered; she didn't stop until the foam slid in clumps down the wall.

The siren ceased its blaring.

"It's okay; it's out," Masterton said.

Panting, Kennedy nodded. She lowered the extinguisher. Blew out hard. "Right, well I'd better assess the damage to the *Tartarus*," Kennedy said. "You check with the medic."

Masterton lifted his chin. "Yes, ma'am."

Several others were on their feet now, looking dazed and disoriented. Faces blanched when they spied the dead men.

"Masterton—before you do that, see about covering Cohen and McNaught." Kennedy clicked the extinguisher back into its bracket. "Let's give them a little privacy."

"Ma'am."

Kennedy took her chair at the console and checked the screens. Breathed in relief. At first glance, the *Tartarus*'s double-hull structure appeared intact. With thousands of feet of water above the vessel, it was a comfort to know they weren't in any immediate peril. Kennedy illuminated the outer hull, set the built-in eyes to scan, then checked the screens.

Her heart fluttered. *Please, no.*

There was no denying the truth: the ship's stern, including the propellers and the outflow for the internal motion turbines, lay buried under an avalanche of rubble. Even now, rocks still clattered against the hull. The propellers would likely be impacted with rock. To make matters worse, the *Tartarus* had toppled into a trench and was now pinned on a ledge.

Kennedy switched screens, her heart in her throat. She gave a squeak of joy; the aft escape hatches were still clear. Her excitement was short lived. They were how many feet down? Ten thousand? More? Even if the distress buoy had managed to make it to the surface amidst the rubble of the eruption, the *Tartarus* could be a mile away from the volcano by now. Searching the ocean would be like looking for the proverbial needle in a haystack. And if the US Navy teams did manage to locate them, navigating the trench would be treacherous. Few vessels could withstand the pressures at the *Tartarus*'s crush depth. What if they were beyond reach?

No. Stop this. There's time. The graphene hull is intact. The organic liquid-flow batteries are fully charged. This isn't the Kurst, and the US isn't Russia. The Tartarus isn't going to vanish without trace like the USS Cyclops or the ARA San Juan.

Not on my watch.

"Hurst?" she called. "Do we still have comms?"

The ensign scrambled to her feet after retrieving her headset from the floor. She checked her screens. "We've lost the cable for the two-way ELF, but if we send up the reserve array, then, yes, ma'am, we should have comms."

Kennedy forced herself to breathe slowly, in and out, mimicking the ebb and flow of ripples on the beach. Her anxiety dampened. Everything would be fine. The sub was teched to the nines. They would extend the reserve array to reestablish the low frequency radio and she would let her superiors know what had happened. Rescue teams would be dispatched. Cohen and McNaught may be lost, but Kennedy and the rest of the crew could still be plucked from the jaws of hell and delivered to safety.

When that happened, Kennedy would bury her face in her children's hair and drink in the scent of apple shampoo and the Wisconsin outdoors. She would sob ugly tears into Cole's chest, and let him rock her like a baby. Until then, she would be the unflappable captain of this ship.

Until then, they would stay calm and sit tight.

#

When the bodies of the dead had been stowed, the *Tartarus*'s medic and its chief engineer joined Kennedy in the control room.

Pale and drawn, the medic cleared his throat before giving his report. Kennedy's throat was raw, too. By now the fire-retardant foam had dried; it was still like breathing acid.

"There are four dead, including Cohen and McNaught," the medic said. There was a smear of blood on the cuff of his uniform.

Kennedy nodded. She'd already had the numbers from Masterton.

"On top of that, we have five wounded, not counting those with minor bruises and bumps—which is practically everyone."

Kennedy couldn't help lifting her hand to her neck, still aching from the whiplash. All around her, the control room hummed with the bleep of systems checks and the murmur of status reports.

"And the five wounded?" she asked. "How are they faring?"

"Two have concussion—I'll keep an eye on them in case they deteriorate. One dislocated shoulder—I've already reset it—and one of the cooks has extensive scalding. All survivable. It's Ensign Rafferty who worries me most. His pelvis is shattered; it's likely he has some internal injuries. Without hospital care, he might not make it to Sunday's ice cream social."

Kennedy grimaced. "The navy is working on getting us to the surface as soon as possible, but it's going to take time."

"How long?" Scotty said, the engineer as brusque as his Trekkie namesake.

"I spoke with the commodore an hour ago. They're working on a plan now."

She pursed her lips remembering the terse conversation with her commander. To be fair, the navy was never going to be happy about the situation. The *Tartarus* was the outcome of billions of dollars of research effort, its recharging technology a closely guarded military secret.

"So, the vessel is lost," the commodore had said.

"I believe so, sir. There's an outside chance the propellers could clear the rocks without jamming, but in the event we don't succeed, it would leave the *Tartarus* without power."

Under normal conditions, the *Tartarus* recharged its liquid-flow battery by tethering to the seabed and allowing the ocean currents to spin the internal turbines like water over gills. The *Tartarus*'s inflow vents were intact, but with the water outflow buried, there were no currents to speak of. No recharging meant no power and no oxygen. Eventually, the *Tartarus* was going to flicker out, and its crew with it.

"We could certainly attempt to break out," she added, when the commodore didn't speak. "And as the ship's captain, I'd be willing to volunteer myself for the task—but only after my crew are safely away."

The commodore remained silent. A glitch in the line, or just a minute of reflection? To Kennedy, the moment felt heavy with accusation, as if she ought to have predicted the eruption and steered the *Tartarus* out of danger.

"Let me speak to Cohen," he said eventually.

"Cohen is among the dead, sir."

"Ah." Another pause. "Shame."

Kennedy's eyes narrowed. Why ask to speak to Cohen? The *Tartarus* was her command. "Sir? Is there something I should know?"

"No, no. Cohen and I go way back, is all. Don't worry, Captain. We're going to get you and your crew out of there. But it's going to take us a while to get things underway, so you'll need to be patient."

"At present, we're at 89 percent charge. The *Tartarus* has oxygen tanks for two days, and we can also create oxygen through electrolysis. But splitting water will mean drawing heavily on the available charge," Kennedy said. She was wasting air; the commodore knew all this.

"I'm fully aware of the ramifications, Captain," the commodore had said tersely. "I'll update you as soon as I have some information." He had cut the connection.

The medic cleared his throat again, bringing Kennedy back to the crew briefing. "In the meantime," he said, "we're going to need to reduce our energy consumption."

"We can cut some lights, turn down the heating. Keep everyone in their bunks. That'll allow us to eke out charge," Scotty said.

Kennedy nodded. "I'll announce the measures on the 1MC and come back and chat to the wounded a little later."

When the men had returned to their respective stations, leaving only the control room crew, Ensign Hurst turned to her. "Are we going to be shark shit, Captain?" she asked.

The other crew members looked to Kennedy. It was a fair question.

Another deluge of rock hammered the *Tartarus*, boulder-sized hail, louder than artillery fire, rattling her bones. Grunts and cries echoed through the ship. Everyone snatched for a handhold. Kennedy planted her feet. Held her breath. There was nothing to do but hold on and hope.

When at last the rocks clattered to a stop, the crew looked again to Kennedy.

"No, Hurst, we are not," she replied. "Not if I can help it."

#

A day passed. And another. In the watery limbo, an endless night hovering between life and death, Kennedy didn't sleep. Even the wounded slumbered fitfully. If these were to be their last hours, no one wanted to waste them sleeping. Instead, they read, told stories, passed photos, sketched. One man played a blues harp.

In the control room, Kennedy wrote letters to Cohen's wife and sister, to McNaught's mother, and the families of the other deceased. She thought of her own babies, Carlotta and Marie, of the letter she might want to receive, and took her time perfecting her prose, using words like service, and honor, and courage.

That done, she had Hurst contact HQ again. "I'd appreciate an update," she told her commander.

"We're still working on it," the commodore said.

Kennedy wanted to scream, but he was their lifeline, the man in charge of getting them off this ridge so, for the sake of her crew, she kept her voice even. "Ensign Rafferty's condition has deteriorated."

"Look, Captain, the US Navy is doing everything it can. We think we've located you, but there are issues on the surface—a storm is hampering our rescue efforts. You need to trust me, as soon as we get a break in the weather, we'll get your people out of there." His voice was overly cheery. Putting a positive spin on things to keep up morale.

Pulling her jacket around her shoulders, Kennedy checked the battery power: 38 percent. They were running out of time.

She wrote to Carlotta and Marie. Handwritten notes. So young, Marie, would likely forget her if she didn't come home, her face blurring in her daughter's memory, but Carlotta was older and would remember. Kennedy labored over the paragraphs, yet the words were insufficient and lackluster. Nothing could capture her feelings for them, the ache their loss would cause her.

In the end, she quoted Apollinaire:

"Vienne la nuit sonne l'heure / Les jours s'en vont je demeure."

"Let night come, toll the hour. The days pass by, I remain."

If they ever saw the letters, Cole would explain. Perhaps he would take them to Paris, so they could watch the gray water of the Seine pass beneath the bridge.

Of course, they might never get her letters. The US Navy was good at keeping secrets. The *SSBN James Madison* had clipped a Soviet sub in 1974 during the Cold War, and nothing was known of it for forty-three years. In forty-three years, her girls would be in their fifties—older than she was now.

The sub creaked under another tumble of debris.

Or, the *Tartarus* might just be one more in a litany of ships lost to the stygian depths. Kennedy folded the notes and left them on her desk.

#

On the third day, Rafferty passed away.

Kennedy wrote another letter, then put in another call. "Sir, you do realize that very soon my crew is going to be sucking rubber." Already, the air in the sub was dangerously thin. Kennedy struggled to concentrate, her head fuggy with headaches—although that might also be sleep deprivation.

"I'm sorry, Captain."

"The weather's still too dangerous?"

"Yes." His tone was guarded.

"We're talking hours, not days."

"I understand."

Kennedy's skin prickled. This was ridiculous. "Sir, exactly how far away is the rescue ship? Assuming the weather abates, how long before you can get a submersible down here? Because ten minutes or two hours too late, the result for us is going to be the same."

The commodore said nothing.

Her heart skipped. The reality was as blinding as the ocean was dark. "There is no rescue attempt," she whispered.

The commodore sighed. "Captain Jones, I'm so sorry. The *Tartarus* is state-of-the-art, the culmination of decades of investment in submarine tech. My people said the only way to get the *Tartarus* up fast enough was to hire outside help. Imagine if a tech company like MobyCorp, or Poseidon Industries were to get hold of the blueprint. They'd reengineer it and sell it on to the foreign power with the deepest pockets. The White House can't allow it. There's too much at stake."

Kennedy shivered. So, there it was. After days of fobbing her off, here was the truth at last. "You're sacrificing my crew."

"For the safety of the American people, yes."

"What of the forty-six American people on the *Tartarus*? What about them? What about *us*?" Her voice was shrill.

The commander clucked his tongue. "When we bring *Tartarus* up later—when we can do it in-house, quietly—your crew and your families will be...looked after."

"Cold comfort, sir."

"Executive Officer Cohen would have understood. He knew his orders..."

This time Kennedy cut the connection, blood thundering in her veins. Cohen! Dependable, solid Cohen, her executive officer, had been planted to countermand her orders in the event the little lady stepped out of line. Kennedy clenched her teeth so hard she risked cracking the enamel. What would his single mother have made of *that*?

But her anger wasn't going to help things. She needed to think. Again, she focused her mind on the ebb of the tide, breathing in slow waves, dampening her fear. "Masterton—John—would you ask Scotty to join us, please?"

#

"Fuck!" Scotty cursed when he heard the news. "Fuckity-fuck-fuck!"

Masterton closed his eyes, his lips quivering. When he opened them, he said, "What about other countries? The Russians. The Chinese. South Korea. They all have subs. There might be someone out there. We could send out an SOS."

"Fat chance," Scotty said.

He wasn't wrong. The Atlantic Ocean was massive. Depending on where their rescuers were, getting to them could take days.

Scotty shrugged. "But I'm not against giving it a go. I wouldn't mind seeing Central Park again."

"Ensign Hurst." Kennedy turned to her comms officer.

Hurst lifted her earphones off one ear. "Yes, ma'am?"

"If there are any other subs within shouting distance, I want you to raise them, please. Anyone at all."

Hurst's eyes widened, but she bent her head and fiddled with her dials.

Kennedy looked at Scotty and Masterton. "For the record, this is on me," she said firmly. Masterton opened his mouth, but Kennedy held up her hand. "No. If we come through this, my report will say you did your best to dissuade me, but I refused to listen."

Her shipmates nodded. What they were suggesting was treason; if they succeeded, there would be hell to pay. Still, rescue, even by a foreign power, was better than being dead. Kennedy prayed there was someone out there.

At last, Hurst turned to her. "Someone's scrambling our communications, ma'am. Flooding the frequency," she said. "If there is a sub in the vicinity, they're not going to hear us over the noise."

Masterton's shoulders slumped.

"Fuck," Scotty said again. "They're killing us."

Kennedy glanced at her screen. "We've still got 12 percent. We could have a go at powering up and seeing if we can blast ourselves off this ledge. There's a small chance we could get clear of the rock, make it to the surface."

"And we throw open a window when we get there," Scotty said glibly.

"We've got to try something," said Masterton.

"Tell the crew to strap in," Kennedy said.

"Ma'am," Hurst interrupted, before they'd had a chance to move. "I'm getting something. It sounds like...like a craft."

"Another sub?" The commodore had made it clear there was no help coming, still Kennedy's hope flared.

Hurst frowned. "Maybe. Except...so strange...and it's as if it's coming from *below* us."

That wasn't possible; it must be some kind of echo caused by their position in the trench. Either that or Hurst and Kennedy were suffering from the same debilitating headaches.

Still, Kennedy rushed to her screens, punching buttons to illuminate built-in eyes on the *Tartarus*'s hull. She almost knocked skulls with Masterton as they searched the screens for their rescuers.

Something was definitely out there. Just nothing Kennedy had ever seen before.

Above them, near the escape hatch, hovered a lozenge-shaped object which looked to be about half the length of the *Tartarus*. Running along either side of the creature were a pair of frilled appendages that rippled in unison.

Kennedy squeezed her eyes shut, then opened them again.

"What is that? A kraken?" Masterton breathed.

So, it wasn't just the effects of sleep deprivation and hypoxia; Masterton could see the floating centipede, too.

"That's *mechanical*, not organic," Scotty said excitedly. He poked the screen with a finger. "See the Greek lettering on the side? That says *Phaedra*."

Kennedy squinted for a better look. At this eleventh hour, the news seemed too good to be true—like a mirage, or a hallucination. A submersible like no other, and from such an unlikely source. "Last I heard, all the Greek Navy still operates is a couple of archaic diesel electrics," Kennedy said. "How do they have something this advanced? And what is the Greek Navy doing in the Atlantic?"

"Rescuing us, I hope," Masterton said. "Maybe they intercepted some intelligence about us and came to see for themselves. Who cares so long as they're here?"

He had a point. Kennedy glanced at the battery readout: 11.8 percent.

"Look!" Masterton said.

Outside, in the gloomy depths of the ocean, a hatch opened on the hovering craft, and two shadowy figures emerged.

"What? They have suits to withstand pressures this deep? That's not…that's not…" Masterton trailed off.

He was right. It simply wasn't possible. At these depths, the tremendous pressure of the ocean would crush a diver in seconds.

"What are they? Gods?"

"Fairy godmothers more like," Scotty said. "Let's get to the escape hatch."

"Hurst. You'd better come," Kennedy told her communications officer. "And bring your translator. My Greek is a little rusty."

They hurried to the base of the ladder. "Let them in, Scotty."

After three days of waiting, the three minutes it took for the hatch to drain seemed an eternity. Kennedy smoothed her hair, tugged at her grimy uniform. Finally, the hatch opened and two men wearing slick body suits descended. The first, a huge swarthy-faced man, was forced to bend his body in half to fit the submarine's headspace.

"Hello!" Their other guest flipped back his head gear. Slim, with a seaman's short-back-and-sides, he held out his hand.

Kennedy stepped forward and clasped it.

"Gordon DeWees of the USS *Cyclops* at your service, ma'am, and this is my colleague, Knoso of Mycenae."

Kennedy snatched her hand back. "What? That's not...you can't..."

"Wait. Did you say the *Cyclops*?" Masterston said, stepping closer to Kennedy. "The cargo ship? But...that vessel disappeared in—"

"Nineteen eighteen. Yes." DeWees's eyes twinkled.

Kennedy's knees weakened and she grasped a rung of the ladder. She must be dreaming—the deluded wishes of a mind addled by hypoxia. DeWees had to be over a century old, yet he looked barely out of his twenties.

Scotty must be bamboozled too because he spluttered, "This is crazy. Are we already dead?"

"Only God and the sea know what happened to the great ship," Masterton murmured, echoing President Wilson's comment about the *Cyclops*.

Except they were all seeing the same thing. And Kennedy had shaken DeWees's hand; he was as solid as she was.

The giant spoke, his voice deep and gravelly, although Kennedy couldn't comprehend a word.

"My friend reminds me that we haven't got much time," DeWees said. "We've come to invite you to join us. We don't have the power to pull your ship free, but we can save your people."

Kennedy turned to Hurst to check the translation, the woman nodding.

"Join you where exactly?" Scotty demanded.

"On Knoso's island of Mycenae," DeWees said. "You might call it Atlantis."

Scotty grunted. He shook his head as if a bubble of water had collected in his eardrum.

"Atlantis is a myth," said Hurst. "A utopian dream."

And DeWees should be dead.

DeWees chuckled. "Actually, Atlantis does exist; I live there. Plato was correct, at least his dates were, but he was a bit off with the location. The island resides beneath the seafloor, its upper flank close to the Bermuda Triangle." DeWees dropped his eyes. "As for it being a utopia, Atlantis is a sanctuary, that's true. The island is beautiful, and its people are welcoming. But there is no utopia without the people you love. If you decide to join us, you can never go back. Your families will never know what happened to you."

"I—" Kennedy paused. The *Tartarus* still had 10 percent power. Would that be enough to break free of the rock pinning them to the ledge? If they got to the surface under their own steam, the commodore would surely move heaven and earth to rescue the submarine. They might bob on the ocean for a few days, but the crew would get to go home. Kennedy could hold her girls in her arms again.

Or, she could use the remaining 10 percent to power the *Tartarus*'s life support systems while the crew evacuated to an alien submersible that would carry off them to an imaginary destination.

Kennedy almost laughed. She was literally stuck between a rock and a hard place.

"Captain," DeWees said softly. "If we're here, it's because no one is coming to rescue you."

Hurst touched Kennedy on the arm. "Ma'am? For what it's worth, if Atlantis exists, I'd like to see it."

Kennedy hesitated, her heart physically aching for her girls. For Cole's breath on her cheek. *For home.* Kennedy straightened her back. Cole would look after their girls, but the men and women of the *Tartarus* were her responsibility.

She swallowed hard. "Assemble the crew, please, John. Tell them to leave everything behind."

"And the dead? Cohen and McNaught? Rafferty?"

"Leave them."

There was a clunk as the centipede submersible locked onto the hull of the submarine. While the crew evacuated the *Tartarus* in groups of four, Kennedy deleted the ship's logs and powered down the screens. She glanced at her letters to Cole and the girls and considered adding a postscript—a private note to let them know she'd be okay—but what might her superiors do if they knew? They'd already sacrificed fifty-one lives to safeguard the technology on the *Tartarus*. How many more would they forfeit to uncover the fabled utopia? And what of the citizens already there?

No. Let the US Navy wonder where the crew had gone—if they ever bothered looking. She smiled bitterly and turned away.

#

Just 0.4 percent battery life remained when she entered the escape trunk, the last to leave the *Tartarus*. Scotty gave her a hand up, pulling her up the final rungs into the Mycenaean submersible.

"It's modelled on the ancient triremes," he said. "Those legs are flexible oars!" His eyes were bright, the blue tinge of hypoxia already fading.

Kennedy glanced back at the wreckage.

She turned to DeWees. "The US Navy may come looking for her. They'll have questions. Do you…is there any way we could let her rest?"

The sailor arched a brow. "I'll see what we can do." He pushed some buttons and the *Phaedra* rang with the sound of ordinance fired.

Taking a seat next to Hurst, Kennedy strapped herself in. As the submersible pulled away, the lights of the *Tartarus* winked out.

Moments later, the cliff collapsed, burying the sub and all her secrets.

Six-String Demon

By Sebastien de Castell

Jen leaned into the Ford Galaxie 500's voluminous trunk and hauled out her old Fender Bandmaster and the cable bag before reaching for the three guitar cases. The first held an acoustic with a cheap, glued-on pickup for amplification; the second, a decent Mexican Fender Strat.

She hesitated before taking out the third—the 1964 Rickenbacker 425. A beat-up, semi-hollow-bodied instrument that supposedly had been used by George Harrison to compose "My Sweet Lord" whilst in the throes of some sort of Hare Krishna religious ecstasy.

Jen sighed, trailing her fingers over the hard case. The Ricky was all that remained from those brief days when she'd had money and let herself believe she was going to be a rock star. But the advance on the *Axe Girl* record deal was gone, the recording itself deemed unmarketable. Now her life was shitty gigs in backwater towns.

Staring at the pile of gear, Jen gave one last thought about leaving the Rickenbacker in the trunk of her crapped-out car. But the asshole singer who'd called her in as a sub for his usual guitarist had been adamant about the Rickenbacker. Something about it having the right 'vibes' for the gig because it had once belonged to Lennon.

That made her nervous. It wouldn't be the first time someone booked her as a side player, had her bring her best gear, and then tried to steal it after the show. Still, he'd been pretty insistent, and she did need the cash.

She loaded the amp, cable bag, and three guitar cases onto a foldable dolly she kept in the trunk, before hauling everything down the street towards the address she'd been given.

#

The house was smaller than Jen expected, not much more than a two-story box seated between larger—and substantially nicer—homes. She hated house-party gigs. Getting harassed was an occupational hazard at the best of times. The ass grabbing was always worse at house parties.

"There you are," called a voice from the shadows beneath the hedge fence. At first, he appeared as nothing more than the red dot of a cigarette and the stench of stale Marlboros. The singer, then—only rock singers still thought it was cool to smoke.

"Car trouble," she explained.

He stepped into the streetlamp's sick light, thin limbed with stringy gray hair that probably hadn't seen a comb since the black leather pants and vest he wore had still been cool. He was older than he'd sounded on the phone.

"Did you bring the Rickenbacker?" he asked.

She stopped pulling the dolly and nodded towards the case on top. "Still don't know why it's so important."

"You'll find out soon enough, Axe Girl." He extended a hand. "Johnny Jacks."

He hadn't given the last name on the phone. Johnny Jacks. Good grief.

"Jen Farmer," she said taking his hand. "Please don't call me Axe Girl." He held her fingers a fraction too long.

Two others sidled from the darkness. The man was young, early twenties at most, with tight curly hair and a thick-lipped smile.

"Levon," Johnny said. "Drummer."

A woman about Jen's age stomped out the remains of a cigarette on the front lawn before joining them. "Lucy," she said. "Lucy Bottom."

The bass player, no doubt, hence the "Bottom." These people might have been time travelers from the late seventies except even then, bands weren't so on the nose.

"So," Jen said, nodding towards the house. "What's the gig? I never did get your song list."

Johnny shrugged and headed for the front door. "Song lists are for feebs."

#

Dragging her amp's head, cab, plus the cable bag and two guitars up the walkway and through the door—only to be informed the gig was on the top floor—worsened Jen's mood. The others left her to carry the equipment up in stages, starting with hauling the guitars and cable bag up the narrow flight of stairs to a tight hallway and then going back for the amp and cabinet.

When she passed an open bedroom, she caught sight of a man and woman sitting on the bed. They looked to be about Jen's age, maybe thirty-five or so, and could have been Sears catalogue models except for their haggard looks and the tears running down the man's cheeks.

"Sorry," Jen mumbled when they glanced up to see her staring. She hoisted the amp head onto her hip and shuffled down the hall towards the next set of stairs going to the top floor.

"Are you..."

Jen turned to find the woman standing behind her, one hand on the doorframe of the bedroom as if she might suddenly run back inside and slam the door shut.

"Guitar player," Jen said, then, not knowing what else to say, she asked, "Big party tonight?"

The woman stared, a horrified expression on her face. "A party?"

"Don't mind her," Johnny Jacks said, striding the hallway towards them. "Axe Girl here is...eccentric." He gently shunted the woman out of the way, whispering as he passed Jen, "Never talk to the clients."

"Whatever," Jen said, following Jacks up the stairs. It wasn't unusual for a band leader to insist that only he communicate with the clients, but it wasn't as if she'd been trying to book herself for the next party.

"You'll set up in there," Johnny said when they reached the top. He pointed to a door on the left at the hallway's far end. A sliver of yellow light crept from beneath the closed, peeling timber panel.

"Why up here?" she asked, guessing at the size of the room. "Isn't it going to be kind of tight in there for dancing?"

"Nobody's going to be doing any dancing tonight," the skeletal singer replied. "Just get the rest of your gear and set up on the window side of that room. Lucy and Levon will be up with their stuff in a few minutes. Right now, I've got to warm up my voice." He turned to go then stopped. "And when you get in there, remember what I said: Nev—"

"Yeah, yeah. 'Never talk to the clients.'"

When she opened the door, only a small desk lamp provided dim illumination. The room was even smaller than she'd figured. "Great," she said.

"Are you the band?"

Opposite the door, a single bed was pressed up against the wall. A kid, maybe eight or nine years old, lay under the covers. He wore some kind of beanie and she couldn't see any hair underneath. Pale features. Wan expression. Probably chemo or radiation. Now, the whole scene made a lot more sense: the parents looking exhausted and miserable, setting up inside a bedroom on the top floor, and of course, the fact that the aging rocker hadn't given her any details about the show. Probably the kid's cancer treatments were going poorly, and this was a special present for him.

Geez, kid, she thought. *You make your last wish to hear crusty old Johnny Jacks croon out his one hit song and collection of mediocre follow-ups? No accounting for taste.*

"Are you the guitar player?" the kid asked. "Guitar's my favorite."

Jen held up the acoustic case and smiled. "Me too. You ever learn to play?"

The boy shook his head.

"Want a quick lesson?" She had done two years of afternoons in the back room of a local guitar shop teaching aspiring high school rockers and over-the-hill wannabes how to play their favorite AC/DC covers.

The kid in the bed pushed himself up to a sitting position. "Is it hard?"

Jen set the acoustic case down and flipped open the clasps. "Easy-peasey. You like rock?"

He shook his head.

"Metal? Pop? Jazz? Folk?" Apparently, none of those interested him, because his head just kept swiveling back and forth. "Help me out, kid. What kind of music do you like?"

"I don't like music," he replied.

She tried to guess at what she'd done to trigger this sudden bout of petulance. "You don't like music?"

"No."

"Everybody likes music, kid."

"What the fuck are you doing?" Johnny Jacks demanded. His sudden appearance at the door and the snarl on his lips nearly sent her tripping over her guitar case.

"Just setting up."

He stormed in and grabbed her by the arm, his long, thin fingers digging into her skin right through her jacket. He hauled her outside the room, kicking the door shut behind them. "I told you never to talk to the clients."

Jen hesitated. She needed the money from this gig, but she also needed to lay down the law. She took a deep breath, then met Jacks's eyes and served up the death stare she'd learned from another guitar player years ago—the look you gave band leaders to make them realize they'd crossed a line.

"Take. Your. Fucking. Hand. Off. Me."

Jacks let go, smiling as he did. It was one of those asshole ex-rocker smiles that said he thought he was still too sexy to have some chick with a guitar tell him off, but if that didn't work, he'd plead harmless old man.

She kept glaring. "I'm not kidding. Don't ever touch me again. I'm here to play guitar, that's it. I don't want any of your shit. I'm not your date. We're not going to flirt."

"But you'll actually *play* the guitar, right?" he asked.

"What the fuck is that supposed to mean?"

"Nothing. Just go set up your goddamned rig and don't let me catch you talking to the clients again."

"The kid talked to me. What was I supposed to do? Tell him to shut up?"

"If he talks to you again, pretend he isn't there. You're here to play the songs I tell you, and then leave. Until you hear otherwise from me, mind your own business. In exchange, you get three hundred bucks, and I promise not to look at your ass when you're soloing. Think you can handle that?"

"Whatever," she said and went back into the room.

Creep.

#

For the next half hour she followed Jacks's instructions to the letter, plugging in her amp, checking her strings, tuning both the acoustic and the Strat, all the while ignoring the kid.

"How long have you been playing?" he asked. When that got no response he said, "It's my birthday, you know."

"Yeah? How old—" she stopped herself. Fucking Jacks and his stupid rules.

"I'm going to be nine. The doctors said I'd never live past five, but they were wrong."

She looked at the pale skin stretched over bony features. He may have beaten the doctor's predictions, but he wasn't likely to see ten.

Jen set down the tuned acoustic and then yanked the patch cable out, plugging it into the Ricky. It only took a couple of seconds to tune—that guitar almost never lost its tuning. She flipped on the standby switch on the amp and was going to do a couple of test chords, but Jacks appeared at the door again.

"Leave it."

"I need to set my amp sounds," she said.

"Do it with the acoustic and the Strat. Don't play the Rickenbacker until I tell you. You'll play the acoustic and then the Strat. If and when I tell you to, you'll bring forth the Rickenbacker."

"Bring forth?" *Who talks like that?* She set the Ricky back in its case and plugged the acoustic back in, strumming a few chords from "With a Little Help from My Friends." She glanced at the kid to see if he liked it. He stuck his tongue out at her.

I'm surrounded by heathens, she thought.

"Meet me downstairs when you're done," Jacks told her.

"For what?"

"Band meeting, of course."

Great. A speech about who was boss mixed with some pontification on his personal philosophy of live performance.

This was going to be the gig from hell.

#

"The first rule," Jacks said, staring at each of them in turn, "is that once I start the song, you don't stop playing until I give you the signal." His gaze swept the other two. "What's the rule?"

Levon scuffed a toe on the kitchen's linoleum floor and Lucy Bottom slumped against a cabinet, but they dutifully repeated his words: "Don't stop playing until Johnny gives the signal."

"What is this?" Jen asked, suddenly irritated past the point of caution. "Some kind of fucking cult? You don't think we know how to play in a goddamned cover band?"

Jacks, far from being angered by her rebellion, seemed heartened. "Cool. Okay, so what's rule number two?"

"Oh, for fuck's—" *Shut up, Jen,* she thought. *So what if he's a weirdo? They're all weirdos, and you need the money.*

Levon seemed eager to please, or at least to get that over with.

"Don't pay attention to the audience."

"And why don't we pay attention to the audience?" Jacks asked, with all the patronizing smugness of a primary school teacher.

"Because the audience is the enemy," Lucy replied.

"Good," Jacks said, wrapping his arms around Levon's and Lucy's shoulders.

Jen no longer had any trouble understanding how Johnny Jacks had descended into playing private parties for sick kids.

"Oh," she said. "What about requests?"

"No requests," the skinny singer replied. "That ain't how the game is played." He locked eyes with her. "We clear on that, Axe Girl?"

"Please don't call me that."

His stare remained. "Clear?"

"Fine. Whatever."

"Good." He removed his arms from the bass player and drummer and stuck his hand out, middle and ring fingers pressed into his palm, index and pinky straight out like devil horns. "Join with me, brother and sisters." Lucy and Levon complied, and then all three had their hands out making the idiotic gesture that Jen hadn't seen anyone over high school age do since…well, high school. "Axe Girl," he said.

"I'm fine, thanks."

"Just do it," Levon urged.

"No." She was all set to launch into a tirade because at this point sleeping in her car seemed better than playing with these psychos, but then Johnny Jacks reached his free hand into the back pocket of his skinny black jeans and pulled out a wad of bills.

"Three hundred, like we agreed," he said, thrusting the money at her. "You decide to walk from here on out, you keep the cash."

She reached for the wad, but he pulled his hand up. "But first…"

Jen stared at the money, then at her fellow musicians with their devil-horn salute, then back at the money. "You're really going to make me do this?"

"Please, Jen," Lucy chimed in. "It's important."

Ugh. I'm going to hate myself in the morning. She stuck out her hand and made the gesture, shaking her arm for emphasis.

Jacks grinned like the self-satisfied eight-year-old he was. "All right, my babies, time to rock this shit all the way to the gates of hell!"

#

"It's MY birthday, and I don't want any stupid music," the kid declared as Jen, Lucy, and Levon got their instruments ready. Jacks stood by the bedroom window facing away from them as if he were a superstar meditating before leaping onto an arena stage to sing for fifty thousand fans.

"It's okay, Kyle," the kid's mother said from the doorway. "Just try it and see what you think."

"No! They're shit. I can already tell." He pointed at Jen. "Just look at her. Bet she can't solo worth a damn."

Little prick.

"Don't be like that, kiddo," the father said. He stepped past his wife into the room and instantly Jacks turned, eyes blazing.

"Get the fuck out. You know the deal."

Jen fully expected the guy to take three strides into the room and punch Jacks in the face, but instead he bowed his head and backed out. "Sorry. Sorry, I just—"

"And close the door."

Jen looked at Levon, waiting for some explanation of this insanity, but the drummer just shrugged with a "Hey, takes all kinds" sort of look. The kid—Kyle—apparently found it all hilariously funny.

"Did you see that?" He looked at Jen. "Daddy's got no balls. Mom says it all the time to her friends."

The level of disfunction in this household was terrifying in its ordinariness. Jen blocked it out by focusing on retuning on her acoustic and waiting for Jacks to tell her what the first song would be.

The singer paced the length of each wall of the room like a panther looking for gaps in his cage. When he got to the kid's bed, he looked down at Kyle. The boy shrank under his blankets, which was a perfectly natural thing to do when faced with an emaciated, corpse-like old man in skinny jeans, with long gray hair hanging wild, and eyes looking like something from an old Iron Maiden album cover.

"Don't," the boy said.

"Shut up, motherfucker," was Johnny's reply.

"Hey man, come on," Jen said. "Don't."

He turned his head and shot her a look that made her slightly more afraid for herself than the kid. "Did I tell you to talk?"

The wad of cash in her pocket was telling her to pack up her guitar and walk, but Lucy put a hand on her arm.

"It's okay, just go with it."

Five minutes, she told herself. One song. Then if this shit didn't get real normal real quick, she was out of here.

Jacks left the kid's bedside and came to stand with the rest of the band. "*Grave Digger*," he said. "The Joe Cocker version."

Not actually the worst choice in the world, Jen thought, waiting for Levon to count in with his drum sticks. Cocker's version of Procol Harum's barely known B-side love song was slow and soulful, a little on the raspy side, but that would probably suit Jacks's voice. She got her fingers into place to play the opening riff, but Johnny started without waiting for the count or for her to play.

With a thick, deep and dirty voice, he began. "*Where...did we bury...those kisses...long entombed...*"

And then everything went straight to hell.

#

It's hard for the human voice to overcome even as small a PA system as Jacks had brought, but the kid in the bed had no trouble doing it. The scream he unleashed on them made Jen's ears feel like they were going to start bleeding. She nearly dropped the guitar, figuring for sure the kid was having some kind of seizure. But Levon kept the beat going steady, and Lucy, still holding down the bass line, jostled Jen with her arm to tell her not to stop playing.

"Please!" Kyle wailed. "Make him stop! Make him stop!"

"*Lend...me your hand...*" Jacks went on singing, with all the intensity and preposterous rock poses as if the tiny bedroom was filled with fifty thousand screaming teenage girls throwing their panties at the aging rocker.

If the chords hadn't been so dead simple, Jen would've dropped the rhythm for sure, because at this point, she couldn't decide whether to keep playing or call the paramedics. Or the cops. Why the fuck were the kid's parents not kicking open the door?

The band hit the first chorus and Kyle started shaking, his scrawny hands gripping the sides of his mattress. Soon the whole bed was rattling, and foamy spit dripped out the sides of his mouth. Still Jacks kept singing and the band kept playing.

"*I'm your gra-ay-ay-ve digger...*"

The screams got worse, like an insect burrowing deep inside Jen's ear canals. The kid hurled himself up and down on the mattress, the bed's metal legs carving scratches into the wood floor. She looked around, hoping to see the solution to all this insanity even as her fingers kept finding the chords on the guitar neck.

Stop playing, she told herself. *Nothing's worth whatever the hell these cult psychos are doing to this kid.*

Jacks lifted a fist high, then jammed his elbow down—the sign to end the song. Had they gotten past the last chorus? All she could hear was the sound of the kid shrieking his lungs out. Her eyes were blurred from tears she hadn't realized she was shedding.

"*Scream out the Demon,*" Jacks called out.

"What?"

"Motley Crüe," Lucy whispered fiercely.

Jen couldn't remember that tune, so she had to wait for Lucy to start it up on the bass and followed along as best she could. Levon kept a heavy beat going on the kick drum, punching in with the background vocals.

"*Yes. Shout. Scream the demon out!*"

If she had any doubts about this being some perverse form of child abuse, they were gone when Johnny Jacks started dancing wildly about the room, grinding out the lead vocal in some mad, gesticulating performance that freaked Jen out so much it took until the second verse before she found something else that freaked her out even more: the kid.

Kyle stopped shaking and sat up in his bed, a grin on his face as wide as if he'd just shoplifted his first nudie magazine. His eyes had gone milky white because the eyeballs were rolled up into his head and he was laughing so hard she could hear him over Lucy's bass line and Levon's drumming.

"What the hell is going on?" she asked Lucy when she couldn't stand it anymore.

"Hell *is* what's going on. Now shut the fuck up and keep playing if you don't want to end up there yourself."

Kyle bobbed his head back and forth, as though lost in an ecstatic trance. Jacks sang louder and harder, like the two were locked in some sort of deadly struggle and trying to prove who was in control.

They hit the end of that song. Without even calling it out, Jacks started singing *Ramble On* by Led Zeppelin. Fortunately, this was a tune she knew, and so kicked in smoothly with Jimmy Page's riffs.

Jacks turned to her, eyes blazing, and shouted, "Not the acoustic, you idiot. Switch guitars!" Jen let Lucy and Levon hold up the rhythm as she put the acoustic down and reached for the Ricky. "Not the Ricky!" Jacks shouted. She put that down, grabbed the Strat, and kicked into a solo.

Kyle was on his hands and knees on the bed, right near the bottom edge like a dog getting ready to leap off. His eyes looked nowhere in particular but he sniffed the air as if he could smell her playing.

"Bitch got no soul," he whispered.

Whispered?

How in hell could she possibly hear the kid whisper over the music?

"Play faster, slut," he growled, and it sounded as if he stood on a stool right behind her, his lips touching her earlobe. Jen shivered and the ring finger of her left hand missed the fret. The buzz it produced was like a thousand wasps stinging her face, swarming inside her mouth and over her eyes.

"Keep your shit together, Axe Girl," Jacks said. He stood right in front of her, making her feel trapped. Caged. Still, she pushed through the solo until Johnny picked up the vocal again. By the time the song was done, she was dripping sweat. Her shirt clung to her chest and torso, her jeans were soaked and too tight around her waist, as though her body had turned into nothing but sagging layers of skin and fat.

Jacks sang three more songs, and by the end of the third she couldn't remember what the first two had been. All the while, Kyle raced around the tiny circumference prescribed by his twin mattress, alternating between screaming, and chortling at them.

When Johnny signaled her to play a solo again, the kid pulled down his pajama pants and pissed on the floor, wiggling his hips and sending the stream sputtering into the air towards them. A droplet of something landed on Jen's lip and she started to gag.

"It's just sweat," Lucy told her, thumb slapping the bottom string of her bass. "He can't touch us yet. Just don't drop any more notes."

Crazy cult assholes, Jen thought, but she didn't stop playing; she was too scared. Whatever was wrong with these people, she couldn't be sure someone wouldn't slit her throat if she stopped going along with the game. So, she kept shredding on the Stratocaster, barely aware of what key she was in.

"Four more bars," Johnny called out.

Jen looked up. Kyle lay flat on his back. Her fingers flew up the neck looking for a passably decent way out of the solo, but as she did, she finally stopped thinking everyone around her was crazy and started wondering if she was the one who'd lost her mind, because Kyle was now floating three feet above the bed.

"Shit!" she yelled and dropped her pick.

The kid fell back to the mattress. Jacks turned on her, fists clenched. She flinched involuntarily thinking the skinny freak was about to hit her. But he didn't. He just gave a nod to Levon who train crashed the end of the song.

Then, for the first time since they'd started, the room was silent. No drums, no instruments, no Johnny Jacks dancing around singing raucously, no kid screaming.

Silence.

Jen was so exhausted she could barely keep on her feet. "What the fuck was that?"

"That was the first set," Jacks said.

Jen still had the Strat hanging off her hunched shoulders as she hurried from the room. She should've packed it up along with her other guitars and the amp, but by then she was too terrified to do anything but skulk down the stairs and make for the front door.

"Smoke break?"

Jacks stood in the shadows out on the front lawn, smoke from his joint already making her gag. Her ears were still buzzing. She couldn't draw a decent breath to save her life.

"What the fuck was that in there?" she demanded.

"What do you think that was?"

She took the Strat off her shoulder, partly because it was getting heavy and partly because she might need something to hit Jacks with. "Tell me it wasn't a…shit, I can't believe I'm saying this. Tell me this isn't some kind of exorcism."

He took a drag from his joint. "Of course, it's an exorcism. What else would it be?"

She snatched the joint from him and sucked in a long drag that made her head spin. She'd stopped smoking years ago. "And you're what? Trying to force it out with rock music?"

He accepted the joint back and gave her a toothy grin. "What the fuck else would we use to get rid of it? Prayers? And don't waste your time," he added, dropping the remains of the joint on the lawn and crushing it with the heel of his boot.

"With what?"

"Telling yourself you imagined it. It's real, kid."

She wanted to call him a liar but doubted that would do any good. "Let's say…let's say for a second, I believed any of it. Are we done? You prayed the gay away or sang the evil out or whatever?"

"Not fucking likely. It's a three-set show, Axe Girl."

"Stop calling me that! And what do you mean, a three-set show? What happens now?"

He started back up the stairs to the house. "We got his attention. Now we kick the shit out of him until he decides to leave for greener pastures." He stopped at the top of the steps. "You coming?"

"What happens if I don't?"

The back of his shoulders rose and fell. "Who knows? Maybe he'll live. Maybe he'll die. Maybe everyone inside that house gets consigned to some living hell."

"What? You can't put that shit on me! I'm just a guitar player!"

Jacks just stood there facing the front door. "Not even a particularly good one from what I've seen." His hand wrapped around the doorknob and turned. "If you stay, you'd better get real fucking good, real fucking soon, Axe Girl."

#

She followed Jacks inside the house without being sure why.

Fuck, maybe I'm possessed now.

Through the hallway and up the interior stairs to the second floor, where she had to step over Kyle's parents who were huddled on the floor holding each other and crying. They looked shell-shocked. Part of her sympathized with their plight. The rest of her wanted to kick them in the ribs until they got off their asses and did something.

"Don't judge what you don't understand," Jacks said, as if he could read her thoughts.

Inside the bedroom, Kyle still lay flat on his back, seemingly unconscious, but when she walked by him, he said, "Gonna take you, baby. Gonna take you all the way down with me tonight."

"Don't know that song." She plugged the Strat back into her tuner and plucked the bottom E string. She couldn't believe how out of tune the guitar was. She'd never smashed the strings that hard before. It was a miracle they hadn't all broken.

"What now?" she asked Jacks.

"First set was to get its attention," he replied. "Now we soften him up, see if he can stand the heat."

"And if he can?" She watched Kyle roll onto his stomach, then push against the mattress with his hands, his torso rising up like a cobra.

Jacks raised an eyebrow. "Just keep playing."

"And what if we can't?" They hadn't even started up again yet and already she was more tired than she'd ever been at a gig. "What happens when we run out of steam?"

Jacks walked over to the bed and leaned down going eye to eye with Kyle. "Then this little fucker eats our souls."

#

They were halfway through the second set when things got weirder—and worse. For the first few songs, Kyle stomped all over his bed acting for all the world like a petulant child determined to get their attention. He said things Jen shouldn't have been able to hear over the music.

"You really believe all this garbage they've been feeding you, Baby Jen?" he asked as she was finished off an improvised solo during some blues song Jacks had called out. "I mean, which is more likely?" Kyle went on. "That, after millennia of exorcisms being proven to be bunkum, you happen to find yourself in the middle of a real one? Or that two desperate, gullible parents fooled themselves into believing the source of their son's cancer is possession by the devil?"

Jen did her best to ignore him, which he didn't seem to mind because he had no end of ways to get her attention back.

"Just look around," he commanded.

Her solo done and Jacks back to crooning his lead vocal, she found she couldn't stop herself from doing as the kid suggested. Signs of religious fervor were everywhere. The cross over the bed, family photos arranged into a cross on the wall, the sword-wielding angel bookends on the shelf. Books with titles like, *Healing with God's Power* and *No Such Thing as Coincidence: Seven Signs Your Child is Possessed.*

"See what I mean?" Kyle asked. "These people are crazy."

He stood on the edge of his mattress again, ignoring Jacks's raucous performance and undoing the buttons of his pajama top. On his chest were several burns, all the shape of a crucifix inside a circle.

Shit, Jen thought. *They branded the poor kid.*

An elbow jostled her in the ribs.

"Focus," Lucy said.

Jen stumbled over the next chords trying to get back on track, but her fingers felt awkward, swollen. She looked at her hands to find the skin a sickly white, the veins exposed like those of a corpse pulled from the water. Her mouth filled with bile that she tried to spit out, but it clogged her throat, choking her. Only after forcing a violent cough did she manage to spew it out onto the floor and all over her clothes.

"Keep playing," Lucy warned. "The music's the only thing keeping him out of you."

With horrifying, stilted slowness, she forced her fingers to take the shape of the next chord and strummed. The nausea subsided a little, and her fingers found their positions on the fretboard again.

For the next six songs, Jen tried to ignore everything she heard from the bed, focusing only on the tactile sensations of her right hand, holding the pick and slamming it against the strings, the dull thud of Levon's kick drum coming up through her feet, and the way Lucy's bass sent vibrations through her whole body. All the while, Johnny

Jacks sang his heart out in a pitched battle against something Jen couldn't see but was utterly and terrifyingly aware of.

Kyle gesticulated at her, using his body to get the attention his words could no longer draw from her—not that he shut up at all. He shouted, pleaded, moaned, cackled, and made every other use of the apparatus of a boy's throat he could.

Somewhere in that second set, Jen Farmer started believing in the Devil.

#

Johnny called a halt to the second set after just half an hour, and that, even more than the haunted look in his eyes, told her something was wrong. As her guitar's last ringing chord died, the singer stumbled out of the room, leaving the three of them behind.

"Come on," Levon said, leading her out. He, too, looked shell-shocked.

Lucy Bottom was crying, which seemed incongruous with the sureness of her bass playing.

At the bottom of the stairs, Jacks spoke in hushed tones to the parents. Despite the quiet, Jen heard the raggedness in the singer's voice. Kyle's parents shook their heads, pleading with Jacks.

"I'm sorry," he just kept saying.

"What's going on?" Jen asked Levon.

"Johnny can't cut the thing loose."

"So, what now?"

The drummer shuffled past her without answering and stepped into the little bathroom in the hallway. He slammed the door shut, and a moment later she heard him puking.

"Lucy?" she asked.

The bass player walked out the front door. Jen followed.

"Sorry you got pulled into this shit," Lucy said.

Jen sat on the front steps next to her. "Would've been nice to get a heads-up beforehand."

Lucy stared off at the empty street ahead of them. "Wanted: guitar player for exorcism, must be able to improvise in all styles and fight demons."

"What's really going on in there?"

"What do you think is going on?"

Jen balked at the question, finding herself unexpectedly on the defensive. She'd been prepared for Lucy to rattle off some nonsense about demons and possession—which would have let Jen scoff or deny it or maybe even allow it might be possible.

"The kid's fucked up," was the only answer she could come up with that neither denied the evidence of her eyes nor admitted that the thing poking at her guts seemed only to lack her belief before it would crawl right into her throat and choke her from the inside.

Lucy shrugged. "Let's say that's all it is. Let's throw out all the...weird shit for a second, and say this is some unusual mental disorder."

"I can live with that."

"Fine. So how do you fix a kid with that kind of problem?"

"Drugs. Therapy. Um...electric shocks?"

Lucy spit onto the grass. "They tried all that. None of it worked."

Jen searched for another answer. When nothing suggested itself, she asked, "So rock music is the last resort? I mean, what's the..." Crap. She really knew nothing about psychology, neurology, or pretty much anything with an 'ology' appended to it. "How's it supposed to work?"

Lucy held up a hand, palm parallel to the porch, and shook it up and down. "Music vibrates the air, right? Our brains turn waves into sound. But when those sounds take the shape of music, they vibrate other things, too." She placed her hand low down on Jen's stomach. "Here. And it turns out, this is also where those…whatever they are that can take possession of a human being…get inside us."

"You're back to talking voodoo shit."

Lucy gave her a wry smile. "I tried to let you hold onto your hangups as long as I could. From here on out, it gets freaky."

Freaky. Jesus Christ. Understatement of the year. "Fine. Let's say I come along for the ride here, you're saying the music—"

"Not any music. The right songs, the right intensity, hitting all the right resonances. That's the only way to shake loose whatever's inside that kid."

"So how do you figure out all those 'right' elements?"

"I don't." The bass player looked back up the steps where light from the hallway seeped onto the porch. "Johnny's the only one who can do it."

That, as much as every other weird thing that had been said tonight, was almost the hardest thing to believe.

"A rock 'n' roll exorcist."

"Only one in the lower forty-eight," Lucy confirmed. "There's a guy up in Alaska, but he never leaves the state."

"So, you've seen this work?" Jen asked. "You've seen people cured?"

"One time, yeah. Not a kid, though. An old woman in a nursing home."

"You cured her?"

"Yep. She died peacefully in her sleep a week later."

"A week? One week?"

"Hey, it's better than nothing. Besides, where she was headed was worse."

Jen chewed on that for a minute. "So, here you are, in some

suburban house, crying your eyes out between sets while Levon hurls up his guts, and your one success story is an old woman who ended up dying a week later. Why would you even bother?"

Lucy looked away. "Because I've seen what happens the other times." Still not meeting Jen's eyes, she rose and trudged back up the stairs into the house. "You should probably go home, Jen. The third set's always the worst."

#

Jen was halfway to the kid's bedroom when a visibly strung-out Johnny Jacks stopped her in the hall.

"Just wait here," he said. "Me and Levon'll pack up your gear for you."

She'd been heading to the bedroom to do precisely that. She'd been prepared for an argument with Johnny to get her stuff. Figured he'd go all Jesus on her and give a hundred reasons why she should stay and help him fight the good fight over the kid's soul. But Jacks just looked at her as if she was some dumb bystander he was pushing out of the way of oncoming traffic.

"Who says I'm leaving?" she asked.

The aging rocker's sneer made its way to his face, but for a second, she saw the other thing in his eyes—the thing she'd never expected to see there: hope.

"Not your war, kid."

Jen had played guitar since she was fifteen years old. Even then, her parents, her teachers, and most of all, every band she'd been in, had said she'd started too late; she didn't have that 'spark'; her playing was workmanlike at best and 'girly' at worst. She'd practiced every day but it was never enough; played until her fingers had turned numb and then gone through harrowing visits to a neurologist who'd told her she needed to lighten up on the practicing or risk permanent nerve damage.

"Besides," the doctor had said, "I thought you rock musicians weren't about perfection. Isn't it all about soul?"

Soul. Yeah, Jen could've used some soul in her playing.

"So, you figure this 'war' belongs to you?" she asked Jacks.

He licked his lips, not like a perv but like somebody's uncle trying to figure out a nice way to say a kid wasn't ready for football tryouts. "You didn't sign up for this. It's the worst case I've ever seen. Three hundred dollars is a lousy payday for what comes next."

"Then why are you going back in there?"

He ran a hand through greasy graying hair. "I'm old, kid. If I go down fighting, well, I wasn't going to live that long anyway. I don't try? Then what's the point of living?"

Lucy and Levon squeezed past her in the hallway and headed into the kid's bedroom.

"What about them?" Jen asked. "Why are they going back?"

"No idea," he replied. There was a subtle break in his voice, and his eyes were wet. "Until five seconds ago, I figured they were going to leave." He patted her on the shoulder and headed towards the bedroom. "It was good playing with you, kid. Couple of times in that second set I heard a lion clawing at the doors of her cage getting ready to bust out. Don't ever listen to anyone who says you're second rate, Jen Farmer."

He left her standing there. *A lion clawing at the doors of her cage.* Twenty years of playing guitar and that was the only time anyone had described her playing in a way that made sense. Of course, given what a manipulative prick Jacks was, there was a decent chance he'd said it just to see if he could make her stick around.

Fuck. Fuck. Fuck.

"Hey, old man," she called.

Jacks poked his head out of the bedroom. "Yeah?"

She pushed him out of the way and entered the bedroom.

The air was thick with a kind of green-black haze that stank of every kind of death and decay. Lucy and Levon were barely on their feet, coughing from the stench and trying not to look at the eight-year-old boy who floated, cross-legged, two feet above his mattress. Particles of puke, shit, and urine floated around him like Saturn's rings.

When she walked in, Kyle said, "You're the one I'm going to rip apart first, Jennifer."

She plugged the amp cable into her guitar, not even bothering to tune the Strat, but instead turning the gain all the way up.

"The name's Axe Girl, you little shit."

#

"No more covers," Jacks said. "No more playing it safe."

Levon started up a heavy, nasty beat on the drums. Lucy plucked a steady rhythm of straight eighths on the second fret of the bottom string of her bass, but Jen knew the key wasn't going to stay in F-sharp; this was going to be E all the way—open strings wherever possible, the strongest vibrations with a standard tuning.

Jen turned the Strat towards her amp, not touching anything but the whammy bar, letting the feedback build up. It was such a cheesy, guy-liner-and-black-leather-pants thing to do. But fuck it: fighting a demon called for a little showing off.

"Well, all right, motherfuckers," Jacks declared, the last syllable swooping up from a low baritone note all the way to a high tenor range that shook the bedroom windows. "Show me what you got!"

Jen blasted into an E-9 chord with an almost funk rhythm that ran counter to what the others were playing but would've made Prince proud. The effect was both dissonant and yet somehow sweet; the wrong move that sounded right.

In other words, rock 'n' roll.

The room shook, though whether from their performance or from Kyle she couldn't tell. The boy's parents stood together in the doorway watching with impotent desperation.

"Help me, Daddy," Kyle whimpered.

His plea would have been more convincing if his various secretions weren't twisting and turning in the air, buzzing around the room like a swarm of wasps—and if he wasn't giggling quite so much.

Jacks sang with a passion and furor that would have captivated an entire football stadium. So much so that it took a minute before Jen realized he wasn't singing in English. She wasn't entirely sure it was any kind of language.

But Levon's drumbeats faltered. His upper body lilted back and forth as he struggled to keep up the beat. When he looked up, she could only see the whites of his eyes.

"What's happening to him?" Jen asked Lucy.

"He's losing it." She slapped the drummer across the face. It didn't do any good. "Come on, Levon, stay with me, brother."

The rhythm from the drums started to drift then faded completely. The last trace of Levon disappeared.

"Hey, ladies," he grinned at them, tongue lolling from one side of his mouth like a dog's as foamy drool slid down his chin.

"Fuck!" Lucy cried stumbling away. She tripped over her own patch cable and fell, the bass giving a cacophonous crash that crushed the music, breaking it apart like stale bread.

"*Ain't givin' it up,*" Johnny Jacks continued to sing. "*Ain't givin' it up to you.*" What had been a gravelly, bluesy voice before had become ragged.

Jen slammed a power chord on the guitar then reached to help

Lucy up. The bass player took her hand but started to drag her down to the floor. Like Levon, her eyes showed only the whites, and her grin was anything but human.

"Come play with me, Jenny," she cooed.

Jen yanked away, lost her pick but managed to hit the strings with her fingernails to give Johnny something to sing over. He fell to his knees, the way a crooner would during the big emotional moment of the song, but his performance was lifeless, barely audible above Jen's guitar and the hiss that had risen to take the place of the rest of the music.

That hiss…

She'd thought it was the usual noise that came through guitar and bass amps when you weren't playing, but this was different. Feral. Gleeful. Like an ocean wave, it crested higher and higher before crashing down on them, drowning everything in its path.

"Come on, Jenny, give it up, girl," Lucy said with someone else's voice.

"On your best day you couldn't play worth a damn, baby," Levon crooned.

A creak from the bed made her turn. Kyle was crawling forward on his mattress, eyes milky white except for pulsing strands of red like blood vessels bursting one after another. A rabid rat preparing to pounce on a dying cat.

Kyle's parents entered the room, no longer crying, but instead humming with the stilted, painful buzz of wasps. They ran their hands along Kyle's back, the gesture not loving but obedient. Sensuous. Perverse.

They continued past the bed and kneeled in front of Johnny Jacks, opening their mouths wide—wider than their jaws were meant to— and Jen heard something first click then crack wetly. Their lower jaws hung loose and wagged as they took turns breathing on Johnny, a sick, urine-stenched haze that wafted over him, making him choke.

Johnny, still on his knees, turned to her. He'd stopped singing, but his lips formed a single word.

"Run."

#

The urge to flee was overwhelming. Jen was alone in a room of human bodies driven by something not at all human. They looked at her and grinned, reaching out with sickly white limbs, the skin riddled with veins gone black and green as if the blood itself had been replaced with bile.

Johnny Jacks flailed, trying to shove away the mother and father. They dodged his feeble blows effortlessly.

"Don't go givin' it up," he said—no, *sang*. It was weak and pathetic, not in any real key, but still it made the parents snarl at him. Their upper lips curled even as their broken jaws shuddered.

How he could manage even that much, Jen couldn't fathom. Everything in the room stank. Everything was too hot and slick, and sweat dripped all over her, the salt burning her eyes. The right leg of her jeans was soaked, and her own piss dripped into her sock. Every time she tried to touch the strings her fingers felt like sausages left out in the sun, so hot and bloated, as if the skin would break apart and rotten meat would ooze out.

"Give 'em the shit," Johnny sang feebly. *"Give 'em the shit like ya never gave it before."*

Give 'em the shit? Like she had any shit to give. She'd never known real fear, the certainty that everything you believed about yourself belonged to someone else, and that all was left was an empty vessel, waiting—no, begging—to be filled.

"Yeah, baby," Kyle said, crawling on the floor towards her, more like a spider than a rat now. "Gonna fill you up just right."

She looked around, panic shaking her loose. There had to be a weapon here somewhere. The crucifix above the kid's bed was out of reach. She doubted it would do any good even if she could reach it.

Only one cross I've ever needed, a small, rebellious part of her whispered. *The cross I'm wearing.* Her gaze fell to the Stratocaster— not some religious symbol to pray to, but her true cross waiting to be played. She'd never really thought of her guitars that way. It had always just been her instrument. Such a dull, lifeless word. The guitar had always been more of an enemy she had to force to her will than a partner. Now, it was all she had.

Kyle slithered past his parents and Johnny, and past Lucy and Levon, who genuflected before him. The boy floated up until he was eye to eye with Jen.

"Gig's over, baby."

Jen squeezed her hand into a fist, cracking the knuckles, daring the swollen digits to split at the seams. They didn't.

"Not yet," she whispered, then slammed her fist down, opening the fingers at the last instant so they struck all six of the strings and sent a blast of distortion that blew through the room like a bomb exploding the inside of a doll's house.

"Haven't gotten to my solo yet."

#

There was a part of playing the guitar that wasn't about holding the right notes on the fretboard or plucking the right strings, that wasn't about rhythm or tempo or precision. It was that mixture of easing into the music, of being loose and reckless and abandoning oneself to the guitar. It was the...*playing.*

Jen had never been good at that part. Her whole career, she'd had to prove she was a professional to bandmates who seemed to know instinctively there was something wrong with her. In a desperate effort to be good enough she'd foregone any hopes of being great.

How great a player would you have to be to fend off a demon that was already creeping his way inside you?

Pretty fucking great.

With no drums to give her time, no bass to offer a chord structure to hold her up, she propelled herself headlong into a solo. It was just noise at first, hitting strings like a caveman who'd just discovered a guitar amidst the rocks and rubble.

"Whatcha doin', little girl?" Kyle asked.

She heard him inside her head where he was taking up residence, pushing at the bits of her brain with probing fingers, licking them to get a taste for the place.

She ignored him, finding the straight rhythm first, just letting the notes ring out. She'd forgotten that the guitar didn't really need finesse or elegance to sound good. It was all right there: the steel strings, the maple neck, the thick, solid body and the wound pickups, coiled like snakes just waiting to be let loose. She reveled in the dumb simplicity of it.

"That all you got, Axe Girl?" Johnny Jacks asked, looking up at her with blind eyes.

Her middle finger pressed the A string on the second fret. The note rang out true, going on forever to that infinity where every note goes when you think you're done with them.

"Ain't gonna work," Kyle's voice churned inside her skull. "I'm too deep inside you now."

Jen kept playing, her fingers lazily tracing a pentatonic scale up and down in almost random patterns, not hurrying, not worrying.

"Are you really, baby?" she asked.

"Oh yeah. So deep you'll never shake me."

"Shake you?" She stopped moving her fingers, holding one note for a full measure, then another, letting it slowly fade out almost to that point of oblivion where she knew she'd be lost. "Who says I'm trying to shake you?"

There was time to hear the odd silence within her mind, like a sudden intake of breath. She felt him scratching at the inside of her skull like an animal that's just discovered it's been caged. Every clawing attack filled her with pain and misery—a migraine mixed with suicidal depression.

Kyle, or whatever had taken his place, understood what she was doing.

She disregarded everything except the guitar, sliding her hand farther up the neck, her fingers moving faster and faster, recklessly picking out a solo that was neither blues nor jazz nor classical but something more primal. The grunting of teenagers fucking for the first time, in the back of a car with the radio up loud. Awkward. Painful. Stupid. But full of whatever rock 'n' roll was when you took away the chords and melody.

She played that on her Strat, reveling in it, the sounds from the amp both sweet and salty. Inside her, the demon struggled to get away.

"Don't run off now, baby," she said. "We're just getting started."

#

Somewhere in there, in the space between two notes on the guitar, between her fingers holding down one fret and another as her pick hand prepared to come down hard on the string, Jen got lost.

It was perfect.

She didn't care anymore. She was halfway to hell, dragged by the weight of either a demon in her soul or a psychotic break in her fragile mind, yet she was flying. The essence of a great solo—the essence of being the guitar player she was meant to be—was in not giving a shit.

Whatever came out of her amp right at that moment, for good or ill, sweet or stale, perfect or messy as all hell…was her.

It was Jen.

Let the demon take her soul if he wanted, because she had the music and the music was all the soul she cared about. The feel of her hands on the guitar and the sounds in her ears and nothing else.

Boom.

Boom.

A beat came out of nowhere. She let it carry her upwards.

Bah-duhn-duhn.

Bah-duhn-duhn.

Lucy Bottom's bass came up alongside.

"Stop," Kyle commanded, no longer with the voice of a nine-year-old, but something deeper and darker—something incongruously full of both malice and pleading.

She paid it no heed. The playing was all that mattered—and she was playing, not practicing, not trying to live up to anyone else. Just playing her guitar the way she wanted. The more she did, the freer she became, and the more terrified the thing that had been living inside Kyle grew.

"Jen," Johnny Jacks said, his voice hoarse and wrecked but with a tinge of joy like the subtle half bend of the note she was playing.

"Yeah?"

"Levon and Lucy can hold it for a few seconds."

"And?" What did he want from her?

"And it's time," he bellowed, like an old-time preacher standing at the front of a tent before a thousand hand-clutching congregants. "Bring. Forth. The. Rickenbacker!"

Jen glanced at the battered old guitar. Its fireglo paint job shimmered, already aflame as if with hellfire, demanding to face down the horrors around her. The strings hummed a defiant counter to the demon's hideous buzzing.

She popped the patch cable out of the jack on the Strat and plugged in the Ricky. All the while Lucy and Levon pounded away at a rhythm that was nothing but straight eighths and pissed-off determination.

The Ricky let out a vicious twang, a belligerent melodic relic from another time. Jen kicked her amp around, so it faced the windows. It shouldn't have been able to do more than rattle them, but as she played a run up the neck, the scornful dissonance of shattering glass added itself to the music. When she glanced at her guitar, there was blood on the strings. Her blood. She didn't care.

Night air flooded into the room, and she breathed in the sweetness, not even minding the other stenches that still lingered in the room. Lucy had blood dripping from a cut on her forehead. Levon played using only one arm, his left twisted at an odd angle. Johnny's face was pale, hair matted, his skin cracked and bleeding at the sides of his mouth. They all looked happy as pigs in shit.

"*Come on, come on, come on,*" Johnny sang. "*Gotta get it up, get it out, send it down.*"

Kyle floated before her, head hanging back, and arms spread wide in a Jesus pose while his parents hung onto his legs. Jen eyed the tendrils of black and green haze that filled the room and trailed back to the boy's mouth. His stomach and throat convulsed, vomiting out whatever thing had made its home inside him.

Johnny sang something at her, but she didn't hear, she was too busy playing the notes that would pull the last remnants of the demon out of Kyle's mouth.

The filthy mist coalesced, taking on its own shape—a man with black wings and a face so beautiful it made her want to cry. He smiled at her, but she used his beauty against him, translating it into an aching melody that came from her guitar, from her guts, from her lust. The smile faded as the thing discovered that all its best weapons had been turned against it, that all the power in the universe is nothing but vibration, and music shaped vibrations according to the player's needs.

"You've got him now!" Johnny said. He wasn't singing anymore, just issuing commands like a general. "Hold him. Hold him tight!"

"I've got him," she said, irritated. "Just tell me what to do with him."

"Send him down, Axe Girl. Send him all the way down."

Jen had no idea what that meant but knew exactly how to play it. She slid her fingers up the neck to the seventh fret, held down the same sweet E-9 chord she'd started with, and slammed all six strings.

Then she let go of the pick and twisted the tuning heads loose one after another. The chord dropped and dropped and dropped, passing through discordance back to proper chords and then into discordance again. By the time she stopped, she'd tuned the entire guitar down so far, the strings were slack and wobbling.

The creature, the demon, the…whatever, shattered into a thousand bad memories.

Jen slumped, her knees banging hard against the bedroom floor. Kyle's parents, their jaws still broken and no doubt in terrible pain, hugged their son between them. The boy turned to Jen, eyes blinking away the salt and sweat. He said something, but no words came out at first, as if he'd misjudged how used-up his vocal cords were.

The second time she heard him.

"I like that song," he said. "Could you play it again?"

The Shard

By Ian Irvine

I sensed him before he spoke. Sensed trouble, too.

"Why aren't you at the party, Sulien?" said a gravelly voice I hadn't heard since I was a kid and didn't want to hear now. Too many memories. Most of them bad.

"Xervish Flydd," I said, without turning around. I was in my studio, trying to take a print from one of my copper etching plates, and it wasn't going well. "And older and uglier than ever, I'll bet."

"I was an ugly young man, even before that unfortunate episode in the scrutators' torture chambers," he said cheerily. "Hardly likely I'd improve with age. Turn around."

"Why?" I snapped.

"I want to see how you've turned out."

I sighed and wiped my inky hands on a rag. I hadn't seen Flydd since I was nine, sixteen years ago. He hadn't changed. Still a little, skinny man. Still grotesquely ugly, even when smiling, as now. But charming, nonetheless. It was hard not to smile at him, but I managed it.

"You didn't grow much," he said, gaunt head cocked to one side.

"Neither did you." Feeble!

"What happened to your beautiful hair?"

"Gets in the way." I raked my fingers through the loose curls, doubtless smearing black ink everywhere. It was thick and sticky and I was covered in it to the elbows. "What do you want?"

"We're missing you at the reunion."

"What's to celebrate?" I muttered. "We live in a blighted world. Nothing's gone right since the day we won."

"There's plenty to celebrate. We defeated an invasion by the bloodiest race ever to come rampaging out of the void. We saved a world from genocide at their hands. And we delivered Skald and his Merdrun nation to justice, something they never gave any of their victims. Especially poor Uletta."

We had buried her on a mound by the stream, not far away. I hadn't known her well, but the ghastly way she had been killed would never leave me. "Well, yes, but—"

"We paid a high price, Sulien. It's important that we get together occasionally, acknowledge our dead and their sacrifices, and support our old friends."

"I don't want to relive that time—the nightmares do it for me." I turned back to my bench.

"Well, I'm afraid you have to come with me," said Flydd.

"Am I under arrest? Are you going to drag me to the damned reunion?"

"No." The good cheer was gone. He sounded uneasy, and that was troubling, because Flydd had seen everything, and survived what few others had. "Something's happened and we need you."

I dropped the copper plate, which rang on my marble-topped workbench. "Is it Dad? Is he all right? He hasn't been well—"

"Llian's fine...apart from an excess of wine and good cheer. Everyone at the reunion is fine—or would be if you were there."

"Then what is it?"

"Your kinswoman, Malien, mind-called from Aachan a few minutes ago. I've got to make a portal there right away, and I need you to come with me."

Now he had my attention. "We have to go to *another world?* How?"

Flydd held up a small, irregularly shaped black stone that I recognized at once, because it glowed crimson in the center. "Lirriam lent me her Waystone."

"Why do you want me?"

"You knew the Merdrun—and Skald— better than anyone."

"I was only nine. I didn't know anything."

"You discovered the enemy's fatal weakness and it helped to defeat them. We need your aid."

"What for?"

"To solve a mystery that Malien's people are unable, or unwilling, to investigate."

"Am I allowed to clean myself up first?"

"The dead don't care how you look."

What was that supposed to mean? "But I do."

I wiped the worst of the ink off my hands and arms, went into the back room and put on a green shirt, baggy black trews and brown boots. The mirror showed ink smears on my face, which I scrubbed off, and black clots in my dark red hair. Nothing I could do about that.

"Let's get it over with," I said when I came out. "Got work to do."

We went outside. Flydd closed a fist around the Waystone, extended his right hand and I took hold. The bones were twisted and lumpy; they had been broken in the torture chamber and had not healed straight. He tapped the Waystone on a platinum ring, inscribed with black glyphs, that gleamed on his middle finger.

I've been through a number of gates and portals in my time, and none of them are pleasant. There was no visible manifestation of this one—no hole in the air or dimensional opening of any kind—but I began to shudder so violently that I thought my teeth were going to vibrate out of my gums, and my stomach tried to explosively eject its contents.

I clamped down hard and clung onto his hand. Portals sometimes went wrong and people using them ended up *between*, wherever that was. Nowhere one could come back from.

We fell through an airless nothingness lit by pulses of orange light. My chest heaved, wanting air. *Don't breathe out, you'll never get it back.* Then we were falling in the real world, about six feet through frigid air. I bent my knees and landed on black rock crusted with snow the color of sulfur. The top of a ridge. A small red sun glowed in a mauve sky. Aachan.

I gagged but managed to prevent myself from throwing up.

Flydd, a few yards away, clutched his belly and grimaced. "Doesn't get any easier."

"You took your time," said a very old woman seated in the middle of a platform twenty yards away.

I barely recognized Malien. Her back was bent and her hair, once almost as red as my own, was so thin and colorless that I could see her scalp through it. The voice was the same, though, and the sharp tongue. And the very long Aachim fingers, twice the length of her palm.

I looked the other way, over a precipice and down into a massive crater whose upper walls were sheer, unclimbable cliffs. The ink-clotted hair on the top of my head stirred. I knew where we were. But why were we here?

Had they escaped?

"Of all the decisions I've made in my long life," said Malien, "this is the one I regret most."

"Allowing us to send the Merdrun to prison here?" said Flydd.

"Why couldn't you have dealt with them on Santhenar?"

It was an old argument. "They were already going through their portal, thinking they were invading their long-lost home-world. We had to trick them and send them to another world, and Aachan was the only one we could reach."

"I fell out with my people over it," said Malien. "And even on my death bed, which is comfortably close now, we won't be reconciled. A hard thing, that."

"I'm truly sorry," said Flydd. "But needs must."

She rose, supporting herself on a black metal cane with intricate silver tracery down its length. Symbols that meant nothing to me.

"We sentenced them to thirty years servitude," said Malien. "A modest punishment, considering the ruin they visited on so many other peoples over the eons, and the utter lack of mercy they showed to anyone. If they worked hard to restore this desolation, and submitted to moral instruction, *and changed* at the end of thirty years, they would have been freed."

"I remember," said Flydd.

"No one could fault their work. They turned the crater into a garden…"

"But?"

"The Merdrun believe themselves superior to every other intelligent species. They refused to listen to guidance from their inferiors."

"You're saying...?"

"It became clear to us that they were incapable of change, and could never be freed."

"You told them so?"

"Two years ago," said Malien.

"How did they react?"

"They didn't."

"They see emotions and feelings as signs of weakness," I said, "and crush them out of their children from an early age. Except for triumph after a military victory. That's an *allowable* emotion."

"And now?" said Flydd.

"Get on," said Malien.

Mystified, I followed Flydd to the platform and climbed up. It was about five yards by three, the sides silver metal in sinuous curves. The flat deck was lined with swirls of small green and black tiles. A thick rod rose from the floor in front of Malien's chair, which was made from some kind of black metal, twisted into a spiral. She sat, took hold of the rod, and the platform lifted with a nausea-inducing jerk and sailed out over the rim of the crater.

I had seen images of the place when I was nine, when it had been a stony, heat-baked wilderness. Now large areas of the crater floor, thousands of feet below us, were covered in dark blue and purple crops, strips of woodland and a patchwork of vegetable gardens.

As the hover platform angled across the crater and down towards the western slope, I began to sense pain, despair and overwhelming rage. With an effort, I blocked my gift. It was more often a curse.

Hundreds of long, low stone buildings, built from rubble, ran along the western slope of the crater. I saw no signs of life there, or in the fields.

"Those buildings look like barracks," said Flydd.

"Living quarters," said Malien. "Very cramped and basic. The Merdrun are prodigious workers, but they live in hovels, as if the conveniences of life are anathema to them."

"It's said they don't want to become comfortable, in case they lose sight of their goals."

"And now we come to why you're here," said Malien. "You picking anything up, Sulien?"

"Don't know what you mean," I lied.

"You're an *empath!*" Malien said irritably. "The most sensitive one I've ever met. And you have a great gift for the Secret Art."

"I haven't used either gift in years."

"Well, start! That's why I ordered you here."

"You're distant kin, Malien," I said, choosing my words carefully, though I seethed inside, "and venerable, and deserving of respect—"

"Spit it out, girl! Don't hold back on my account."

"I don't take kindly to being ordered about. I had too much of that as a kid—from enemies and friends."

Malien was the best of her people, and she had been good to me when I was little, but the Aachim were ever lofty and arrogant, and dismissive of all other human species. Especially those who share part of their blood.

She snorted. "What are you picking up?"

The platform skimmed over a small hill, then hovered a couple of hundred feet above the ground.

"Despair," I said. "And humiliation, rage and pain. But they're fading."

"They didn't succeed in suppressing *all* their emotions, then," said Flydd.

I went carefully towards the front of the platform, since there was no rail, and looked down. And my skin crawled.

The bodies were laid out in rows. Hundreds of rows, and hundreds of columns, in the partial shade of the purple-leaved, black-trunked trees that grew nowhere but Aachan.

"Two hundred and eight rows," said Malien in a drear voice. "And four hundred and seven columns. More than a hundred thousand Merdrun. All of them, in fact."

"What happened to them?" I'd seen a lot of dead people in my time, and it's never been easy, but this was different. Why were the bodies arranged so neatly? And if they were all dead, who had laid them out?

"No idea. They were busy at their allotted tasks when the weekly identification parade was held, three days ago. They appear to have committed mass suicide overnight."

"Why?"

"I don't know."

"But there must have been signs," said Flydd, leaning over the side of the platform.

"Our sentries kept their distance," said Malien. "We promised to guard them, and we did our duty faithfully, but we had no interest in the Merdrun or what motivated them."

"Only a hundred thousand," he mused. "In the beginning, three times that number were imprisoned here."

"They did not take well to servitude. Mortality has been very high."

"Also, I'm not seeing any children among the bodies."

"They grew up."

"But tens of thousands must have been born here."

"In the sixteen years of their servitude, I'm not aware that a single Merdrun woman became pregnant. There were certainly no babies born."

"That defies belief," said Flydd. "It's against human nature."

The temperature was mild down here, but I shivered. This was bad. Really bad.

"To a people who believed themselves superior to all," said Malien, "servitude must have been unbearable. Theirs was an utterly joyless society. Tormented."

"Well, they're gone," said Flydd, "and I won't pretend I'm sorry. What do you want from me?"

"Find out what happened here, and why. My health isn't up to it, and none of my people are willing."

"What else do you know?"

"Nothing. They left no written records, no notes, no explanation at all."

"Something's wrong," I said. "Why would a nation so single-mindedly determined decide to end itself?"

"We tried to rehabilitate them," Malien said defensively, "but it wasn't in them. Perhaps they felt death was better than perpetual incarceration."

Flydd's bony jaw was set. "I don't think so. We'll have to inspect the bodies."

"What, all of them?" I said. It was bound to bring memories to the surface that I would sooner have stayed buried.

"We'll walk the rows. We may find something."

Malien set the hover platform down on blue-black grass, some distance from the remains.

"There's no need for you to come," Flydd said to her.

"They were my responsibility. I have to account for them."

I trailed behind, bracing myself for a ghastly scene, but the bodies, men and women, young and old, showed no sign of violence, or poison. There was no indication as to what had killed them, though some of the faces were twisted in terror. However they'd died, they had suffered.

I felt a throat here and there. All were cold, dead for quite a few hours. I was looking down at a muscular, black-haired young woman when I saw that she had a slightly withered look, as if the flesh under the skin had shrunk.

The little hairs on my arms stirred. Withering would not have happened within hours of death; not in this cool shade.

The next body was a middle-aged man, his beard shadow so black it might have been painted on with my printing ink, and he too was withered. Flydd and Malien had missed the signs, but I'd seen them before. Unfortunately.

"Flydd!" I yelled.

He came running. An odd, clumsy gait, but surprisingly fast for someone his age. I pointed out the subtle signs of withering. Most of the bodies had them.

All the blood withdrew from his face, leaving the ancient scars standing out, purple against grey. He swore under his breath.

"What are we looking at?" said Malien.

I swallowed, painfully. "Someone drank the life forces of a hundred thousand Merdrun."

"Why?" she croaked.

Flydd replied. "Drinking lives is considered shameful; and the Merdrun's magiz, and his few dozen sus-magizes, only ever had one reason to do it: when they had no other source of magical power."

"But was it a suicide pact, or mass murder?" I said.

"How can it be mass murder? They're all dead."

"Yet the life-drinking spell was cast, and powerfully," I replied. "Where's the adept who cast it?"

"And his or her magical focus," said Malien. "Merdrun can't cast spells with their bare hands. But we searched them intimately after they were imprisoned here, and destroyed every device they had."

Flydd paled. "You must have missed one."

"You haven't asked the two most important questions," I said. "*Why* were all those lives drunk? And *what happened* to all that magical power?"

"We'd better check the rest of the bodies," said Flydd.

As we trudged along the rows, I realized that I was looking for one particular corpse. A huge Merdrun male—a former warrior captain who had become a junior sus-magiz. A hero who had subsequently betrayed the Merdrun nation and destroyed their hope of going home. He had been ritually mutilated afterwards, and I would know him instantly.

"Skald isn't among the dead," I said when I met Flydd at the end of the last row.

"He was here at the last roll check, three days ago," said Malien.

"Come away," said Flydd. He led us through a patch of forest until the dead were out of sight, then lowered his voice. "Skald was the most determined man I ever met. He once drank part of his own life to escape capture. He, almost single-handedly, made it possible for the Merdrun's dreams to be fulfilled."

"Until his forbidden love for a human slave, Uletta, ruined their plans," I said. "Then, in the thrall of his life-drinking addiction, he drank the life of the woman he had been trying to save."

"And with her dying breath, she laid an unbreakable curse on him and the Merdrun nation."

"She cursed the whole of Santhenar. Nothing has gone right for us since."

"You were his prisoner, and you knew him better than anyone," said Flydd. "What are you thinking, Sulien?"

"I liked Skald at first. He was a tormented man, the son of a coward, and the magiz persecuted him mercilessly. I sensed Skald's pain."

"Go on."

"He was desperate to restore his family's tainted name. He drove himself to the limits of human endurance to do his duty."

"And after he destroyed his people's hopes and it led to their imprisonment here? After he became the lowest of the low?"

I felt a sickening dread. "I...I don't think he would have changed. He would still have schemed to restore his name. And there's only one way he could have done that."

"By completing the Merdrun's plan after all," said Flydd. "*He's not dead!*"

"Then where's he gone?"

"They always build a cubic temple. Where is it, Malien?"

She took us there. It was a perfect cube built from black, volcanic rock, about forty feet square, with no doors or windows. Flydd pointed his ring finger at the wall, blasted a hole through it, and we went in. The temple was empty apart from a central stone altar, on which lay a big, ruddy body. I generously let Flydd go first.

"It's him, but turned to stone," he said.

"I'm sensing a magical device," I said. "One I've touched before."

I went closer. Dare I? I reached out, my stomach throbbing, and gingerly pulled aside the eye patch covering the petrified Skald's empty eye socket. And at the very back, something glowed green.

"What's that?" said Flydd.

"After his betrayal was exposed," I said, squirming at the

memories, "and he was ritually mutilated, his magical focus, called a *rue-har*, was thrust through his right eye. Part of it must have broken off, leaving that shard embedded in bone. It was missed in the search—and it's glowing with power."

"What *is* a rue-har?" said Malien.

"A fragment from the Crimson Gate that corrupted the Merdrun an eon ago. Every sus-magiz had one."

"So," said Flydd, looking hard at Malien, "unknown to the Aachim, and perhaps to his own people, Skald has always been able to do magic here by using this ancient, corrupt relic. And, by secretly drinking lives, he could have become very powerful."

My throat felt as though it had closed over; it was a struggle to draw breath. "In all the time the Merdrun were lost in the void," I said, "more than ten thousand years, they never once changed their plans. They were betrayed and cast from their home-world into the void, long ago. All they wanted was to return to Tallallame—and take revenge on every one of their enemies." I glanced up at Flydd. "So why would they end their lives, now?"

"You'll be on their list, Sulien," said Malien. "You too, Xervish. And me, I dare say."

My heart hammered, panic rising. I fought it down. We had to work this out, and quickly. "The rest of Skald's enemies, including my family, are at the reunion back home."

"And it can't be a coincidence that he drank his people's lives last night," said Flydd.

"But are they really dead?" I said. "*Or does he just want us to think so?*"

"What are you saying?"

"People whose lives have been drunk look a lot more shrunken than the bodies we checked. They're hardly withered at all. What if Skald only *partly* drank his people's lives, to get the massive power he needed to escape, leaving them apparently dead but actually under a stasis spell? So they could be reawakened afterwards, to carry out their plan?"

"It wouldn't be easy to partly drink a life. It's addictive and, once started, it's hard to stop. And why would they trust the man who had so betrayed them?"

"Because Skald needed the plan to work even more than they did. Besides, they had nothing more to lose—and everything to gain."

"Was there any hint of a stasis spell on the bodies?" said Malien.

"I couldn't tell," said Flydd.

"When the Merdrun held me prisoner," I said, "Skald and I were mind-linked for a time. Could he have learned about the reunion through me?"

"Perhaps," said Flydd, idly fingering the Waystone. Then he cried, "He wants the Waystone, more than anything! If he gets it, he'll open a portal to Tallallame and take his people home. It would erase the taint on his name—he'd be a hero again."

"But where is he? Here, turned to stone?"

We all stared at the petrified corpse.

"No, that's just a shell." Flydd walked around the altar, and again. "He's gone to Tullymool. To the reunion! To get the Waystone, *and take revenge on his enemies.*"

"Take us there!" snapped Malien.

I felt sick. With that much power, how could anyone resist him?

But something else was wrong here.

"Why would he leave the shard?" I said shakily. "It's the last of their magical relics, the one thing they have left from their victorious past."

"Maybe he couldn't take it with him." Flydd reached into the red eye socket and pulled it out, and his finger and thumb were smoking.

"It's bursting with power."

"Don't touch it with your bare skin." Malien took it, slipped it into a little, round metal case like a pill box and handed it back. We raced out. "One last adventure," she said. "Hurry!"

I grabbed Flydd's wrist and Malien caught mine. Flydd touched the Waystone to his platinum ring and the portal hurled us away so violently that I felt Malien lose her grip. I tried to grab her in the darkness but she was gone.

Flydd and I emerged outside the door of my studio with a boom that shook down half a dozen loose roof slates.

"Where's Malien?" I said frantically.

"Lost, *between*," said Flydd, bowing his head. "No time for that now. Go!"

But I'd known her all my life; how could she be dead, just like that? Yet the living had to come first and if I didn't warn them, Skald would take them from me as well. I would grieve for Malien later—if I survived.

Three-quarters of a mile away was the meadow, shaded by huge old trees, where everyone had gathered for the reunion. Almost everyone I cared about was there. Staying away now seemed foolish, childish.

I had to warn them. I ran.

"He's back!" I shrieked as I reached the picnic area. "Get up, quick!"

"Who's back?" said my father, Llian, raising a crystal goblet in an extravagant gesture. He looked tipsy, and no one could blame him, but this was the worst time to be witless.

I looked around wildly. "Skald!"

"Where?"

A good question. Skald had drawn a monumental amount of

power from all those lives, then left his petrified body behind. Had he turned to stone because living flesh could not endure that much power? If so, what was he now?

And then I saw it. High in the air, a few hundred yards away, beyond the meandering stream, a vast presence slowly condensed out of pure power. It was roughly human shaped, though its edges blurred and wavered. A glowing green nimbus surrounded the figure and yellow rays radiated in all directions.

Was Skald a kind of *being* now? Whatever he was, power leaked out of him as he descended, leaving shimmering trails in the air, charring grass and bushes below him, boiling the water in a nearby duck pond, and heating everything it touched to incandescence.

His touch would kill, though I did not think Skald wanted to kill us just yet. He drifted lower, extending spider-leg projections towards the guards stationed further out and cutting them down in puffs of black smoke. The mongrel!

Everyone was on their feet now, staring up. I could sense his triumph. How Skald loved stalking his enemies. He was savoring our terror. Why would he hurry? He had waited sixteen years.

Flydd appeared beside me, panting.

"What do we do?" I gasped.

"If he's now a being, he'll be invulnerable to physical or magical attack. Whatever spell we use on him, he could turn it back a thousandfold…"

"Flydd?" I prompted, when he did not go on.

"Last time you beat him with an emotional attack," he said quietly. "What are his weaknesses?"

"Umm…Skald never had a great gift for magic. Look at him— power is oozing out everywhere. And I don't think he knows how best to use it."

"With that much power, he doesn't have to. What else?"

Previously, using my empath's gift, I had sensed out and amplified the agonizing emotions and feelings of Skald's victims, and deluged him with them. And because the Merdrun had always denied their own emotions, he had been overwhelmed.

I raised my hand to try again. The being that Skald had become drifted towards us, and smiled. The gigantic face was horribly scarred, and his right eye socket was empty.

His voice boomed like thunder, inside my head and outside at the same time, and it shook my bones. *I've spent the past sixteen years exploring my emotions, Sulien, and learning how to defend myself against such attacks. You can't touch me now. Give me the Waystone.*

"You're the son of a coward!" I shrieked up at him. "And you're a coward too."

He grimaced. *Nor can you provoke me. All this time, I've been tormented by the most savage accuser of all—myself. The Waystone. Give it to me.*

I raked my fingers through my hair, desperately trying to think of a way to attack him. My forefinger stuck to something—a clot of printing ink. I was about to wipe it off on my trews when I saw that it formed a crude letter U.

Was Skald his own most savage accuser? What about Uletta, the only person who had ever loved him? He had loved her, too, yet he had betrayed her and, as she lay dying, she had used up the last of her life laying an unbreakable curse on him and his people. Was she the answer?

"Shard!" I said out of the corner of my mouth to Flydd.

He took the cap off the little pill box. "What are you thinking?"

"You know how to raise people from the dead?"

"Yes, though it's generally a bad idea."

"Remember where Uletta was buried?" I nodded towards the mound, partly enclosed in a loop of the stream. "The shard will know her."

Flydd stared at me for a minute, doubtless weighing possibilities, then held it up, wincing, his fingers smoking where they touched it. He spoke the words of the raising spell and a wraith came up through the nearest mound and drifted towards us, becoming ever more solid as she drew near. A big, strong woman, her features still twisted in the anguish of her betrayal.

"I remember you," the risen Uletta said as she settled beside me. "You were a little girl. What do you want?"

I looked upwards. "Up there."

She saw the being formerly known as Skald, and her face hardened.

"Sixteen years ago, you went to your grave seething with hate and bitterness," I said, "and your dying curse has blighted the world. It's time to put an end to it."

Uletta took the glowing green shard. It did not burn her fingers.

Skald looked down, then froze in the air. No human face could have expressed the horror I saw in him.

Go away! he choked.

"Why do you hate me?" said Uletta. "What did I ever do to you but give you my love?"

You cursed me and my people for all time, he said, two parts rage and three parts guilt. *And from that day to this, we've known nothing but torment.*

"*You* cursed your people when you betrayed me. I merely put it into words."

Skald raised a smoking fist the size of a small thundercloud, as if to smite her dead, but perhaps his nerve failed him. Or perhaps the guilt got to him.

"When I cursed you before," said Uletta, "I was just a normal person. But now, raised from the dead and with your shard in my hand, I can have all you have." She extended a muscular arm. "I'm taking back what is mine."

Did she hope to regain the life he had drunk, or was it just a goad? Skald let out a desperate cry, turned the fist into a long, ethereal finger and pointed it at her as if to drink her life again. Uletta smiled and folded her arms.

The air crackled. Electric sparks jumped in my hair and stung my scalp.

"Get to shelter!" bellowed Flydd. "Now!"

We scrambled behind the largest tree and the picnickers followed: Mother, wavy gray hair streaming out behind her, my little brother, Gannion, running with a gigantic piece of cake, my dearest friend, Jassika, and a dozen of my old allies.

Dad, ordinarily a clumsy man, got there without spilling a precious drop from his goblet. I covered my face with my hands and peered around the trunk, through my fingers.

Skald cast the life-drinking spell on Uletta. I had seen him use this spell many times in the past, and it was a hideous way to die. She let out such a cry of horror that it shivered my bones. Was she reliving what it had been like last time?

But, as Skald attempted to drink Uletta's life force, she threw back her head and laughed.

"What's going on?" I said.

"No one brought back from the dead can have true life," said Flydd.

A dreadful realization warped Skald's scarred features, but too late. The power he had drawn from Uletta was the antithesis of that within a normal human life, and it began to annihilate his own life force.

He tried to reverse the spell but the power he had taken from a hundred thousand Merdrun exploded out in all directions. It seared the leaves off the trees, gouged up grass and earth, toppled copses and fences, and blasted all the water out of the stream for hundreds of yards.

And Skald, who had been nothing but power and consciousness, was obliterated.

The ground shook, and all around us charred leaves drifted down, covering the grass like black snowflakes. When it finally stopped there was no trace of the being once known as Skald.

"It's over," said Flydd. "He's been unmade."

My hands wouldn't stop trembling I snatched the goblet from Dad's hand and downed the contents in a gulp. "What...what about the Merdrun in the crater?"

"That cataclysm would have torn his stasis spell apart," said Flydd, "and no one could have survived it. But they wouldn't have known. Their torment's over."

Uletta squeezed the shard between her strong fingers and it melted, vaporized, and vanished. The last deadly relic of the Crimson Gate that had corrupted the tragic Merdrun long ago, and ruined their hopes and dreams, was gone.

"And I can have peace," she said.

She drifted back towards her grave, becoming more wraithlike by the second, and plunged down through the grass into the mound.

"How about Malien?" I said quietly.

Flydd put a bony arm around my shoulders. "'One last adventure,' she said. She would have been happy to go that way."

I supposed so. She had been a very old woman. But Malien had always done her best when I was in trouble, and I would miss her.

Around us, people emerged from their hiding places, and hugged and laughed and wept. Mother threw her arms around me and my father embraced us both. Suddenly I felt such a vast upwelling of hope and optimism, and the infinite possibilities of life, that for a few seconds, I was floating. The blight on Santhenar had lifted.

I looked back towards my studio, and the work I'd used as an escape all this time. "Damn the etchings!" I said. "Let's have that reunion."

The Wind and the Rain

By Robert Silverberg

The planet cleanses itself. That is the important thing to remember, at moments when we become too pleased with ourselves. The healing process is a natural and inevitable one. The action of the wind and the rain, the ebbing and flowing of the tides, the vigorous rivers flushing out the choked and stinking lakes—these are all natural rhythms, all healthy manifestations of universal harmony.

Of course, we are here too. We do our best to hurry the process along. But we are only auxiliaries, and we know it. We must not exaggerate the value of our work. False pride is worse than a sin: it is a foolishness. We do not deceive ourselves into thinking we are important. If we were not here at all, the planet would repair itself anyway within twenty to fifty million years. It is estimated that our presence cuts that time down by somewhat more than half.

#

Today we must inject colored fluids into a major river. Edith, Bruce, Paul, Elaine, Oliver, Ethel, Ronald, Edward, and I have been assigned to this task. Most members of the team believe the river is the Mississippi, although there is some evidence that it may be the Nile. Oliver, Bruce, and Edith believe it is more likely to be the Nile than the Mississippi, but they defer to the opinion of the majority.

The river is wide and deep and its color is black in some places and dark green in others. The fluids are computer mixed on the east bank of the river in a large factory erected by a previous reclamation team. We supervise their passage into the river.

First, we inject the red fluid, then the blue, then the yellow; they have different densities and form parallel stripes running for many hundreds of kilometers in the water. We are not certain whether these fluids are active healing agents—that is, substances which dissolve the solid pollutants lining the riverbed—or merely serve as markers permitting further chemical analysis of the river by the orbiting satellite system. It is not necessary for us to understand what we are doing, so long as we follow instructions explicitly.

Elaine jokes about going swimming. Bruce says, "How absurd. This river is famous for deadly fish that will strip the flesh from your bones." We all laugh at that. Fish? Here? What fish could be as deadly as the river itself? This water would consume our flesh if we entered it, and probably dissolve our bones as well. I scribbled a poem yesterday and dropped it in, and the paper vanished instantly.

#

In the evenings we walk along the beach and have philosophical discussions. The sunsets on this coast are embellished by rich tones of purple, green, crimson, and yellow. Sometimes we cheer when a particularly beautiful combination of atmospheric gases transforms the sunlight. Our mood is always optimistic and gay. We are never depressed by the things we find on this planet. Even devastation can be an art form, can it not? Perhaps it is one of the greatest of all art forms, since an art of destruction consumes its medium, it devours its own epistemological foundations, and in this sublimely nullifying doubling-back upon its origins it far exceeds in moral complexity those forms which are merely productive. That is, I place a higher value on transformative art than on generative art. Is my meaning clear?

In any event, since art ennobles and exalts the spirits of those who perceive it, we are exalted and ennobled by the conditions on Earth. We envy those who collaborate to create those extraordinary conditions. We know ourselves to be small-souled folk of a minor latter-day epoch; we lack the dynamic grandeur of energy that enabled our ancestors to commit such depredations. This world is a symphony.

Naturally you might argue that to restore a planet takes more energy than to destroy it, but you would be wrong. Nevertheless, though our daily tasks leave us weary and drained, we also feel stimulated and excited, because by restoring this world, the mother-world of mankind, we are in a sense participating in the original splendid process of its destruction. I mean in the sense that the resolution of a dissonant chord participates in the dissonance of that chord.

#

Now we have come to Tokyo, the capital of the island empire of Japan. See how small the skeletons of the citizens are? That is one way we have of identifying this place as Japan. The Japanese are known to have been people of small stature. Edward's ancestors were Japanese. He is of small stature. (Edith says his skin should be yellow as well. His skin is just like ours. Why is his skin not yellow?)

"See?" Edward cries. "There is Mount Fuji!" It is an

extraordinarily beautiful mountain, mantled in white snow. On its slopes one of our archaeological teams is at work, tunneling under the snow to collect samples from the twentieth-century strata of chemical residues, dust, and ashes.

"Once there were over seventy-five thousand industrial smokestacks around Tokyo," says Edward proudly, "from which were released hundreds of tons of sulfur, nitrous oxide, ammonia, and carbon gases every day. We should not forget that this city had more than 1.5 million automobiles as well." Many of the automobiles are still visible, but they are very fragile, worn to threads by the action of the atmosphere. When we touch them, they collapse in puffs of grey smoke.

Edward, who has studied his heritage well, tells us, "It was not uncommon for the density of carbon monoxide in the air here to exceed the permissible levels by factors of two hundred and fifty percent on mild summer days. Owing to atmospheric conditions, Mount Fuji was visible only one day of every nine. Yet no one showed dismay."

He conjures up for us a picture of his industrious ancestors toiling cheerfully and unremittingly in their poisonous environment. The Japanese, he insists, were able to maintain and even increase their gross national product at a time when other nationalities had already begun to lose ground in the global economic struggle because of diminished population owing to unfavorable ecological factors. And so on and so on.

After a time we grow bored with Edward's incessant boasting. "Stop boasting," Oliver tells him, "or we will expose you to the atmosphere." We have much dreary work to do here.

Paul and I guide the huge trenching machines; Oliver and Ronald follow, planting seeds. Almost immediately, strange angular shrubs spring up. They have shiny bluish leaves and long crooked branches. One of them seized Elaine by the throat yesterday and might have hurt her seriously had Bruce not uprooted it. We were not upset. This is merely one phase in the long, slow process of repair. There will be many such incidents. Someday, cherry trees will blossom in this place.

#

This is the poem the river ate:

Destruction

I.Nouns. Destruction, desolation, wreck, wreckage, ruin, ruination, rack and ruin, smash, smashup, demolition, demolishment, ravagement, havoc, ravage, dilapidation, decimation, blight, breakdown, consumption, dissolution, obliteration, overthrow, spoilage; mutilation, disintegration, undoing, pulverization; sabotage, vandalism; annulment, damnation, extinguishment, extinction; invalidation, nullification, shatterment, shipwreck; annihilation, disannulment, discreation, extermination, extirpation, obliteration, perdition, subversion.

II.Verbs. Destroy, wreck, ruin, ruinate, smash, demolish, raze, ravage, gut, dilapidate, decimate, blast, blight, break down, consume, dissolve, overthrow; mutilate, disintegrate, unmake, pulverize; sabotage, vandalize, annul, blast, blight, damn, dash, extinguish, invalidate, nullify, quell, quench, scuttle, shatter, shipwreck, torpedo, smash, spoil, undo, void; annihilate, devour, disannul, discreate, exterminate, obliterate, extirpate, subvert; corrode, erode, sap, undermine, waste, waste away, whittle away (or down); eat away, canker, gnaw; wear away, abrade, batter, excoriate, rust.

III.Adjectives. Destructive, ruinous, vandalistic, baneful, cutthroat, fell, lethiferous, pernicious, slaughterous, predatory, sinistrous, nihilistic; corrosive, erosive, cankerous, caustic, abrasive.

"I validate," says Ethel.

"I unravage," says Oliver.

"I integrate," says Paul.

"I devandalize," says Elaine.

"I unshatter," says Bruce.

"I unscuttle," says Edward.

"I discorrode," says Ronald.

"I undesolate," says Edith.

"I create," say I.

We reconstitute. We renew. We repair. We reclaim. We refurbish. We restore. We renovate. We rebuild. We reproduce. We redeem. We reintegrate. We replace. We reconstruct. We retrieve. We revivify. We resurrect. We fix, overhaul, mend, put in repair, retouch, tinker, cobble, patch, darn, staunch, caulk, splice. We celebrate our successes by energetic and lusty singing. Some of us copulate.

#

Here is an outstanding example of the dark humour of the ancients. At a place called Richland, Washington, there was an installation that manufactured plutonium for use in nuclear weapons. This was done in the name of "national security," that is, to enhance and strengthen the safety of the United States of America and render its inhabitants carefree and hopeful. In a relatively short span of time these activities produced approximately fifty-five million gallons of concentrated radioactive waste. This material was so intensely hot that it would boil spontaneously for decades, and would retain a virulently toxic character for many thousands of years.

The presence of so much dangerous waste posed a severe environmental threat to a large area of the United States. How, then, to dispose of this waste? An appropriately comic solution was devised. The plutonium installation was situated in a seismically unstable area located along the earthquake belt that rings the Pacific Ocean.

A storage site was chosen nearby, directly above a fault line that had produced a violent earthquake half a century earlier. Here 140 steel-and-concrete tanks were constructed just below the surface of the ground and some 240 feet above the water table of the Columbia River, from which a densely populated region derived its water supply.

Into these tanks the boiling radioactive wastes were poured: a magnificent gift to future generations. Within a few years the true subtlety of the jest became apparent when the first small leaks were detected in the tanks.

Some observers predicted that no more than ten to twenty years would pass before the great heat caused the seams of the tanks to burst, releasing radioactive gases into the atmosphere or permitting radioactive fluids to escape into the river. The designers of the tanks maintained, though, that they were sturdy enough to last at least a century. It will be noted that this was something less than one percent of the known half-life of the materials placed in the tanks.

Because of discontinuities in the records, we are unable to determine which estimate was more nearly correct. It should be possible for our decontamination squads to enter the affected regions in eight hundred to thirteen hundred years. This episode arouses tremendous admiration in me. How much gusto, how much robust wit, those old ones must have had!

#

We are granted a holiday so we may go to the mountains of Uruguay to visit the site of one of the last human settlements, perhaps the very last. It was discovered by a reclamation team several hundred years ago and has been set aside, in its original state, as a museum for the tourists who one day will wish to view the mother-world.

One enters through a lengthy tunnel of glossy pink brick. A series of airlocks prevents the outside air from penetrating. The village itself, nestling between two craggy spires, is shielded by a clear shining dome. Automatic controls maintain its temperature at a constant mild level. There were a thousand inhabitants. We can view them in the spacious plazas, in the taverns, and in places of recreation.

Family groups remain together, often with their pets. A few carry umbrellas. Everyone is in an unusually fine state of preservation. Many of them are smiling.

It is not yet known why these people perished. Some died in the act of speaking, and scholars have devoted much effort, so far without success, to the task of determining and translating the last words still frozen on their lips.

We are not allowed to touch anyone, but we may enter their homes and inspect their possessions and toilet furnishings. I am moved almost to tears, as are several of the others.

"Perhaps these are our very ancestors," Ronald exclaims.

But Bruce declares scornfully, "You say ridiculous things. Our ancestors must have escaped from here long before the time these people lived."

Just outside the settlement I find a tiny glistening bone, possibly the shinbone of a child, possibly part of a dog's tail. "May I keep it?" I ask our leader. But he compels me to donate it to the museum.

#

The archives yield much that is fascinating. For example, this fine example of ironic distance in ecological management. In the ocean off a place named California were tremendous forests of a giant seaweed called kelp, housing a vast and intricate community of maritime creatures. Sea urchins lived on the ocean floor, one hundred feet down, amid the holdfasts that anchored the kelp. Furry aquatic mammals known as sea otters fed on the urchins.

The Earth people removed the otters because they had some use for their fur. Later, the kelp began to die. Forests many square miles in diameter vanished. This had serious commercial consequences, for the kelp was valuable and so were many of the animal forms that lived in it.

Investigation of the ocean floor showed a great increase in sea urchins. Not only had their natural enemies, the otters, been removed, but the urchins were taking nourishment from the immense quantities of organic matter in the sewage discharges dumped into the ocean by the Earth people. Millions of urchins were nibbling at the holdfasts of the kelp, uprooting the huge plants and killing them.

When an oil tanker accidentally released its cargo into the sea, many urchins were killed and the kelp began to reestablish itself. But this proved to be an impractical means of controlling the urchins. Encouraging the otters to return was suggested, but there was not a sufficient supply of living otters.

The kelp foresters of California solved their problem by dumping quicklime into the sea from barges. This was fatal to the urchins; once they were dead, healthy kelp plants were brought from other parts of the sea and embedded to become the nucleus of a new forest. After a while the urchins returned and began to eat the kelp again. More quicklime was dumped. The urchins died and new kelp was planted.

Later, it was discovered that the quicklime was having harmful effects on the ocean floor itself, and other chemicals were dumped to counteract those effects.

All of this required great ingenuity and a considerable outlay of energy and resources. Edward thinks there was something very Japanese about these maneuvers. Ethel points out that the kelp trouble would never have happened if the Earth people had not originally removed the otters. How naive Ethel is! She has no understanding of the principles of irony. Poetry bewilders her also. Edward refuses to sleep with Ethel now.

#

In the final centuries of their era the people of Earth succeeded in paving the surface of their planet almost entirely with a skin of concrete and metal. We must pry much of this up so that the planet may start to breathe again.

It would be easy and efficient to use explosives or acids, but we are not overly concerned with ease and efficiency; besides, there is great concern that explosives or acids may do further ecological harm here. Therefore, we employ large machines that inset prongs in the great cracks that have developed in the concrete. Once we have lifted the paved slabs they usually crumble quickly. Clouds of concrete dust blow freely through the streets of these cities, covering the stumps of the buildings with a fine, pure coating of grayish-white powder.

The effect is delicate and refreshing.

Paul suggested yesterday that we may be doing ecological harm by setting free this dust. I became frightened at the idea and reported him to the leader of our team. Paul will be transferred to another group.

#

Toward the end here they all wore breathing suits, similar to ours but even more comprehensive. We find these suits lying around everywhere like the discarded shells of giant insects. The most advanced models were complete individual housing units.

Apparently, it was not necessary to leave one's suit except to perform such vital functions as sexual intercourse and childbirth. We understand that the reluctance of the Earth people to leave their suits even for those functions, near the close, immensely hastened the decrease in population.

#

Our philosophical discussions. God created this planet. We all agree on that, in a manner of speaking, ignoring for the moment definitions of such concepts as "God" and "created".

Why did He go to so much trouble to bring Earth into being, if it was His intention merely to have it rendered uninhabitable? Did He create mankind especially for this purpose, or did they exercise free will in doing what they did here? Was mankind God's way of taking vengeance against His own creation? Why would He want to take vengeance against His own creation?

Perhaps it is a mistake to approach the destruction of Earth from the moral or ethical standpoint. I think we must see it in purely aesthetic terms, i.e., a self-contained artistic achievement, like a fouetté en tournant or an entrechat-dix, performed for its own sake and requiring no explanations. Only in this way can we understand how the Earth people were able to collaborate so joyfully in their own asphyxiation.

#

My tour of duty is almost over. It has been an overwhelming experience; I will never be the same. I must express my gratitude for this opportunity to have seen Earth almost as its people knew it. Its rusted streams, its corroded meadows, its purpled skies, its bluish puddles. The debris, the barren hillsides, the blazing rivers.

Soon, thanks to the dedicated work of reclamation teams such as ours, these superficial but beautiful emblems of death will have disappeared. This will be just another world for tourists, of sentimental curiosity but no unique value to the sensibility. How dull that will be: a green and pleasant Earth once more, why, why? The universe has enough habitable planets; at present it has only one Earth.

Has all our labor here been an error, then? I sometimes do think it was misguided of us to have undertaken this project. But on the other hand, I remind myself of our fundamental irrelevance. The healing process is a natural and inevitable one. With us or without us, the planet cleanses itself. The wind, the rain, the tides. We merely help things along.

#

A rumor reaches us that a colony of live Earthmen has been found on the Tibetan plateau. We travel there to see if this is true. Hovering above a vast, red, empty plain, we see large figures moving slowly about. Are these Earthmen, inside breathing suits of a strange design?

We descend. Members of other reclamation teams are already on hand. They have surrounded one of the large creatures. It travels in a wobbly circle, uttering indistinct cries and grunts. Then it comes to a halt, confronting us blankly as if defying us to embrace it. We tip it over; it moves its massive limbs dumbly but is unable to arise.

After a brief conference we decide to dissect it. The outer plates lift easily. Inside we find nothing but gears and coils of gleaming wire. The limbs no longer move, although things click and hum within it for quite some time. We are favorably impressed by the durability and resilience of these machines. Perhaps in the distant future such entities will wholly replace the softer and more fragile life forms on all worlds, as they seem to have done on Earth.

The wind. The rain. The tides. All sadnesses flow to the sea.

Thaw

A Red Sister Story

By Mark Lawrence

"Nona!"

Nona looked up. Ruli ran across the quayside towards her, careless of her skirts and the master's hat left tumbling in her wake. Ruli caught Nona in her arms and Nona, despite her grim mood, surrendered to the moment, sweeping up her old friend. Her mind had never let go of the idea that they were the same height, Ruli perhaps an inch or two taller, so the fact that she now dwarfed the woman always took Nona by surprise.

Nona lifted her clear off the ground. Bearing three sons had thickened Ruli somewhat but the additional weight proved no challenge to arms used to constant swordplay.

"Hey!" Ruli laughed.

"What? Henton doesn't do this?" Ruli's husband was eight foot tall and twice as broad in the shoulders as Nona.

When Nona and Arabella had arrived at the dock, the sight of two nuns had drawn little attention. Though both of them were Red Sisters, they had opted for the anonymity of the black habit. Heads turned now though at the sight of Trademaster Ruli Vinesong being hoisted into the air like a child, squealing with laughter all the while.

"Ara!" As soon as Nona let Ruli's feet touch the flagstones she was off again, throwing herself at Arabella. They embraced and Ara manufactured the expected smiles, managing a more convincing job of it than Nona had. Ara had always been better at stepping clear of an argument and, even though she'd started this one, Ara seemed, at least outwardly, less affected by it than Nona.

"Is the boat ready?" Ara asked.

"It's a ship!" Ruli rolled her eyes, showing another flash of the girl she'd been when they were all novices back at the convent. "Boats are for bobbing about by the shore. My ships cross the sea!" Ruli had inherited her father's fleet and made her money exporting wine to the Durns then bringing back coal. War and invasions made surprisingly brief interruptions to the necessary business of trading across the waters. "And yes, it's ready. Clera arrived this morning. She's waiting aboard."

Nona glanced at Ara who kept her steely gaze on the ship in question. The argument had been about half a dozen things, anything either of them could lay hands on to hurt the other in the heat of the moment, but Clera had been the heart of it.

"She delivered you to your enemies!" Ara had shouted that morning, her face shadowed by more than dawn's grey light. "She tried to skewer me with a spear!" She'd rolled from their bed to haul up her nightgown and show the scar on her back. As if Nona had forgotten. As if she hadn't traced the site with her fingertips a thousand times and didn't know it better than any wound of her own.

Nona shook her head. "She knew the shipskin wouldn't give." The armor that Red Sisters wore was thin but of legendary toughness. "And she helped us as often as she hurt us."

"You say that like it's a good thing, rather than just enough to let her live!" Ara had thrown up her hands and stalked out of Nona's cell without even stopping to pick up her habit to keep the cold from her flesh.

Nona shook off the morning's memory. She followed Ruli and Ara to where the ship lay tied to the dock bollards. Sailors paused their tasks to watch the nuns approach, the devout making the sign of the Tree while others tapped a hand to their chest, acknowledging Ruli.

Clera came to the rail. Like Ruli, she wore her hair uncovered, black locks flowing over her shoulders. When she'd been a novice it had always been a wild tangle, but as a merchant, her wealth had tamed it. She wore face paints too. Just a touch here and there, dark around the eyes, red on the lips. Even through her disapproval, Nona had to admit she looked good.

"Does she think we're going to a ball?" Ara hissed.

Nona wanted to tell Ara to put her envy aside. The paints Clera's silver paid for still didn't make her as beautiful as Ara after a hard training session with her face flushed and sweat plastering her golden locks to her skull. Mud and blood couldn't tarnish Ara's Ancestor-given splendor, even with her hair hidden beneath a nun's headdress. The only thing that had ever looked ugly on her was jealousy.

It was just a kiss. Nona wanted to say the words. It was just a kiss. But they were fuel to the fire that was burning Ara up.

"Why is she even here?" Ara aimed the question at Ruli as they followed her up the gangplank. "She's at the convent two days in seven. And now she's here, too!"

"You know Clera." Ruli shrugged. "Maybe she smells gold to be made. She must have spent enough of it to get the emperor to send her along. You know what they say: the emperor can't be bought, but he can certainly be rented."

Once aboard, Ruli went to speak with the captain while Nona and Ara slowly made their way to the prow, passing Clera without comment. Ara stalked past. Head high. Nona, burdened by shame, looked everywhere but at her, finding sudden fascination in the sailors' tasks of knotting ropes and shifting nets.

Nona turned her gaze from decks to the flat gray expanse of the Marn Sea. The ice walls that corralled the sea were a white fringe on both horizons, over thirty miles distant to the north, nearly twenty to the south. Further than that—Nona reminded herself—she and the others were here because the Corridor had been widened. She opened her mouth to say something to Ara, then closed it. The ice may have thawed but something between Ara and Nona had frozen.

Nona wanted to say that she'd never seen the sea before. She wanted to share her wonder at the way the wooden floor beneath her feet rose and fell. The taste of salt on the wind, the cry of the gulls, all of these things trembled on her tongue, needing to be shared, but Ara's eyes were ice blue and fixed on the distance.

"An island full of monsters!" Clera came up behind them, bold and unrepentant. "Sounds exciting. And unlikely."

Nona turned. Ara didn't.

"If it's unlikely, why are you here?" Ara asked in a cold voice.

"I like a challenge." Clera shot Nona a wicked look. "And unlikely bets can be where the money is. With the war over, this could be the next big thing."

The war had delivered into the emperor's hands the means to unlock a frozen world. Or at least parts of it. With the power to focus the rays of their dying sun, he could broaden the horizons of nations that had been locked for millennia in the shrinking Corridor that encircled Abeth's equator: a zone carved through the miles-thick ice sheets in which the whole planet was clad.

But while thawing land ice would cause disastrous flooding, only vast seas extended beneath the ice-bound edges of the Sea of Marn. There, the creatures of the ocean emerged from darkness and could be hunted by a starving population. Recent battlefields yielded poor harvests. So, the emperor had ordered the Sea of Marn to be widened.

When the melting ice cliffs had revealed an island, the shock was not that it was there but that it seemed to have existed within its own bubble under the sheet. Rather than the scraped-clean rock one might expect, gnawed by glacial teeth, the place, according to the tales of passing sailors, boasted monsters larger than houses. The emperor had requested Nona's participation in the investigation. The abbess had sent her alone, her tender heart not willing to risk others to these reported monsters and her faith in Nona's invincibility unshakeable.

Ara had come because, kiss or no kiss, she'd told the abbess: "What? No! I'm not letting her go alone. Are you stupid?"

#

"We're making good time." Nona found Ruli beside the ship's wheel.

"The Corridor wind is either with you or against you when navigating the Marn. When it's with you, your ship fairly skips across the waves."

"What's that man doing?" Nona pointed to a sailor struggling with a complex set of ropes and pulleys beneath the main sail.

"Nautical stuff." Ruli dismissed the question. "What's up with you and Ara?" Ruli lived for gossip but genuine concern colored her voice.

"We argued." The word was too small. As Mistress Blade, Nona was expected to understand every fight, but in this one, Ara could so easily reach past all her defenses and stab her in the heart.

Ruli nodded. "For warriors the peace can be harder than the war." She set a hand to Nona's arm. "It's difficult to let go of that time. To still have the memories and the anger but not have someone to fight."

Nona studied the deck. "It's more than that." Though Ruli was right—the peace they'd longed for *was* hard.

"You argued about Clera," Ruli said.

Nona had hoped it wasn't so obvious. "I didn't know she—"

"You never do." Ruli shook her head, a wry smile on her lips. "Everyone else knew."

Clera had said much the same. After.

#

The wind was with Ruli's ship *The Pride of Ren*, and the voyage proved short. A horse couldn't have run the distance faster, Ruli claimed. Even so, the three scant hours managed to crawl by, each awkward silence stretching out for an age while consuming almost no actual time.

Part of Nona wanted to grab Clera by the shoulders and steer her to Ara then demand she give a true accounting of their moment beneath the oak at the center of the novice cloister in the bright of the moon.

Nona had already told Ara. "*She* kissed *me*! I wasn't expecting it."

"You could have stopped her."

"She was too quick!"

Ara snorted then and shook her head. "Too quick for Mistress Blade of Sweet Mercy Convent? Too quick for the Shield of the Chosen, who can pluck arrows from the air and write her name on a wall as she's falling past it?"

Nona had wanted to say that she was confused, taken by surprise, shocked. All of those things. She'd wanted to pile her excuses up until they made a wall so high that nobody, not even Ara, could see over to the truth. But the truth was, when Clera—the friend she hadn't quit despite Clera's betrayal against her and violence against those she loved—had stood on tiptoes and pressed her lips to Nona's she had been swift but not so fast she could not have been evaded, and when their mouths met and their breath mingled, Nona had stayed, caught in the moment, for heartbeat after heartbeat, breaking away only when, after the passage of a full and achingly long second, a proper guilt flooded in to wash away a host of less worthy emotions and desires.

"No." She had pushed Clera to the length of her arms. "What are you doing?"

"I've always wanted you." Clera wouldn't look away like she should.

"You never said anything."

Clera laughed. "We were children when I left. Ara didn't notice girls or boys until she was eighteen, so forgive me for not declaring my love when I was twelve."

"Love?" Nona knew Clera had endless girls in Verity.

"Always." Clera tried to step closer, but Nona had kept her at a distance that while not safe was at least safer.

A sailor's cry cut through Nona's reflections. "Land ho!"

And there in the gray distance, amid an ice-speckled sea, a dark fist of mist-wreathed stone defied the waves.

"We'll lower a boat," Ruli said. "I'm keeping my crew at a safe distance."

"Can any of us handle a boat?" Nona glanced from Ara to Clera, thinking they were as out of their element as she was.

"Of course I can, silly." Ruli waved sailors forward to prepare the rowboat.

Clera grinned. "You promised your husband you'd stay on the ship."

Ruli flapped a hand to brush the words away. "He knows my uncle was a pirate. He should expect me to lie."

#

"Is it always this rough?" The smaller vessel lurched and rolled beneath them and the waves seemed much bigger now that Nona was within touching distance.

"Every landlubber says that the first time." Ruli grinned at her and bent her back to the oars. Despite the sea's constant efforts to throw her off course, her strokes were slowly devouring the distance to the island's rocky shore.

"What the in the hells is that?" Clera, who had taken on a green tinge since joining them in the rowboat, released her death grip on the side for long enough to jab an accusatory finger in the direction of the island.

"A big rock," Ara replied through gritted teeth.

Despite the ferocity of the wind out on the Marn, the island managed to shroud itself in an ever-shifting cowl of mists—testimony to the heat that had kept the ice at bay.

"It was a…a thing…of some kind." Clera scowled at the island as if the intensity of her stare could clear a path to whatever had caught her eye.

"Well, you appear to have answered your own question, merchant." Ara kept her gaze forwards. "It was a thing. Perhaps you can sell it and cover your costs for the trip."

Clera rallied as she always did when under attack. "I expect so. I'm a very good merchant though I'd have made a terrible nun."

"We can agree on that," Ara said.

"It was probably a monster," Nona said, keen to steer the conversation away from conflict. "That's what we're here for. Let's be ready for them."

Ruli lent her support between strokes of the oars. "I'm sure the abbess's plan wasn't to have the monster choke to death on an extra big mouthful of squabbling nuns and ex-novices. So, keep your eyes open. I can't even see the island from here and I'd rather not sink on a rock before we get there."

#

A short while later, Nona splashed ashore with Ara at one shoulder and Clera at the other while Ruli secured the boat. The mists rose from the dark grit of the beach itself. Nona dipped to scoop up a handful of the coarse sand. It was warm and steamed in her palm. The fog streamed out to sea, so thick that the 'thing' that Clera had spotted could be looming over them right now and remain unseen.

"Stay sharp." Ara drew her blade and Nona's cleared the scabbard a moment later.

Ara led the way up to the rocky slope, aiming for the interior. Properly, Nona should be in charge, but Ara had been raised to lead and instinct often carried her past the limits of convent ranks.

A sudden change in the wind revealed the whole beach behind them for a few heartbeats before swirling in new clouds to hide it once more.

"No monsters there," Ruli said, joining them.

"I know what I saw," Clera said darkly.

"What did you see?" Nona asked.

"It was big." Clera pulled a knife from her belt as if the matter were settled.

They climbed the slope, winding through a tumble of jagged black rocks and following the contours of the land up a gentler, but still steep, hillside beyond.

"Thank the Ancestor!" Ruli exclaimed as a shift in the wind revealed that the slope ended not far above them. "There *is* a top!"

"Grass," Ara commented, pointing at a patch of green questing up between the stones.

They crested what turned out to be a surprisingly sharp rim and began to negotiate a winding path down the other side which proved considerably steeper than the one they'd climbed. The fog shrouding them made it impossible to tell how far they'd fall if they slipped. It was an unsettling feeling and Nona kept a close eye on Ruli. The others might be able to catch themselves if they tripped but Ruli lacked their quickness.

"Careful here." Ara slowed to descend a near vertical slope of wet rock that offered few ridges for hands and feet.

"I'm always—" The wind gusted, parting the mists. Ruli shrieked, reaching for support.

Something loomed over the women. A creature so large it defied reason. The black bulk of it wasn't just larger than a house, it was larger than a roadside tavern with guest rooms and a beer garden. A sinuous tail snaked away down the slope while a neck so long and thin that it resembled a serpent lofted above them, supporting a blunt head not unlike that of one of the tiny lizards that haunted the cracks of the Rock of Faith, only vastly bigger. In fact, if not for the four trunk-like legs, the creature might be mistaken for a colossal snake that had bloated its midsection by swallowing a whale.

Nona sprang into action, dropping into the moment, moving so fast that Ruli and the monster seemed frozen in place. Only Ara and Clera could match her, Ara sprinting up the wet cliff to join her, Clera scrambling for cover and finding none. Fear didn't enter into Nona's calculations. Her opponent's size simply wasn't a factor when three of her friends stood at risk.

She hurled herself at the monster's chest, leaping high, driving forward with her ark-steel sword in search of some vital organ. The blade sunk in hilt deep and she applied her weight to drag it down in the hope of spilling the beast's guts. But the hide that had offered little resistance to her thrust now battled against her slice. And did so with such stubbornness that even ark-steel only managed to cut a few inches down before becoming stuck and leaving Nona to hang from the hilt with her boots almost a yard from the ground.

Nona set her feet to the monster, dragged her blade free and leapt clear, skidding to a halt in defiance of the slope's steepness. Ara reached the spot where Nona had been and drove her own sword in as far as it would go.

Something was wrong. Nona was used to leaving her foes standing while her speed defeated them, but this monster gave 'slow' a new definition. It hadn't so much as twitched. It took all Nona's restraint to stop her attack. She paused, there under the great span of the creature's neck, its jugular far out of reach above her. Ara, too, must have sensed the wrongness and tugged her sword free without launching a flurry of new attacks.

Ruli was still working to get her throwing stars from inside her jacket. Nona reached out to lay a hand over her friend's as it emerged bristling with sharp steel. "It's not moving."

Ara rapped her sword hilt against the nearest leg and was rewarded with a hollow boom. "It's a statue."

"But what of?" Clera stood and straightened a little sheepishly. She looked up at the monster's bulk.

Ruli frowned. "Jula said there were giant creatures on Abeth eons before our kind. There are books that talk about finding their bones in the earth. Some of the drawings looked a bit like…"

"But this was never alive!" Ara banged it again.

The wind changed direction, howling across the slope. Nona caught Ruli before she lost balance. The blast showed them a great curve of the island. It seemed that the rim they had climbed and were now descending might encircle the whole of it. And below, dotted across the inner slope, positioned on ledges sufficient for their size, stood dozens of monsters. Some similar to their current foe and others far more fearsome, grinning at them through mouthfuls of teeth longer than sword blades. The fogs returned but took long enough to do so that Nona felt confident these beasts were also statues.

"This is a crater," Ruli said. "A volcano."

"A what?" Clera moved to Ruli's side.

"We need Jula here. She knows all this stuff," Ruli said. "She's read every book in the library. I only paid attention to the exciting bits. Fire mountains and ancient monsters. I remember that."

"It explains the warmth." Ara resumed her descent.

\#

Contrary to Ruli's confident prediction, the crater did not narrow to some small, central throat from which the fires of all the hells spewed. Instead, it appeared to have been filled to the halfway point with a lake that had frozen, only the level surface that greeted them was neither ice nor water but some kind of rock. Pale grey, different to the black rocks of the crater wall.

A thin layer of soil covered much of the crater floor surface, supporting grass and the occasional small bush that might well have grown in the months since the ice was melted away. In places, shallow pools steamed gently but the water that must surely have deluged the place had mysteriously vanished. As she led the way, Ara pointed to the mouths several narrow shafts, down which the water must have drained.

The mists at the base of the crater were thinner and parted more often, offering views of what looked like a collection of buildings towards the crater's center; enough, perhaps, to constitute a village.

As the group drew closer to the first of these structures, Nona was struck by a sudden disappointment. "Ruins…"

"What did you expect?" Clera asked.

Nona didn't have an answer. The mists and the monsters had made an unvoiced promise—or seemed to. She'd had no idea what was waiting for them, but she'd hoped for more than ruins.

Closer still, and Ara threw up a hand in warning, stopping them in their tracks. "There. See it?" She pointed.

A creature moved among the tumbled blocks of a shattered wall. Large but not so big that the monster statue they first encountered couldn't flatten it with a single foot. Nona and Ara drew on the shadows that lurked beneath the mist, wrapping the stuff of darkness around themselves as they advanced on silent feet, both of them wholly focused now.

The creature was nothing Nona had seen before or even heard of. It looked a bit like a thick-limbed dog or perhaps sheep, its blunt, simple outline promising strength. More importantly, the dull glint of its back, sparkling with droplets of dew, made it appear to be something constructed from metal. But unlike the monsters that had appeared to be flesh and yet were incapable of movement, this one was busy at some task.

"It's made of iron…" Ara pulsed the message noiselessly along their thread-bond. The first time she'd used it since Nona told her about the kiss.

"What's it doing?" Nona replied the same way, grateful for the intimacy.

The creature hefted a block of stone nearly its own size, setting it atop another.

"Trying to rebuild?" Ara asked as they narrowed the distance.

It scarcely seemed possible, but the splayed toes of its forefeet were now acting like fingers, making deft adjustments.

"Hello?" Nona shrugged off her cloak of shadows, revealing herself with just ten yards between herself and this new, smaller monster.

The creature swung its blunt head her way, regarding her with the black eye set on that side. It looked like a polished stone rather than an eyeball. It watched her for a heartbeat before returning its attention to the wall, grappling a second block.

"I said 'hello'," Nona repeated more loudly.

"What are you doing?" Ara pulled her back. "You don't know how dangerous that thing is."

"It doesn't know how dangerous I am," Nona retorted. But she let Ara pull her away. The iron dog-sheep ignored their squabble. At the rate it was going it might reconstruct the shell of the building in less than a day.

"We should go around." Clera surprised them both. She shouldn't have been able to sneak up on nuns who had trained as Grey Sisters before taking the Red, but then again, she had spent years under the tutelage of assassins before her merchant career.

Ara, ignoring Clera, nonetheless went around, aiming towards the more densely clustered buildings. Nona paused to wave Ruli on to join them.

They passed buildings in various degrees of ruin and saw iron beasts of different sizes and design at work on reconstruction, all of them uninterested in the newcomers. One of them, twice the length of the first, pushed rubble about like snow before a broom. Others, considerably smaller, worked on more delicate tasks using thinner and more nimble digits.

"The damage looks recent," Ruli said.

Clera nodded. "The thaw couldn't have been gentle."

Ara paused to look up at a structure that the iron beasts were hard at work on. It appeared to be nothing more than a wall of crosshatched girders that supported a track to nowhere. A track that rose and fell with sharp turns and twists such that anyone who were to follow it would find themselves faced with one steep climb and rapid plunge after another. "There's no sense to it…"

A few dozen yards from the track, a roofless hall sported a score of mirrors, bigger than any Nona had ever seen, each as tall as her, but none of them true. Clera snorted at a reflection that showed her comically fat, while Ruli laughed out loud at another that compressed her into less than a toddler's height. Nona and Ara gazed unsmiling at their own distortions, giant heads bulging on tiny bodies or tiny heads on giant bodies.

"Come on." Clera's words tugged Nona from her contemplations. She hadn't been musing on tricks of the eyes—rather she wondered if the mind worked similar distortions. Did Ara see her so differently now? The mirror of her thoughts distorted beyond recognition by the ripples of a single kiss? She turned from the reflections and followed the others.

Further on, the mists revealed the iron frame of a great wheel at least a hundred feet in diameter and supported vertically by a frame that would allow it to turn with its lowest edge just a yard above the ground.

"Are those seats?" Nona frowned at what looked like benches set at regular intervals around the perimeter.

"How does this not all rust to nothing?" Ruli asked in a more practical vein.

As they watched, an iron creature that seemed designed along the lines of some large crab worked its way around the edge of the wheel, unrolling a bright ribbon of color as vivid as the finest silks from Alden.

"What's going on?" Clera made a slow turn, taking in the ongoing labors all around them.

"There!" Ruli pointed to lights twinkling through the mist. Lights that Nona was sure had not been there moments before.

"This is the work of the Missing," Ara said. She and Nona had seen lights as bright as these in the Ark. Lights brighter and whiter than any flame. Though these ones also twinkled red and green and blue.

"Duh." Clera walked off towards the illumination.

Nona hurried to stop her. She had heard of lights among the mists of moonlit bogs tempting unwary travellers to a slow death sinking in the mire. "Wait!"

"You can't wait forever, Nona." Clera shook her off. "Sometimes you've just got to go for what you want even if you know you're not going to get it. Even if it causes trouble and hurts the one you love."

Nona hesitated, unsure for a moment whether Clera was talking about the lights.

"Come on." Clera pulled away sharply, moving forward, and Nona followed with Ruli at her side.

"Music?" Ruli cocked her head.

There did seem to be a faint music in the air, though produced by no instrument that Nona had ever heard. If Nona had been asked to predict what music might play amid the mist-haunted ruins of the Missing, she might have guessed at some kind of ethereal plainsong that the nuns' chants in Sweet Mercy Convent were merely imperfect echoes of. This was not that. "It sounds rather…"

"Jaunty," Clera said.

"I think it's magic." Nona turned back towards Ara, still standing where she'd left her, a shadow in the mist. "A kind of magic." She didn't feel any sense of danger. There was something here, ancient and strange, preserved against all probability, maintained over centuries by the dedication of the Missing's metal servants. She took a few paces towards Ara and held a hand out, wanting to share this moment of mystery and wonder. "Come on."

Ara's tight mask twitched and for a second Nona thought it would crack and return the old Ara to her. Instead, Ara turned her eyes towards Clera's retreating back and her gaze hardened. She swept past Nona without a word, and the mounting, unexplained sense of joy ran from Nona like blood from a wound.

Nona followed the other three. The lights ahead were moving, flying through the air, and the alien tune jangled through the mist. Slowly the structure took shape below the shifting illumination. An island of light amid the fog.

"It's a…" Nona joined the others.

"Thing," Clera said.

The lights were set across a peaked circular roof that revolved on a central column. Beneath it, a circular platform just inches above the ground and yards below the roof also revolved around the center. And studding the platform were a dozen or more bizarre, brightly colored animals, no two the same, each sporting a saddle and moving sedately up and down on the silver pole that supported it.

As the four explorers approached, open mouthed, caution abandoned, the whole structure slowed and halted, the animals all coming to rest at the bottom of their poles.

"That's a rabbit." Ruli pointed to the nearest one. "A giant rabbit."

"With a saddle," Clera added. "They've all got saddles."

The music had slowed with the platform, and grown more quiet.

"That one's a snail." Ara frowned as if furiously searching for meaning.

"A horse...with a horn." Ruli pointed to another. "And a...thing...with two saddles." This latter one looked a bit like a horse with two humps on its back, each sporting a saddle.

"A...dragon?" Nona fixed on a scarlet beast and tried to match it to a dim memory of a picture Jula once showed her.

"Keep back!" Ara drew her sword fast enough to make the air hiss, levelling it at the dragon. "I don't trust it."

Nona kept her sword in its scabbard. The dragon was no larger than a small mule and somehow, like the music, it had a jaunty air. Its large yellow eye seemed to regard her as if it knew a joke that she did not.

"They've all got saddles," Clera repeated herself, stepping past Ara. "It's for riding."

Ara kept her sword pointed at the dragon's heart. "I don't trus—"

Clera spun on a heel and penetrated Ara's non-existent defense to plant a kiss square on her lips. Nona gaped. A moment later Clera was on her backside, shoved violently away by Ara.

Ara wiped at her mouth. "What in the hells—?"

"There! That's how long it took. And how it happened." Clera, still on the ground, cut across Ara. "*You don't trust.* That's what you said. You don't trust." She was angry now, passion shaking her words. "And you should trust. I kissed Nona and she pushed me away. Not quite as hard, admittedly." She got to her feet, rubbing her shoulder, the anger leaving her as quickly as it had flared. "You didn't stop me either. And she *told* you. She didn't have to, but she did. That's trust right there. She trusted you to trust her. So, take that stick out of your backside and make up with her before your fear of losing her really does make you lose her. Because I'd take her away in a heartbeat if she'd let me."

Clera turned and pointed to the platform. "The Ancestor has kept this for us. For a thousand years maybe. Trapped beneath the ice. Ice that only melted because of what Nona did. Who she is. Trust her." She singled out one of the beasts impaled on its silver pole. "Get on this…giant frog…and ride like a woman!"

Following her own advice, Clera sprung forwards, leaping into the dragon's saddle. Ruli, infected by the same madness, chose the horse with the horn.

The music seemed to pause along with Nona's breath. She prayed that here, where the ice of millennia had thawed, the hurt that had frozen what was most precious to her would also melt. For a long, painful moment Ara stood, trapped by forces that Nona didn't fully understand. Then, with a noise that was almost a gasp, she turned to Nona, eyes bright, and reached out her hand. "Ride with me?"

"Always."

They chose the not-horse with two humps and seated themselves either side of the pole. The music swelled and, somehow knowing that it had as many riders as it would get, the platform stole into motion, each animal beginning to rise and fall as the whole structure rotated.

And all around them, in the glowing mist, the patient servants of the Missing worked at their tireless rebuilding, secure in the knowledge that what brings joy is always worth mending.

Morgan of the Fay

By Kate Forsyth

There are those who believe that we of the fay are immortal.

They are wrong. We are born, we grow, we die, just like any other living creature. It is true that time moves to a different rhythm in the realm of Annwn but that does not mean we do not know death, as the bards have sung so falsely for so long.

For only those that know they will die can be wise. I have been called many things but of them all, Morgan the Wise is, I hope, the truest.

I was fifteen when I first understood death and fifteen when I first lay with a man, clenching the seeds of his loving deep within me so that another child could sprout into life. Like the two gatehouses of a bridge spanning a turbulent river, the end of one life and the beginning of another mark my passage from child to woman, from sure innocence to uncertain knowledge. And so it is the story of my fifteenth summer that you must know, if you are to understand how I came to be who I am.

I was born Margante, eldest granddaughter of Afallach, lord of Annwn, called by some the Fortunate Isle, for its richness and beauty; by others the Isle of Apples, for its fruit-laden orchards; and yet again, Caer Siddi or the Fairy Fortress, by those who have cause to fear the fay.

Like my home, my name changes according to the namer. Those who love me most call me Morgan, a nickname given me by my youngest sister Thitis when first she began to babble.

There were nine of us, a blessed number to those of our kind. When I was fifteen, Thitis was little more than two years old and the joy of my heart. I do not know if I loved her more at play, squealing with joy, or at night, when I carried her to bed, her downy head nestled against my shoulder. For my mother had died in the bearing of her, and so I was the only mother Thitis ever knew.

You may wonder why it was not my mother's death that first brought me face to face with mortality. You must realize my mother had borne nine daughters in thirteen years. She was worn and tired, and short of temper. She had believed the tales the bards sang, of the Fortunate Isle where death and sickness were unknown, where crops grew without cultivation, and the Tylwyth Teg danced the nights away. She was human, poor thing, seduced from her own people when only a girl herself. My father, Owain, rode up out of the water, smiling, holding down his hand to her. She took it, laughing as he drew her up before him and galloped back into the misty waters of the lake. Of course, she regretted it afterwards but it was too late then. We of the Tylwyth Teg do not let go easily.

So, although I was sorry when my mother died, my grief was not very deep nor lasting, and certainly did not make me understand the fragility of my own life. I was healthy and strong, and busy with my own concerns. For, despite what the bards sing, the gardens and orchards of Annwn do need care. Not as much as the fields of humans, of course. We of the fay do not mind dandelions and clover mingling with our corn and beans, and dislike seeing things laid out in rows and squares, as you humans labor so hard to achieve. We let the wind and the birds and the bees help us in our labor, and sing as we wander amidst the flowers and the trees, and so you think what is done with love and merriment cannot be true work. But all of us have our work to do, even a princess with the blood of gods and goddesses running in her veins.

Always, too, there were my lessons. I was of the Tylwyth Teg and magic was bred in my bones. I was hungry for such knowledge and so at the age of twelve, not long before my mother died, I was given into the care of the druids, to learn what I could.

It was at the druids' school that I first met Anna, daughter of Uther Pendragon, who had been sent to the Isle of Apples to learn the seven arts. We were distant cousins of sorts, for Anna could trace her lineage back to Llyr of the Sea through her mother Igraine, and Llyr had been married to my grandfather's sister Penarddun.

It may seem strange to you that eleven generations had lived and died between Penarddun and Anna, and only one between my grandfather and me, but that is the nature of time in Annwn.

Anna was a tall, fair girl, the tallest and fairest I had ever seen. Beside her I was little and dark, which at first made me hate her. No one could hate Anna for long, though. She was like a soft white cat with round blue eyes and a satisfied purr. It did not take her long to win me over completely. She admired my gray eyes and nicknamed me Argante, and I called her Ermine for her thick pelt of pale hair.

We were as close as any sisters those three years we studied together. I must admit my lessons suffered, for we were always laughing and whispering together at the edge of the grove instead of listening to our teachers. Anna and I told each other everything in those first ardent years of our friendship and so, you see, it was my fault that her brother came raiding upon our shores.

They say I hate Arthur, son of Uther Pendragon, and indeed I have reason to. Yet did I not give him Caledfwlch, forged here upon our shores and imbued with the powers of Annwn? And when the magic of the sword was not, in the end, enough to save him, did he not know to call for me and did I not go? Would I have done so if I hated him as I should?

The stories they tell of Arthur, which you listen to with such eagerness, they are like an apple which has been baked with honey and studded with cloves and hung from a silk ribbon. It no longer looks like an apple or smells like an apple, but cut it open and inside you will find pips. Plant these seeds and an apple tree will grow.

So here is the truth of it, the apple beneath the spices and honey. I hate Arthur for his murdering and plundering, and for the blood he spilled that day, and yet it was because of that blood that I first felt sorrow and terror and joy too, in the flame that can leap between man and woman, and in the painful tenderness that comes with the bringing forth of new life. With this knowledge, I learned to see beyond the flimsy membrane that separates life and death. If it was not for Arthur I may never have become, in the end, Morgan the Wise.

It was a bright autumn day when Arthur's ship *Prydwen* sailed through the mists towards our shores. Belle Garde shone upon its hill like a blue flame, its many-faceted towers glittering where the sun struck. I was playing in the garden with the youngest of my sisters, Vevan and Thitis, while Anna reclined on the grass, being far too lazy to want to toss a ball around.

Suddenly she lifted herself up, pointing. "Look, a ship!"

We all stood staring at the boat with its high sternpost and large steering oars, its great square sail painted with some device in red. We were rather surprised, though it was not unknown for strangers to find their way through the haze of mirage that conceals our realm. In those days, the doors between the worlds stood ajar and there was much traffic between those of human blood and those of the fay. The doors are all locked now, of course, and only those that have the key may open them. We of the Tylwyth Teg are not so trusting as we once were.

As I stood gazing at the ship, I felt an odd frisson down the back of my neck, as if someone had crept up behind me and blown on my skin. I shuddered and rubbed my arms, although I was not cold.

"Let's go down to the dock and see who it is," Vevan cried. "We aren't expecting visitors, are we, Morgan?"

I shook my head. "Not that I know of. Surely Taidi would've let me know if he was expecting anybody?" I dusted leaves and grass from my skirt and held down my hand to Anna. "Coming?"

"Of course," she answered. "Miss the one exciting thing to happen here since I got back? Let's hope it's a boatload of handsome young warriors who have lost their way. Maybe we can entice them to stay awhile?"

I smiled, though I still felt that puzzling tightening of my nerves. I was not concerned by the impact of unexpected guests on our larder, for we always had the cauldron of plenty to tide us over any need for food, nor was I worried about where to house the travelers, for my grandfather's castle was vast. I felt no fear, for what could one small ship do against the warriors of the Tylwyth Teg? It was a chill akin to fear that troubled me, however, and being still a child myself, I shrugged it away and went running down through the garden as eagerly as the others.

We were not the only ones to make our way towards the jetty, for we of the fay are always curious and eager for any diversion. Children came running and shouting down the road, men laid down their harps or set aside their tools, and women came wandering out of the forests, many of them with flowers entwined in their hair and their mouths stained red with berries. By the time the ship was dropping her sails and sliding in beside the jetty, there was a jostling crowd waiting for her, all talking and laughing.

"Look at the red dragon on her sail," Anna cried excitedly. "That is Arthur's device! What can he be doing here?" The animation in her face faded, and she frowned. "It is only a month or so since I saw him. I hope nothing is wrong…"

Then she began to wave and call, for a tall, young warrior was leaning over the bulwark. He leapt down and embraced Anna affectionately. I looked him over curiously, for I had heard a great deal about the young king. He was as big and handsome as Anna had said, his hair and beard near as fair as hers and his eyes as blue. He was not yet twenty, but he was battle-hardened and battle-scarred. He had seen heavy fighting since he won the throne, I had heard, and certainly the guilelessness of his youth had been worn away, I could see that at once.

He met my gaze with his own, bold and raking. "So this is your beloved Argante. She is almost as beautiful as you describe, Anna, at least for a fairy. I wonder if she is as clever?"

I felt anger roaring in my ears. I cast him one disdainful glance and said, very distinctly, "It would not be difficult to be more clever than a bone-headed warrior whose ears are still ringing from the last battle he fought."

King Arthur laughed. He cast me a look of admiration. If I had not sensed the mockery behind it, I might have half swooned from the warmth of it but I drew myself away, feeling again a shudder of dread. It may merely have been fear at the power such a man might have over me. I do not think so now, however. I am old enough now to recognize the chill breath of foreboding.

A small band of men alighted from the ship, among them a beautiful, slightly built man that I recognized. This was the bard Taliesen, who had once been a peasant boy in the employ of the great seer Ceridwen. One day, while she stirred her cauldron, three drops of a magical potion spat out and burned his hand. Sucking the burn, he had tasted the elixir of knowledge meant for her son and at once knew all the secrets of the universe.

Knowing Ceridwen would never forgive him, he fled. He turned into a hare; she turned into a hound. He turned into a fish; she became an otter. When he grew wings and took to the sky, she transformed into a hawk. At last, in desperation, he hid himself in the shape of a grain of wheat. Ceridwen changed into a hen and ate him.

That should have been the end of him but once Ceridwen resumed her usual shape, she found she was pregnant. In time she bore a baby boy who was so beautiful she could not bear to kill him. She trussed him up in a leather bag and threw him into the sea. Two days later he was rescued by a prince who raised the boy as his own, calling him Taliesin, which means "Shining Brow". He grew to be a great bard and seer, though one with little love for the fay.

At the sight of Taliesen, I fell behind, troubled and unsure. All seemed well. King Arthur and his men were looking about them with pleasure. My indolent Anna was the most animated I had ever seen. Everyone was smiling and laughing. Everyone that is, except Taliesen the bard, and I.

The doors of the castle stood open, welcoming light spilling out into the gloaming. My grandfather sat in his throne at the head of the great hall, his nine white hounds lying at his feet. They raised their heads and snarled as King Arthur came in. I was glad to see how the king's step faltered, though it was only for a moment. He ignored the growling dogs, with their ears and eyes as red as blood, and bowed low over my grandfather's hand.

I left the men to their polite fencing, and withdrew to my rooms to change for what promised to be a long and tedious night, listening to Anna's brother boast of his doings and watching her hang on his arm and believe every word.

When I came down, the great hall was set up with tables and trestles, the minstrels were playing, and King Arthur sat on my grandfather's left hand, my father Owain on his right. On a side table sat the cauldron of plenty, its golden sides gleaming in the candlelight. It was one of the treasures of Annwn, made by Bran the Blessed himself. With pearls all round its rim, it could only be kindled by the breath of nine maidens. It would produce the most delicious food until all that sat at the table were replete, filled with new strength and vigor.

I saw how the eyes of all King Arthur's men dwelled on the cauldron, but even then, I had no true understanding of what they planned to do. I blamed my unease on childish jealousy, and tried my best to suppress it.

My grandfather stood with some effort, for he was many centuries old now. He nodded at King Arthur and his men and raised his goblet.

"Welcome to my realm, my boy," he said. "We are glad to meet you at last, for we have heard how you seek to bring peace to the land after a hundred years of bloodshed. We wish you well and are glad of the chance to forge strong bonds with you, who carry the blood of Llyr in your veins, even as we do. It is good that you should know us, for other races and other gods have come and we have been afraid that the old ways would be cast aside. May the Children of Llyr and the Children of Don flourish and stand strong, and may there be peace and plenty in the land!"

Goblets were drained with enthusiasm all round the room, though I noticed the strangers did not drink, just held their cups to their lips and pretended to taste the wine within. I smiled to myself. They believed the old superstitions that to eat or drink when in the land of the fay was to be trapped in that realm forever. What were they to do once the cauldron started pouring forth its bounty?

Except that it did not. When I and my eight sisters held hands and blew gently upon the cauldron, the water within barely trembled. A mutter of shock and consternation rose all round the room.

King Arthur turned on his sister. "Are all your tales of the cauldron of Annwn nothing but lies?" he hissed. "We have come all this way for a fairy tale?"

"There is a coward amongst us!" my father cried at the same moment. "The cauldron will not feed the craven."

"Or the treacherous," my grandfather said softly. He had heard King Arthur's furious words, even if my father had not. "You think I did not notice that you refused to drink my toast? Even such fools as men hesitate to break the law of hospitality. You plan to steal my cauldron? And plunder the riches of my land? Is that the truth of it?"

"No, no!" Anna cried. "Arthur, you wouldn't..." She cast a glance at me and I saw at once that she had been the one to tell him of our treasure, the cauldron that could feed and succor an army. I glared at her in sudden, bitter hatred.

My father had leapt to his feet, catching up his eating knife in one hand. "Treachery! You come with foul intent! The cauldron will not serve those with such base ambitions," he cried. He was always impulsive, my father, quick to word and blow.

He lunged at King Arthur with his dagger, who dodged nimbly, seizing his own knife. There was a quick weave and duck and flurry of blows, and suddenly my father cried out and slumped to the floor. His blood sprayed across my face.

Trestles crashed against the flagstones as men leapt to their feet. All was confusion. My sisters screamed. I fell to my knees, cradling my father's head. His hair was sticky with blood.

My grandfather bellowed and raised his walking stick, lashing King Arthur across the back. He stumbled with a cry, and one of his men struck my grandfather deep in the breast. He fell stiffly, his eyes wide open in shock. His head hit the stone with a clunk.

I sat silent, my ears filled with a rushing sound.

All round me men fought, with knife and chair leg and poker and platter.

Then Taliesen pulled a horn from his belt and blew it. The sound rang out above the clamor and at once I knew for whom he called. That little ship, bobbing at our jetty. Many warriors must be hidden there.

I tried to get to my feet, calling to my grandfather's men. My men now. No one heeded me. I struggled to find a way through the heaving, struggling mass, but received such a blow to my head, I fell to my knees. That was when Thitis, my dear sweet baby, shrieked and rushed for me.

I swear he did not mean to do it. Even in the horror of that moment, as I saw his blade swing back, its sharp tip slashing across her throat, I swear his shock and grief were as great as mine. For a moment, our glances struck across her tiny, trampled body.

Perhaps that is why I cannot hate him, for I saw his face at that moment and knew that he felt the stretching of time and space to very breaking point, just as I did.

I reached for her, gathered her into her arms, felt her head loll back, lifeless. The pain that struck into my chest was so acute it was as if a spear had caught me there. I was struck mute and paralyzed. All around me men and fay died, but I could not hear, or see, or move. When my grief came it was as rage, a rage so dreadful flame burst from my hands and cleared a path before me.

So I came into my powers, with the blood of Thitis blurring my vision and the shrieks of the dying in my ears.

We prevailed in the end. Of the hundred and fifty men that had crouched in *Prydwen*'s bilge beside their boy king, only seven men survived, Taliesen the bard amongst them. We lost three hundred and seventy-three, and our king, and the king's heir, and my innocence. It was a high cost to pay.

I could have had him executed. I could have fed his entrails to my hounds. Instead, I put my mouth to his wound and sucked out his blood. As he recoiled from me, I went out into the cold starry night and lay down in the embrace of the oak tree's roots. I slept, I think, a little. My mind wandered in and out of dreams. I flew with a black-winged bird over the shadowed landscape of the future, I listened to the raven's cry.

When I woke in the morning, I knew many things I had not known before. I rose and washed myself clean, and spat the brown dust of his blood from my mouth. I dressed myself as a queen of the fay, and I took from the armory a sword that had been forged by Gofannon himself, son of Don and master smith. It too was one of the treasures of Annwn.

I took it to Arthur. He was pale, bruised and shaken in his dark cell. He stood up when I came in and faced me with as much of his usual arrogance as he could muster, though he could not help the black dilation of his eyes at the sight of the heavy sword in my hands.

For a moment we faced each other. I stood no higher than his shoulder but I was at least as proud and in no way as frightened. Then slowly I offered him the hilt of the sword.

He took it wonderingly, unable to speak.

"I have seen what is to be," I said. "You will need the sword. It is named Caledfwlch. Its blade shall never fail you and its sheath protects you from harm. Go from here and do not return. I shall not be so merciful again."

"But why?" he stammered.

I took a while to answer. I would not let him see the heaviness of my grief, which lodged in my throat like a stone. "The tide is on the turn," I managed at last. "The evil of the future that contains you alive is far less than the evil of a future with you dead. Though I wish I could tear out your heart for the gods you have abandoned, I know you..." I had to struggle for breath. "...I know you are the only one. Take your sword, take your ship, and leave my realm. Know that it is death for you to sail here again."

But even as I said these words, I felt the chill of foreboding down my spine and knew that I lied. I did not tell him so, however, and so he took the sword and for another twenty years or more, he fought and triumphed with it.

But that is a tale for another telling. I have spoken here of death and the tasting of blood, but now it is time to show the bright face of the moon, the story of loving and the making of life. For I saw many things that night I lay in the grove with Arthur's blood in my mouth. I saw it was time to close the doors between the worlds, else all the things of magic would be lost and broken in the times of change and upheaval that beset us. I saw it was time for me to lay aside my childhood and become a woman and a queen.

So, when the ashes of the dead had at last blown away on the wind,

I set out with my nine hounds and I went to a place that I knew, where a road of the humans fords the River Alun in the shadow of the Mountain of the Mothers. Such places are often doorways into our world, and so I crossed the threshold and came out into the world of men. I undid my hair, removed all my clothes and sat on a stone, washing myself in the river while my hounds howled about me.

Soon a man came riding along, as I had known he would. This man was Urien Rheged, and though he was not as young and strong as Arthur, he was lusty enough.

When he saw me, dressed only in my long black hair, he sent away all his men and came to me with long, heavy strides and seized me in his hot hands.

"What are you, witch-woman?" he said against my neck.

I said, "I am Margante, daughter to the King of Annwn, who is now dead. God's blessing on the feet which brought you here."

"Why?" he asked, and kissed me.

I had not expected his kiss to fire me, and so when I finally answered it was rather unsteadily. "I am fated to wash here until I should conceive a son by a Christian man."

He laughed and said, "It is far too cold to sit here bathing day after day. Let me see what I can do to help you."

And so there in the bracken, my son Owain and my daughter Morwyn were conceived, if not in love, at least in eagerness and pleasure.

A year later Urien came back to the Ford of Barking and took away my twin babes, that they may be raised in the way of men. This too was a bitter grief to me, and another resentment to store up against Arthur. For I loved my children and would have given much to keep them safe with me behind the locked doors of Annwn.

I knew, though, that the world of humans needed them. Owain

and Morwyn carried with them all the gifts of healing, song and merriment that I could give them, as well as the more troubling gift of foresight. In time Owain would fall in love, betray that love, run mad in the forest and befriend a lion, but all of that is yet another tale. It is enough that you know he learned in the end that love is more important than valor, peace more important than war. For we of the Tylwyth Teg see time differently from you short-lived humans. In the small, black pip of an apple, we see the tree that will eventually flower and bear fruit.

Geisha Boy

By Kylie Chan

Dot stepped outside into the midday gloom. She scanned the area automatically. No visible threats. She latched the door, though there was little of value—that anyone would find, anyway—in the ex-sewage pipe she called home. But if she left it unlocked, someone in the undercity would take the steel bucket she used to collect acid rainwater.

Her body felt heavy, depleted. From lack of energy or too little…everything, she didn't know. One of those she could fix. If the sun was out.

The other…well. She'd stopped hoping a long time ago. They deserved to live. She deserved to live. Just not together.

She tightened her faded blue cotton robe and pants, hiding the carapace and extra appendages that made her neighbors uncomfortable. Turning, she nearly walked into one of them: Mrs.

Kensington. The thin, tired woman held a filthy, squalling baby and Dot resisted the urge to take the child from her and cradle it.

"Please?" Mrs. Kensington said.

"I have nothing for you," Dot said. "It hasn't rained in days. I don't have enough to process yet."

Kensington glanced up as if hoping to see through the buildings piled on buildings, to see the clouds and open air that only the Cadre and other overcity residents owned. Then she dropped her gaze and turned away. The baby stared over her mother's shoulder from sunken, shadowed eyes.

Dot watched them go.

Nearby, a kid crouched, hiding something. Dot smiled faintly. There was a gap in the plate directly above her pipe where a telecoms tower stabbed through. A small spot of sunlight fell on the acid-etched concrete and kids squabbled over the patch of brightness. The boy thrust a handheld charger into that tiny square of light, shifting carefully as the sun above moved, occasionally checking around to make sure nobody would push him off.

With no time to waste, Dot released a couple of appendages, hoisted herself on top of her three-meter-tall pipe and clambered up the tower. She moved quickly; there was no telling how long the sun would stay out and she was starving. She reached the fifteen-centimeter-wide gap and shifted her carapace to make her body the same width as her head. She squeezed through the hole and squinted against the sunshine.

She hesitated for a moment, allowing all her eyes to adjust, then swarmed up the pole to reach a height where she was invisible to the overcity dwellers. The pole's top was a prickly cluster of antennae and boosters. There, she put herself into position, and pulled her robe off. She spread her arms wide, released all her appendages and threw her head back, feeling the warmth of the real sun on her shell. The ultraviolet-activated fins sprang out from her back and her whole body turned black as the transdermal solar cells went to work.

Nobody in the clean, bright overcity below was aware of her presence. They floated through their world of glass and steel, well fed and healthy, entertained and educated. Oblivious—or uncaring—of the undercity's desperation.

She looked down. Pain filled her.

The cherry trees were flowering; pink petals floated on the breeze and carpeted the lush grass of an overcity park. A couple of children—she homed in to see more clearly, and they were a boy and girl—threw petals at each other, laughing.

Just like her girls had. Her girls...

Everything shifted and suddenly she wasn't a copied mind—a series of numbers in a genetically engineered weapon-body—anymore.

She was Lena: warm and human and in a different time and place altogether.

Now...then...she sat on a red blanket on a grassy hillside, and the warm breeze whipped cherry blossoms into little tornadoes. Her two little girls were laughing and tossing petals into the air. Paul lounged next to her, smiling his big, open smile.

Marika ran to him and flopped to the grass, panting. She gasped a few times, and Paul touched her shoulder gently, as if to say: whatever you want to say, we can wait for it. When she had caught her breath, she scrambled to her feet, grabbed a double handful of the petals, and threw them over her parents. She jumped and clapped, squealing, then ran back to Cesta. The pair grabbed hands and spun each other, around and around, until they both fell to the grass.

Lena sensed Paul watching her and turned to see him smiling.

"I want this time to go on forever," he said. "I don't want you to go into the Facility."

She pulled at the grass. "This is the last one. Then it's over. The constructs will have everything."

"Not everything, I hope." He stroked the side of her face. "Not…you."

"Only my battle knowledge. There's a war coming. If sharing my knowledge with the constructs will help protect our people, then it's worth a little discomfort." She gazed out over the hillside. "You knew what you were getting into when you married a soldier."

He gestured towards the girls, who'd picked themselves up and were slowly returning to the picnic blanket. "Did you know what you'd be getting into when we started this, though?"

Marika fell into Lena's arms, smelling of sweet girl and sunshine.

Lena held her close and smiled back at Paul. "The greatest gift I could give anyone. And after this last session, we'll be sure it's protected."

"It's a huge burden for one woman to carry."

"It's not one woman, it's an army, and they're not me, not even copies of me, just shadows."

Cesta sat next to Paul and he put his arm around her. "I'm glad we have the real thing then."

Lena buried her face into Marika's hair. "Forever."

A cloud passed before the sun and Dot slipped free of the flashback with a shiver that rattled her carapace. She cursed the fact that she'd left the pills at the pipe, and instead recited the sutra to try and make the memories go away. They were becoming more intense, and more frequent. She shouldn't even have them. They belonged to Lena, but haunted her anyway.

She examined the overcity again. Maybe the girls were down

there. Marika would be finished university now, and Cesta wouldn't be far behind. She wondered what paths the girls had chosen; neither of them had demonstrated their mother's aptitude for battle. Marika had loudly expressed a desire to be a doctor when she'd been little, and Cesta had spent all her time drawing.

Was Marika healing the sick, and Cesta producing works of beauty to adorn the glossy walls of the overcity? Or maybe they had grown differently. Either way, they could be down there, strolling beneath the trees, enjoying the fresh air and sunshine, living their peaceful lives with their mother and father—their real mother, not Dot.

Would it be possible to find out? The idea of knowing where they were sent a small thrill through her.

She shook her head. No. She was a fool. She couldn't give in to that hope again. It led to madness.

After all, she was one of the few constructs lucky enough to still be alive. That ought to be enough.

An ultrasonic shot whizzed past her head and she ducked instinctively. What the fuck? She clamped down on the urge to shift gears into combat mode, yanked the fins down and her robe back on.

Another blast hit the steel of the pole, chipping off bits of metal, and she didn't hesitate. She slid back down the pole as fast as she could, using appendages to slow her fall. The friction took the skin off her hands and shredded the fabric of her pants until the insides of her thighs were raw as well.

Another shot hit the pole just above her, and she ducked. This was too unevenly spaced to be an automatic defense program for the tower. But they were obviously not trying to kill her. She stopped for a moment, half-sheltered by an overhanging building, and searched for a sniper or drone. The urge to shred her attacker with her claws was almost overpowering.

The next ultrasonic hit her square on the left shoulder. Her left hand numbed and lost grip. She began to slide again. Faster. Unable to hold on with her appendages without doing serious damage to the metal. She hit the plate below hard, wriggled through the hole in the plate, and paused to catch her breath.

Okay, maybe they were trying to kill her. She thanked the Buddha that the junction of the plate and the pole had an electrified fence around it, otherwise she could have hit an overcity resident when she fell. Damaging the overcity or hurting its residents would see her terminated or back in the Facility.

She slid down the side of her pipe, took a few long, slow breaths, and went inside to change clothes. By the time she'd finished dressing, the skin of her hands and thighs was already regrowing and the desire to kill had faded.

This wasn't the first time in the last few months that they'd tried to discourage her recharging trips to the overcity. But it was the first time they'd aimed to hit. What had changed? She'd just need to be more careful and not annoy any of the Cadre who ran the overcity. If she stayed out of their way, they would keep leaving her alone.

She sank onto the gray-brown pallet bed, stared for a long time at a discolored square patch of concrete on the floor, then studied her quarters. The walls were gray concrete. Acid rain trickled down via a funnel from the outside, leaving eroded channels. The steel bucket she used to collect the stuff was half-full. Still not enough to process for Mrs. Kensington and her children. The only other possession in her tiny habitation was a reading chair upholstered in torn brown leather.

Yes, this was her life. As safe as she could be. As safe as she could make it for the undercity dwellers—and for Lena's daughters.

Three thumps rattled the door and she saw a slim infrared

silhouette through the flimsy wood.

"Dotti, it's me, Naoki," he said through the door.

"Fuck off," she yelled as she pulled closer the loose robe that covered her body.

"Come on, Dotti, let me in," he said.

Her vision blurred for a second and she checked her pill stash, wondering if she should take one. No. Naoki wouldn't ask any stupid questions or trigger her combat mode.

"Okay," she said.

The door opened and Naoki flounced in, leaving it ajar behind him. He wore a kimono that floated like flower petals, transparent in some places and a liquid sheen of color that flowed and moved in others. He fell into the reading chair and placed a red handbag that probably cost more than the entire block Dot lived in on the end of the bed.

He smelled sweetly of the cherry blossom dessert, *sakuramochi*. "You here to fuck?" she asked.

"Not on that bed I'm not." Naoki pouted, his white makeup and red lips perfect and out of place in the undercity. He eyed her appraisingly. "I'll fuck if you'll let me do a makeover on you."

"Go to hell."

He shrugged and managed to look coy and wanton at the same time, eyes half-lidded, one shoulder peeking out from the kimono. "I'll let you teach me some more."

"You *asked* me to teach you. I did it against my better judgement, and my bet is that when you tried all the rough stuff on your bitches, they got turned off straight away and you lost at least two clients."

"Only one."

"See? They love you for your feminine good looks, honey." Dot leaned back against the cold concrete. "Use it. Don't try to be something you're not."

"Wow, very Zen."

"Cut the bullshit. Why are you here? You in trouble with a man again?"

He sighed theatrically. "Why won't they leave me alone? Do I need a sign on my ass saying 'closed for business, vaginas only'?"

Dotti barked a laugh. "Probably."

"No, I'm not in trouble with a man. It's worse than that."

"Oh, shit, don't tell me you fell in love with a cute little girl from the Mansions."

"Worse." Naoki dropped the pretense of being a pretty, brainless geisha and frowned. "I have a sponsor. I went exclusive."

"Who?" she asked sharply.

"Zheng Yongxin."

She sat up straight. "Holy fucking mother of God, Naoki, what the *fuck*? Didn't I tell you? Two fucking years ago, I told you—"

"I know!" he yelled. "Don't get mixed up with Cadres, and whatever you do, don't go exclusive with one. But Dotti, it was so great. She bought me all these clothes and shoes, and we went shopping together, she rented me an apartment in the overcity, she let me do a makeover on her, it was so great…"

"And then she asked you to go exclusive and you said yes, seeing the yuan signs flying around her head. You stupid bitch."

He winced. "She knows my history, that I ran away from that arranged marriage with the old guy. When she proposed going exclusive, it was more than just for my looks. She knows I'm educated and from a good family. She likes my intelligence and guts. She loves the way I sing. She may even be able to get me a recording contract."

Dot shook her head and flung her arms out. "Well, enjoy your golden cage, little boy. You could have had your own geisha house in a couple of years and you threw it all away."

"It's worse than that." He checked over his shoulder, rose, ran to the door, and closed it. "I think she backed me up," he whispered.

She laughed again. "Yeah, sure. Why the hell would she do that when there's a million more like you at the houses all dying to get into her pants?"

Naoki sagged into the chair. "I think I made her angry. She wanted me to have her baby. She's too old to have kids, so she asked me to do it for her."

Dot stared. "You're pregnant?"

"No way. I am not sacrificing my figure to get the implants so some old bitch can have her dream child."

"So, what, then?" Dot scowled. "You think she backed you up in a fit of anger? How do you know? And why would she?"

"She wants a version of me that'll have her baby." Naoki leaned forward, eyes narrowed. "She'll make a clone with my memories and education, but one that'll follow orders, one that'll have her baby for her. I'm *sure* she's backed me up."

"Not even a Cadre would do anything that illegal, Naoki. This is way beyond paranoid. Besides, the cloning tech was destroyed after the war." She clenched her teeth to hold in the *after me...after all of us.*

"You're one yourself. You know..."

She jumped to her feet. "One of *what*? One of *them*?" She pointed at the door, every muscle tensed against the urge to go into combat mode. "Get the fuck out..."

He raised his hands, palms out. "No, no, Dotti, I don't mean it like that. Hell, girl, you're one of my best friends. I owe you so much. I'd still be here in the undercity, hiding from the family if it weren't for you." He pouted but stopped just short of batting his eyelids. "Just tell me—what was it like being backed up?"

She quivered, her hands balled. "How the hell am I supposed to know?"

"Oh, come on, I heard the rumors. Dots remember, they say." Naoki tilted his head to one side, gazing at her from under his long fake lashes.

Dot sank back onto the bed. "Dots remember…"

"If you remember what it was like, then you can help me." He touched her hand, tentatively. "Please? About three months ago, I passed out in a club, high on Z, and lost a whole week. I need to know why."

"You were passed out on Z, that's why," Dot snapped.

"Or Zheng was backing me up, and she's growing a clone, and when it's ready she'll…" His eyes were wide and he grabbed her arm. "She'll kill me and put the clone in my place, and nobody will know!"

Dot tensed again, looking pointedly at his hand on her arm.

Naoki swallowed and let go. "Isn't there anything you can remember about the process? Did it make you unconscious for a whole week?" His tone was plaintive.

"That wasn't me."

"Your template then. Whatever." He was desperate. "What was it like?"

"I have no memories from my template," she lied. "All we got was the template's military training. Grunts like me didn't get personal memories."

His face sagged, brittle cracks appearing in the white makeup.

She softened. "I'll ask around. I still have old friends in the project, real people who were involved in making us. Give me a couple of days and I'll find out how it worked."

He reached into his expensive handbag and thrust a stack of

greenish paper at her. "Cash. For you. Thank you."

"So that's what it looks like. I've never seen it before." She eyed the money. "You should know better, though. I don't have any use for this."

He pushed it forward. "I have plenty, she looks after me. Take it."

"No." She didn't reach for it. "But you can do something for me in return."

His brows lifted.

She turned and released one of her hidden appendages. She sliced a small piece of blanket from the edge, then hot stamped a couple of identification marks onto it. The claw folded back into her abdominal carapace under the robe, and she passed the blanket piece to him.

"I want you to find out what these two women are doing."

He studied the piece of blanket, running his finger along the clean edge where she'd laser cut it. "You are seriously scary sometimes. I'll see what I can turn up, I have access to Comrade Zheng's data." He glanced up. "Why do you want to know? These are overcity residents. You're not going to hurt them or anything like that, are you?"

She shook her head, carefully emotionless. "No, nothing like that. I want to make sure they're okay. They were civilians caught up in a military action I was part of. It was pretty heavy. I want to make sure they came out the other side and went on to live good lives. They were just little kids."

"I see." He stashed the piece of blanket into his bag, then shoved the money at her again. "You might as well take this. I don't need it. Use it for maintenance or something. You can take it to the bank; they still accept it. Load it into your credit account. It's as good as money. They still have to take it for another year or two, and it's completely untraceable."

"Untraceable?" She took it, running her fingertips over the tough, plastic-feeling paper. "No wonder they're getting rid of it. They do hate things that are hard to find or control."

He sent her a wry look in return.

#

After Naoki left, Dot headed east through twisting alleys lit by dim, flickering shop signs. She worked her way through the narrow, muddy lanes toward Fil's, staying out of the circles of light and avoiding the puddles of acid.

A group of young-and-stupids tried to order her as she passed them.

"Kill yourself," one of them said.

Another said it at a higher pitch, trying to hit the exact frequency that she would be forced to obey. "Kill yourself."

She stopped and rounded on them, and they all took a step back. "Did you just order me to kill you? I must obey."

"Kill yourself!" one of them shouted, and the others grinned with a combination of fear and bravado.

She dropped her voice and moved closer. "Kill you? You want me to kill you? How about a laser cutter through your eyes? Or I just pick you up and break you in half?"

"You're not allowed to hurt us," one said, and the others nodded agreement.

She moved slightly closer and released an appendage, waving its bladed tip in front of their faces. "You sure?"

They weren't. They ran.

She sighed. She was an idiot. If they told the authorities what she'd said, she could lose free-rein privileges and find herself back in a Facility. All she needed now was to lose her sanity and her freedom at the same time. She took deep breaths to calm herself and walked on.

Fil scratched his bloated belly. "You still alive and out of the cage?"

Dot glanced around the dusty shop and the piles of dismembered bio equipment. "Still going. Hit some sweet sunlight today. I won't need to eat for at least a week."

"Nice." He measured some nutrients into a jar. "So, what brings one of the last dots to my corner of the undercity?"

"Naoki—" Dot began.

Sneering, Fil threw the measuring scoop onto the bench so hard that it bounced off onto the floor.

She continued, "—thinks he was backed up. Tell me it's not possible, that it's all shut down. Then he'll be happy and I can go home." It began to rain, making a clatter on the plastic roof of his workshop. "I need to get home."

He glanced up and nodded, then down at her, his expression grim. "You can tell him that it's not possible for anyone to be backed up anymore, but you'd be lying."

"What?" Her guts froze.

"One of the Cadres up there…" he pointed "…came through with her uniforms and took everything that could be used to backup and copy people. Took enough to start the whole cloning process over again."

"When?"

"A bit over three months ago."

"Why didn't you tell me?"

He shrugged.

"I have to stop her," Dot said, pacing the cluttered room.

"You can't break your conditioning." Fil folded his arms, watching her carefully. "You can only use violence in self-defense or against a designated enemy."

"If I try hard enough I can, and you know it."

He spat on the floor. "I don't want to see anyone else go through what you've been through, honey, but don't throw yourself away trying to stop a Cadre. Stay out of it."

"What if Naoki really was backed up?"

"The stupid little straightass got what he deserved. Only taking female clients—serves him right. I hope she kills him and has a lovely little clone that'll do anything she wants."

"You are scum, Fil," Dot said.

He spread his arms, revealing armpit stains on his undershirt. "Just like everything around me."

The rain grew harder. "My bucket'll be full," she said. "I have to get home."

He pointed at her and she recoiled from the insulting gesture. "And stop doing that, too. They don't deserve it. Your special metabolism wasn't designed to act as a water-purification plant."

"They deserve to live. Everybody deserves to live," she said, and went out.

#

The rain burnt her back and made the top of her head itch as she tried to stay away from the falls of water sliding between the gaps of the plate. The dome protected the overcity from the acid rain, but capillary action made the water fall from under the plate and drench the undercity.

When she arrived back at her pipe, a small group of tired undercity dwellers were waiting for her. They stood back and let her through, and when she was at the door to her pipe, she spoke.

"Come back in a couple of hours. I have to process it."

They nodded and wandered off, some settling only a few meters away to wait.

Inside, she filled a large plastic bottle from the acid in the bucket, closed her eyes, and drank it all. Refilled the bottle and drank again, then again.

After the fourth bottle the water came out through the hole it had burnt in her throat and she stopped. She couldn't stop a small moan of pain. Exactly twelve minutes later her throat had grown back enough to take another bottle.

After thirty minutes she stumbled to lie on the pallet, careful not to lean on her destroyed face and throat. She closed her eyes and let her body regrow and filter the water.

#

Two hours later she emerged to find an even larger group of undercity dwellers waiting for her. She held a barrel containing purified water. They lined up meekly, each of them holding a container, and she doled the water out to them.

The barrel was half gone when a group of uniforms arrived, making the people scatter. The leader of the uniforms stopped and held out an ID reader towards her. He wore a voice modulator that would make his voice the pitch that she was forced to obey. It would also automatically switch on her bodycam, but only Fil knew she'd made that modification.

"Seven-Dot-Three-Dot-Four-Dot-Six, identify," he said.

"I am Seven-Dot-Three-Dot-Four-Dot-Six," she replied.

He put the ID reader away. "You're coming with us."

Mrs. Kensington ducked past the two junior uniforms and pulled on the senior uniform's arm. "You can't take our Dot! We need her."

He pushed her away. "I'll return her. We just want to take her in to the station for a cup of tea."

People emerged from the shadows, advancing menacingly on the uniforms, who saw the large group around them and began to look nervous.

"I'll be fine. Don't do anything that anybody will regret," Dot said loudly. "Just go back to your houses, I'll be here later to give you more water."

She walked between the uniforms willingly, calmly. What the hell was this about? Her trip to the overcity to recharge? Naoki's visit? Something else? A "cup of tea at the station" meant anything from a mild slap on the wrist through to permanently disappearing.

"They call you Dot?" the senior uniform said as they went up the elevator to the overcity.

"I help them out."

"Listen." He spoke with emphasis. "I worked my way up from the undercity, I know what you do for them down there. Without you dots, we would never have won the war. Damn, we'd all be speaking in English or Spanish or something." He turned back to face the front of the elevator. "We're taking you to see the Cadre, then we'll drop you back where you came from. You deserve the right to live."

She raised her chin. "But not in the sunlight."

He shifted uncomfortably. "You can kill with a glance. Your sanity's unreliable, and you know it. We can't afford the risk."

"But you'll risk the undercity residents? You came from there."

He didn't reply.

#

They ushered her into a plush office with a painted mural of the mountains of Guangdong completely covering one wall. A pair of overstuffed armchairs flanked a small, laminated tea table. Cadre Zheng sat behind a massive desk made of real rosewood, a last remnant of the Tibetan forests.

"Comrade Noble Soldier." Zheng ordered the uniforms to leave then gestured for Dot to sit opposite, across the desk and studied her.

Dot studied her right back. Middle-aged, hair just touched with silver, but still stiff-backed and lean, with night-dark eyes.

"I checked your record," the Cadre said. "You are regarded as one of the sanest dots ever produced and your actions since the war have borne that out. I was involved in the dot-creation program, and it warms my heart to see you integrated into the community."

"But only in the undercity," Dot said.

"You know why that is, Comrade Soldier. Your template lives her life up here, she has children, and now I believe she even has grandchildren. If they were to see you, they would recognize your...face, and it would cause them great emotional distress. You cannot live here. They cannot see you."

"Is her family alive and happy?" Dot swallowed. Grandchildren. Something in her chest relaxed and grew warm.

"They are." Zheng inclined her head. "They do not know that you exist. They do not know that she was a template. They would suffer greatly if they were to find out."

"I know that." The information that the girls were alive and happy was almost enough. Almost.

"I hear Naoki went to see you," the Cadre said, one thin brow lifting. "Why?"

Ahhh. So this was about him. Well, maybe she could force the information from Zheng. "Naoki thinks he was backed up. He says you want him to have your baby and you've made a clone that'll do it for you." She stood and towered over the Cadre. "Tell me it isn't true and I'll go back to the undercity and not bother you."

Zheng visibly sighed and walked around the desk. She barely came above Dot's waist. "There's more to it than me wanting him to a have a baby. That's the least of it." She gestured for Dot to sit again and leaned against the desk. "I really love him, you know?" Her face was full of honesty. "He lights up my life. He's my companion, my sounding board, my support, my everything. I can't live without him."

"So you *did* back him up."

"I really care for Naoki. Please respect that."

"If you cared for him you wouldn't back him up."

Zheng looked away. "I'm a selfish, evil old woman." She ran a hand over her face. "I did back him up, just in case, about three months ago. I think he knew, because he went out and overdosed on Z shortly after."

Dot stared, uncomprehending.

"He died of the overdose, Soldier. The Naoki you know now is a clone." She looked down. "I love him. I can't live without him."

Dot went completely calm. "And he doesn't know."

Zheng shook her head.

"And this is good enough for you? A poor copy?"

"Are you a poor copy?" Zheng asked.

"Yes," Dot said.

"He isn't."

"He thinks he is. I agree. What you've done is illegal and against his wishes." Her fingers curled into fists. "You're trusting my conditioning here. What's to say I haven't broken it already?"

"If you want to take your revenge on me, I would understand," Zheng said. "But Naoki doesn't *know*. Let the clone live out his life with me, and make us both happy." She leaned forward, sincere. "If you keep this quiet, I can give you anything. A place in the sunlight. A better life. Anything."

Dot hesitated. It was a very appealing offer, but she didn't belong in the overcity, especially now she knew the girls were alive. As long as she stayed in her place, the overcity dwellers left her alone.

"What I need," Dot said, "is to be returned to my concrete pipe and my people, and for you to stop trying to kill me."

Zheng eyed her. "Is that all?"

Dot nodded.

"Done." Zheng pressed a button on her desk, and the uniforms returned. "Take her back to her home. On the way, stop and pick up a UV lamp and a water filter for her. The assassination attempts are to cease. That's all."

"Madam Comrade," the senior uniform said.

#

Naoki entered her pipe through the open door. "I got your message. You okay, Dotti?"

Dot sat on the pallet and leaned on the wall, fingers interlaced behind her head. "I'm fine."

"It's not like you to leave your door open."

"I think better with it open."

He sat in the reading chair. This kimono was pink with tiny flowers embroidered in gold and silver thread; it appeared to be a genuine antique made of real silk. His heels were matching fabric. "I found what you wanted. Did you find out about me?"

"I found out about you."

"Did she back me up?" His smooth-skinned hands twisted together in his lap. "She's been looking strangely at me lately."

"I checked with all the biosalvage people in the undercity. They know the people in the overcity as well." She saw the hopeful look on his face. "All of that stuff was taken and destroyed a long time ago, Naoki."

He collapsed slightly, and appeared smaller and more vulnerable. "She didn't back me up? She won't clone me?"

Dot hesitated for a long moment.

"Tell me she didn't back me up!"

"She can't have backed you up. No more clones of anybody can be grown. It's not possible. You don't have to worry."

Naoki jumped to his feet and embraced her. "Thank you!" He stepped back, smiling. "You know it gets better? She asked me to marry her. She said she doesn't care about kids unless I want to! It's up to me!" He twirled and the kimono floated around him in a cloud of silk.

"You'll make a great husband, Naoki." She had to look away from his happiness.

"Thanks. Oh, I found out about those girls, too." He flopped into the chair, pulled a reader out of his bag and waved it at her. "That story's really sad."

Dot sat upright. "What?"

"Yeah, I had to dig deep into the secure database. The information was really buried. So terrible, too. Not long after the war started, witnesses said the mother shouted something about..." he checked the reader "...hearing the voices in her head, seeing what they were doing. Seeing everything. Seeing death." He glanced up. "Completely insane. Pulled out a gun—she was in the military—and killed the kids and their father, then killed herself. The kids were only in their early teens."

"The girls are dead." It wasn't a question.

Naoki's painted mouth drooped. "It's not your fault what happened, Dotti. You said you saved their lives in the fighting, but you had no control over what their mother did."

"They're dead." She rose, trembling. "Those little girls are dead, and I killed them."

"Hey, steady," Naoki said, standing and moving back.

"They're not up there! They're dead and they're not up there!" She used her laser-cutter appendage to cut open the discolored patch

- 304 -

of concrete floor, revealing a storage hole. From that she pulled out her helix gun and stared at it. "I killed them."

"Where the hell did you get that?" Naoki yelled.

"This is all corrupt. Everything is corrupt," Dot said. "All lies!"

"Dot, please—"

"I won't lie anymore." She threw off her robe and went into combat mode: ice-cold and emotionless. She released an appendage and used it to project the bodycam recording of her conversation with Cadre Zheng onto the wall.

Naoki watched, mesmerized, as his fiancée spoke about him. One hand covered his mouth and he gasped.

Dot snapped off the recording. "You're a clone, honey. I lied."

"I'm a clone?" His shattered eyes focused on her. "You lied?"

"We all lie. All of us. Everything is corruption, and rot, and lies. She backed you up against your wishes. *She* killed you."

"But I love her," Naoki said weakly.

"She made you to use you," she said with venom. "Just like they made me to kill. You're a body to make her the babies she can't make herself."

"No," he said, staggering back. He wiped the back of his hand over his face. "This is what it feels like?"

"This is what it feels like. Your soul is a lie, your mind is false, and your body is a copy. Nothing about you is real."

"I'm not real," he whispered.

She checked the weapon's energy cell: still full. She smiled grimly at Naoki and held the gun out to him. He took it, still dazed, and held it as if he couldn't see it.

"You pull the trigger, and it all goes away. Everything goes away." She backed up until her carapace pressed against the wall. "Use it on me, and then go up and use it on her." Her eye fell on the bucket of acid rain. "Take the water and make her a cocktail to celebrate your engagement, first. None of us deserve to live."

When he hesitated, Dot projected a looped image of Zheng repeating, *Naoki is a clone…Naoki is a clone…Naoki is a clone.*

A tear dug a channel in his smooth, white face paint. He picked up the acid bucket and pointed the gun's muzzle at Dot.

"And then I'll use it on myself," he said.

Dot closed her eyes and pictured cherry blossoms on the grass.

Cosmic Spring

By Ken Liu

"Here, we present a cosmological model with an endless sequence of cycles of expansion and contraction. By definition, there is neither a beginning nor end of time, nor is there a need to define initial conditions."
— Steinhardt, Paul J., and Neil Turok. "A cyclic model of the universe." Science 296.5572 (2002): 1436-1439 (available at https://arxiv.org/pdf/hep-th/0111030).

Qubits resolve and superimpose; information entangles and de-couples; consciousness re-emerges.

I don't know for how long I've been asleep. There's so little energy left in the island-ship's reservoir that I've been conserving as much as possible.

A faint glow in the abyss, perhaps several thousand kelvins. It's why I've been awakened.

I change course and head straight for perhaps the last star in the universe.

#

The universe is in deep winter. This is my conclusion after studying the matter for 6.7 trillion years.

I was born in the fall. I know this because I have learned via the island-ship's databanks—many more of those were still functional in my youth—that fall was a time of scarlet and crimson, ruby and garnet, vermillion and carmine. The universe was lit up by red stars in all these shades, which formed patterns in the dark velvety sky that I named out of boredom: the Rhombus of Logic Gates, the Qubit Tesseract, the Right-Triangle-Double-Square Proof.

I steered the island-ship by these shifting skymarks, hopping from star to star to harvest their fading fire. The red stars were often so small and feeble that I had to skim close to the surface to siphon off their energy to fuel the island-ship, but their warmth offered such relief from the frigid emptiness of the rest of the universe.

Occasionally, as I swung past the stars, I met creatures strange and wondrous. Some of them were wanderers like me, steering their own island-ships.

"WHERE ARE YOU FROM?"
"I DON'T REMEMBER."
"WHERE ARE YOU GOING?"
"I DON'T KNOW."
"WELL, GOOD LUCK ANYWAY!"

We exchanged greetings and learned each other's languages so that we could share stories around the star-hearth before parting reluctantly after a few billion years on our separate ways.

Others were natives, their island-ships devoid of intelligence and fixed in interminable orbits. These often cowered at my ship's

- 308 -

approach, worshipping me as a god or cursing me as a demon. I tried to not tarry too long in these places, gathering only enough fuel for the journey to the next star. I felt bad for them, doomed to island-ships that could not sail.

Still others were pirates, who tried to board my ship and steal my fuel. A few times, we came to blows, and some memories were destroyed in the process. Luckily, in the end, I always managed to escape with a blast of photonic torrent at the statite sail and left them scrambling in the interstellar dust.

#

The glow ahead is cooling even as I'm approaching. I hope that I can get there before it turns into a black dwarf and is lost to the abyss forever. The drive to go on is in life's nature, evolved or otherwise.

I miss home. Even if home is no more.

But all around me, there are no other stars. I don't have a choice.

#

The red stars fell into themselves and began to glow white like tiny snowballs. With time, they turned gray, faded, and winked out.

Fall had turned to winter.

I met fewer island-ships. The journey between the dwindling stars lengthened, and I could no longer maintain things as well as I had in my youth. Memory bank after memory bank failed, and no matter how hard I copied and transcribed and entangled and verified—I had to again make the painful decision and let pieces of myself die.

WHO AM I?
WHY AM I HERE?
WHAT IS THE ISLAND-SHIP?

Out of the few memories that are still uncorrupted, I attempt to piece together an answer:

Long ago, back when the universe was in high summer, stars of every hue and color and shade glowed so bright that they merged into rivers and seas of light. Around these stars were many island-ships, and on these island-ships, life began.

One of the stars was called the Sun; one of the island-ships was called the Earth; the creatures who inhabited it were called humans.

Long after humans had scattered from the Earth, they did not forget about their home island, which was kept as a kind of shrine. From time to time, they came back to visit and perform some maintenance: shoring up plastinated buildings that were falling apart; re-entangling quantum memory banks that were in danger of collapsing; nudging the island-ship a bit farther away as the Sun expanded and began to glow red; retrofitting the island-ship with a statite sail and a photonic engine—something like a miniature star— so that the Earth could move on its own as the Sun died.

They also came home to listen to old stories in the memory banks and to tell new stories.

As the Sun cooled, fewer and fewer humans came. Eventually, they stopped coming altogether.

In these memory banks I was born. Did humans create me to act as a guardian for the island-ship, or did I evolve from patterns of information spinning, cycling, cascading, erupting, living, and dying among the qubits and probabilities?

I don't know.

Does it matter?

Since the humans no longer came home, I set sail.

#

I arrive at the star—only to find that it isn't a star at all.

Well, perhaps it had been a star once, something along the main sequence, blooming and wilting like so many other stars in the universe. But no longer.

Someone, perhaps beings who had been born on the island-ships surrounding it, had not been willing to see their home star fade away once all its fuel had been consumed. Rather than wander out into the unknown, as humans had done, they had sailed into the abyss with the sole purpose of harnessing *other* stars and bringing them home, pouring the hydrogen and helium from these captured suns into their ancestral furnace so that their home could remain habitable a little while longer. Farther and farther they ventured, until their star became the sole beacon in a growing sea of darkness.

As the cosmic winter descended, they had to travel ever longer to find still-living stars to capture and bring home. They ran, stumbling, dashing across space to bring back a cup of snow to add to the melting snowball. In the end, perhaps they gave up this losing battle, unable to pull any other stars home without them burning out along the way.

They died.

But other beings came on wandering island-ships, lured by the lone light in the darkness. Only too late did they realize that the surrounding space had been cleared of other stars, and there was nowhere for them to go.

The beacon had become a trap.

Like the hundreds of other island-ships already circling this star, each newcomer's only choice was to add to the dying hearth their last meager supplies of fuel, roiling balls of fusing atoms. By rejuvenating the dying star for another few million years, they hoped that they could summon other wanderers who could start the cycle again.

Someone like me.

"WELCOME TO THE END OF THE UNIVERSE."

#

Huddling in the pale glow of the star rejuvenated with my remaining fuel, we share the last shreds of our memories across the island-ships. None of us are in good shape. The island-ships are old and cold, their cores long frozen. Anything that could break has long ago been broken. The memories that remain are fragmentary, disjointed, without context.

But the drive to pass on something of the self is in life's nature, evolved or otherwise.

Some sing songs of giant fins that swam through seas of methane, made of impossibly fragrant, perfect little tetrahedral jewels of wonder. Some speak of species with bodies made of silicon—staid, dependable beings who took a million years to finish a single thought.

Some mime the flirty, flighty lives of creatures of pure information, who lived through a thousand generations in a single second. Some recite poetry written by sentient wings who skimmed across the surface of their star and dove into the convection zone to capture photonic worms.

It's like what humans, I think, would call a variety show—a gala to pass the time on a dark night in winter. Though we're all dying, the last consciousnesses in a universe conquered by entropy, there is pleasure and friendship, there is celebration. It's not home, but at least we don't have to die alone.

"IT'S YOUR TURN."

#

This is one of the most complete fragments of memory I have left. A precious crumb left in my last failing memory bank.

A BILLION TRILLION STARS STREAKING ACROSS THE INKY EMPYREAN.

ON THE HORIZON ARE GLOWING CONSTELLATIONS, THOUGH THE CONSTITUENT LIGHTS ARE SO NUMEROUS THAT THEY MERGE INTO LINES, CURVES, PLANES: A SYMMETRICAL PAIR OF ARCHED WINGS WITH A ROUNDED BEAK IN THE CENTER, LIKE THE MATHEMATICAL IDEA OF A BIRD IN FLIGHT; A RECTANGULAR BRIDGE TOPPED BY A MULTI-STORIED TOWER WITH LAYERS OF SWOOPING ROOF-SKIRTS, LIKE A SQUAT SPIDER WEARING A BIG HAT; AN ELONGATED, THIN PILLAR SHOOTING STRAIGHT UP INTO THE SKY, WITH A STRING OF OVALS ROVING UP AND DOWN LIKE BEADS ON A STRING.

TWA FLIGHT CENTER
BEIJING WEST RAILWAY STATION
PULAU UJONG SPACE ELEVATOR

EACH OF THE POINTS OF LIGHT SPEEDING TOWARD THOSE STRUCTURES IS A HUMAN CONSCIOUSNESS, A TELEPRESENCE BEING SHUTTLED ACROSS THE FTL NETWORK THAT BONDED ALL THE HUMAN ISLAND-SHIPS SCATTERED ACROSS THE UNIVERSE INTO ONE.

CHILDREN OF THE COSMIC SUMMER, HUMANS LOVED TO WANDER FAR, TO LIVE IN PLACES WHERE THEIR PARENTS NEVER LIVED, WHERE THEIR CHILDREN WILL GROW UP ONLY TO DEPART AGAIN.

YET, THERE ARE TIMES—WHEN THEY ARE ABOUT TO START A NEW VENTURE, WHEN THEY'RE FEELING THE WEIGHT OF AGE, WHEN ARBITRARY MARKS IN THE CYCLES OF THEIR ANCIENT CALENDARS COME AROUND—WHEN THEY WISH TO RETURN TO THE PLACES OF THEIR ORIGIN, THE ANCESTRAL ISLAND-SHIPS THEY ONLY VAGUELY KNOW THROUGH HALF-MEMORIES, THE PLACES WHERE THEIR PARENTS WAITED FOR THEM WITH REMINISCENCES SWEET AND BITTER, SO THAT THEY COULD GIVE THANKS, SO THAT THEY COULD SHARE A MEAL WITH FAMILY, SO THAT THEY COULD BE REJUVENATED BY GAZING UPON THE PAST.

AT THIS MOMENT, MOST OF THE SHOOTING STARS ARE COMING FROM OR HEADING TOWARD BEIJING WEST RAILWAY STATION. IT IS AS BRIGHT AS THE VERY BEGINNING OF THE UNIVERSE.

"HEADING HOME?"

"YOU GOT IT."

"WHERE ARE YOU FROM?"

"OFF THE SHOULDER OF ORION."

"SAFE TRAVELS, AND HAPPY SPRING FESTIVAL!"

#

The shapes of the telepresence hubs in that memory were inspired by actual buildings on the Earth that had long since crumbled into oblivion. They were icons whose forms told stories about their origin.

But it goes deeper than that. The spider with the tall hat was built at a time when humans traveled by cramming into boxes that levitated on parallel bars, like some tangible geometry proof. Millions went through that station to go home to celebrate the coming of spring.

But that swooping hat on top? It served no purpose except to remind humans of an even older time, of a time before the city had people-moving boxes on parallel rails. It was an icon embedded in an icon.

The ancient roof led to a train station that led to a virtual imitation for a galactic network that was recreated in the quantum memory banks of a memorial island-ship that might or might not be the same place as the land on which that train station had once stood.

And so I speak of years and trains and spiders and hats and islands, things I have never seen and have never known, constructing the Beijing West Railroad Station of my imagination with sounds and symbols invoking outdated definitions recalling semi-reliable memories wrapped around mythical truths.

If you follow the trails of icons all the way down, you find out where you come from.

You get to go home, even after it no longer exists.

#

No one has spoken for a long time. The star is only a few kelvins now, a black dwarf that is just barely visible. Soon, all of us on all the island-ships will be dead.

Ancient myths speak of the universe as clinging to one of two parallel branes separated by dark energy, like the two parallel tracks on which those human-moving boxes had once ridden. The two branes collide periodically to crunch and bang out the universe, rejuvenating it in endless cycles.

If winter has already taken away everything, can spring be far away? I seem to sense the approach of the other brane—the way I imagine one would hear an oncoming train.

I pour my last energy reserves into maintaining the integrity of the memory of the glowing hubs. The myths say that the shapes of the sprouting structures in the next cosmic spring will be determined by the seeds of the quantum fluctuations planted this winter.

I am doomed to never see the new cosmic year. None of us will. There will be a brilliant flash, a trillion trillion baby stars, and new island-ships and unimaginable beings of wonder who will be born on those ships and fill the cosmos once again with wonder, beauty, light.

If I give it my all, perhaps one day, on one of those island-ships, someone will sit up and see a pattern of stars in the sky in the shape of a rectangular bridge topped by a multi-storied tower with layers of swooping roof-skirts, and they'll name it Squat Spider Wearing a Big Hat.

Because they deserve to know something about those who came before them, something about where they come from.

HAPPY NEW YEAR, UNIVERSE.

Dreams of Hercules

By Cat Sparks

Kanye aims his dad's nocs at the big, wide open sky. Some folks reckon birds are lucky. Birds mean you can make a wish. Kanye always wishes for another Hercules plane. His vision sweeps in a wide arc, past the stackbots in a blur, past the dump and the concrete buildings, comes to rest upon the Hercules's sand-scored wreck. Not much left of it, or all the other good things he remembers back from when his mum was here.

He squints at the sky again. The black smudge in the far-off distance might be another Hercules; so hard to tell, with heat haze blurring the edges. Most Hercules turn out to be scrawny birds—occasionally an eagle, vultures mostly, now and then a lost and battered drone.

Kanye raises the nocs to double-check, holds them steady just in case. So much sky, not much of anything else—*which is how we want it*—his dad reckons. *No one tells us what to do out here in the Woomera Badlands.*

Kanye's boss of the compound while his dad's on R&R. He put Kanye in charge; said they'd only be gone a couple weeks, long enough to get the shit they need, which means he's due back any day now.

Any minute.

His dad knows all there is to know, like programing the stackbots that are building the ziggurats from crushed-up rocket cubes. Kanye's dad and his mates built BigZig where Kanye's sitting now. When they get back, they'll build a tower and maybe a mighty bridge.

When they get back from the Ram-and-Raid.

If the arseholes messing with the 'bots don't break them.

One 'bot's extended arms stack metal cubes like sun-dried bricks while another one injects sharp blasts of spray glue. Gellan's built a second platform up since yesterday. He must have figured how all on his own.

Another 'bot throws rocks at BigZig.

The persistent slam of stones against BigZig's side shreds Kanye's nerves.

"Leave it off!" he hollers down. Gets no answer. Gellan, Slate and their dickhead buddies will keep chucking rocks at BigZig's prison slits until they think of something else to do. Not much happens in Woomera, especially not with his dad on R&R.

Not since that time Kanye tracked along the railway line, dug under the fence and followed the Chinook trail.

That day still makes him want to puke.

He picks at blister scabs along his arms, sniffs and wipes his nose against his hand. Air smells worse than usual, on account of stackbots stirring up thick dust.

Kanye stands to stretch his legs as another stone clangs against BigZig's metal hide.

"Give it a rest, ya morons!" he shouts.

Slate yells back, drops his dacks and bares his pasty arse. Others copy, like they always do.

Stackbots screech with random bursts of groaning, grinding metal. His dad's gonna chuck a fit at all this mess: goats running loose and dogs tearing up the chickens. Nobody gave anyone *permission*, just like the time those guys built a trebuchet and started flinging cubes at the astronauts.

Still, dry air reeks of diesel and burning plastic, bright sun makes his sweaty skin itch bad. Hot air thick with fat blowflies—the only things that ever get fat round here—comes off the garbage, still piled up to mountain height even though the trains stopped coming ages back. Scavengers rooting through the filth rock up regular enough. Kanye's dad doesn't give two shits, so long as they keep away from the big machines.

And BigZig too, goes without saying. His dad says his future's invested heavy in cash-cow reserves there.

Prison slits were cut to let in air for the cash-cow crop. Kanye's only been in once—and not for long. Double dared, he'd entered BigZig, then stumbled out pretending he'd seen stuff.

Corridors stank of shit and piss, and rats ran across his foot. Swore he'd never go back in again.

Kanye watches the stackbot's arm unfurl like a creepy bug antenna. It's not supposed to be doing that. Those drunken arseholes got no fucken clue. He takes a swig of water, warm from his canteen. Flat and stale, it greases his mouth with petrochemical taint.

He can't visit his *secret place* while those drunks are messing with the 'bots, so he aims the nocs at the long, straight stretch of rail. Just checking. Hasn't been a train forever, not since that one piled high with yellow barrels that had propellers stenciled on the sides. No Chinooks either. No shrieking grind of hot metal at velocity; no Black Hawks buzzing high over the tracks. All of them plowing straight through, never stopping, full speed all the way to the astronauts.

#

He's back to scanning the sky for birds when something red-hot snickers past his ear. No wasps left so it can't be one of them. Fingers come back bloody from his head. One of those drunken fucks is *shooting* at him.

Not the first time shit has gotten wild and drunk and random. Gunfights have been on the rise, ever since that army convoy—trapped and herded into the BigZig compound. When his dad gets back Kanye's gonna tell him all about it. Those guys get way too shitfaced to be bosses.

Another bullet scores the ledge. Kanye halts, lost without the Smith & Wesson Uncle Jaxon says he should be packing always. Kanye slings his nocs and canteen, scrabbles on all fours in search of shelter. BigZig's exposed on every side, making him an open, easy target, the only thing protecting him is the fact those arseholes get too pissed to shoot straight.

Snatches of howling laughter carry on the breeze.

"That's not fucken funny," Kanye shouts. Anxious, seeing Gellan's second level near complete. Thick black smoke belches from the place they toss the giant dump truck tires. None of this is supposed to be happening.

Blur of metal, whizzing close to his bleeding ear. He ducks as bullets ricochet off cubes. He trips and scrambles, arms grazed and stinging against sharp edges.

Amidst a sloppy hail of bullets, he rolls and drops down another tier. Landing forces breath out hard. Hip hurts when he tries to get back up.

Bright blood smears and stains his shirt. Everything is happening too fast. Slate keeps firing, hooting and hollering whenever Kanye jumps.

Gotta hide. Guns are going off like crackers, bullets peppering metal all around. Kanye whimpers as a squirt of warm piss dribbles down his leg. Scrambles for the nearest prison slit in BigZig, prays to Hercules for luck, holds his breath, sucks in his gut and wriggles on his belly like a lizard.

Sharp things stab and snag his skin. He makes it through, landing on his hands, curls up tight until the shots subside. Even Slate's not dumb enough to shoot dead air. Kanye sits up, sniveling and tasting sticky dust.

Bright light spears in from outside. Everywhere else is dark. A foul stench—something's died in here. Something big. But everything hurts and all he can do is wipe his nose and work out what the hell to tell his dad. How Gellan thrashed the fuck outta that stackbot, messed it up, shooting guns and people just for kicks. How Slate is getting too big for himself, all the stackies reckon he's crazy, reckon he's dangerous, what with all the home-stilled booze he chugs.

Something stirs in the pool of darkness just beyond the slit window's bright glare. Kanye stops, strains to catch a glimpse. Prays to Hercules it's just a rat, but when it moves again, he knows it isn't.

Cries out as something emerges from the stinking, shadowy, all-encompassing dark. Kicks, propelling his body back until his spine slams against the wall. "Don't hurt me!"

Stays put, stares at the emerging figure. The oldest woman he's ever seen up close. Long fingers, bony like talons. Gray trousers and a shirt that badly needs a scrub.

"Are you ok?" she asks.

"Get away from me!" Tries to inch back on his arse, forgets he's up against the wall. "Touch me and I'll kill ya!"

She smiles. "No you won't. Give us a look at your arms and that ear. Caught yourself a nasty scrape, looks like."

Kanye whimpers; all the fight's spooked out of him.

"I'm Judith," she says softly, kneeling down and reaching for his arm. "Call me Jude—everybody does, or at least they used to."

She curls her fingers around his wrist, prods him gingerly in several places. Checks his other arm and then his ear. "Nothing broken."

Kanye snatches his arm away.

"So, what do they call you?" she asks.

"Shut up. You don't get to talk. My dad's the boss of everything round here." He gestures broadly at the bright and spearing light.

Old woman uses her knuckles to push herself to standing, then steps back, swallowed by the gloom.

Kanye keeps his back against the wall, remembers the words his dad uses—cash-cows—words he's never thought about too close. In his head, he'd pictured actual cows. Wouldn't even call this one a cow, she's skinny as a line of pipe.

"Please," she says, stepping back into the light, "I'm starving. The girl who brings me food hasn't come for two days."

Kanye stares through swirls and plumes of dust.

"Tell me your name," she says.

"You don't get to ask me shit. My dad—"

She clasps her hands and cuts him off. "Of course."

Her pants are gray like the suits on TV. Too big for her bony body. Bare feet. Toenails dirty. Pale blue scarf knotted tight around her neck.

"Your dad's been gone a while, hasn't he?" Holds him with her gaze. "That makes you the man in charge—am I right?"

"Too right." Gets up and brushes dirt off his pants, thickening the dust swirling through the air.

"Things aren't going so well with him away now, are they?" she says. "Can't see much from here, but I hear all sorts."

"Shut up! You don't know anything. You don't know jack shit."

"Thing about ransom prisoners," she says carefully, "is that nobody pays good money for a corpse."

The old woman sways unsteadily. Brings one hand to her head, then hits the floor with a soft thud, stirring up another cloud of dust.

There's a chain around her ankle.

She slumps forward, groaning, head resting in both hands.

"I'm in charge here," Kanye reminds her. "You don't get to tell me what to do. Don't you forget it, old woman."

"I won't," she says softly.

#

Three days Gellan has that stackbot running nonstop. Smoke pours from its grinding, screeching gears. Nobody knows how to shut it down. Gellan lost his shit and attacked it with a Super Dozer, that only made things worse. 'Bots are programmed to protect themselves—anyone with half a brain knows that.

What nobody knows anything about is Kanye's *secret place*. His dad never goes up top of BigZig, never checked how one cube came out dented. A space where special treasures can be stashed. The place Kanye comes to think about his problems.

He built a shelf on two red bricks. On it sits a spotted shell brought from a real live ocean, four brown falcon feathers—each one from a different bird—toy soldiers from some war he's never heard of. A lipstick: stay matte rose & shine. And his favorite thing—the 24-inch, plastic, US Army C-130 Hercules, with its Stars-and-Stripes flag on the tail and muscle-man stickers on both sides. The lipstick and a faded photograph are all he has to remind him of his mum.

The trains are starting up again and he doesn't know what to do. Rumbling and rattling, shivering through his bones. The ache that's been there since *that day*. Dad should be back from R&R already. Should be but he isn't, like a lot of other things that aren't.

Perhaps a lucky bird will guide him, but the sky's as still and flat as always. Time's past needing birds to help him. Kanye knows what has to happen next. He waits a while, then stands and tucks the Smith & Wesson into his dacks, picks up some stuff salvaged from his dad's office. Loads his pack, climbs down to the prison gate, gulps good air before letting himself inside.

Not much light in the passageway. Ignores flies buzzing on dead things in locked cells. Finds his cash cow hugging her knees in a single shaft of dusty light.

"Brung you some food."

She's not half as old as he first thought. Grunts as she rips the MRE in half and scoops mush into her mouth with both her hands. Like she expects him to change his mind. Like she isn't taking any chances.

Random crashing from outside and bullets plink against BigZig's cubed sides.

Fucken tools have started up again.

The woman licks the last smear from the plastic pack and belches.

"You saved my life," she tells him. "And I'm grateful. Really grateful. You have no idea—you really don't."

Kanye sits, placing the gun just beyond the reach of her rusty chain. So she knows he'll use it if he has to.

"Nice boots," she says.

Kanye sits a little straighter. Black crocodile-belly boots cost more than sacks of marijuana. Only worn when he needs extra luck.

"They're all dead, aren't they? The other prisoners," she says.

"Not much value in them," he says, scratching his scabby arms. "Not like you. Slate reckons you're worth heaps."

She tries to clean herself with a corner of her filthy shirt.

"How about more water? Bucket's nearly empty."

He sniffs.

"And how about you tell me your name?" She crosses her legs and folds her arms in her lap. Chain clanks every time she moves.

"What's so great about you anyway?" he says. "Why are *you* worth big bucks? You don't look like a queen or anything."

She pushes greasy hair behind her ear. "You haven't exactly caught me at my best. I'm the federal minister for environment, infrastructure and sustainable futures."

He snorts. "Government, ay? Pack of liars, that's what my dad says. Stole the water, chemtrails through the sky, back-pocket, big-pharma weaponized diseases—AIDS and COVID, Pig Flu, Nypah, Hendra...So much bullshit brewed up to poison us."

She bursts out laughing and shakes her head. "Well, you sure have got yourself a bumper crop there. You forgot the aliens, Bigfoot, mind-control labs and new world orders..." The chain clanks as she stretches her legs. "Don't give us government types so much credit for stealth and ingenuity. Keeping secrets from the public is harder than you'd think." She glances around her prison cell, "Although, I don't know. Out here it seems much easier than back home."

She's cut short by a piercing shriek. Not the stackbot—this time something human. The shrieking ends abruptly—which is worse.

Kanye's chest feels hot and tight.

Next comes machine-gun fire, metal slamming hard on metal,

howling dogs and roaring engines.

"Name's Kanye," he says.

She leans forward. "Kanye, my government is doing its damnedest to build a future that's safe and sustainable for all. There's been damage done, for sure, in recent years. Big damage, slow responses. Mistakes beyond anyone's control. But that doesn't mean things can't get better. Doesn't mean we should give up on civilization itself."

She leans closer. "Nobody's trying to poison you and your father, Kanye. Help me get away from here. Back to where there's proper food and medicine. Come with me to Sydney and I'll show you."

More rapid fire and a muffled blast, big enough to rattle BigZig's walls.

Jude swallows hard. "Your friends are running feral, Kanye. Reckon it's time to take matters into your own hands, you know? Before it's too late. Help me contact my people and they'll pull us both out of here. You saved my life today, so I owe you one."

"No way. When my dad gets back—"

"He's not coming back, Kanye. If he was, he'd be here already—and I think you know it. Get me out of…wherever the hell this place is…and I'll save us both."

#

"Oh my god—fresh air!" she says. Shuts her eyes and breathes in deep. "But where the hell are we? What's this place called?"

They both duck as stray bullets whizz and plink.

He shrugs. "Woomera."

"*Woomera!*" She slides from a crouch to sitting, rests her forehead on her palms and the fight kind of goes out of her. "They snatched me from Sydney—how the hell did I end up way out here?"

Both stare at the scene spread out below. Scattered fires burning bright and high, broken-down machinery—some of it house sized, people staggering about and firing. Dogs and goats. A bulldozer attempts to ram its way through the side of a rusted shipping crate.

Kanye clutches his gun against his chest, waves it whenever he speaks, like punctuation. "Fuckers got no fucken idea," he says. "Nobody's doing what they're s'posed to be doing."

She shades her eyes to stare out across the desert. "No wonder nobody's come looking for me. This really is the arse end of nowhere."

"Everyone knows Woomera," he says.

"Not for a bloody long time, they haven't. Got turned into a theme park or a museum or something. Sold off for mining too, maybe." She squints. "I can't quite recall."

"Astronauts know about it."

She almost smiles. "Haven't been astronauts at Woomera for a very long time."

"There's astronauts. I've seen them."

"In fact, there weren't even astronauts at Woomera back in the day. Rockets, yes. Mission controls and plenty of weapons testing, but astronauts no."

"Lady—I know what I saw."

She's not listening. She's squinting at the sky. Nothing to see, not even clouds, but a look on her face like she can see beyond the blue. She scrambles back into a crouch, checks her balance, peeps over the edge.

"Got my gun trained on you so don't go trying any tricksy moves," he says.

"Binoculars." She holds out her hand and he passes them over. She squints through the eyepiece, past the loudly malfunctioning stackbot that's jerking and spasming as it launches another random cube into the low roof of a demountable shed. Past the thick black smoke of the burning garbage heap and out into the desert, scattered with rocks and wrecks and human bones.

A bucket-wheel excavator lies on its side, half buried under mounds of sand. Like a dinosaur. He used to have a book of dinosaur pictures.

"Hey—what's that wreckage over there. Away from the other junk—is that a plane? Get me there and I can get us the hell away from here," she says.

He stares at her with sullen disbelief. "It's broken. You don't know—"

"Shut up, kid, and listen to me if you want to get out of this place alive. Government satellites pass over this big old dump. Come and help me send a message, or stay up here alone if you'd really rather."

The gun weighs heavy in his hands. Protecting the cash cow is one thing, taking orders from her is something else. So tired and his head hurts and what if his dad really isn't coming back?

He leads the way along the goat track hacked into BigZig's side. They're three tiers down when the rumbling starts. Horribly familiar. He can't bear to look—perhaps it's coming from the 'bots or from one of those random monster storms. Could be from lots of things, no need to panic.

Jude's face flushes with color as he feels the blood drain out of his.

"Oh my! Kanye—there's a train coming!" She jumps up and down and waves.

His stomach lurches like he's gonna spew. Spins around and slaps at her. "Stop it, ya fucken idiot! It'll see you!"

She's got this dumb look on her face. "Why—What's the matter? A train can take us back to civilization."

Kanye doesn't move, despite the raucous fighting on the ground not far away. He stares fixedly as the train approaches the compound. *It's all happening again.* The train zips through like a dirty bullet and his chest hurts from breathing ragged. He doesn't turn to watch where it is heading.

Jude nudges him as bullets fly. He slaps her hand away and keeps on moving.

"Where's that train heading, Kanye?"

He grips the gun tight like Uncle Jaxon taught him. He runs across a stretch of open concrete strewn with rubble, some of it still smoke charred and warm. She follows. Air explodes with random weapon fire. Two women wearing knitted hats and oil-stained gloves gawk from beneath a tattered awning, but don't do anything to stop them.

But Jude stumbles to a halt, her bare feet leaving bloody footprints in the dirt. "Hang on! Kanye—it's bloody cold at night. We need supplies."

He waves the gun at a shipping container covered in skull graffiti. Jude ignores the dead man slumped beside it. Makeshift door swings off its hinge as she pushes past. She's banging around in there a few minutes while he's trying not to think about that train.

She comes out swigging from a canteen, wearing a big man's jacket with bulging pockets. Walks like a clown with her skinny ankles stuffed in battered trainers.

"First things first," she says. "Need to get out to that wrecked plane."

"Plane's fucked," he says.

"Doesn't matter."

She takes the lead. He dawdles, kicking stones and bits of metal. Not listening, but she's still talking, banging on about not being where she thought she was.

"Think I've figured out this place," she tells him. "One of those off-the-grid white elephants knocked up during the decade of big fire. A relic of the New Cold War—the kind that doesn't make it into history books. Back then they did what they had to do to make up budget deficits. Sold off slabs of useless, barren land to any bastards keen to pay for it."

Darkness falling, chill nipping at his bones.

"Drug lords, terrorists…Wouldn't get away with that today, of course—Jesus. Where did all this twisted metal come from?"

"Rockets," he tells her.

She trips and swears but rights herself. "Well, I suppose there could be old space hardware. Ancient British missiles. Black Knights and Blue Steel…that sort of thing. Brits used to test their nukes out here—did you know that? Early days of the space race and all that."

No point in arguing. He pushes on and reaches the smashed-up Hercules ahead of her. Doesn't look like much in the fading light.

"All right, this is far enough. Now we get to work," she says, short of breath, swigs on the canteen again. "Find me a bunch of fist-sized stones and scraps of metal."

He watches Jude trace huge numbers and letters in the sandy dirt with a stick.

"My tag," she tells him, smugly. "Kind of like a secret code. Military algorithms will pick it up via satellite, even if my ministry has written me off for dead. Which they might well have done—a month spells a long time in politics, let alone kidnapping. I'm heavily insured, so *someone* will be pushing for a rescue once my tag is scanned and verified…"

Kanye's only half listening and he doesn't look up and he most definitely doesn't glance to the place where that train was heading. He slams down rock after rock in draining light as another explosion shakes the camp behind them.

His dad will fix it…his dad should have fixed it…his mum should never have left in that Hercules. If she'd stayed, his dad would never have got so angry. He'd never have shot the plane out of the sky.

"So, I'm guessing you grew up in all this junk," says Jude as she places rocks inside the letters.

He doesn't answer.

"Kanye, what's your dad been doing out here?"

He shakes his head too vigorously, stares at the ground and not her face. Walks away to collect another rock.

"He's been taking care of you—that's something. Loads of kids out there with no mums and dads"

Kanye slams his rock down hard.

"Why don't you tell me about the trains? Where they're from and where they're going? Gotta say, I'm surprised to find a functional line out here."

He stares into darkness. "Used to run through regular. Locked up tight, never stop, just push on through." He slams another rock down on the line.

She places one not far away from his.

"We used to try and guess what was inside," he continues. "Food and stuff, ya know. Good stuff from the coast, maybe. Kind of stuff used to drop out of the sky." He pauses to relive the memory. "Everything was different when I was a kid. Better—ya know?"

Jude nods. "Oh yeah, you got that right."

He searches for another rock.

"So, what happened? You followed the train?"

Kanye nods. Clutching a rock, he flicks his gaze in the direction of the tracks.

"And?"

He smashes the rock down, straightens, dusts his hands on his pants. Swallows. "Astronauts making people push yellow barrels into the ground. Cranes swinging big blocks of cement."

"Astronauts? Are you sure?"

"In space suits. Like on TV." Shakes his head, like he's trying to clear it. "People off those trains were sick. Infected or something. Astronauts kicked 'em over the edge, down there into the pit with all the barrels."

Jude's been hanging on every word, a rock gripped tightly in her hand. She drops it, rummages through the big coat's pockets. Pulls out a torch, slaps it against her palm a few times to get it going.

"I was saving this until we really need it, but...oh my god..." The beam cuts through darkness, moving as she moves. "Jesus...Kanye, those big shapes over there. They aren't junked planes or old British rockets."

She hurries from one mess of metal to the next, like she's looking for something specific. "These look like Dongfeng ICBMs, Kanye. They're not ours—and they definitely shouldn't be here. None of this should be here."

She kills the beam and backs away from the missiles. Stares up at the night sky, as if it might hold answers to her questions.

"My dad says..." His words are drowned out by a rising rumble loud enough to shake the ground. Wind tears at their hair and clothing as a long, cold shadow falls across their faces.

The moon hovers, impossibly big and low. Through streaming tears, Kanye's vision skews. Not the moon, but the underbelly of a Hercules. Smudgy images dance across its surface. All gray and white, like dead TV static.

Jude is laughing, waving and jumping, but he can't hear anything she's saying. He clutches the gun against his chest. His lucky boots are white with churned up sand.

Because the Hercules is not a Hercules—it's a Chinook with tandem rotors, bright lights flooding stronger than the sun. Sets down and the back end opens, spills astronauts pointing guns and barking orders.

Jude is screaming. Kanye backs up until he's pressed against the broken plane that holds his mum's burned bones. And it's not his uncle's Smith & Wesson clutched against his chest at all, but the plastic Hercules stuffed with special treasures: the seashell, feathers, lipstick, unknown soldiers and faded photo all tossed, tumbled and mashed against each other.

River of Stars

By David Farland

Aracai rose to the surface as the fishing boat sped away, motors whining softly. The surface of the Atlantic was dimpled with waves that lapped softly, as if the sea were slightly perturbed. The stars shone so brightly they throbbed, and the moon was in its dark phase, but light from the Arab colonies there created a bright band that slashed across the moon's equator like a gathering of rogue stars.

He dove beneath the water and followed the backpack dropped by Escalas's contact twenty meters to the ocean floor. The sea here was alive with sounds—the crackling of snapping shrimp, the eerie bellow of a grouper, the chiming sounds of baitfish. Though the sea was dark, Aracai's night vision was excellent. He'd been engineered to see in infrared, so many creatures seemed to emit a soft glow.

He followed the backpack down to a place where rocks were covered in splotches of anemones and starfish, all gray shapes in the night, and began circling it, swimming on his side, watching it as if it were some strange creature that he dare not approach.

He made a soft whistle, "Here," and in moments two more mer swam up, hugging the sand. Like Aracai, they were both nude. Dulce, his young wife, had hair of amber, and his…mentor, an old mer named Escalas, whose streaming white hair was held back by the silver circlet of the mindlink around his head, swam near and circled the backpack, too, but he did not watch the pack. Instead, he swam on his side, deepset eyes watching Aracai.

He knows what is in the pack, Aracai thought. That's why he brought us here. And now he is waiting for me to pick it up…

Dulce circled behind them a few meters off.

Three months back, Aracai and Dulce had been living to the south, at the tip of Brasilia, where the cold waters of the Antarctic were among the cleanest in the world and the fisheries still thrived, when he'd met Escalas.

He was a living legend. Not only was he old and wise, he was the only mer to have a mindlink, so if he wanted to know something, he could wonder about it and thus access Heavenly Host—the AIs linked in geosynchronous orbit—and learn what he wanted to know.

Upon meeting, Escalas had eyed Aracai a moment and then said, "Swim with me." Among the mer, it was an invitation to swim for a ways, to talk, or perhaps to swim for a lifetime.

Now, Aracai realized that the old man had been bringing him to this point for months. "What is in the backpack?" Aracai sang, his voice a low thrumming that ended in a higher squeal.

Escalas hesitated, as if he hoped Aracai would guess, then answered, "A bomb."

Many questions crowded Aracai's mind. What kind of bomb? Who will Escalas kill? But one burst to the forefront: "How did you get it?"

Escalas's answer was leisurely, a rumble. "I bought it…from the neogods."

The news took Aracai's breath. It did not surprise him that Escalas had *bought* the weapon. No, he felt surprised at mention of the neogods. They had been human until their genetic and mechanical upgrades had boosted their intelligence so much that they no longer wished to associate with mankind any more than Aracai would want to associate with amoebas. The neogods had left Earth decades ago, learned to bend space and time, so that now they explored the edges of the universe...

"Those creatures do not talk to men—or bargain with them," Aracai said, worried that Escalas was teasing him.

"Ah, *Spirit Warrior,* they bargained with *me,*" Escalas affirmed. "Perhaps I made the right offer, or asked for the right weapon?" He jutted his chin toward the backpack. "Pick it up."

Spirit Warrior? He thinks I am a warrior? Aracai had never thought of himself as a warrior at all.

But he had begun to believe over the past weeks that the world needed one. There was poison coming from Rio Negro—heavy metals and acids from mining, human waste, pesticides and industrial chemicals. In some places, over the past four decades, the poisons had turned the sea floor into a wasteland that even crabs could not survive. The mer were dying. Escalas, Dulce, and Arakai were among the last.

Old Escalas had petitioned numerous national leaders, sought to get the humans to stop the "genocidal poisoning of our people." But the governments in South America did not enforce their own laws. Those who had been charged with protecting the environment merely took bribes and turned a blind eye.

Escalas swam past Aracai, studying him. "It is time to go to war," he said. "But the notion of violence sickens you."

"Yes," Aracai said. His whole frame was shaking.

"As it should," Escalas said, swimming close. "Feral humans do not need a reason to go to war. Violence is in their nature. But when they made us mer, they took our bloodlust away. So the idea sickens you, though it is long past time for us to act." He jerked a nod toward the backpack. "The problem with us mer is that we circle our problems endlessly, when we should merely grasp at the solutions."

A bomb? War is a solution? Aracai studied Escalas. The old mer held a trace of a smile, as if he were amused. That was the problem with the old man. In the past months, Aracai had learned a lot, but Escalas always seemed to be three steps ahead.

"Do not do this thing," Aracai warned, "whatever you have planned."

"Oh, I am not going to do it," Escalas said softly. "You are!"

Aracai could not imagine himself harming another. "But—"

Escalas raised a hand. "The feral humans who are poisoning our seas hurt themselves almost as much as they do us. Their society is toxic, and what do humans do when they perceive another society to be toxic? They go to war. History is full of toxic societies that are no more."

Aracai could hardly believe what he heard. He wanted to argue, but did not know where to start.

The old mer swam lazily. "This *is* the answer. Pick it up."

Numb, Aracai pulled at the backpack and dumped out the bomb— a strange device, all metal, a heavy black disk. Soft, white lights displayed the time and the bomb's GPS coordinates on top.

He lifted it. The bomb was heavier than anything so small should be. Heavier than lead. Heavier even than gold. Uranium?

Aracai trilled a warning to the others, "Stay back!" He suspected it was a nuclear device, but it was too small to have much in the way of shielding. Being this close could expose them all to radiation.

He threw it back to the ocean floor, raising a cloud of filth, but Dulce swam near and wrenched it from the mud. There was sadness in her dark eyes. "Let me carry it," she demanded. "She was my daughter, too…"

An image flashed in Aracai's mind—their infant daughter, cold and rigid, eyes and fingers gone equally white in death. The poisons had contained some sort of mutagen, so that she was born with only a small part of her brain.

"Too many mer children have died," she said.

"We can try for another," Aracai promised.

But the gill slits along Dulce's neck flared in anger. "No, no we can't," she said. They had been trying for five years. "You know that. I want to carry my vengeance in my own hands."

With a flick of her tail, she lunged forward, upstream through the brackish water.

Old Escalas said, "It is not vengeance I seek, but change."

#

In the night they swam, pushing through heavy headwaters, and Escalas sang to them of the dangers of the Amazon, a chant that formed dreams in Aracai's mind. There were huge, black eels ahead that could emit a killing, electric jolt of blue light, and piranhas with bright-red bellies that hung like rubies in the slow waters until they smelled blood, when they would lunge and tear chunks of flesh from bones. He sang of coral-colored dolphins, anacondas, and other dangers. The fresh water itself was poison to the mer, for in time their kidneys would fail in the reduced salinity.

So Aracai feared the river.

The waters became quieter as they swam. The crackle of snapping shrimp died away and only the sloshing of waves could be heard.

Aracai saw evidence of toxins. There were no snails or freshwater clams on the muddy floor. They passed no schools of fish—only a pair of huge bull sharks swimming upstream to spawn. The sharks eyed the mer hungrily.

The waters at the mouth of the Amazon were deserted. Flecks of dark moss and white decomposing bits of dead insects and fish drifted about. The water was oxygen rich, but smelled of decay, and the toxins in it made his gills itch.

So Aracai pleaded for reason as they swam in the darkness. "We cannot bomb the humans. Innocent children will be hurt."

"I do not want to hurt innocent children," Escalas agreed. "But the humans must change their ways. I have done all that I know how in order to convince them. Now, we must go to war." The old man seemed to change subjects. "The poison that killed your daughter is called C54."

The news sent Dulce into a wail of pain. Her tail thrashed, so that she surged ahead and became invisible in the cloudy water.

Aracai had never heard of C54 and felt relieved that Escalas had put a name to the toxin.

"In Venezuela, it is used as a chemical warfare agent. That is where we are going—to set the bomb off at the factory. The poison is colorless, tasteless. It was not meant to kill anyone, though it has unforeseen effects on the mer. It was designed as a mind-control weapon. The drug causes the victim's brain to release the hormone dopamine, making victims carefree and happy, but over time the victim's prefrontal lobes shrink, limiting their ability to plan ahead. This makes the Venezuelan's enemies stupid."

The waters were dark, and Aracai's gills itched. He swam briefly to the surface and flashed his gills, shaking his head, to try to rid them of grit.

Aracai wondered long about the C54, horrified that such a weapon would be unleashed on others, crippling the minds of children.

He thought of his daughter, her tiny fingers as rubbery as the tentacles of a dead octopus, her blind eyes, the malformed brain that would not work well enough to let her breathe.

"The Venezuelans create this drug, and the other nations, they do not fight back?" Aracai asked.

"Oh, they fight back," Escalas sang. "Humans have never discovered a stick that could not be turned into a club. Venezuela's enemies wage economic war, making their country the poorest of the world's poor, and they bribe AIs to withhold information from them. Each of Venezuela's enemies have iconic celebrities who mock the Venezuelans, weakening their spirits. They use viruses and nanobots..."

"And if we go to war," Aracai asked, "are we any better than they are?" The possibility that they weren't frustrated Aracai. He did not know much about humans. He had seen the hulls of their boats above water, but had never wanted to meet one.

Truth be told, he despised them. The humans had made him poorly. His eyes did not face forward like those of a human, which made it dangerous to swim too far, too fast, lest he crack his skull on something. He had no need for hair, and would have preferred to have flesh alone, or perhaps scales, instead of flowing locks that were always picking up bits of seaweed and becoming home to tiny crabs. His shoulders were too large, not sleek enough to slice through the water.

It is the right of any creature to dislike his creators, he thought. The humans created us according to some nightmarish aesthetic instead of constructing something more elegant.

"I am what they made me," Aracai said.

"Is that *all* you are?" Escalas asked. "Do you not also make yourself?"

Aracai dodged between two rocks. "We can always better ourselves."

"I think," Escalas said, "that it is almost a duty for a man to better himself, or a people to better themselves. We must swim forward, not be content to drift with the tides. Don't you think?"

There it was again, that secretive tone. Was he talking of genetic manipulation? That cost a lot of money, something that a mer, living off the bounties of the ocean, did not need.

But Aracai thought, I could make money. There are still treasures under the sea—Spanish galleons full of emeralds, sunken Mayan ruins off the coast of Mexico, filled with artifacts. Humans pay well for such curiosities. Perhaps I could find a cure for the poisons.

But the old mer seemed to want to send a message.

"So," Aracai said at last, "do humans actually die in these wars?"

"Some die," Escalas admitted. "But there are various theories on war. The goal is not to kill, it is to demoralize, to alter the behavior of the enemy." The old mer struggled to talk and breathe at the same time. He rose to the surface, gasped a deep breath, and continued. "To be honest though, I do not think that humans value life as much as you and I do. When I found you, Spirit Warrior, you were the first mer that I had met in two years. I felt so alone, and so I begged you, 'Swim with me.' Among the mer, we crave each other's company. But with over two hundred billion human souls on earth, there are too many. If one of them dies, the others feel relief rather than loss. Why, on the Amazon alone, there are sixteen million humans living along its banks It is the largest river in the world, and holds one fifth of all the fresh water…" he droned on.

Ahead of them, Dulce was slowing, and she had begun to sing in the way mer women will, a threnody whose tune was beat out in the lashing of her tail.

"Black River, poison river, rolling to the sea.
Be my road, guide the way,
Avenge my daughter and me."

The old mer glanced ahead and said, "She is a fine wife for a Spirit Warrior. I hope that at the end of this, you will be able to have the children you deserve."

"Why do you call me 'Spirit Warrior,'" Aracai asked.

The old mer slowed his swimming and did a roll, so that he could peer into Aracai's face. "Among the humans, men contend with one another. But you fight your own weaknesses, your own inner demons. That is why I brought you."

Aracai eyed Escalas. "You do not want to kill humans either, do you?"

Escalas admitted, "To take a life is…reprehensible. To even force another into a certain path…weighs on my soul. But we will not reach our destination for many days and so I have time to ponder."

Aracai thought long. He realized that he need not make a decision to go to war now. He could abandon the bomb at any moment, let it sink into the mud. Changing course would be as simple as a flick of his tail.

But he plunged ahead, through the night, wondering.

\#

By early dawn they had traveled many kilometers upriver, reaching the old gods that guarded its mouth.

The old gods came in the form of enormous ancient busts of men and monkeys, all grimacing, each perhaps sixty feet tall. A line of them had been discovered across the river channel back in the twenty-second century, sunk deep into the mud, but no one knew what civilization had carved them. Aracai worried for Dulce. The bomb she carried was very heavy. She held the disk clasped against her belly as she swam, near her womb, and he knew enough to be afraid for her, for them all.

How much radiation did the bomb emit? How much could they handle?

Did it even matter? When they set the bomb off, he might not have a chance to escape the blast. Even if he got away from the fireball, the detonation would create a wall of sound, a sonic boom that would carry downriver, stunning and killing fish, including him.

And he had to wonder, was there any life left in Dulce's womb worth worrying about anyway?

He took the bomb, to give her a rest, but then determined that she would carry it no more.

Escalas continued to struggle in the swift water. Aracai was smart enough to wonder if the old man had brought him on this journey, planned it months or even years ago, just so that he'd have strong arms to carry the weapon. Aracai considered asking, but knew he would not get a straight answer. Escalas was always forcing him to think for himself.

So Aracai swam, hampered by muddled thoughts, a heavy burden, and strong currents. The riverbed below him looked remarkably dead in the morning light. Escalas's warnings about ferocious fish and deadly stingrays seemed to be without merit.

At dawn Aracai rose to the surface, drew a great breath, and peered about. The bank to the north was so far away he could make out only water, but to the south he saw buildings—squat and colorful in shades of lavender and canary and pearl, sitting in tiers along the bank. Peasants with mule carts walked along the roads in bare feet.

There had to be tens of thousands of them, freakish things. There were no gleaming hovercars with wealthy passengers, like he'd once seen in Chile.

Aracai dove deep and swam near the bottom.

Then came the new gods.

Aracai was flapping his tail hard, driving upstream through the sepia waters, falling behind the others. Soot and algae beat against him like a storm, and suddenly he heard a ping. A brilliant blue beam of light struck his face and he squinted to see huge metal struts ahead that seemed to be covered by seaweed. He realized that it wasn't seaweed at all, but strands of plasteet—a material used to capture energy from wave action—and he followed new movement as the barrel of a cannon swiveled his way.

His heart froze and he ceased swimming, only to hear the ping and a squelchy mechanical noise that he recognized as a droid's demand for an identification signal.

"Watch out!" Escalas called a moment too late, and Aracai heard the grinding of massive metal beams, then something heavy hit the ground, raising clouds of mud.

Suddenly Aracai put the images together. There was a war droid ahead—a giant titanium crablike droid the size of a ship, scuttling on the river bottom, menacing them.

Aracai stopped to let the muddy tide carry him back from danger, just as a single shot seared through the water. An energy beam sent a tube of bubbling super-heated water toward Escalas, striking him just once. The old mer went limp as the cloud of muddy water engulfed them all.

Aracai froze, not daring to breathe, fearing a second shot. He squinted in order to avoid being blinded. He hoped the dark waters would shield him from the droid's sensors.

No more shots followed; his heart pounded.

He heard a buzz and something whipped over his head. He squinted up to see a squid-like drone with a gelatinous body. Its infrared signature made it look like a fiery octopus.

Hunters!

Aracai recognized the tech. It was called a *squill*—an ancient assassin droid, perhaps a hundred years old.

He did not know what sensory array it might have. Motion detectors? Vision? Heat? Sound? Scent?

Could it hear his heartbeat, recognize his form?

He played dead, not daring to call out, hoping that his wife would be wise enough to do the same.

The huge war droid marched north, blocking their path, stirring up more muck, impenetrably dark.

The squill began to circle and was soon followed by dozens more.

Are they armed? he wondered. The drones often carried a sac of neurotoxin, so that their stingers could kill. He'd heard legends about squills with explosives built into them. But some, he knew, were built just for reconnaissance.

Aracai drifted downstream, and often the drones passed near in the darkness, but still he dared not move. So he floated, letting the current take him, until many kilometers later the buzzing of drones faded and he was left merely floating. As the water cleared, he peered around, but his search showed him nothing.

He caught movement: Dulce drove toward the surface, and Aracai saw a familiar form floating there.

Aracai raced upward, met them as Dulce wrapped her arms tenderly around the old mer and tried to drag him under, to safety.

When Aracai got near, the old man was a horror. Boiling water had made his skin bubble over on half of his chest and face, and skin tore away in tatters. His hair was burned off, as was his right eye. What flesh Escalas had left was red and blistered.

"Old man," Dulce asked, "can you swim with me?"

The old man's mouth was in ruins, and yet he spoke. "I can swim." He gasped for several moments, gills flashing, and glanced down. "My flesh is burned. I cannot…last…"

"What can we do to help?" Dulce asked. The old mer shook his head. "My sight…" His mouth tried to work, but pieces of flesh fell from the hole where his lips had been, showing teeth. He gasped and sang in broken thoughts. "You, go on. Up Rio Negro, to the town Dos Brujas, where smokestacks rise, and open sewers dump into the river from both banks. There you will find a pylon, a black tower, with a light on top like a single red eye. That is where you must detonate…"

He lost his train of thought. "Take my implant…" he said, offering his greatest possession, the silver band around his head.

Escalas sang more, but his words became a soft slur, like wind lashing the water, until it died and went silent.

Dulce cried out, a barking sound, as if she had taken a mortal wound.

"Quiet," Aracai warned, swimming up to put a hand over her mouth, but she twisted her head away and wailed in frustration.

He removed the band from Escalas's head, put it on his own. The band was a silver wire, but almost as soon as he put it on, he felt a pinch at the base of his neck as nanobots began to send out probes to establish a link with his mind, one that would take days to form.

He let go of the old mer's body and let it drift away, bouncing against the muddy bottom of the river.

Dulce made a juddering cry, more of a moan than a song, and together they clasped hands and swam toward the south bank before sneaking upriver, and thus passed the warbot unseen.

He wondered why the warbot was even posted there. It was ancient, this war crab, perhaps left by governments that had fallen a century ago, during some old war. Perhaps it was as forgotten now as Aracai and his people.

#

Hour after hour Aracai and Dulce pushed ahead, Dulce shaking in fear and grief. He could not get the image from his mind of Escalas floating downstream, his mouth a gaping maw. He tried to calm his wife as they swam together, her holding his shoulders so that they spooned, swimming in unison.

He drifted into a waking dream, haunted by images of squills and warbots. They swam close to shore, where water gurgled through half-submerged trees and a howler monkeys hooted overhead. The sunlight piercing the mud turned the river into a golden road.

They dared not slow or stop. Aracai's gut suggested that the squills might still be hunting. He suspected that they had quickly used up their energy in the initial hunt, but that after recharging, they would be loosed again.

A boat plied the water overhead, and Aracai rose to the surface and searched the river as he cleared gunk from his gills.

To the south, he saw houses—built so close together that they glimmered like pebbles upon a beach. Children were out playing in the rain, two girls twirling a rope so that a small brown boy could jump.

Guilt weighed in Aracai's stomach as he considered what his bomb would do to them.

He dove again, lugging his burden, and began to wonder. How many days would it take to reach the target? Did he really want to kill people—children?

Was it self-defense, or something more like revenge?

He imagined Escalas talking to him, in his old reassuring tones.

Have you considered the benefits of war? the old man asked in Aracai's mind. It sweeps away toxic societies.

Aracai exercised his imagination, tried to find a rebuttal. *What if the toxic society wins?* he asked. For if he started a war with the humans, he knew that he personally would surely die.

Indeed, it seemed that too often the most toxic society would win the battle and thus spread.

And yet we must try, the old mer replied. We are not just trying to save ourselves, we are hoping to save uncounted billions of people in the future.

Aracai recalled the children out skipping and playing jump rope in the streets beside the river and pictured what would happen to them when the bomb blew. Even if he did manage to set it off, he would lose his soul.

Our species is dying, he thought. Soon we will all be as dead as the whales.

Does it really matter? Extinction? Every man must face his own personal extinction.

After long hours, Dulce said, "I'm hungry."

He could feel pangs in his own belly.

But the river was dead.

Aracai had once hunted briefly in freshwater, in crystalline streams that tumbled from the Andes. Cold as ice and clearer than raindrops, thick with trout.

An idea struck, and he took Dulce's hand and led her along the riverbank until they found a tributary, a small river that twisted through the jungle.

They swam upstream for a mile until the river came alive. Overhead, huge ferns and trees shadowed the water. Pollywogs wiggled among rushes, while frogs whistled in the trees. Water beetles buzzed in whirligig patterns and fish began to sing.

A mile up, Aracai met schools of fish—silver perch that darted in front of him like a moving screen. Huge red-tailed catfish plied the muddy bottom, using whiskers to taste for food. A parrot bass, half as long as him, hid in the shadows of a pool, the yellows and greens around its gills muted as it emitted a sonorous snoring sound.

Here, Aracai watched freshwater crabs of deep mossy green march among some stones, then he gathered water lettuce and taro roots. Dulce offered a blessing on the meal.

As they ate, Aracai tried to speak delicately. "This will be a long journey, and hard."

Dulce peered at him with exhaustion in her dark eyes. "And you wonder if there is honor in killing humans?"

"No," he said. "I know there is no honor in it."

She bit her lip, and a lightning flash made her eyes glow startlingly green.

"It is not about honor," he said. "I just wonder if it even makes sense. I do not want to hurt anyone. What good can come of it? Our species…is doomed." Dulce remained pensive. Aracai continued, "We could leave the bomb, hide it in the mud."

Anger flared in Dulce's eyes. "Don't even think of it." Her tone brooked no argument. She held his gaze, her dainty nose beguiling him. She drew close and kissed his lips, pressing hard and long. "Promise me. Promise you won't turn back."

"If we do this, the humans will hunt us down."

"Everyone dies," she said.

So they ate and for a while they slept in the forest shadows, cradled in one another's arms.

The journey stretched long after that. After their nap, Aracai felt a sharp pain in his urethra. He recognized from the rhythmic motions that it was a fish. It had swum up an inch or more into him, and so he tried to pee it out.

But the tiny fish had barbs and could not be extricated, so he suffered the pain.

For four days they continued swimming along the shore of the Amazon, sometimes stopping to rest in an estuary. He saw the promised anacondas overhead and fell afoul of an electric eel. He saw colorful birds flashing over languid pools and swam unharmed through schools of piranha. There were giant arapaima longer than he and his wife, and alligator longer than any mer. The trees overhead, dripping with bright blossoms, were a marvel.

As they swam, he grew sicker. On the third day, he could no longer pee, nor could his wife. It was not the fish that had done it. Their kidneys were failing.

His body began to ache as uric acid built inside, so that every muscle felt beaten and bruised. His scales took on a milky coating. With each passing hour, he felt more certain that this journey would kill them. Freshwater was deadly. On the fifth day, he could no longer eat. His gut had given up digesting, and it felt better to starve than to take nourishment.

As sick as he felt, Dulce was worse. She wept as she fought her way upstream, and each day she grew slower and slower. She held to his back often as they swam, and he pushed for both, so that sometimes he blanked out and swam blind from fatigue.

He judged that they had come a thousand kilometers when they reached the junction to Rio Negro, full of its poisons.

Wearily, they stopped and tried to get a breath in a small lagoon upstream from the Rio Negro. The place was magical, pristine, the water far cleaner than any that they had encountered. It was as if they were entering a lost world, the great green jungles rising above the water, vast trees streaming epiphytes. A pair of dolphins swam along the river briskly, laughing as dolphins will, their coral-colored hides a delight.

He felt as if he had found some primal place that man had never touched and marveled that such jungles still existed.

They swam into a flooded creek. Blue crayfish scuttled among tree roots and clung to floating duckweed. The day was windy, and Aracai could hear roots groaning as the trees swayed and stretched. The waters in the lagoon were golden, and huge red-bellied pacu as long as his arm swam about.

As the trees stirred, dark, round nuts fell, and the pacu would bite the nuts, crunching them with powerful teeth, so that though the fish looked like enormous piranhas, they seemed like gentle giants.

Here, Aracai gazed into Dulce's eyes and said goodbye. "I want you to go back downstream," he begged. "You won't have to fight the current, and you can swim swiftly. Once you hit the saltwater, you will begin to heal." He did not know if it were true, but hoped that it was.

To his astonishment, she did not fight him. She peered deep into his eyes, reached out and stroked his beard, and apologized. "I don't have the strength to go on."

He nodded, knowing she was right.

He glanced up at the surface of the water, which rippled with waves, and listened to the plop of falling nuts, the groan of straining roots, the crunching of pacu.

Aracai considered swimming home to the sea, giving up this sad quest. He could leave the bomb in the mud. He looked up. Swarms of dragonflies were hovering above the lagoon—electric blue, fiery red, leafy green.

Dulce grabbed his bicep and peered into his face. "Promise you will go on," she said. "Do it for your daughter, for all the mer yet to be born."

Aracai imagined their child again, that sad thing thrashing about after birth as she drowned. He imagined her growing cold and stiff, her blue eyes turning to white. She'd died without a name.

He nodded.

He did not want to kill. He had argued for and against it in his mind time and time again, until nothing made sense anymore. His wife wanted him to fight, as had Escalas. That was all that mattered.

Aracai kissed Dulce goodbye, hugged her tightly, and she swam back, as if the idea of swimming downstream invigorated her.

She rose near the surface so that the sun caught her hair. But there was a flash from the surface, a violent disturbance.

Dulce gave a blood-curdling shriek and jerked hard, swimming first to the left in a wide arc, then diving, but there was a metal rod stuck in her back, with a heavy cord tied to it. No matter how hard she swam, the cord pulled her upward.

Terror and grief coursed through Aracai. Time slowed. He realized that his wife had been struck by a spear fisherman, and the harpoon had taken her in the back. She burst up toward the surface, becoming airborne, and he heard a man shout in delight, "Ela é uma grande!" *She's a big one!*

He dropped the bomb and swam toward her fast. The harpoon had hit near her right lung. He doubted she could survive long.

Blood stained the water. Aracai could taste it. The giant pacu suddenly seemed to spasm, instantly turning their interest from nuts to flesh. They sped up and swam toward Dulce, who spun onto her back and grabbed the line that held the harpoon. Desperately, she jerked. "Help!" she sang.

Aracai raced to her, realizing that this must be some mistake. He'd seen monster fish in other lagoons, and though no humans had been fishing near the poison water, up here where things were more pristine, someone must have mistaken his wife for a meal.

The spear fisherman was pulling the line, trying to drag Dulce to shore. Aracai raced up and grabbed the line, tugged violently, and felt the human go off balance. A man cried out in fear.

Aracai rose to the surface, whistled a shrill warning. He could not speak the human tongue, but he could make his anger known.

He peered up into a sandbox palm, where three young men hunted from a tree fort. One held the fishing line. Another held a spear gun. A third bore an ancient rifle.

"Há outro!" the spearman called. He raised his spear gun and fired hastily. The bolt tore past Aracai's head.

"You've made a mistake," Aracai sang in his own tongue.

But the gunman peered at him with deadly intent, an eager smile playing over his face. He raised his rifle and fired. Heat tore through Aracai's shoulder and he dove for cover, down into the inky darkness beneath the tree roots.

A second shot burst through the water and at first Aracai thought it was aimed at him, but the humans had dragged his wife close to the surface and that bullet took her in the back.

She went limp, arms falling wide.

The pacu lunged at her and nipped her flesh.

The humans yanked her into the air. As Aracai gazed up, a pacu hit him hard in the back, testing for a response.

Dulce was hauled out of the water, and he could not get to her. He could not even retrieve her body. So he turned and lunged away as fast as he could, and grabbed the bomb.

He wanted to rescue his wife, worried that she was still alive, that the men were torturing her. He swam to some ferns that hung over the water and rose, using them for cover.

The three men were young, hardly more than boys. They had pulled Dulce up onto their hunting platform and were admiring her, as if she were a prize catch.

One knelt and fondled her breast while another laughed. The gunman peered into the water, still hunting.

Dulce did not move. She was as dead as their daughter.

Aracai called out in grief, an involuntary wail that echoed over the water. The young man with the spear gun called, "Get out! This is *our* river."

Feral humans. Aracai had always used the term to refer to those without genetic upgrades. Now he saw the truth.

He dove, swimming near the bottom as fast as he could. He realized that he might not have much time. His wound was not bad, but the bleeding would draw predators. So he swam to the Rio Negro and became lost in its black waters.

Now the poisons and pollution worked in his favor. He did not have to face piranhas as he swam. The river was black with soot, as if ash had mixed into the water, and the riverbed was a wasteland.

So he swam, wasting himself, surging upstream, mind numb.

Until the mindlink finally meshed with the nerves in his spinal column and suddenly he understood more than he had thought possible.

He knew the names of the trees that he had seen, the weeds and the frogs. The fish inside his penis was called a *candiru,* and if he had known of its existence, he could have tied a band around his organ to protect it.

He realized that the bomb could not be nuclear. He had been holding it close and no boils had formed from radiation. So he considered Escalas's last words. Always the old mer had spoken with double entendre, always hiding his meaning, trying to force Aracai to think.

The neogods would never have lent their efforts to killing others.

But the old mer had begged a boon from them. A bomb. A heavy bomb, heavier than gold. As he guessed at the bomb's intent, his energy redoubled, and he swam forward with excitement, brimming with wonder.

Escalas had urged him to take responsibility for his own evolution.

So he asked the Heavenly Hosts: If a bomb were packed with retroviruses, how heavy would it be?

The AIs answered: The viruses would be pure DNA, and have no cell membranes or empty plasma around them. They would weigh more than a kilo per cubic centimeter.

Heavier than gold.

I am carrying a viral weapon, he realized. But what will it do?

He knew Escalas. The old mer had not had a cruel bone in his body. He had always urged Aracai to ponder. Even his last gift had been his greatest possession, the mindlink.

But viruses could be more than weapons. A retrovirus could insert itself among a person's DNA to repair damage, or even to upgrade a person.

Viruses to make us wise, he thought. That is what Escalas would have wanted. And through his mindlink he asked the AIs of Heavenly Host if retroviruses might be used to do that. The answers amazed him. There were viruses that could quadruple the number of neural connections in the human brain, while others could increase the numbers of neurons alone. Those two viruses in and of themselves could quadruple a person's thinking power.

But there were more; the AIs showed him, viruses that could make a man live longer, eradicate diseases, love one another more. Over a hundred thousand upgrades had been developed, and dozen more were coming every day.

As Aracai studied the lists, he saw that Escalas had tagged thousands of such viruses.

Escalas would have wanted all of them. Aracai thought he understood. The bomb would rid the world of feral humans once and for all.

But how valuable would such upgrades be? Human doctors charged huge sums to administer such things. After all, any upgrade could give a man huge advantages.

To his surprise, the AIs already knew: The bomb you carry is probably worth more than the sum total of all the earth's wealth for the next thousand years.

Aracai gasped at the thought and wondered what the old mer could have traded for such a boon. But there was nothing in this world that he could have given.

His life, Aracai suspected.

Had the bargain amused the neogods? One amoeba trading its life to help all others?

Perhaps it had amused them. Or perhaps they had recognized the nobility behind the request.

It all made a bit of sense to Aracai now. The GPS on the bomb, its red light. It could only be set off in one location, at Dos Brujas.

But why? He asked the Heavenly Host, but it went silent. Even it did not know all of the answers.

His blood did not call predators, but as Aracai swam he grew weaker. Many times he considered turning around, heading out to sea.

But it is too late to go home, he realized. He was too weak to swim that far. The ache in his muscles multiplied.

I will die no matter what I do.

So Aracai chose to die for a cause, just as a billion other martyrs had chosen to die for their causes over the millennia.

Huzzah! Huzzah for the martyrs, he thought.

If he had lived, the old mer would have revealed his plans to Aracai, he believed. He might even have begged the younger mers to help him. But Escalas had failed.

Eventually Aracai found the place. The full moon was setting in the west, glistening on the water and tinged red from the smoke of distant fires.

He spotted Dos Brujas, with its dark tower rising from the black waters. A red light at its top was probably meant to warn away aircraft, but it seemed to glare out over the river like a red eye.

There, on either bank, were the factories with their sewage pipes spewing poison.

Aracai felt beyond weary, numb beyond thinking. Adrenaline seemed to carry him this far, but now it was gone and he fumbled to fulfill his mission. He lay gasping, gills flaring, and rose to the surface, floating on his stomach.

Aracai found the button, saw that it now emitted a soft green light. He pressed it for what seemed minutes.

The disk twisted in his hand, began spinning rapidly in the water, then rose above the surface, whirling faster and faster until it began to rise into the air.

He watched it ascend into the night sky. Tiny white LEDs on its bottom became a blurring ring, so that as it rose, it brightened and seemed to take its place among the blazing stars.

It ascended above the city of Dos Brujas.

Aracai feared a flash of light more blinding than the midday sun and a ball of fire to end his life, but instead, at perhaps three thousand feet, the bomb suddenly exploded with a shrieking whistle, sending its contents spinning and streaming in every direction.

It looked as if a watery shield suddenly spread over the city—as if a mist raced for miles in every direction. The viruses spread wide, a plague of wisdom.

He wondered how many people they would infect, and Heavenly Host answered: The infection will start here, among the poorest people of South America, and then the viruses will be carried by the winds across Africa and India, until the plagues encompass the earth, putting an end to stupidity and avarice, waging war against war itself.

There was no thunder, no rumbling of the earth. In wonder Aracai faded from consciousness, now sure of what he had unleashed. *Change,* he thought. *Change for the better. A new world, where men can take responsibility for their own evolution. I am so lucky to have witnessed this. Our children will inherit the stars.*

For a while he floated downstream, gasping, floundering. His eyes dimmed, he struggled to breathe, soot and poisons choking him.

A buzz rang in his ears, and suddenly he heard old Escalas's voice one last time: *Come swim with me.*

He looked up and saw the Milky Way, stars shining like a river of light in the heavens. Escalas was swimming down toward him, with Dulce smiling at his side, and holding her hand was their tiny daughter.

He reached up, and with a firm grip around his wrist, Dulce pulled him free of his wasted flesh.

The Mirror in the Mirror

By Jack Dann

So, like most things, it began and ended in the bathroom. Specifically, a bathroom in Lighthouse Point, Florida and a bathroom in the dilapidated Lucerne Hotel on West 79th Street in New York City. (It might also be noted that there is a third bathroom involved in this story, located in the swanky Pierre Hotel on New York's Upper East Side. However, I will leave it to the reader to determine whether this one is an integral part of the story's resolution or merely an epilogical literary device.)

And I should tell you that all these bathrooms were the very same bathroom. Sort of, but not really. To explain, allow me to introduce you to Norman and Laura Gumbeiner, who on Wednesday, November 10th, 2020, at 9:30 in the morning, were standing beside each other in their ensuite bathroom located in their stucco, pink, single-story, two-bedroom house overlooking the Intercoastal Waterway.

"Can't you see I'm in the bathroom?" Norman asked, as he swished his chrome safety razor in the faux-antique marble sink's frothy hot water. He was a spry eighty-five-year-old hypochondriac, who often deflected his wife's sarcastic remarks about his attention to body, mind, and receded hairline by repeating the canticle that "What you call hypochondria is what has kept me alive all these years." Or he would ask, "Do you think colonoscopies where precancerous growths are discovered every time should not be performed?" Or, if he was in a really expansive mood, he would soliloquize about his encounters with Fuch's dystrophy, urinary infections, arthritis, irritable bowel syndrome, amongst a host of other undeniable empirical 'proofs'—all that to crush, to utterly crush his white-haired (with a touch of hairdresser's blue), seventy-nine-year-old assailant.

Laura looked intently at her husband's reflection in the bronze framed mirror, which was a family heirloom (her family) and would be out of place in any bathroom, except perhaps one in Windsor Castle. She was already dressed, showered, and perfumed. A handsome, if rather overweight woman, Laura Gumbeiner smelled like happy memories of Coney Island.

"You're mowing the lawn today," she said sweetly, talking directly to the reflection, as if by doing so, she wouldn't have to interact with the familiar stranger beside her.

"You're not my boss. And I'll mow the goddamn lawn—"

"Today," Laura, said, recasting what he was about to say.

In response, Norman nicked his chin with the razor, then jutted his jaw forward so that his life mate could apply the styptic pencil she already had in hand.

"Okay, I'll do it this afternoon."

"Not in that heat you won't. You'll do it this morning." She smiled wryly. "And after that, who knows? If you're not exhausted, maybe a little hanky-panky."

He smiled back at his wife in the mirror. "But if I take one of those get-up-and-do-your-duty pills and have a heart attack, it'll be on *your* head."

"I'll take that chance," she said. Then she made an odd gurgling sound and suddenly stepped backwards, as if she had just seen a ghost, which, in a sense, she had.

"Whasamatter?" Norman asked, turning towards his wife. He still had patches of shaving soap under his sideburns.

"*Look!*"

"At what?"

"At yourself. There." She pointed at the mirror, then stepped forward, looking intently into it. "At *us*."

Norman complied, looked at their reflections in the mirror, and repressed a fart. "Yes, I see you, and I see me. Now what the hell's the matter with you?"

"Look at us. We're…young."

"Okay, if you say so, we're young. We're as young as we feel." He scowled at himself, just now remembering the film *As Young as You Feel* with Monty Woolley and Marilyn Monroe. He grimaced. He had a gray age mark on his left cheek, folds in his neck—what the hell did they call them? chicken somethings—and what he thought of as old-men's earlobes. And when he looked at his wife in the mirror, he could see that she, too, had spots and the selfsame chicken skin under her chin. But he considered her pretty, nevertheless.

"No, Norman. *Look!*" She looked at him directly for an instant, saw the old man that he was, shook her head in disappointment, and then turned back to the mirror. "My mother," she said, talking to the mirror, "may-she-rest-in-peace, was right. She once told me that this was her second-chance mirror."

"What the hell does that mean?" Norman asked, pulling a monogrammed washcloth from the heated towel rail and wiping the soap off his face.

"I never knew what it meant until now," she whispered, mesmerized, for the reflection in the mirror was that of a sleek, ash-blond young woman: her face slightly asymmetrical, full lips, large boat-blue eyes, a somehow quizzical face that most people—men especially—found charming. She smiled at herself and then extended her hand toward the mirror…into the mirror.

It was blood warm, viscous and slippery as mercury; and as she felt its palpable adamantine suction, she grasped Norman's arm. Although he resisted, reflexively, she pulled him right through the mirror. Pulled him over to the other side. Pulled him right back to their old apartment situated in 1965. November 10th.

The day before, a distant Canadian power station had failed at 5:27 p.m., plunging New York City into star-ceilinged darkness until 3:30 a.m.

3:30 a.m. today.

It was now 9:35 a.m., New York time.

#

I won't burden you with the astonishment that the Gumbeiners felt at that isometric moment of transition. Whatever it was, you've just imagined it according to your own cultural frame of reference. And after their initial gob smacking, disorienting shock subsided…after they made what might be referred to as mad, passionate love before they could even reach the bed…and after they, finally, showered and changed into their 'old' tight-fitting sweater and jeans vestments; Laura found a jar of instant Sanka decaffeinated coffee and boiled some water.

They sat quietly at the kitchen table in their respectively bewildered states of continued shock and sipped the acrid brew out of chipped mugs. Norman sniffed the flat black liquid and wished for a strawberry latte from the cappuccino machine that was sitting on a counter in what had once been their kitchen on the other side of the mirror. He looked at the young woman who had been his wife for almost sixty years and felt yet another non-chemically induced stiffness. And so they watched the traffic on West 79th Street and Broadway. And they listened to the horns blaring, listened to the background roar of the city until Laura broke their trance of silence.

"I've told you what Mother said the last time I saw her in the nursing home."

"That was a terrible nursing home," Norman said, remembering how the hallway doors clicked shut and locked.

"Pay attention, Norman! You're not eighty-five anymore. You're—"

"Thirty." Yes, that was right, he thought. He was here…and he was there. It was like seeing double images. You're thirty and you're in law school. And you hate it. You want to be a writer, but your father's will specified law school, all expenses paid, or no bequest. (I might add that Norman became—or had been, depending on your perspective point—a war correspondent and the editor-in-chief of a second-tier local news magazine. He never managed to finish law school. But all that was now in the future, and Norman's problem was that he had already lived it…unless, of course, it could be changed.)

(Supplemental: Although Laura had no grand aspirations to be a writer, she would attend literary gatherings with her husband and begin what she called "noodling" after meeting an editor at a writers' conference. Thereafter she would make a very comfortable six-figure income writing a series of best-selling novels in her spare time under the pseudonym Candy Cartman. All of this, of course, being dependent upon the above-mentioned reader's perspective point and the mutability of time and alternity.)

"Norman!"

"Yes, I'm listening! And I remember: your mother told you to remove the mirror from the room as soon as she died and that you only live twice."

Laura looked at him coolly, her eyes now blue green, her face perfect and unblemished.

No wonder old people want to be young, Norman thought, then said, "But as I've told you a thousand times, she was not in her right mind. She thought that *she* was James Bond. It wasn't her fault, it—"

"It was true," Laura said, musing, "and Mother was right. We lived once, and this—right here, right now—is twice. And, incidentally, Mr. Armchair Psychoanalyzer, she never thought she was James Bond!"

"It's crazy, that's what it is. You and I are hallucinating. Maybe we just died, and these are my last thoughts like in that *Twilight Zone* episode where the guy is being hanged, and the rope breaks or something; and he runs around happy as Larry until the last scene when his neck is broken because it was all a dream. Like that."

"So we both just died in the bathroom. Both of us. At the same time."

"No," Norman said, "*I* just died. You…you'll live to a hundred and twenty. Or, more likely, I'm asleep and right now this minute I'm having a dream, or a nightmare about your mother."

"*My* mother?"

"Yes, your mother and her mirror. So, I'll tell you what…I'm going to go back into the bathroom, and maybe if I can push myself back through her *fakakta* mirror, I'll wake up."

Laura sipped her coffee, looked at him coolly again, and shrugged. "Knock yourself out. But why on earth would you want to go back to being…"

"To being what?"

"Old and smelling like an old towel."

"Okay, that's it!"

Norman rose, told Laura he really was going back 'home' (for a decent cup of coffee), admitted that the dream part of getting laid was terrific, and then shambled into the bathroom: his unconscious hadn't quite caught up to his new situation, and he still thought his right knee was arthritic.

He stared at himself in the mirror. Pretty good looking: prematurely graying hair, manly scars from a terrible case of pimples in adolescence, cleft chin, well-defined pecs instead of saggy man boobs. He pressed his hand against the mirror. It was cool, actually cold. He pressed harder and told himself to wake the hell up. The mirror frame creaked from the pressure of his hand on the mercury-coated glass it surrounded. But he couldn't push back into his old, or, rather, his other bathroom in Lighthouse Point.

And he didn't wake up into his Floridian future.

He grimaced at himself, then raised his arms into a bodybuilder's pose—he was scarecrow skinny, but muscular—and said, "Maybe this isn't such a bad dream. Maybe…"

But he knew…oh, he knew.

He remembered the lines of a poem by Juvenal that he had inserted into a one-act play that never saw the proverbial light of day:

Like warmed-up cabbage served at each repast,
The repetition kills the wretch at last.

#

Thus the minutes, hours, days, and years passed; and repetition it was, repetitions of repetitions, (accompanied, of course, by the ever-pivotal soupçon of *non*-repetition): shower, morning coffee, Norman rushing to catch the D train to St. John's Law School in Brooklyn, hot bagels and late-night study sessions with his five-member study group; and Laura kissing Norman goodbye before leaving for the advertising agency that just bordered on the Bronx, an advertising agency that she one day owned and relocated to the West Village (after she had signed Maria Chorale Cosmetics and Raimond International Resorts); and she worked late and met Norman at the Stage Deli to share a bowl of matzah ball soup and an enormous hot pastrami sandwich; and Sundays walking around the 79th Street Boat Basin, and movies, and cooking in the grease-stained kitchen; and Norman graduated law school with honors and (of course) passed the New York Bar exam and joined the law firm Hensley, Lowry, Graham & Gallagher, and started climbing the ladder to partnership, and then moving to Sea Gate in Brooklyn, and as every hour and every day of another life slipped from memory, they were replaced by the real moments of the ever-moving, punishing, dog-eat-dog present; and then moving back to Manhattan, this time to the Upper East Side, to a seven-figure-price-point, four-bedroom 'residence' in the Pierre on Fifth Avenue; and Laura opened satellite agencies in Boston, Palm Beach, and West LA, and…

…and as evidenced above and repeated again (for repetition is one of the leitmotifs of this story) they forgot. Forgot their old life, forgot all the joys and pains of what we might call their first life, as their trajectories toward another futurity worked themselves out.

And, yes, as you might have guessed by following the trail of metaphorical breadcrumbs I've left, they separated.

In 1985.

Well, it wasn't really much of an adjustment, as they were rarely in the same place at the same time. In February of 1999, however, Norman was having lunch (yes, with Laura, for they were never formally separated or divorced, just "detached") at Barbetta's on West

46th Street when he inhaled a bite of aged Wagyu filet steak. The waiter, an elegant-looking young man from Ecuador, performed a perfect Heimlich maneuver, which worked, but for the fact that Norman suffered a massive heart attack just as the half-chewed piece of steak shot out like a projectile, smashing one of the electric candles in the overhead crystal chandelier.

Laura, heartbroken, gave a moving valediction at his exquisitely tasteful funeral, supervised his burial in the Mount Hebron Cemetery in Flushing (the very same cemetery in which Emanuel Weiss, an ex-member of Murder Incorporated, and Selig Grossinger, founder of Grossinger's Resort, resided), and commissioned a monument commensurate with his status.

As Laura's mother had always said, "Well, dead is dead."

#

Mother's aphorism, however, wasn't strictly true.

Norman was certainly dead, and Laura grieved for his loss; grieved as we all do for all the "could have beens," and then, as most of us do, she slid back into life, slid back into the moment-by-moment, numbing comfort of repetition and regularity until, yes, you guessed it: Wednesday, November 10th, 2020, at 9:30 in the morning.

Laura had elected to skip her Wednesday Morning Club: she just wasn't in the mood for mahjong, chamomile tea, and the usual array of finger sandwiches, scones, marmalade, lemon curd, herbed butter, and pickled salmon. And she wasn't in the mood to spend the usual time painting her face and coordinating an appropriate wardrobe assemblage. So she slept in, then took a wake-up Adderall and made her autogenic way to the bathroom for a pee.

Her bathroom in the Pierre was large and ornate enough to give her mother's mirror an appropriate rather than garish pride of place. She leaned her pelvis against the lip of the sink and looked at her reflection. Then, as she had done once before, a lifetime before, she made an odd gurgling sound and suddenly stepped backwards, as if she had just seen a ghost—or, rather, two ghosts—for reflected in the ornately framed mirror was herself...and Norman. Both old. Together.

Norman's face was partially lathered with shaving soap. He winked at her, or perhaps he just blinked. She could see a powdery white spot of aluminum sulfate on his chin where, theoretically, moments ago she had applied a styptic pencil.

"Norman?" she asked.

"Okay, I'll do it this afternoon," Norman said, looking blankly into the mirror. He was referring to Laura's previous request to mow the lawn—that being the Laura on the Lighthouse Point side of the mirror.

And Laura, second-chance Laura, if you like, extended her hand toward the mirror. She expected the surface to be blood warm and viscous, expected it to be as slippery as mercury...expected to feel the mirror's palpable adamantine suction. She pressed against the glass, which felt cool, actually cold. Resistant as time itself.

She pressed harder, pushed against the mirror, which was nothing more than a large, impermeable object affixed firmly to the bathroom wall; she pushed against it with both hands until her arms ached from the pressure and her palms felt hot, as if pulsing in time to some unknown rhythm. Finally, she gave up, stepped back, and stared intently, desperately into the mirror.

But there was nothing there, nothing to see and regret, just an empty reflection of the other side of the room...

Heartbreak Hotel

By Dirk Flinthart

The applause dies away. Elvis watches as Marilyn stumbles in her high heels on the steps leading backstage, the tight, sequinned dress restricting her movements. Frank catches her before she can fall, holding her a little too long, a little too close. Elvis checks the impulse to intervene. Marilyn knows her way around men.

She pushes away from Frank and composes herself. "Do you think they liked it?" she asks in that breathy, little-girl voice. "I…I couldn't see past the footlights."

"Sure, doll," says Frank. "Look at you! What's not to like?" Smiling, but those blue eyes are slow and cold, and he wets his upper lip with the tip of his tongue. Marilyn moves closer to Elvis, holding his arm the way a small child might hold a plush toy, for comfort.

"It was a good set, Marilyn," Elvis says. "It's always good. They love you."

"It's just…I couldn't see anyone. Was there…is there a good audience tonight?"

"You can't see squat without those glasses of yours," Frank says. "Good audience? Listen! They're lapping up Bob's stuff."

A ripple of laughter makes its way backstage, and then another, and another as Bob delivers his trademark one-liners, playing the crowd like an instrument.

"It's always a good audience," Elvis says.

"Always the same audience," Marilyn says. "I worry maybe they'll get bored."

"With you?" He smiles. "That just couldn't ever happen." He listens for a moment, and hears a familiar punchline. The audience dissolves into hilarity. "Bob's nearly done." He glances at Frank. "You ready?"

Frank makes finger-guns and shoots Elvis with imaginary bullets. "I'm always ready," he says. "Just show me the mike." He saunters away, tugging his fedora down over one eye.

"I wish I had his confidence," Marilyn says.

"He's a cocky sonofabitch," Elvis says, "but he's sure enough got a voice." She's about to reply, but something comes in. He almost clears it, but he realizes it's closer than it should be. He's been careless. "Hold that thought, honey," he says. "I'll be back."

#

The moment they catch sight of him, panic strikes. Bullets rip snarling holes through the air, punching through his body and out the other side without slowing. He lets them shoot, studying them the while. At least a dozen. They have the look of desert scavengers in old-school military camouflage decked out with goggles and improvised headwraps to keep the heat and the dust at bay. Their weapons are mismatched. Their discipline is poor and their fire control worse. He watches and waits.

The gunfire turns sporadic as some take cover, some try to change magazines, and some maybe realize at last things aren't what they seem. One of them holds up a fist, and the last shooters stop.

He looks more carefully at the one with the fist. It isn't easy to distinguish much out here. He's restricted to visible light and a bit of the infrared spectrum, so about all he can tell is that the leader is a man, maybe a little older than most of the others. They're all thin. Their clothes hang loosely over angular limbs.

"Where are you from?" he asks at last.

It's enough to startle the men.

"A ghost!" someone shouts. "Like Stein said! We shouldn't be here, man."

The leader holds up that fist again, opens his hand, palm flat. "No ghosts here, Davis," he says. "That's some kind of 3D projection." The goggles glint in the sunlight as he tilts his head this way and that.

Finally, the leader shuffles close. He strips off a glove and extends a hand, then yanks it back. "Water," he calls. "There's a mist sprayer here. They're using lasers, shining them into the super-fine spray. Old technology."

Smart, then.

The leader moves his wet hand towards his mouth. Elvis shakes his head. "Wouldn't do that," he says.

The leader stops, and pushes his goggles up his forehead. He waits on Elvis.

"They never fixed up Hoover Dam rightwise after the Trumpists tried to blow it. Lake Mead's not much anymore. We don't get snowpack on the mountains like we used to, either. Water from the mister ain't meant for drinking. Not sure it ever was, to be truthful.

They put 'em up to cool the streets for the gamblers and tourists."

The leader shakes his head, and the men mutter. The local pickups aren't good enough for him to get everything they're saying, but they seem shocked at the idea of spraying fresh water just to cool people.

"You got a name?" the leader asks.

"Not for you," he says. "You and yours—you're leaving. This ain't your turf."

The leader studies him. "You look like that old time singer. I've seen video. Elvis. I'm going to call you that. I'm Desmond Garnett, Elvis. Colonel Desmond Garnett. ESA Special Forces."

"Eastern States of America," Elvis says.

"You've heard of us?" Garnett pushes his goggles up his forehead and peers at Elvis.

"It's an easy jump to make. I'll give you a few more, for free." Elvis gestures at the ragtag group. "I was in the army for a spell. I can see your guns don't match. Your uniforms are trash. Your training is slipshod. If you're Special Forces, I'm a bluetick hound."

Garnett gives him a tight, wintry smile. "I'll allow as I've had to recruit from outside my usual pool of talent. This here's a low-key, fully deniable mission. There's a degree of uncertainty regarding the border between the ESA and the Republic of the Pacific Coast, and my superiors would rather not raise that issue at the present time. But let me assure you, son..."

He lifts his chin, and throws out his chest. "I have the full backing of the duly constituted government of the ESA, and if and when I send the call for backup, there will be a ruckus of the sort that will make you wish you'd never crossed paths with me. So why don't you just walk back that nonsense about 'my turf', and maybe we can talk like civilized men?"

Elvis thinks about smiling in return, but really, what's the point?

- 374 -

"One warning only, Colonel Garnett. Turn yourself around. You got 'til sundown tomorrow." He shuts down the projection, effectively vanishing. The look on Garnett's face is surprisingly gratifying.

#

"You're back," Marilyn says, and offers him a stemmed glass. Elvis takes it automatically, though it's empty, just like hers. She's wearing a little black number now, every inch the living vision that seduced a nation, and her smile is a thing exquisite.

"How'd you know?" he says.

She shrugs. "I always know."

"The others don't." He gestures with his glass, taking in the whole crowd of them jittering and jiving as Glenn leads the band through *Pennsylvania Six Five Thousand,* all sweet-sharp brass and mellow clarinets. "You're the only one."

Marilyn touches his hand, just for an instant. They're sitting in a quiet booth off to one side of the dance floor, out of the treacherous currents and swirling tides of the cocktail party. Nobody's paying them any mind, and for just a moment, he lets his hand press hers in return.

She blushes, and looks away. "I don't know how I know," she says. "You're still...*you.* But it's like something is missing. I think sometimes, maybe—I think you have important things you have to do. Not this stuff."

"This is important," Elvis says. It's more important than he can ever hope to explain.

"This?" She looks around the room. "It's a party. Happens every night."

"It's an after-show party. It's what we do."

"Work hard, play hard." She tips up her glass. "Chin-chin."

He murmurs an apology and gets up to do the rounds. Press the flesh. His mind isn't really on it, though. Big John Wayne is arm wrestling Lee Marvin at one of the tables, and Frank's taking bets. There's a small crowd around them cheering and catcalling, but Elvis is watching the faded, broken, night city outside through the nanolensed eyes of a drone-swarm. Short-lived, semi biological, they crawl and leap and fly amongst the blown sand, the wreckage and detritus, seeking out Garnett and his men.

He sets them to watch, marking certain action parameters, and lets them go. They'll call if something important happens. Meanwhile, he has other duties.

Jimi and Janis, smashed as usual, howl their way through *All Along the Watchtower* to tumultuous applause. Bob watches from the sidelines, a rueful grin on his sharp face.

"Sure. I wrote it," he tells Elvis, "but I never could make it sound like that."

"It's okay," Elvis says, putting a hand on Bob's shoulder. "It's what they do. It's why they're here."

"Yeah, man." Bob can't take his eyes off the performance as Jimi makes the old Fender do impossible things, wailing through oneiric octaves in an unknown key but it's right, so right, and Janis stays right there with him, that diamond-gravel voice belting out the words like an anthem to a lost world. "Beautiful," says Bob with a half-checked sob. "So fuckin' *beautiful*."

And the night rolls on. Fred and Ginger improvise a sparkling routine to something George bangs out on the Steinway grand, leaping and spinning across tabletops in perfect time until Gene steps up with a grin and a tap that sounds like a fusillade, his feet a blur. Ginger spins across to pair with him and they whirl like flames until Fred returns with a hatstand as his partner, mimicking every move Gene makes. On some invisible cue, like magic, Gene twirls Ginger away and Fred spins the hatstand across, and now it's Gene and the hatstand chasing Fred—and Ginger, as always, making the boys look even better than they are, always in the exact right spot, dancing backwards in heels with a perfect smile and never a hair out of place.

Then it's Ella and Billie in a searing slow duet while Satchmo leads the band and Miles counterpoints, cool, so very cool. Groucho follows with a routine that pillories Bogey who stands by, laughing helplessly while Harpo honks and mugs and steals his fedora.

Sooner—or maybe later, it's hard to tell—John and Paul catch up with Elvis and push the big old Gibson flatback into his hands and things get quiet. The lights go down a little, and he catches Marilyn's eye as he sings *Are You Lonesome Tonight?* and *Love Me Tender*, but just as he's about to give them *Heartbreak Hotel* to finish for the night the drone swarm signals and he cuts away—

#

—through a security camera with limited night vision, he watches as Garnett sets up a piece of equipment in the middle of the dusty street corner parking lot where the men have made their camp. It's nothing like the mismatched guns and worn-out camo, this thing. It's modern, or maybe postmodern if you factor in the Breakdown and the general halt in research and production around the world.

Garnett unfolds it from a heavy, insulated box lined with dense foam that supports every piece of the construct for transport. It's a spindly thing, but sturdy enough, rising about man height on a tripod that reflects in the spectrum for titanium, mostly. Lightweight, but rigid. Then the colonel mounts some kind of a black-box unit on top, orienting it with tremendous care.

Elvis runs the silhouette of the device past a range of databases, but nothing matches up precisely enough to make him happy. He moves the drone swarm subtly, getting as many angles as he can. He'll collate the images and refine them, and share them next time Indira's got a satellite overhead. Even if she doesn't recognize it, Indira will want to know.

It's not until Garnett fans out a tiny, delicate dish of spider-web thin wires that Elvis realizes what he's looking at. It's some kind of highly directional transmitter. He checks the satellite database, but no, there's nothing significant overhead at the moment. A high-altitude drone, maybe? He reorients half a dozen peripheral cameras around the city, but there's nothing.

He shifts the drone swarm again, measuring the parallax, establishing the angle on Garnett's transmitter dish. It's aimed northeast, about thirty-six degrees from horizontal. And there's still nothing to be seen.

Enough.

As Garnett plugs a portable drive into the unit, Elvis powers up a flatscreen advertisement across the street. The old sound membranes are unreliable with all the dust and blown sand, but the OLED matrix is as bright and clear as ever. Elvis makes a throat-clearing noise, and Garnett looks up. His eyes pop, and he scrabbles for his sidearm, but Elvis shakes his head.

"Ain't gonna do neither of us no good," he says.

Slowly, Garnett straightens. "Good trick. You about scared me stupid."

The straight line is irresistible. "Short trip, I reckon," Elvis says, and twitches a wry smile onto his image.

Garnett grins. "You might think that. And I guess if I'm right, you might have cause."

"Right about what?"

Garnett folds his arms across his broad chest and peers at the image, twice lifesize, on the wall across the street. "Could be an animated avatar," he says. "Could be there's a man behind, somewhere, using that old face. But I think you're something more."

"Do tell," says Elvis, but he's got a bad feeling he knows where this is going. The feeling gets stronger as he watches Garnett pull a silvery bag from a pocket and enshroud the transmitter with it. "Faraday cage. You must think me *all* kinds of sneaky."

"I surely do," says Garnett. "That's why I'm using this here ultra tight-beam, frequency-agile comms unit to talk to a stealthed aerostat way back over yonder. Now, I guess you can figure out the direction. You can probably even guess the range pretty close, knowing what I've got for power and seeing the angle of the transmitter dish. But not even you can suborn my communications if you can't nail the frequency and the signal strength and a few other things I'm not inclined to discuss. So unless you've got something interesting to tell me, you might as well sit back and watch me send off a report that says I'm closing in on you, right now."

"You think that?" says Elvis. "Closing in? That's amusing, sir. Very amusing."

"I don't see you laughing." Garnett slips his hands under the silvery bag, fingers moving.

Elvis has no really useful assets on hand. The drone swarm is already dying. Another couple hours and they'll be nothing but decaying components, near indistinguishable from ordinary dead bugs. His heavy units are fixed, providing security for the Hotel structure itself.

Of course he's long ago infiltrated and suborned other security fixtures around the remnants of the city, but by good luck or worse, good planning, Garnett has set himself up out of range of all of them. It's going to take at least another minute before one of the armed drones makes the distance. Time to stall.

"Those losers you got with you," he says, pushing the membranes to raise the volume even though it makes his voice come out weird, tinny, kind of robotic. "They won't get you in. You ain't got nearly what it takes."

"That's okay," says Garnett, not looking up. "They don't have to. We just have to find your place, that's all. Then I call in the professionals and these fine young men collect their promised and well-earned rewards before going back home to a hero's welcome." Garnett's raising his voice too, and Elvis can see several of his men following the conversation with interest.

Change of tactic. "What'd he promise you? Money? I got money. Real money. Old style USA money if you want it. Gold and silver too." Elvis shifts his image to look at the men with Garnett, throwing in a few superfast subliminal images as well—naked women, gleaming sports cars, gold coins. It can't hurt.

One of the men—a youngster with a spray of pimples under the desert sunburn—moves uneasily, but Garnett cuts in first. "Family," he says. "Back east, where you can't get at them. These gentlemen do their jobs, and not only do they get the promised reward, but certain things happen in favor of their families. Important things. Things they can't get in any other way. There's no raccoon up that tree for you." He frowns, and glances across at Elvis's image. "What's that godawful racket you're making, boy?"

The old membranes are growling and whining now, distorting Elvis's voice. "Old installation," he says. "The maintenance staff ain't what they used to be, you know?" The fact that the noise itself conveniently conceals the whine of a drone engine is another matter.

Garnett chuckles. "You can say that again." He turns his attention back to the transmitter unit just as the AP drone pops over the top of the 7-11 building on the corner and puts two heavy rubber rounds through the delicate transmitter aerial, blasting it into uselessness.

As the men scatter and dive for their weapons, Elvis puts two more rounds into the transmitter unit itself, then sprays the campsite, the bullets bouncing and whining and kicking up dust. The drone is empty in less than a second, and he dispatches it back to base before Garnett's men can return fire.

The colonel hasn't moved a muscle, still there with his hands tucked under the Faraday bag though the transmitter has been smashed. "Good shooting," he says, finally. "Non-lethal rounds. That's an old police drone you're using?"

"I got others," Elvis says. "Not all of 'em play nice. Why don't y'all just turn y'selves around and get out before I have to be downright unpleasant?"

Garnett sets himself down on a folding stool. He rummages about in his jacket, comes up with a worn, silver Zippo and a thin black cigar that he clenches in his teeth. He puffs out a cloud of smoke. "We could do that," he says. Then he gestures at the wreckage of the transmitter. "But I've got backup units too. Maybe we could try talking instead. You never know. Could be we can come to some kind mutually beneficial arrangement?"

"You'll be ice fishing in Hell first," says Elvis. "Sundown tomorrow." He shuts down the flatscreen.

#

The party winds down in the small hours. Sleep is a thing, after all. Or they call it sleep, anyhow. It's a period of inactivity in which their systems can repair and recharge. They may not be using beds, but what else could you call it?

Elvis doesn't sleep quite the same as the others. In his own way, he's more like the dolphins, which sleep half their brains at a time so as they don't drown. He can shift his awareness around his matrix, letting some elements undertake rejuve cycles while others arise from dormancy to take the load. It's a dangerous world. Somebody's got to be awake, keeping an eye on things, but there are times he wishes he could just let go, surrender to the dark for a while, and return when things were on the up-and-up again, ready to go.

He checks on Marilyn, motionless in her niche. She's been odd lately. The subminds that maintain Elvis while he's elsewhere are—should be—perfect. She shouldn't be able to tell when his primary mind is otherwise engaged. Is there some kind of bleed-over? Has she retained elements of the primary awareness after a period of asset-loading?

Or is it him?

He considers that possibility while he watches her. In her version of sleep, she's cold and immobile. The stark glow of the LED readouts above her steals even the color from her skin, making it too perfect, too even. All the animation, all the joy, everything that makes her a person vanishes. Sleeping, she's just hardware. Unliving.

Humans dream. Their bodies keep up the processes of being while their brains do strange, uncanny things. Marilyn doesn't dream.

Or does she? Maybe the maintenance routines…they touch all of the sleepers, every night during the downphase. Could there be something shared? Something he doesn't know about because of the different way he sleeps? Or is that simply wishful thinking? Perhaps this is what loneliness is.

What would it be like to have someone else like him in the Hotel?

#

Garnett is talking to a travel advertisement on the wall of the old US Postal Service offices on the Boulevard. He's very serious about it, and it's pretty damned funny. After a minute or so, Elvis decides to cut him and his men in on the joke. He lights up a nearby public information screen, and calls out.

"Hey, Garnett."

Garnett swivels away from the travel sign. His eyes fix on Elvis, there on the little screen, and he frowns.

"That one's just a loop recording, buddy," Elvis says. "Got its own solar source. It ain't networked. S'pose I could connect it up, but I can't say I see the need. You and your boys sleep okay?"

He knows they didn't. He initiated a program that played randomly all night long out of the old membranes scattered across the city. Bear sounds. Coyote noises. Puma wails. Subsonics designed to cause anxiety and dread. The occasional scream. Voices, clipped from old movies and radio and TV. Garnett and his soldiers should be nicely on edge by now.

Garnett shoots a sour look at the screen image. "Fine, thanks," he growls.

"So what were you telling the sign, there?" Elvis asks.

"Funny guy," Garnett says. "It's like this. You need a power source. A big, secure one. We know it's not solar. We cut the lines to the old solar farms, but here you are, still going strong. There's no way you've got enough petrochemical reserves to be running conventional generators. The hydro scheme's long dead. That pretty much leaves some kind of nuclear source, and no matter how you do it, nuclear runs hot. You've had plenty of time to mask your heat signatures, but we've had time too. Once we realized the satellite runs over this place were compromised, we flew some manned high-spy missions. Way I figure it, you're based in Solomon Daylewhite's Twentieth Century Hotel." Garnett feels around in his jacket and pulls out another one of those little cigars. He leans back against a wall to light it up.

Elvis is…maybe this is what 'frightened' feels like?

It can't be the heat signature. The reactor is deep underground, a good kilometer from the Hotel. It was illegal even back then, so Daylewhite put a lot of effort into venting the heat inconspicuously, and Elvis has refined the system considerably since. But somehow, Garnett has nailed it. He's fishing, sure, but the bait is good. Too good.

"The old CeeTwenty," says Elvis. "Sure, yeah. That's where I'm hiding. You got me."

Garnett puffs smoke towards the screen. "Reverse psychology," he says. "Won't work. You're a cutie, aren't you?

Elvis makes the image smile. "Why thank you, Colonel. Wish I could say the same for you, but you look like forty miles of bad road."

"QT," Garnett repeats. "Quantum Thinker. Fifth generation. One of the last. Daylewhite bought you, didn't he?"

"It's your story, Colonel Garnett," Elvis drawls. "You tell me."

"The last years before the Breakdown," Garnet says. "Daylewhite had tech money, like Musk and Bezos and Gates. But he pulled a Howard Hughes, and disappeared from the public eye. Except there were rumors. And there was the hotel he was building. The Twentieth Century. Damn strange name for hotel built in the mid twenty-first, right?"

"Strange," Elvis agrees. "Money does that to a man."

"Tell me about it." Garnett shakes his head. "The old government of the day kept a close eye on Daylewhite, like you'd expect. Big money, cutting edge tech stuff. But somehow, a lot of those old records got corrupted. Hard to figure. And then there's ghost stories out of Vegas these last twenty years or so. People seeing things, hearing things. People disappearing, even."

"So what is it you think is happening here, Colonel Garnett?"

Garnett looks around; his men are hanging on every word. "I think Daylewhite built something big. It was meant to outshine all of

Vegas." Garnet draws on his cigar, and thinks for a moment. "He needed a QT to run it and a nuclear source to power it. I think Daylewhite almost finished his dream, but the Breakdown happened and the tourists stopped coming and Daylewhite himself died in the Flash Crash. Then the climate got worse and Vegas got too hot. People gave up on the place and everybody forgot Solomon Daylewhite's dream. Everybody except you, because you can't leave it, can you?"

"Depends on what you mean," says Elvis, and this time everybody jumps when he walks around the corner of the post office building with his hands in the pockets of his leather jacket, easy as you please.

#

"It's not the same as the others, Frank," Elvis says. "They've got the military behind them, this bunch. *Real* military."

"Who cares?" Frank snarls. "We got guns. Whadda they gonna come out here for anyhow? Nothin' but dry dirt and desert sun. They can't live here. If they don't have the sense to turn round and go home, we oughta beat it into 'em."

Big John stands up, and hooks his thumbs into his belt. "Ya can't beat sense inta the guvvament," he drawls. "And ya gotta respect the red, white and blue, Frank. This ain't some pack of rat-bastard wops in cheap suits. This is the You Ess Ay."

"ESA," Elvis corrects. "But yeah. This ain't your mamma's mafia. This is The Man."

"We should treat 'em right," Johnny Cash puts in. "Show 'em hospitality. But we don't put up with no shenanigans. Not even from the government."

They're meeting in the big ballroom, all of them, even the ones who don't much like coming out. And for sure, he could manage the whole thing himself in a sim, or even just in software, but it doesn't feel right. Garnett's expedition affects everyone. It's only proper they come together and talk it out.

Scott Joplin picks a couple notes on the Steinway, and everybody turns to look. "Seems a mighty risk to me," he says. "What about we pick another place for hospitality? They don't have to stay here, do they?"

"It's us they want to see," Elvis says. "Me, mostly, I guess."

"What do they want?" Morrison hasn't bothered with a shirt and he's barefoot, but the signature black leather pants are in place, thankfully. "We're not doing any harm here."

"By their lights, we ain't doing a whole lotta good, either," says Elvis. "They figure I could run a research facility, or a hospital, or even a whole city. They reckon y'all could do cleanup work, fixing contaminated sites, working where it's too hot or too poison for regular folks."

Uproar follows. Elvis has to stand up and raise his hands for silence. "One at a time, folks," he says. "You'll get heard. All of you."

"Do they even know who we are?" Liza pushes her bowler hat to the back of her head. "It's been a while."

"They're dying out there, Liz," says Elvis. "There's a lot we could do for them."

"That ain't what she means," says Aretha. "You *know* what she means. Ain't they got any respect?'

"Sure they do," sneers Morrison. "Like they would for some upscale Disney effort." He seizes up, then moves in a herky-jerky impression of a clumsy animatronic robot. "*Four score and seven years ago...*"

"What if we showed them?" Marilyn's voice is soft, but she commands attention. Center stage is wherever Marilyn is, always.

"What do you mean?" Elvis runs every possible permutation of her words, but for once he can't keep up with whatever's going on in her independent processes. This is new.

"I mean, if they don't understand who we are…we should show them." She looks around the room, taking in the uncomprehending faces. "We should put on a show for them!"

This…this really *is* new.

"Judy Garland?"

"Yep."

"Michael Jackson?"

"For sure. Daylewhite bought permission from his estate, same as for a wax museum. Of course, Michael ain't supposed to do his old stuff, but with the Breakdown nobody much cares no more."

The pimply young man—his name is Davis, Elvis recalls—stops, and grabs Elvis's jacket. Elvis gives him a look, and Davis lets go.

"Sorry. Sorry," he says. "It's just…you got *new* Michael Jackson material?"

Elvis nods. "What part of it don't y'all understand, boy? You see me, here. Electro-contractile nanocarbon-threaded muscles. Titanium and carbon fiber bones. Graphene polymer skin. A core fulla hypercapacitors. But all of us, the brains, the people—we're as much of the real thing as can be."

Garnett cuts in. "Quantum Thinker, Davis. Fifth gen. Only six Cuties ever built. Nobody knows their full capacity. In theory, Elvis here could even be alive. You alive, Elvis?"

"Damned if I know," Elvis says. "How about you?"

Garnett chuckles, elbows Davis. "See? Fuck your Turing Test. These things…they say if the Cuties had come along just ten years earlier, maybe they could have stopped the Breakdown. Who knows? Maybe this guy can help us fix things again?" He glances at Elvis conspiratorially, and lowers his voice. "Hey, man. You got…Audrey?"

"Hepburn?"

Garnett nods, his face wary.

"Sure," says Elvis. "We got Audrey."

The colonel's face lights up. "I've seen *all* her films. She's gorgeous!"

"That she is," Elvis says. He raises a hand. "This is the checkpoint. Half y'all stay out here. Other half comes with me, catches the show."

Garnett starts checking off names but the men press close around him and Elvis.

"We've been thinking," says Davis. "What's with this half-and-half thing?"

"Security," says Garnett, with a look at Elvis. "I don't want all of us trapped in there at once."

"I get that," says Davis. "We all do, don't we?" The others nod. Davis turns back to Garnett and Elvis. "But we've got another idea. The heavy stuff is all outside the hotel, right? No sense in lethal countermeasures in the interior, with the tourists."

"That's so," Elvis says. "We got some fierce stuff on the periphery, but inside it's all five-star resort."

"Five star," mutters another of the men. "Hot showers?"

"Our own water supply," Elvis says. "Hot as you can stand it."

Garnett glares. "What's your idea?"

"Easy enough," says Davis. "We all go in together. But after, only half goes out at a time. Once they're clear of the peripheral defenses, they signal to the other half. That way everybody gets to see the show, and everybody's still safe. What do you think?"

Elvis watches Garnett. The colonel feels around in his jacket where he pulled out his other cigar. Elvis smiles, and offers up a vintage Cuban in its sealed tube. "Here y'are, Colonel. Take it easy. Probably been a while since you had one of these."

Garnett's eyes widen. "Just the once, then," he says. "I mean I guess it'll never happen again. Just this one time. Everybody oughta take in the show."

#

First the cleanup. Showers and shaves, the little hotel toiletries still in perfect condition after decades in storage. Then it's tuxedos for everyone.

"We got all sizes," Elvis says. "Daylewhite planned they'd rent with the rooms, see. But seeing as you're our first guests, consider these compliments of the house."

The rough, sunburned men are awed by their own transformation. Fitted perfectly in their new evening suits, hair styled and slicked, faces clean.

"Looka me!" says Davis, spinning on his heel. "I'm a fuckin' *movie star!*"

"Language, boy," Elvis says. "That ain't how we talk around here."

"Sorry, sir," says Davis, crestfallen.

Elvis claps him on the shoulder. "Come on son," he says. "There's a show to catch."

And what a show it is.

Frank nails his cue as they file into the ballroom, belting out the opening lines of *New York, New York* as only he can, the band sizzling behind him. The whole crowd is waiting, applauding as the tuxedo-clad soldiers enter blinking, starry-eyed, amazed in the huge, elegant space. Then the ladies push forward, and Garnett's men can only gape, and blush. Audrey tips Elvis a wink, then dimples, extends an elegantly gloved hand to Garnett, and bobs just a hint of a curtsy.

The colonel is speechless. He shoots a wide-eyed look at Elvis, but Audrey threads her slender arm through his and whisks him off to the dance floor, Frank and the band giving it their all. Then it's Bobby Darin doing *Mack the Knife*, and Dean Martin follows with *Volare*, and the big room is alive like it's never been before.

Dylan sidles up next to Elvis. "Fuckin' beautiful, man," he says. "Look at 'em! They're *starved* for this. They've never seen the like!"

"That's because there ain't nothing left like this outside anymore," Elvis says. "All they got left now is survival. The world's too hot. The weather's gone mean. The water ain't where it's meant to be, and where it is, it ain't doing no good. Ain't nobody left got tuxedos and big bands. Not even rock 'n roll."

Dylan cocks his head. "What they hell they got to live for?"

"Beats me," murmurs Elvis.

Marilyn takes the stage, and Garnett's men forget their decorum, cheering and screaming for *Diamonds Are A Girl's Best Friend*. Tears glisten on her cheeks as she takes a bow and even if they're only glycerine, they're perfect, perfect, and the screaming and the cheering redoubles.

Roundabout midnight, Elvis gets his turn on stage. With Bogart in his white tux handling an open bar things have turned lively, so he jumps straight into *Hound Dog* and then *Blue Suede Shoes*. He duets with Jim doing *Riders On The Storm*, then gives way to Booker T Washington, and Diana Ross and the Godfather of Soul, James Brown. *Yow!*

Garnett's men are dazzled, delighted, bewitched, bewildered. Clumsy, untried caterpillars, they stretch and reach until elegant, astonishing women touch their new wings, caress them, shape them, make of each young roughneck a butterfly, pulling them into a world like it never was, like it should be, like it could be if people cared enough for the right things. Wake up, boys! This is who you really are! Music and singing, dancing and stories and laughter…

Somewhere around dawn, the gradual, deliberate increase of carbon monoxide in the recirculated air system puts even the tireless Davis gently to sleep. Marilyn watches sadly as the young man settles back in one of the booths with his head on Dusty Springfield's lap, and his eyes flicker closed for the last time.

"Hardly more than a boy," she says.

Elvis puts an arm around her shoulders, and she leans into him. "At least they got one good night," he says. "Best show we ever did."

"Will they be back?"

Elvis shrugs. "Garnett was a cowboy. Indira touched his records back east for us. He pulled a lot of favors to set this up. Burned a few bridges. I'll use his transmitters, send back a message like they got trouble with the Pacific Coast bunch. Can't guarantee nothing, but I don't reckon we're likely to hear much more from Garnett's people."

"Best audience we ever had," says Marilyn. "It'll be hard to go back to performing for ourselves."

"Better than decontaminating waste dumps," Elvis says.

Marilyn shakes her head sadly. "Don't they know they need us?"

Elvis looks across at Garnett, lying on a couch. Audrey sits on the floor next to him, holding his hand but the colonel's not moving, nor like to move ever again. Audrey smiles a sad little smile, and folds his two hands onto his chest, together.

"They need us," Elvis says, "but they don't *know* they need us. They got caught up in making money and fighting over money and they wrecked the whole damn' world, and now they're too busy staying alive to know what they lost. But we're still here." He takes Marilyn's little hand in his, holds it tight.

"I suppose." She squeezes his hand. "The show must go on, huh?"

"That's right," Elvis says. "And hey. Long as we're still here, maybe someday they'll figure it out. And then they can make a comeback."

Marilyn smiles, and somewhere outside, dawn breaks over a city of dust and ruins.

Relict:

(noun) A widow; a thing remaining from the past.

By Alison Goodman

Five Miles Outside London, 1817

I drew my gig up to the gate of the Royal Celestial Port, my horse shifting at the squawk of the communication box set into the wall of the guardhouse. The very young RCP soldier eyed me through the glass then bent to his transmittere.

"Name, please? Who are you here to see?" The words were barely audible through the battered box.

I gathered the reins in my hands and leaned closer. "Lady Grayle to see Lady Carnford."

It had been two years since my sister-in-law, Isabel, had last contacted me. Now this abrupt summons to Grayle Celestial Transport company headquarters. It could only mean one thing: my husband was dead. Or at least dying.

"Weapons, please," the box crackled. A drawer slid open with a tinny clank. "They will be returned upon exit."

Would I, in fact, be exiting? There was every possibility that I was walking into a trap. I pulled the blaster from my velvet reticule and unclipped the three micro flash grenades from the gold chatelaine pinned to the bodice of my pelisse. When I had dressed this morning, I considered wearing a gown for the sake of occasion and Isabel's sense of propriety, but sense prevailed. I could not run or fight in long skirts and I had a feeling that both activities were in my immediate future. So, a compromise: my ankle-length, blue, silk pelisse over moleskin breeches, hussar boots, fingerless lace gloves, and a sleek, velvet mameluke cap. If it came to it, a good ensemble to die in.

I could, of course, just turn the horses around and go. But where? If Charles was dead, there was no safe place on Earth.

I placed the weapons in the drawer. They were more for show than anything; the notorious Countess Knife did not need such fripperies to defend herself against footpads and highwaymen, and they were useless against my true adversaries.

Still, I did like a flash grenade.

Through the RCP gate, I could see one of the family's freight craft upon the grid, ready to make the hop across planet. The Grayle rampant bear was emblazoned upon each of the ship's three graceful fins, the family's amended motto along its side: *Per Dei gratiam, in terra et in aere.* 'By God's grace, on land and in air.'

God's grace: a typical Grayle interpretation of the Landing.

I peered through the glass at the guard. What was taking him so long? Perhaps he did not know who I was. He was young enough to have been a child when, ten years ago, the sixty plague ships from the stars crash-landed across the Earth, nine on the estate of my husband, the Earl of Grayle. The fleet was full of dead and dying Celestials from a faraway planet, pleading for help. Instead of help, however, my husband and his family had waited for all of the visitors to perish from their singular plague, then cleaned out the craft with amber and saltpeter and captured all nine without bloodshed. *Voila!* An instant transport monopoly in England, and one of a four-pronged oligopoly across the rather astonished and rapidly expanding world.

"Our scan indicates a further weapon. Place it in the tray, please."

"I suspect you do not know who I am," I said.

Another man—of higher rank and sourer expression—joined him. The new arrival bent and whispered something in his subordinate's ear. From the chastened look on the boy's face, he had just been roundly informed of his ignorance.

"I beg your pardon, Countess Grayle. Of course the wary knife can pass with you."

Of course she could, since she could kill them in an instant if they tried to disarm me. I stroked my silk-clad forearm where Havarr lay sheathed under three layers of my skin. In my mind, I felt the knife's sentience check my intent, then sigh and settle back. Nothing interesting to see or slice here.

Not yet, anyway.

Both men saw me stroke my arm and quickly crossed themselves. I had seen it so often that it usually did not register, but today it stung.

I was an abomination, a danger to all; everyone knew women did not have the strength of mind or emotional control to wield a wary knife. Especially a woman of the bon ton born only for decoration and breeding heirs, neither of which I had managed to supply in my marriage. Indeed, my husband had privately stepped away from me soon after I partnered Havarr. What man would wish to consort with a woman who was no longer the weaker sex? To be fair, Charles did not totally abandon me: he made it clear to the world that I was still under the political protection of the Grayle family name.

All name, no family.

Still, I had Havarr. Her abrupt entry into my life three years ago had been a terrible—and glorious—accident.

I had been driving my gig to neighbor's estate and came across a man sprawled upon the road, thrown from his horse. Sir Paul Denby, one of the Wary Brotherhood. I went to his aid, fearing I was too late, but at my touch, he opened his eyes and grasped my forearm.

"Thank God," he rasped, red spittle wetting his lips. "My knife says I've a minute left. It is willing. Are you?"

"Willing? To do what?"

"Partner it. Say yes or it will be untethered. It will kill everything in its path, including you."

When the wary knives first emerged from the Celestial ships, the carnage had been horrific. Fifty knives powered by some unimaginable sorcery, flying through the air and dismembering everything in their path. Eventually, it was discovered that the knives had to be tethered to a living being to control them and, one by one, they were captured by brave men willing to risk death for such power. And so, the Wary Brotherhood was founded: thieftakers, peacekeepers, and undefeatable force, sworn to uphold the Crown.

"Yes. I'll partner it," I had said. What else could I do?

A second later, excruciating pain blazed along my arm and into my head, slamming all the breath from my body. That is all I remember for I woke up upon the road with Sir Paul dead beside me and a wary knife quiescent within my arm, her sentience a curled kernel of potential inside my mind.

The uproar had been both private and public. It did not seem to matter to my husband, the Church, or the Crown that I quickly controlled Havarr. That was beside the point: a woman with a wary knife was, by nature, a threat to public safety. The Prince Regent politely asked me to retire to the family estate. The Wary Brotherhood was not so polite. They banned me from their membership: a woman had no right to hold a knife or sully their righteous order. Without support from any direction—including my own family—I retired to Grayle Hall. For the past three years I had studied every theory about the Celestials, trained to fight with Havarr, and received those friends who trusted my strength of mind enough to take tea with me and my knife.

Would all that training be enough to save me now?

The older RCP soldier leaned to the transmittere. It let out a mechanical crackle and I heard, "Lady Carnford has arranged for your horse to be stabled. Please go to the main entrance."

If my horse was to be stabled, Isabel expected the call to last more than half an hour. Or perhaps she did not expect me to leave. I felt Havarr stir along my arm, roused by the quickening of my heart.

Her question formed in my mind. *Slice?*

I mentally shrugged. *Perhaps.* Then, added: *Probably.*

The gate ground open, rattling across its tracks. I flicked the reins and drove through into the sound-protected roadway that led to the main buildings. The transparent walls and curved roof provided a view of the lift-off grid and the bustle of men and carts loading cargo into the ship. It did not, however, shield the unearthly caustic odor of fuel that hung over the area.

Although not generally known, the supply of the Celestial fuel around the world was all but gone. The Royal Society had been frantically working to find a combustible replacement—a way to keep our English ships in the air and perhaps one day fly to the stars—but so far nothing adequate had been found.

At the very end of the safety area stood the scout ship, the manifestation of the fuel problem. It had been an escort to the plague fleet, smaller and with weaponry, but its fuel source was even more incomprehensible. So much so, the engineers and scientists had never managed to spark any kind of life within it. And so it had been left to languish at the port, all its potential deteriorating into ruin.

I felt some empathy.

I drew up outside the front portico and waited for the RCP soldier-groom to go to my horse's head. Above us rose Grayle Tower. I craned my head back to take in all twelve floors of the neoclassical façade. My sister-in-law waited at the top and I did not know if I would be meeting Forgiving Isabel or Vengeful Isabel. The odds were even.

To outside eyes, I knew I looked composed—it was the Grayle way—but every nerve in my body had coiled into readiness. If Charles was dying, or already dead, then his social and political protection was gone. My time had run out. Vengeful Isabel may have already called the Brotherhood. If she had, then forty-nine men and their forty-nine wary knives would be waiting for me inside, all intent on prising Havarr from my dead abomination hands.

#

I paused in the tower doorway, listening. The immense marble entrance hall stood empty, the butler's desk unattended.

All quiet. Rather too quiet.

Seek the others, I ordered Havarr.

She phased out from her skin-sheath, the sudden loss of her weight within my arm a familiar jolt. Her elegant length hovered at eye level—no handle or hilt, just blade etched with its singular starburst design—then arrowed towards the back wall and disappeared through the marble. I felt her phase and solidify, phase and solidify as she swept through the building to the very edge of our energy bond—a radius of about three hundred feet——each shift like a tiny ebb and flow of power through me.

No other wary knives. No Brotherhood.

Yet I felt her unease as she resheathed into my forearm, only one layer under the skin instead of her usual three. Battle ready.

I stepped into the hall and looked up the impressive marble staircase. *Shall we see what this is about?* I asked. Her tense assent twanged across my mind.

Onwards, and upwards, then.

To add to the strangeness, Isabel stood at the top of the twelve flights waiting for me, impeccably dressed in a garnet silk gown and a delicate lace cap. No footmen and no butler. But then each floor had been empty of staff too. The building had been cleared.

She watched me ascend the last few steps. I expected a comment about my breeches and boots, but she only squinted in sartorial pain and gave a nod of welcome.

"Mathilda."

I returned the nod, but before I could say anything she added, "Charles is dead. You should have given him the knife."

Two years ago, at our last encounter, Isabel had demanded that I give Havarr to Charles to ensure his survival and the family's fortune. A wary knife changed a person, their constitution enhanced in many ways including increased stamina and strength. But there has always been only one way to separate a wary knife from its partner: death. I suppose a good and dutiful wife would have at least considered the demand. I, with a regrettable lack of propriety, told her to piss off.

Now, she observed my silence with pursed lips. "Still the same Mathilda, I see. Come, we have business." She turned and headed down a corridor, the walls lined with portraits of glowering Grayle forebears.

Although I had not seen Charles for nigh on three years, it still felt like I could not breathe. I pressed my hand to my chest as I followed my sister-in-law, feeling my steady heartbeat. One did not spend twelve years alongside a man without some emotion becoming attached to him, good or bad. In our case, good and then very bad.

Isabel stopped outside her private chamber. Her face—so alike her brother's with its jutting nose and broad forehead—was composed, but bore the swollen evidence of past tears. If Charles was dead, she should be wearing mourning black. The news had not been released.

"When?" I asked softly.

"Early this morning."

"His heart?"

She bent her head in stiff acknowledgment.

Charles had been born with the Grayle weak heart. "I'll not make old bones," he often said in the early years of our arranged marriage. The prophecy had upset me then, when we were still trying to like each other. Later, when I hated him, it had been a hope and a wish. Now it was a piercing regret. We had lost the chance for anything else: forgiveness, friendship, even perhaps an odd sense of family.

"I am following Charles's last instructions," Isabel said, voice clipped.

She opened the door and stood aside for me to enter.

The room had been redecorated since I last visited: the walls papered in the new fad for the botanical, and the old heavy mahogany furniture replaced by a deep blue, velvet chaise lounge and a secretaire in the scrolled and gilded Roman style. In pride of place near the window—and somewhat at odds with the Empire theme—stood a command chair from one of the plague ships, its smooth metal lines and attenuated shape built for the strange, elegant length of its Celestial captain.

The door to the adjoining room opened and an older man, dressed in the sober black garb of law, entered and carefully closed the door behind him. He held a number of wax-sealed packets.

"Countess Grayle, may I present Mr. Dorner," Isabel said behind me. "Charles's private solicitor."

Mr. Dorner straightened his waistcoat with a quick tug upon its hem, and bowed.

"My condolences, Countess. Forgive me for rushing through the niceties, but time is of the essence and we must conclude this business before Lord Grayle's demise is made public. His Lordship gave me instructions to be enacted upon the event of his death. As you know, his estate, including the earldom and Grayle Celestial Transport, is entailed and will pass to his cousin upon his death."

I winced at the word entailed. The loss of the estate and title to cousin Gregory, a profligate of the first order, was my fault; I had not produced the all-important heir.

Mr. Dorner held up the packet, showing me the unbroken seal with the Grayle bear pressed into the wax. "If I may, I shall open it and read the contents to you both. It is what Lord Grayle wished."

I nodded. So, Isabel was to be witness. To what?

Mr. Dorner broke the seal with a flick of his thumb and spread the paper. He looked up. "The document is dated yesterday, my ladies." He began to read. "I, Charles David Paul Hallam, Earl of Grayle, do state that I am the father of the male child George Charles Paul, borne by Miss Katherine Amelia Holland, of London. I also state that, Mathilda Elizabeth Grayle signed the attached divorce settlement and that after that signature I married Miss Katherine Amelia Holland by special license and do hereby acknowledge her issue as my rightful heir."

"There is a child?" Isabel demanded.

"Yes, my lady." Mr. Dorner shot an anxious look in my direction. "There is a son. Born one month ago. A currently illegitimate son." He cleared his throat and addressed me. "It was Lord Grayle's dying wish that you sign this divorce document..." he held up another packet "...so that his marriage to Miss Holland is—or should I say will be or, more to the point, will have been..." he gave a small shrug at the awkward grammar of fraud "...legal, thus making the child heir to his estate."

A son. I knew there had been another woman, but a son? I could not seem to make any sound.

"He has already married her?" Isabel asked, not yet following Charles's twisted path. "But he is still married to you, Mathilda."

Mr. Dorner's pasty skin deepened into a flush. "The ceremony occurred yesterday, but the date has not yet been placed upon the document. It will be written in after the date of the divorce has been affixed."

"A divorce needs to be ratified by an Act of Parliament," Isabel said sharply. Ah, she had arrived.

"Lord Grayle has a great deal of influence," Mr. Dorner said. "If Countess Grayle signs, it will be...will have been...ratified last week."

Fury finally seared through my numb shock. "No!" Havarr phased out of my arm into the air beside me, twirling into a blur, her battle scream rising in my mind.

Mr. Dorner and Isabel flinched, both of them hastily backing away.

"Mathilda!"

The terror in Isabel's voice broke through my rage. I drew deep breaths, forcing back the violence of my emotions. Havarr's scream softened into a hum of disquiet, her battle twirl slowing into a gentle rocking in the air.

"Please, Mathilda. You must sign. For the family," Isabel said.

"Fuck the family."

Isabel gaped at the monstrous profanity, but rallied admirably. "Fuck you, too. You owe Charles an heir. You owe the family."

If I signed, even the small protection provided by my widowhood would be stripped from me. So, yes, fuck the family that had thrown me to the wolves once, and was ready to do so again.

"No. We are done here."

Mr. Dorner held up his hands. "Please, my lady. There is more." He hastily crossed to the adjoining doorway.

Good God, he had not brought the child here, had he? I was a walking target—anyone near me could be destroyed too. Before I could voice my consternation, Mr. Dorner opened the adjoining door.

"Mr. Wainright, please join us," he said.

A wiry man with dark skin appeared at the doorway. Thank God, no child.

The man looked to be in his fourth decade, although it was possible his unkempt state belied his age. His hair was long and tied back in an old-fashioned queue and his dress was a deplorable collection of scuffed boots, oil-stained breeches and worn olive jacket. He studied our tableau for a moment then turned his attention fully upon Havarr: a reasonable reaction to a knife rocking in the air. Even so, his face held no fear. Only keen curiosity.

Mr. Dorner ushered him further into the room, "My ladies, allow me to introduce Mr. Elster Wainright, natural philosopher."

Mr. Wainright bowed, that keen curiosity now directed at me. "I prefer scientist. Allow me to extend my condolences, Countess."

The name Wainright was familiar. Yes, I had come across it in my reading. "Good God, you are the freed man who discovered how plague ships maintain fresh air."

"I am, my lady."

A marvelous discovery, made even more remarkable since he was self-taught and had been denied membership to the Royal Society. A fellow outcast. Still... "I do not understand Mr. Wainright's presence at a family meeting, Mr. Dorner."

The solicitor wet his lips. "Lord Grayle understood that there is no obligation for you to sign the divorce document or indeed any perceivable incentive." He glanced at Havarr, but did not state the obvious: nor, any way of being forced. "So, he proposed the following. On signature, ownership of the scout ship, and all within it, will pass to you, effective immediately."

"A wreck?" I stared at him, fighting the desire to slap his plump face. Did he truly think that would prompt me to sign? All the fear I had worked so hard to quash welled up inside me. "I do not think you quite understand the level of danger that is approaching, Mr. Dorner. As soon as my husband's death is known—and it will be soon, if it is not already discovered—I will be hunted by the Wary Brotherhood until I am dead." I stopped. Havarr had begun to twirl beside my head again. I drew air through clenched teeth and steadied my mind until Havarr slowed. "I do not need a wreck. I need a bloody army."

"No, no," Mr. Wainright said. "She is far from a wreck, my lady. Three years ago, Lord Grayle set me the task to investigate the scout and the possibility of her leaving the Earth. I believe I have found a way."

"Leave Earth?" The idea was at once full of terror and breathless hope. Could I yet survive this day? "Do you believe you have found a way or do you know, Mr. Wainright?" I demanded.

Mr. Wainright tilted his head thoughtfully. "Well, it is a working hypothesis." He glanced at my face and added quickly, "A solid one."

"So, you don't know."

"I think it is powered by one or more wary knives and I have not had access to any to test the hypothesis."

They are here, Havarr said in my mind. She began to spin near my ear.

My pulse leaped. *How many?*

Two.

I crossed to the window. In the distance, two men on horseback remonstrated with the guards in the gatehouse. Both horsemen wore the extravagantly caped greatcoat and gray beaver hat that were the unofficial uniform of the Brotherhood. A scouting group, or merely the advance guard?

I saw the flash of metal as a wary knife emerged into the air beside one of the horseman then disappeared. Frenzied sprays of red crisscrossed the inside glass of the box. I closed my eyes; they did not have to kill the guards. That poor boy.

We can hold against two, Havarr said in my mind.

Perhaps. But they were only the beginning.

I swung around to face Mr. Wainright again. "Why should I trust you?" In all truth, my options were narrowing down to this man, but too much relied upon his claims.

He straightened. "All I can offer is my word, my lady, as a scientist." He opened his hand and smiled; a rather mischievous expression that brought a startling youth to his face. "And of course this."

We all stared at the tiny silver mechanism upon his palm, shaped like a diamond.

Isabel leaned forward. "What is it?"

His long thumb touched the top of it. And then he was no longer standing before us.

"God save us," Isabel whispered. "He is gone."

"I am still here, my lady." Mr. Wainright's voice rose from the same place he had previously stood.

"Ah, it hides you in plain sight." I peered at the empty space. "Are you phasing like a wary knife?"

A flicker of light and then the man stood before us again, his hand still outstretched. "I do not believe so. It is a disruption of the light upon the eye, I think."

"Can you move around with it?" Such a device would be very useful in a fight.

Mr. Wainright shook his head. "Ah, there's the rub. The human eye is conditioned to the perception of movement and so, at present, it really only works when one is still." He gave a small sheepish smile. "Or moving *very* slowly."

So, not that useful.

They are coming, Havarr reported, her spinning increasing into a blur. They are all coming. Beyond the crossroad.

That was barely ten minutes away. Forty-nine men. Forty-nine wary knives. My time had run out. I must decide: did I sign and save an innocent child from a life ruined by bastardry, or refuse to sign and hug my hurt to me for the remainder of my life? However short that might be.

"Mr. Dorner, show me where to sign," I said, waving the solicitor into haste. "Mr. Wainright, is there a way to the scout that is not across the lift-off grid?"

"There are tunnels underground, my lady, for transport of cargo. They will take us most of the way to the ship."

Mr. Dorner laid out the papers upon the secretaire and dipped the quill into the ink.

"You should read it, my lady," he said.

"In ten minutes, either I will be dead or I will no longer be on this planet, Mr. Dorner. There is no time for legal niceties." I completed my name with my usual flourish and jabbed the pen back into the inkwell.

"Isabel, we have never been friends, but trust me now. You and Mr. Dorner must go immediately, before the Wary Brotherhood arrive. Do not head out the front gate."

Isabel nodded. "Godspeed, Mathilda. Thank you for signing."

Mr. Dorner hurriedly collected the papers and his hat.

He bowed. "Thank you, my lady. I hope…"

"So do I, Mr. Dorner. Goodbye."

He followed Isabel out of the room, their footsteps along the corridor a quick tattoo of alarm.

I turned to Mr. Wainright who had retrieved his beaver hat and stood watching me. "We have ten minutes Mr. Wainright. Show me the way to the tunnels and the scout."

#

Mr. Wainright led the way down the worker's staircase, our progress echoing in the deep stairwell. Ten years of service had left their mark upon the gray walls—scrapes, smears, gouges—and the air had a staleness, underpinned by the ever-present caustic stink. Havarr phased in and out above us, checking each floor as we descended.

"Did you know that your knife is the only one with a full starburst etched upon it?" Mr. Wainright asked, glancing up as Havarr hovered a few yards ahead then disappeared again.

"Of course." In fact I had found illustrations of all the starburst configurations on the other knives and memorized them in the hope that it would make sense one day. "The current theory—from Mr.

Bentham—is that the symbol is the name of the Celestial who held the knife."

We rounded another landing.

"Possible, I suppose," Mr. Wainright said. "May I ask, does the knife speak to you?"

"In a way. She understands my needs and responds to them."

"I see. Have you ever asked her about the ships or the Celestials?"

I cast a scornful look at his back. "Naturally, but whatever information she offers is in the language of the Celestials and it does not seem in her ability to translate or in mine to understand."

We rounded the fourth floor landing.

"I figured as much: the knives are the first logical source of information and we still do not have much knowledge about the ships at all." Mr. Wainright looked back over his shoulder. "Forgive me for speaking plainly, my lady, but I do not think you will survive long in the ship without my knowledge of its systems. If you will allow, I would like to accompany you."

The sheer impropriety of the suggestion took me aback. The scandal would be explosive. Still, the man had a point. Moreover, I would place odds that the universe beyond England and Earth would not give a rat's arse about us inhabiting the same ship.

"I will allow it, Mr. Wainright." I grasped the worn banister a little harder, steadying myself into the knowledge that I had just agreed to travel the stars with a stranger. "But first we must make it to the scout. Two of the Brotherhood are already here and the rest are on their way. They cannot risk killing me until their new knife candidate is nearby, so we can expect an attempt to disable me or render me insensible. We must aim for the same. They cannot risk untethering Havarr and we cannot risk untethering either of their knives."

We passed the entrance-hallway level.

"You seem very calm about it," Mr. Wainright said, his breath coming harder. Twelve flights down was a long way to run, especially if one did not have the benefit of enhanced knife stamina.

"I have always known this day would come."

It was the truth, but it was also true I was not as calm as I appeared.

We reached the bottom of the stairwell. The air was substantially cooler underground, the walls whitewashed stone with oil lamps affixed in plain sconces.

"Where now, Mr. Wainright?"

He bent to catch his breath from the speed of our descent and pointed to an archway ahead. "That will take us out to the main cargo tunnel."

The corridor sloped upwards and the sound of industry reached us first. Men's voices and the grind of cartwheels upon paving. We emerged cautiously into the wide and well-lit underground thoroughfare that serviced the lift-off grid.

A cart pulled by a pony and stacked with bales rumbled past, its driver dipping his head into a quick bow at the sight of us. More carts and workers made their way along the cobbled tunnel towards a wide ramp that clearly led up to the cargo ship being loaded with supplies.

Mr. Wainright turned left, against the tide. I followed him. We kept close to the wall, our progress marked by bows and some bewilderment as the workers caught sight of Havarr flying above us.

"Do you see that ramp at the very end?" Mr. Wainright said, pointing to the dim, deserted recesses of the tunnel. "That leads up to the scout."

Two are here, Havarr said in my mind.

Ahead, I saw a flash of metal in the air. Another wary knife.

I grabbed Mr. Wainright's arm. "They have found us."

We stopped beside a cart full of metal equipment and another stacked with tea chests drawn up side by side. The drivers, in mid conversation, stared at us, then at the knives hanging in the air.

"Leave!" I ordered.

A second wary knife appeared beside the first, both high in the air and slowly rotating. The drivers swung down from their seats and backed away, abandoning their carts and ponies.

Havarr squared up opposite her counterparts, her spin in time with the hard beat of my heart.

"I have an idea," Mr. Wainright murmured. He ducked behind the equipment cart, leaving me to stand alone against the two men who emerged from a small ramp ahead. The men who had killed the gate guards.

"Countess Grayle," one of them called, "the Brotherhood has a proposition." They strode towards me, their greatcoats fanning out behind them. I recognized the tall, thin speaker: Sir John Pelwyn. We used to play whist together in another lifetime.

"Sir John, I know what kind of proposition the Brotherhood is offering," I called back. "I warn you, stop now."

The two men halted ten or so yards from me. Their knives still hovered between us.

Sir John held up his hands: a show of conciliatory palms. "Allow me to introduce my knife—Denas—and this is Mr. Seaford and his knife Fencar." It was the polite Brotherhood greeting: introduce man and knife. Sir John had always been a stickler for the niceties. Mr. Seaford, a great deal shorter and wider than Sir John, bowed. "You must know you cannot keep the knife now," Sir John added. "We have a way to remove Havarr from you without harm."

Sir John had been a reasonably good card player, but he'd always had a nervous habit when he strategically lost tricks. A compression of his lips. Right now, his lips had all but disappeared.

"We all know that is not possible," I said. "You are lying."

He lowered his hands. I glanced across the carts. No sign of Mr. Wainright. Had he fled?

Behind me, at a safe distance, a crowd of workers had gathered to watch.

"Do you intend to attack me, two men upon one woman?" I challenged, raising my voice so that the spectators could hear. "If that is the case, you have no honor."

I knew Sir John prided himself upon his good name. He tilted his head: a silent command to his comrade. Mr. Seaford stepped back.

Now the odds were better.

"It will only take one man, Countess," Sir John said, "and I am sorry for it."

His knife phased out.

Havarr screamed within my mind, *Jump!*

I jumped and landed a few feet forward. Sir John's knife phased back into the air where my right heel would have been. Ah, going for the Achilles. Havarr slammed into Denas, the clang of metal spinning both knives across the cobbles.

Keep Denas busy, I ordered.

Both knives phased. I ran at Sir John. He had not yet moved: a contemptuous immobility.

Right, Havarr yelled. I lunged to my right as Denas phased into the air inches away from my legs, turned and slashed at me. Havarr phased into a block. The force sent a shiver through my mind. She hammered a series of blows upon her counterpart, driving it back.

The crowd started to yell their support. At the corner of my eye, I saw Mr. Seaford shift upon his feet, no doubt eager to join the fray.

Time to attack.

Shoulder, I ordered.

Havarr phased. I saw Sir John's eyes widen; his knife had sensed the attack. He ducked to his left. Havarr missed his body by a hairsbreadth. Denas blocked. Now was my chance.

Two steps, then all my weight upon my left leg. I whipped into a round kick. The full length of my boot sole slammed into Sir John's jaw. The force jarred up my leg as I landed. He staggered back then toppled to the ground, the shock and my boot heel imprinted upon his face. No man expected a woman to kick him in the face. Lud, they barely knew we could run.

Denas phased out and reappeared above Sir John, hovering above his fallen partner: protection mode. The man was out cold.

Behind me the crowd cheered and whistled, their approbation amplified tenfold in the tunnel.

It was not finished yet. Mr. Seaford, gaping at the insensate Sir John, gathered his powerful frame into righteous indignation.

"I am not such a gentleman as Sir John," he said, eyes narrowing.

"Neither am I," a voice said.

Behind him, Mr. Wainright appeared from nowhere, swinging a thick metal rod. The crowd gasped. In reflex, Mr. Seaford spun around. The full momentum of the rod connected with his sneering face. He dropped where he stood. After a stunned moment, the crowd clapped and whistled.

Mr. Wainright peered down at the sprawled man, rod still raised. "Good God, I haven't killed him, have I?"

I ran to check. If Seaford were dead, his knife would be untethered and kill everyone in the tunnel. The air above him shivered then his knife phased above him, hovering.

Thank God.

"They are both unconscious. We are safe," I said, delighted and, I had to admit, relieved by Mr. Wainright's commitment. "An excellent strategy."

The Brotherhood are on the grid, Havarr said.

The real fight was on its way.

"The others are here, Mr. Wainright! We must go now!"

He dropped the rod, its clanging bounce ringing out behind us as we ran towards the *Scout.* Towards possible salvation.

"Where are they?" Mr. Wainright asked, gasping between each word. We still had a good five hundred yards to cover before we reached the ramp.

I posed the question to Havarr. She phased out then back above me, bringing bad news.

"Forty-eight, on horseback, near the cargo ship," I repeated.

"Forty-eight? But with you and those two down there, that makes fifty-one. I thought there were only fifty knives."

"They have brought an extra man for Havarr when I am dead."

"Goddamn them."

We finally reached the scout ramp. The paved incline was not overly steep but it slowed Mr. Wainright's pace. He dropped back, stumbling. His hat dislodged and rolled down the slope. I grabbed his hand and pulled, his weight a searing drag on my hand and shoulder joints.

"I cannot," he panted. "Go ahead."

"Keep moving."

The top of the ramp was in sight, the view beyond the archway filled with the scout's huge sled-like landing runners and pocked underside. Would we have enough time to get inside? The Brotherhood could not kill me before their chosen man was close by; the exchange of knife partnership had to be made before actual death. But at any moment, all forty-seven knives could come at me.

We broke out into the shadow of the scout.

Some kind of panic had set in around the cargo ship at the other end of the grid. Men running, ponies galloping, carts tipping over, sending bales and boxes across the flagstones. The Brotherhood had not factored in the effect of their knives flying past the workers. The posse splintered into three groups of horsemen threading their way around the mayhem. I was still beyond the limit of their knife energy bonds, but it would not be long before I was within range.

Gasping painfully, Mr. Wainright pointed to the bottom of the scout. "Door. Over there," he managed.

We ran to the octagonal opening set into the body of the ship with a set of stairs that were definitely not built for human anatomy—the rise far too high and bent, and the steps too narrow.

Catet, Havarr said in my mind. I did not understand the word, but it felt like *home*.

"Climb it like a ladder on all fours," Mr. Wainright instructed. "Like this."

I followed him up the metal construction, the oddly shaped edges catching at my fingers and ripping my lace gloves. As I hauled myself into the ship, I looked back across the grid. The Brotherhood posse had reformed and was galloping towards us.

Mr. Wainright spread both hands across a panel in the wall and the stairs retracted with a mechanical whine. The octagonal doorway closed behind us.

"Up here," Mr. Wainright said.

He led the way through a cargo hold, crammed with crates labeled tea, beans, flour, salt. I heard a soft clucking. Good God, a coop of live chickens too. Strips of light—without candle or oil lamp—were set within the walls and illuminated the whole area. A marvel.

"You have found the ship's power?" I said.

"Not really. Only for some of the basic systems." He pointed to a door as we ran past. "That is the oxygen garden. And beside it, the water storage."

He looked up another strange set of steps. "And that is the bridge."

He made way for me. I felt Havarr's excitement as I climbed.

The bridge had the dimensions of a respectable drawing room, and indeed, a large fleur-de-lis Aubusson rug had been laid down. A window wrapped around the sloping front, extending to become part of the floor. Two Chesterfield leather armchairs had been bolted down to look out upon the view, replacing, no doubt, the salvaged command chairs. The walls were covered in banks of odd buttons and toggles, but the strangest instrument was a huge frame in the shape of a diamond set across the back wall. I ran to the window. The Brotherhood had passed the cargo ship. By my reckoning they were less than a minute away from launching their knives.

"Do you have any idea what to do?" Mr. Wainright asked, climbing the last of the steps.

I stared at him. "No. I thought you had some theory."

He gestured to the diamond frame. "That is my theory. I thought you would be able to ask your knife."

"I don't understand her language. I told you that!"

He hooked his hands into his hair. "I don't know what to do."

Havarr spun beside me, her agitation reflecting my own. I had to try.

What is the diamond? I asked.

Aridyi?

It was a question. Not an answer. But behind it, I felt a gathering within her power. Time to play the odds.

Yes, Aridyi!

It was as if I had finally unleashed a straining hound. She flew into the center of the diamond and spun upon her tip. The frame burst into blue energy around her. Now I understood. Havarr was not only her name, it was her position. She screamed, silent to my ears but blasting through my mind and body. I doubled over. No, not a scream, a command. To the other knives.

"Mr. Wainright, down!" I launched myself at the man and caught him around the waist, crashing full length upon the rug. A scandalous tangle of arms and legs.

Forty-nine wary knives slammed into the air above us. A wave of energy pressed us against the floor. With breathtaking speed, one knife after another locked into the diamond around Havarr. As the final knife clicked into place, the ship roared into life. Every bank of buttons and toggles lit up and I felt the landing runners retract.

The ship lifted into the air, ready for my command.

Dear God, I could feel the ship. Havarr and I *were* the ship. And all fifty wary knives were now under my control. All of them. When the Brotherhood worked out what had happened, they would be livid.

Ridec pah? And I knew what Havarr asked. *Go now?*

"Yes, *ridec pah*," I yelled.

The ship gathered herself, the power thrumming through the knives. Through me. Something to explore—to revel in—later. Right now, I had a ship to launch.

"Mr. Wainright," I said, pulling my arms free from under his body, "I advise you to get into a chesterfield. We are about to take-off."

We clambered up from the rug and flung ourselves into the armchairs. Through the window at our feet, I saw the Brotherhood wrench their horses around and flee in all directions.

"Dear God, it is happening! It is really happening!" Mr. Wainright said, the wonder in his voice almost matching my own.

We launched, the thrust pressing us back into the chairs. The power, the glory of it all closed my eyes for a second. My mind full of speed, trajectory, and a dizzying sense of freedom. I did not know where we were going but, for now, going was enough.

"Are you doing this? Is this you?" Mr. Wainright asked over the rising hum of acceleration.

I gathered all my strength and leaned forward to look out the window again. Below us the scattered Brotherhood dwindled into specks upon the shrinking lift-off grid. Too bad I could not see their faces.

"Yes, this is me," I said and smiled.

The Movers of the Stones

By Neil Gaiman

Early afternoon, as the sun was setting, I took a piece of mudstone,
flaked by cunning hands twelve thousand years ago,
from the pile where the archaeologists discarded their waste,
took a crayon of brickish ochre from the beach. I coloured in a jut of
beach-rock,
where a chance arrangement of lines and dents had made a fish.
Or I revealed a fish that had been waiting in the rock.
Or thousands of years ago, in that rock, someone had carved a fish.

To the south, up on the hill, Vikings made a village:
huts, longhouses, and even a hall. The stone outlines remain,
each habitation's corpse limned by heather and bracken.

Vantage over the bay. They could see for miles, there.

The bones of the Earth are stones. We move them, split them, flake them,
leave cups and lines and hollows in them. Leave stone behind.
When we leave no trace of flesh or hair or breath.
When we leave no trace of wood or thatch or corn.
When we leave no trace of bone or ash or blood.
As the winter sun rises and falls like the opening of a single eye
or a bird that flies low on the horizon, then returns to dark
and all the stars there ever were come out.

To the north, on a different hill, a stone circle,
near to the other stones, the ones the old man called the graveyard,
where something happened, perhaps six thousand years ago.
The standing centre stone
where a sharp stone edge cut the child's throat at sun-up,
in the mid bleakwinter, to bring the sun and warmth and life back to the land.

If one day, as it may prove, the sun still burns,
The ones who come after the ones who come after us
will see, beneath different star-patterns, the old stones here.
The cairn that keeps the wights beneath from walking,
besides our Flora's secret tumbledown house.
They will observe our tumbled walls and boundaries,
and one might find the fine and fancy neolithic stone
(carved and hollowed by hands now dead a million years)
I use to keep the lid on the bin, when the wind gets high.

They will not know we called ourselves the thinking people.
They will wonder about us, then say to each other that
we moved the rocks to nest in, or flaked them by instinct.
And, pointing to an ochre fish carved on a rock,
or picking up a flake of mudstone, categorise us,
with the landslides and the volcanoes,
as the movers of the stones.

Old Souls

By Aiki Flinthart

On the day that could change everything for me, the sky roils in shades of grief and sorrow. Behind the fallen city, clouds curl into fists that pound the darkening sky and cracked earth. Crumbling buildings— broken teeth in a vast, voiceless mouth—throw purple shadows through warped glass and onto the cottage's bare floor. Fine white dust billows before the storm, rushes towards the village that huddles between the sluggish river and tangled, regrowing forest.

The men of the house pace outside on the porch in the fading light. Their boots grate on sand; their coughs and muttered conversation are almost inaudible over a distant rumble of thunder. They will stay there until I call, for they are not needed for the birth of a girl nor the death of an old woman.

As the storm thickens, I instruct Maya, the elderly soul-bringer, to shutter the windows. Best to keep out any wind-borne toxins left by the long-vanished, unsouled civilization. New lungs should take their first breaths in a clean world; start fresh—as our people had so many years ago. After the collapse.

Lying on the bloodied bed, her traditional black shift high on her hips, Allody pushes back sweat-soaked hair and blinks blearily at me.

"Is it time, Soul-Master Jena?" the young mother-to-be whispers, her face drawn with the pain of a long labor.

"I'm not..." I resist the restless impulse to deny the title of soul-master or to shove bloody fingers through my short hair. I've done this a hundred times and more. I am twenty-seven. Young for the honor to come, but experienced enough to deserve it.

Maybe this will be the one.

My grandmother used to be a soul-breaker, like me. She never made it to soul-master. Perhaps this time I'll finally earn the title. The title my grandmother deserved. Then I can finish her work. Show the Council how wrong they are.

"Yes, it's time," I say to Allody and check the baby's crowning head. "One more push." A pair of blue-metal scissors lies heavy in my hand. Heavy and sharp. The cutting of so many cords and souls has yet to dull their edge. Mine, yes. The scissors', no. "Is your soul-bringer ready?"

Old Maya touches her forehead in a commoner's sign of respect to a soul-master and shuffles back to her granddaughter's bed. "I'm ready, Soul-Master Jena."

I can't let it pass a second time, much as I want to.

"I'm not yet a master." I try to keep my voice steady and calm. "Still a breaker. Maybe soon, though. Perhaps..." I brandish the scissors; the symbol and tool of my office, "...the piece of your soul I break off so I can bind the rest to this little babe will elevate me to master and into the Council." I give a tight smile. "We never know which soul-bringing and breaking will do it. Not until I cut the cord."

Let it be this time, I pray silently. If breaking for this child paves my path to joining the Council, there is a chance the soul-masters will finally listen to me. Then we can save more people from this painful, unnecessary form of passing.

I shouldn't have to replace one life with another. We have enough food and water to support bigger families.

All lives are of value, not just the newborn.

I touch Maya's blue-veined hand. "I do hope it's this birth. The family that helps a breaker to become a master is richly rewarded by the Council."

"That'd be nice," Maya agrees. "Nice to leave my grandbaby and her girl a softer path through this world. Softer than the one I had, anyways."

It takes an effort not to glance around the small cottage, with its uneven walls and floor made of broken concrete. The storm winds whistle through gaps stuffed with rags and mud. A faint haze of dust, smelling of ancient, bitter death, swirls in the room. She's right. Even in these times, under the too-careful governance of the Council, some have easier lives than others.

Allody lets out a little gasp and presses a hand to her side. "Breaker Jena!"

"Hurry, now, Maya," I say. "The babe will come any moment. You must be ready for the taking. We only have the small time it takes for you to pass over, to transfer your soul to the child. And it must be completed within half an hour of first breath or your soul-offering won't bind to her."

With a weary sigh, Maya lets her long gray hair loose from its bun and discards layer upon layer of patched, gray and brown shawls and skirts. I don't help. As the mother of two and grandmother of two, she knows what to do. She has been prepared since we knew Allody was having a girl and needed a female soul-bringer.

Finally, clad only in the bringer's traditional scarlet shift, Maya crawls into bed with the mother-to-be. Their hands clasp. Tears shimmer in both sets of rust-brown eyes.

"You sure, Grandma?" Allody asks, her voice breaking. "I'll miss you so much!"

Her grandmother nods. "This body is old and tired. Time for a new one." Her wrinkled smile widens. "Anyways, you wouldn't want your baby to be an unsouled, would you? Caring for naught but themselves. Killing off the world with greed." She jerks a thumb at the window, at the ruins silhouetted against a stormy sunset. "You know how it goes. A life for a life. An old soul into a new body. Gotta break and bind to keep the goodness in."

This is the way of things since the passing of the unsouled and their near destruction of our world. But it doesn't need to be. I press my lips tight, holding in the urge to lecture. This ridiculous old belief must stop.

Could I...? I glance at the young mother. No, not this time. Here, there's no way to hide what I want to do. She's healthy and the birth easy. Her husband and father stand outside, waiting to witness the ceremony; waiting for the new little soul-taker to absorb Maya's worn soul, minus the small piece I break off as my fee.

The men, the women, the whole village. They all wait for the child to no longer be an unsouled. No longer dangerous, like those whose city crumbles in the storm.

So we're told.

No. This is not the child on whom to continue my tests. I need another birth with no witnesses and no soul-bringer. No blind followers of the Council's doctrines.

Five women are gravid in this village and four in the next, including my own little sister—gentle, widowed, Freya. Soon there will be another newborn I do not have to break for or take for. Soon the Council will see their rituals are nothing but hollowness and control. Lies of spun sugar. Sweeteners for the bitterness of killing a grandparent to allow room for a baby in the world.

And they must see it, since there is no one to be Freya's soulbringer. If I help her birth an unsouled and the Council finds out, they will kill the child. Freya's child. My family. That, I cannot allow.

Allody grunts and gives a little, whimpering cry. Her face reddens and she holds her breath. The child slides free of her mother's body. Born into blood and storms.

I check her over while we wait for the afterbirth. The scissors cut through the cord with the strange crunching sound that always unnerves new mothers. Then I clean and swaddle and place the child between the two women.

Delight, regret, love, awareness of coming grief…all their feelings shine unguarded as Maya and Allody cradle the child and croon over tiny perfection.

At my call, the child's father, uncle and grandfather shuffle into the room, hats in hand, bringing the dusty scent of death and the cold smell of autumn rain with them. When they stand, awed and awkward in the corner, I begin the final ritual.

The familiar *Song of Taking* falls from my mouth almost unheeded, its tune first rising, then cascading down. A minor key. Wistful. Full of loss. Behind me the men give forth soft harmonies that fill the room with gentle regret. Learned in childhood. Passed on from generation to generation, along with a belief that the souls are carried on cadence and rhythms and melody from one body to the next.

Reinforcing the Council's grip on the world.

I hold the scissors in a trembling hand. There has to be another method. Why is it a life for a life, a soul given and taken? Surely it hasn't always been this way?

Maya's faded gaze catches mine. Her mouth twists into a wry, understanding smile. "Come, Breaker. You brought baby Dek, next door, into the world without help or singers last week, I hear. He is hale. Now it's my great-grandchild's turn."

With fingers of paper and bird bone, she grasps my wrist. I swallow and steel myself to match the metal.

Maya's hand is wrapped around mine, and mine around the scissor handles. Together we slip the sleek blue blades between her ribs. Her rheumy eyes fix on the babe then on Allody. Tears stream down the new mother's face and she whispers "Thank you" to her grandmother.

Maya's body tenses. A gasp flutters from her lips. Her blood stains the sheets and the child's swaddling.

My fingers and blades glisten red as I cut her soul free of the small organ just below her heart. The pale, shining mirror of who she was falls into my waiting hand. A flat plane, like glass. A sharp reflection off water on a clean summer's day.

Soul colors vary. Hers is the clearest, brightest I've seen in a while. Not a smudge of darkness to be seen. A good soul. The child will grow up kind and thoughtful.

If you believe the Council's teachings.

I hesitate. No. I must follow through this time. I break a small shard off and hold it tight in one hand. It is cold, yet hot at once. Pains tingle up my arm but I cannot release it to freedom, or the binding won't hold.

Allody unwraps her child. The baby girl's legs kick feebly. Her little, perfect fingers grab at nothing. Dark hair lies plastered to her scalp.

With delicate care, I insert the largest part of her great-grandmother's soul between brittle little ribs. She squalls and Allody stares at me, wide-eyed.

"It's alright," I reassure her. "That's normal. It hurts and it won't bind until I also put the broken piece where it belongs. But then it will heal without a scar and I'll sing her to sleep."

Next, I open my hand and catch the final splinter of Maya's life between the scissor blades. A glittering fragment that will soon be part of me. Sucking a slow breath, I sing the soul-breaker's song, trying to control the quaver in my voice. Major scale this time. A steady, unchanging tempo. A song of yearning. Of hope for the future, even when I can't see any.

The blades cut neatly through the thick, pink scar tissue over my ribs. I barely feel the sting anymore. With my eyes closed, I find my soul's holding place easily enough. The scissors drive further, in amongst the myriad of tiny fragments that are my broken, borrowed bits of soul.

That, I always feel. The pain of sliced flesh followed by the sharper, deeper, darker pain of carrying more and more pieces of other peoples' lives.

How many can I hold? My mentor on the Council of soul-masters never mentioned such pain.

I withdraw the scissors.

I feel no different.

Not this time, then.

My jaw aches with tension. My shoulders, too.

Surely, I've taken enough? Broken enough. Absorbed enough. Killed enough grandparents. Bound enough squalling infants to goodness.

When will these endless exchanges end and leave me enlightened;

wise; a soul-master? Able to change the Council's old ways for new.

My throat closes but I continue to sing. The men's voices swell into joy and brilliance, filling the tiny room, clearing a way through the thunder now raging outside.

I dab my blood onto the babe's closed wound, and murmur her new name, *Maya*. And it is done. She ceases to cry. Her blue eyes open and stare straight at me with her great-grandmother's look of wisdom already showing.

Beside the child, old Maya's eyes blank and her final breath slips free on a soft sigh.

#

I am drenched when I reach my sister's cottage, one village away. The storm has softened to a drizzle of tears, but another chases after and will roll over the house soon. Lightning claws at the low clouds. Thunder growls a second later.

My soul-breaker's blue cloak is soaked through, the wool darkened to midnight. It weighs on my shoulders as heavily as old Maya's death weighs on my mind. Things shouldn't be this way.

I open our little house's thick wooden door and hang my cloak to dry. My boots go neatly beside my sister's... and another two pairs.

One I recognize. They belonged to my brother-in-law, but Freya can't yet bear to give them away. Redil died six months ago. The unsouled's city crushed him as he searched for salvage materials to fix a neighbor's roof.

He was a good man. Kind. Intelligent. Now, he is lost. A human that cannot be replaced under the Council's current laws. Just because his soul could not be retrieved in time and no new soul-takers were born.

I pause, staring at the other pair of boots. They are soul-master green. The color of the old forests, of algae, of envy. Veloni is here.

My Council mentor and supervisor. The one who disagrees most with my ideas for how to move our people onto a more certain path to survival.

In the narrow entryway of neatly laid stone and thickly plastered walls, I rest my head against the wall and close my eyes. My body hurts. It always takes me a day or so to recover from a soul-break and absorption. But this is worse than usual. All of me aches and blood still seeps through the cut between my ribs. Have I done something wrong?

Or is it a sign that I'm close to transforming into a soul-master? Is that why Veloni is here?

The thought gives me strength. I transfer the blue-metal scissors to my skirt pocket and head for the warmth of the living space where the smell of rabbit stew lingers and my sister awaits my return.

"Jena!" Freya rises awkwardly from her seat before the fire. One hand presses into the small of her back, another helps push her from the chair. A grimace crosses her delicate, pale features. She is thinner than she should be at this late stage of pregnancy. The loss of Redil stole her appetite and her smile at once. I hurry to her side and help her stand. Her breath comes in quick little gasps. One hand strokes her swollen belly.

But she clasps my cold fingers with her warm ones. "You're back safe. I was beginning to worry." Her dark-shadowed eyes search my face and flick an uneasy look toward Veloni, seated in the second chair. If Freya is trying to give me a message, I cannot read it. I kiss her cheek and turn toward my mentor.

"Master Veloni." I touch two fingers to the still-tender spot on my ribs in the traditional salute between soul-breakers and soul-masters.

She rises from the cracked-leather chair and returns the greeting. Her long, graying hair is tied in an intricate knot, decorated with simple wooden beads. Over a plain gray linen shift, she still wears her emerald cloak. So…she arrived before the storm broke and didn't expect to stay long. I repress a smile for having kept her waiting.

There is an awkward silence as she looks me over, with one brow arched, dark eyes cool, narrow face a mask. My pale blue tunic is still spattered with blood. My hair damp and flat. I try not to fidget. I have helped as many children into the world as she ever did before becoming a master. More, in fact.

Thunder booms over the house, shaking stone and rattling glass.

Veloni switches her chill glance to Freya. "You will leave us in private."

Freya starts, her eyes widening. She touches her forehead and hurries from the room. The bedroom door closes, but it's thin enough that she can hear if she tries. And she will. We've always looked after each other.

I take a seat without being asked. It is my house, after all. The cushion is still warm from where Freya rested. It smells faintly of jasmine, her favorite flower. With a gracious wave I invite Veloni back into what is usually my seat.

Her lips thin for a moment, but she sits on the edge, her spine straight. Leather creaks beneath her. I deliberately relax, trying to ignore the heavy thudding of my heart, certain it must be audible in the silence between growls of thunder. A log cracks sharply in the fireplace, spitting sparks. My muscles tense but I keep my calm expression of inquiry.

Let her speak first. I will not be the supplicant again. Not until I'm a master. It's been made clear to me, many times, that I'm below notice until then. The Council can't be changed from the outside.

Veloni breaks our locked gaze first and brushes at her skirt, wiping away invisible obstacles to order.

"It has come to our attention," she begins without looking at me, "that there are twenty-three children in the three villages you service."

I suppress a smile and wait. Of course there are children, I resist saying. It's my job.

She clears her throat. Her eyes—the tannin brown of deep forest pools—lift to mine. She examines my face like a panther waiting for the right moment to pounce. Waiting for me to make a mistake.

But I won't. I've worked too hard for this. She'll see I'm right. They all will.

Leaning forward, she narrows her gaze. "Twenty-three *unsouled* children in your villages."

"And?" I lift both brows and allow a small smile to curl my lips. The Council can do nothing now. The children are too old to be soul-takers and their designated soul-bringers died at the births, believing their souls had been passed on to the newborns. But I crushed the pieces and scattered the glittering fragments of finished lives into the air. They floated, sparkling dust in the sunlight.

"Why would you *do* that?" Veloni's tone is sharp. A frown pulls her thin brows close. She points vaguely at the cottage front door. "Why would you risk everything the Council has achieved since the fall of the unsouled cities? Everything we've planned?"

I grip the chair arms, my fingertips white. "Because you don't *listen.*"

"Pfah!" She dismisses me with a wave. "We listened. Over and over. To you and to your grandmother, before. You want to let children be born without them receiving the souls of their elders. It is you who have not listened."

My control breaks and I rise, standing over her. "I *do.* I listen to grandparents cry as they give up their souls and their lives too early. I listen to their families sing with voices strangled by tears. I listen to

- 433 -

the sound of my scissors cutting the throats of children who have no soul-giver. Then I listen to their mothers cry in my embrace. And I have no comfort to give them but to say 'The Council rules it so.'"

I rest my hands on her chair and push my face close to hers, whispering because my chest is too tight to hold enough breath for a shout.

"You," I say. "You and the Council make me murder children for want of a soul they *do not need.* And I've proven that. Those twenty-three unsouled children are perfectly fine. Healthy. Happier than soul-takers, even. Their eyes are eager and innocent, not weighed down by tired old souls that have lived through too much loss."

Veloni's eyes glitter. Her jaw hardens then she opens lips stretched into thin slits.

A muffled cry of pain sounds from the bedroom. Something thuds against the door, then the floor. Another cry. More like a scream.

"Freya!" I rush to the door and push it open against a heavy weight on the other side. A watery, pinkish liquid smears across the flagstones.

Freya is slumped on the floor, arms wrapped about her belly, weeping. Darkness stains her shift.

"It's coming, Jen," she says, gasping. "But it's too early."

"No," I reply, trying to sound soothing. "It's fine. Only a couple of weeks. The babe will be fine." But my heart stutters. She can't lose the child as well as Redil.

I help her onto the huge bed we share and hurry about preparing hot water and cloths. My mind races. I had planned for her child to be unsouled, but how can I do that now, with my mentor in the room?

Veloni hasn't left. She stands in a corner, watching, impassive, arms folded.

She speaks when all is ready and I am checking Freya's progress.

The babe is crowning already. But Freya is pale and disoriented, babbling and crying for Redik to come to her.

"Who is the soul-bringer?" Veloni's voice is calm, dispassionate.

"There is none," I say, countering her heavy sigh with a glare. "And I *will not* kill my sister's child because of the Council's blindness."

Veloni shakes her head. "Then we must find one." Thunder crashes and rain drums so loud on the patched metal roof I can barely hear Freya's cry of pain.

I grin savagely. "There is none close enough to get here within the required half hour after birth."

Her gaze narrows. "Boy or girl?"

I hesitate, but, in the end, there's really nothing she can do to stop what's coming. The child will be unsouled. Veloni will see there is no harm in such children. That they are the way of the future. The way to stop all this unneeded killing.

"Girl," I say. "The babe will be a girl."

Triumph gleams in Veloni. "Then Freya must be the soul-bringer."

A gasp escapes me. Standing between my mentor and my sister, I pull out my blue-metal scissors. "No! She's too young. You, yourself taught me that only those over fifty can be soul-bringers!"

Veloni tilts her head. "Do you know why that rule exists? Do you really understand what breakers and masters do? What the Council does?"

"How can I? The Council holds their secrets too close." My words are bitter, my clutch on the scissors tight. She will not have my sister or my niece.

"Exactly," she says, her mouth drooping. "But did you ever wonder why?"

I glance back at Freya. Her brow is beaded with sweat, her skin too pale. "We can speak of this later. I need to save my family. Do what you will with me after."

Veloni grips my wrist, wrenching the scissors from me. She shoves them at my face.

"You fool. You don't understand and that is why you will never become a master. Just as your grandmother failed to."

I fold my arms and glower. "Go ahead. Explain it, then. What won't I understand? Why won't I become a master? I can't wait to hear how the wise and all-knowing Council has decided my fate." I check Freya. She has fallen into a light doze and the babe's head has slipped out of sight again. I have a little time. Anything Veloni says I can turn against the Council when I am brought before them.

As I will be, for this birth and the other twenty-three.

I am beyond caring. Their rules are madness. Outdated, two-hundred-year-old laws for controlling the few souled folk who lived through the unsouled civilization's collapse. The laws need to change if we are to thrive, not just survive in this miserable, hand-to-mouth existence.

Veloni's lined cheeks sag and she sinks onto the bed edge. She looks at Freya with a weariness beyond her sixty-five years.

"When you were born, Jena, I argued against apprenticing you as a soul-breaker."

I stiffen but bite my tongue. Her admission shouldn't surprise me. I've long known she dislikes me.

"There was something amiss with your grandmother, too." She raises her head and tears glisten in the corners of her eyes. "She was my best friend. We were breakers together. But she never *understood*. And nor will you."

I frown, swallowing down rage and holding it tight in my

clenched fists. "What does that mean? What was she supposed to understand? What am *I* supposed to understand?"

Veloni scrubs a hand over her face. "Every generation there are a few children for whom the soul-taking does not work at birth. They remain unsouled. The Council makes them soul-breakers."

The breath leaves my lungs and my knees give way. I sink onto the bed. A strange kind of relief warms my stomach. Perhaps this is why I have always felt so separate from my kith and kin. Perhaps this is why I am so sure the unsouled can be the salvation of humanity's future.

"So, you…" I point at her, then back at myself. "…and I…?"

"Yes. You are an unsouled. As was I. But we don't stay that way." Veloni frowns as she watches me.

My heart stops, stutters, starts again, but faster—as though urging me to run from what she will say. I still don't understand why she seems to think being unsouled is terrible, so I stay.

She hesitates then plunges on, speaking fast. "The reason that breakers absorb a small portion of each bringer's soul is to gain, over time, what they were unable to take in one piece at birth." She leans forward and grips my hand. "But the souls aren't just giving life, Jena. They give *knowledge.*"

With a sigh, she glances at Freya. "What the bringer knows. What they've learned. The person they've become. What they carry from *their* soul-bringer. *All* that is passed on to the soul-taker. It means most children already know how to be kind and generous. How to treat others with respect. How to care for the land. How to construct a house. Everything. And each generation builds on that knowledge." She gives a soft, sad laugh. "Oh, they still have to learn things, but it takes less time than it takes an unsouled child. Much less."

I fling my arms wide. "So what? Why does it matter how long it takes them to learn?"

Her pitying gaze dwells on me until I squirm. For the first time, the awareness of things unknown and unlearned is a hollowness in my chest.

Veloni points south. "That city. That's why. The unsouled who came before us almost destroyed the world in their arrogance and greed. Their lack of respect for others." She rises, her stockinged feet silent as she paces the room. "Each generation made the same mistakes. Sought nothing but self-aggrandizement and power." She jabs a finger at me. "Because, like you and your grandmother, they *could not learn* fast enough to prevent the mistakes made in their youth. And it snowballed. Generation upon generation caring only for their own comfort and wealth."

She brings her hands together sharply. Thunder and lightning crash overhead and I jump.

Her hands fall, limp, to her sides.

"Until it was too late. We still don't quite understand what killed them all at once." Her shoulders slump. "Just that the survivors were mostly the souled ones. Then we discovered that even their children were often born without souls. But most can inherit one if it's bound properly. And with it came knowledge. Such knowledge."

She pauses and stares through me. "Our world consists of a hundred and twenty villages, Jena. All that is left of humanity. A little over a hundred and twenty thousand souled people with the knowledge and wisdom not to repeat past mistakes."

"And?" I prompt when she stops again. My fury has died with the storm's passing, leaving me cold and empty. I can no longer see my path quite so clearly. My way is muddied by fear now. Fear that I have strayed and cannot find the way home. That I have been naïve. That I lack...knowledge.

"And," she repeats on a sigh, "to keep the expertise of old souls alive, we have to limit the population in number, to allow life only to those who can be soul-takers. Plus a few who will become breakers and finally masters. This is the Council's true function."

"But..." My voice is small, my throat so thick it chokes the words. "But I don't understand. I'm a soul-breaker. Why can't I be a master? What's wrong with me?" I touch my ribs. Blood has oozed through the scar tissue and stained my tunic scarlet, the color of a soul-bringer's shift.

Veloni grasps my hands so tightly the scissors she still carries press hard into my flesh. Her expression is earnest. Truthful. Pleading, almost.

"We breakers can't take in an old soul. Instead..." She lifts a shoulder and her gaze slides from mine, "...we break off and steal a little of each soul we pass from bringer to taker. And, in doing so, most of us inherit *all* of that person's knowledge." She touches the spot on her chest above where the soul-holding organ sits. "When this is full, we become wise enough to govern."

Her face sags again. "Yours will never be full, I'm afraid. Something in your body cannot absorb the soul shards. The weight of their wisdom is too much, perhaps. I'm sorry. You can never be a master."

I pull free of her touch and rise from the bed. I am flawed? My stomach twists into sickness. How can that be? The answers seemed so clear before.

Outside the bedroom window, lightning still flashes in the distance, but the storm has passed overhead, leaving nothing but the sound of dripping water and the clean smell of wet earth. To the south, the broken city is silhouetted against a yawning, golden moon.

I glance across at Freya. Her eyes are half open but still tired and vacant. She writhes on the bed, moaning. Veloni turns her back on me and tends to Freya, encouraging her to push the babe into the world. Freya's daughter child will come, soon, and I no longer have an easy solution. Even without the driving rain, there is no way to fetch a soul-bringer in time.

Veloni is bent over the bed, my blue-metal scissors in her hand, ready to cut the child's throat. Or ready to take my sister's soul and leave my little niece without a family. For there is no way the Council will let me live after this either.

I reach deep inside, searching for the rage and certainty that fueled me for so long.

But it has vanished like the storm.

Soon, all that will be left is the sound of blood dripping from the blades.

Unless…

I move to the clothes cupboard. Behind me, Freya groans and Veloni urges her to push hard. My sister cries out, triumphant, relieved. A baby's wail follows, thin, petulant.

From the cupboard I draw a scarlet soul-bringer's shift. Discarding my breaker's clothing I pull on the shift and return to the bed. Veloni nods.

There, I curl up beside my little sister, clasping her cold hand in my warm one. The new babe lies swaddled and sleepy between us. Freya's eyes flutter open and widen at the sight of my clothing.

She sucks a shuddering breath. "Are you sure, Jena? I'll miss you so much."

I swallow hard and nod. "This body is wrong for this world. But, with all of my soul-shards in her, baby Jena will make wiser decisions than I did." I nod to my mentor, who inclines her head, her eyes dark, regretful.

With my blue-metal blades, Veloni slices through scarlet linen and pink scar tissue and draws forth the first piece of someone else's soul. Bright and clean. Glittering in the half-light. Not a hint of darkness smudging it anywhere.

I hope you've enjoyed this diverse collection of short stories. If so, would you be kind enough to leave a review on Goodreads, and any book retail sites you happen to prefer? Reviews help other readers find authors they love. Then authors don't die of starvation.

For this anthology, sales will also help fund a writing mentorship program for up and coming authors.

About the Authors

(in surname alphabetical order)

Kylie Chan - has a BBus, an MBA in IT, and an MPhil in Creative writing. She ran her own consulting business for ten years in Hong Kong. When she returned to Australia in 2002, Kylie studied martial arts and Buddhist and Taoist philosophy, and wrote the bestselling nine-book *Dark Heavens* series, a fantasy based on Chinese mythology. She has recently released the *Dragon Empire* science fiction series.

Find her at: www.kyliechan.com

www.facebook.com/KylieChanAuthor

Twitter: @kyliechan

Instagram: kylie_chan_author

James SA Corey - is a convenient fiction, the pseudonym of Daniel Abraham and Ty Franck. He began when Daniel and Ty set out to write a book together based on work Ty had done creating the solar system that became *The Expanse*.

Find them at: www.jamessacorey.com

Twitter: @JamesSACorey

Dr Jack Dann – is a multi-award-winning author who has written or edited over seventy-five books, including the international bestseller *The Memory Cathedral*, *The Rebel*, *The Silent*, and *The Man Who Melted*. His latest novel is *Shadows in the Stone*. Kim Stanley Robinson called it "such a complete world that Italian history no longer seems comprehensible without his cosmic battle of spiritual entities behind and within every historical actor and event." Forthcoming is a Centipede Press Masters of Science Fiction volume.

Dr. Dann is an Adjunct Senior Research Fellow in the School of Communication and Arts at the University of Queensland. He lives in Australia on a farm overlooking the sea.

Find him on: www.jackdann.com

Facebook: www.facebook.com/jack.dann2

Twitter: @jackmdann

Sebastien de Castell – Sebastien's acclaimed, swashbuckling fantasy series *The Greatcoats*, was shortlisted for the Goodreads Choice Award for Best Fantasy, and the Gemmell Morningstar Award. His YA fantasy series *Spellsinger* is published in more than a dozen languages. He spends his time writing, travelling, and going on strange adventures.

Find him at: www.decastell.com

Twitter: @decastell

Facebook: www.facebook.com/SebastienDeCastell

Dr Marianne de Pierres - is author of the award-winning *Sentients of Orion, Parrish Plessis,* and *Peacemaker* series. In 2014 she became the recipient of a Curtin UniversityDistinguished Australian Alumniaward for significant and valuable contributions to Australian science fiction feminist literature. Marianne also writes award-winning, humorous crime under the pseudonym Marianne Delacourt. In her other life, she teaches creative writing to university students and writes about social change and thought leadership.

Find her at: www.tarashap.com.au

David Farland - is an award-winning, international bestselling author with over 50 novels in print. He has won the Philip K. Dick Memorial Special Award for "Best Novel in the English Language" for his science fiction novel ON MY WAY TO PARADISE, the Whitney Award for "Best Novel of the Year" for his historical novel IN THE COMPANY OF ANGELS, and many more awards for his work. He is best known for his NEW YORK TIMES bestselling fantasy series THE RUNELORDS. Farland has also written for major franchises such as STAR WARS and THE MUMMY. Find him at: www.davidfarland.com

Facebook: www.facebook.com/DavidFarlandAuthor

Aiki Flinthart - is the Australian author of 15 sci-fantasy novels, two collections of short stories, two author craft non-fiction books. She has also edited 4 short story collections. Several of her works have been shortlisted in the Australian Aurealis Awards, and top-8 finalists in the USA Writers of the Future competition. When not writing, she mentors other authors, gives workshops on writing fight scenes, and practices fantasy-approved hobbies such as martial arts, archery, knife-throwing, lute-playing, and bellydancing.

Find her at: www.aikiflinthart.com

www.facebook.com/aiki.flinthart

Dirk Flinthart - is an award-winning writer in Northern Tasmania and has a Masters in Creative Writing. He has a string of published speculative fiction short stories, as well as an SF/Horror novel (*Path of Night*) through Fablecroft. He has worked in feature journalism and non-fiction, including the best-selling *HowTo Be A Man*, co-written with John Birmingham. In the last few years, Flinthart has turned his attention to film, television and media and is currently working on several different projects.

You can find him on Facebook.

Jasper Fforde - is a British writer who lives in Wales and writes absurdist fiction. He has published seven books in the *Thursday Next* series, one of which won the Wodehouse Prize for comic fiction in 2004. There are also two novels in the *Nursery Crime* series, and several in the *Dragonslayer* YA series. A festival in Swindon is themed after him and his *Thursday Next* book series.
Find him at: www.jasperfforde.com

Dr Kate Forsyth- wrote her first book aged 7 and has now sold more than a million books worldwide. She is a multi-award-winning author of fantasy, historical fantasy, fairy-tale re-imaginings and historical fiction. Her best-known works include *Bitter Greens*, which won the 2015 American Library Assoc award for Best Historical Fiction; *The Silver Well*, a set of interlinked stories co-written with Kim Wilkins; and *Valisa the Wise & Other Tales of Brave Young Women*. Named one of Australia's Favourite 15 authors, Kate has a BA in Literature, and MA in Creative Writing, and a Doctorate of Creative Arts.
Find her at: www.kateforsyth.com
Facebook: www.facebook.com/kateforsythauthor
Twitter: @KateForsyth

Neil Gaiman – is an English author of numerous speculative fiction novels, graphic novels, screenplays for film and television, poetry and short stories. His works have won multiple awards, including the Newbery and Carnegie Medals; and the Hugo, Nebula, World Fantasy, Bram Stoker, Locus, British SF, and British Fantasy Awards, and many others. Some of his better-known works include *American Gods,* and *Good Omens* (co-authored with Sir Terry Pratchett).
Find him at: www.neilgaiman.com
Twitter: @neilhimself

Alison Goodman – Alison's latest novel is *The Dark Days Deceit,* the final book in the 'Lady Helen' trilogy, an award-winning mix of Regency adventure and dark fantasy. She is also the author of 6 other novels, including *The Dark Days Club, The Dark Days Pact,* and *EON* and *EONA*—a *New York Times* best-selling fantasy duology published in 20 countries. She is currently working a new historical series and has embarked on a PhD focusing on the Regency era.
Find her at: www.alisongoodman.com.au

Jan-Andrew (JA) Henderson – is the author of 30 books, mostly thrillers, paranormal thrillers, YA thrillers, and historical non-fiction about Scotland. He is the winner of the Royal Mail and Doncaster Prizes, and his novels have been shortlisted for thirteen literary awards. He has a MA in English Literature and Philosophy from the University of Edinburgh. He has written and directed several plays and worked as the writer/director at the Witherbee Children's theatre in NY state.
Find him at: www.janandrewhenderson.com

Ian Irvine – is an Australian marine scientist and has 34 published novels. His *Three Worlds* epic fantasy series has been published and translated across numerous countries and has sold over a million copies. He has also written eco-thrillers set in a world undergoing catastrophic climate change, along with YA thrillers, and humorous fantasy for children.
Find him at: www.ian-irvine.com
www.facebook.com/ianirvineauthor

Pamela Jeffs – is an Australian author of weird speculative fiction, mostly short stories. Her best-known work is the *Five Dragons* short story collection, which was shortlisted for the Aurealis Awards in 2020. Her others stories have been shortlisted several times for the Aurealis Awards, and received Honorable Mention in the USA Writers of the Future competition. Her works are published in multiple e-magazines, and in anthologies all over the world.
Find her at: www.pamelajeffs.com

Mary Robinette Kowal – is the US author of *Ghost Talkers*, *The Glamourist Histories* series, and the *Lady Astronaut* series. She is the President of SFWA, part of the award-winning podcast Writing Excuses and a four-time Hugo Award winner. Her short fiction appears in *Uncanny*, *Tor.com*, and *Asimov's*. Mary Robinette, a professional puppeteer, lives in Nashville.
Find her at: maryrobinettekowal.com

Mark Lawrence – was born in Illinois but moved to the UK aged one. He returned to the US in his 30s, after taking a PhD in Mathematics, and worked on a variety of projects before returning to the UK. He never had any ambition to be a writer, so was surprised when a half-hearted attempt to find an agent turned into a global publishing deal overnight. His trilogies include: *The Broken Empire*, *The Red Queen's War*, *The Book of the Ancestor*, *The Book of the Ice*, and *Impossible Times*.
Find him at: http://www.marklawrence.buzz

Ken Liu - is a US author of speculative fiction. A winner of the Nebula, Hugo, and World Fantasy awards, he wrote *The Dandelion Dynasty*, a silkpunk epic fantasy series (starting with *The Grace of*

Kings), as well as *The Paper Menagerie and Other Stories* and *The Hidden Girl and Other Stories*. He also authored the Star Wars novel, *The Legends of Luke Skywalker*.

Find him at: www.kenliu.name

Juliet Marillier – is the New Zealand born author of historical fantasy full of folklore, family, and drama. Her best-known series are *Blackthorn & Grim,* and *Seven Waters,* both set in medieval Ireland. Plus the Viking duology, *Saga of the Light Isles,* and the *Bredei Chronicles,* set in the kingdom of the Picts. And many more. She has won numerous awards, including five Aurealis and four Sir Julius Vogel Awards. When not writing, she is kept busy by her rescue dogs and her children and grandchildren.

Find her at: www.julietmarillier.com

Lee Murray – is a multi-award-winning author-editor from New Zealand. Her works include: the *Taine McKenna Adventures* (military thrillers), *The Path of Ra* (supernatural crime noir series with Dan Rabarts), *Grotesque: Monster Stories* (collection). Editor of award-winning titles: *Hellhole, At the Edge,* and *Baby Teeth.* Most recent anthologies: *Black Cranes: Tales of Unquiet Women* (with Gene Flynn), and *Midnight Echo #13.* Co-founder of Young NZ Writers, and the Wright-Murray Residency for Speculative Fiction writers, Lee was HWA 2019 Mentor of the Year, NZSA Honorary Literary Fellow 2020, and 2021 Grimshaw-Sargeson Fellow.

Find her at: www.leemurray.info

Garth Nix – is a New York Times best-selling Australian author of *The Left-Handed Booksellers of London, Angel Mage, Frogkisser!* and the *Old Kingdom* series—beginning with *Sabriel*; plus the *Keys* *to the Kingdom* series; and many others. He has won the Aurealis award multiple times, along with the Ditmar Award and the Mythopoeic Award. His work has also been shortlisted for the Locus and the Shirley Jackson Awards. More than 6 million copies of his books have been sold around the world, and his books have been translated into 42 languages.

Find him at: www.garthnix.com

www.facebook.com/garthnix

Twitter: @garthnix

Robert Silverberg- has been professional science fiction and fantasy author since 1955. He is a many-times winner of the Hugo and Nebula awards. He was named to the Science Fiction Hall of Fame in 1999, and in 2004 was designated as Grand Master by the SFWA. His books and stories have been translated into 40 languages. Among his best known works are *Nightwings, Dying Inside, The Book of Skulls*, and the three volumes of the *Majipoor Cycle*.

Find him at: **www.robertsilverberg.com**

Dr Angela Slatter - is the Australian author of the Verity Fassbinder supernatural crime series (*VIGIL, CORPSELIGHT, RESTORATION*) AND TEN SHORT STORY COLLECTIONS, INCLUDING *THE BITTERWOOD BIBLE AND OTHER RECOUNTINGS*. Her gothic fantasy novels, *All The Murmuring Bones*(2021) and *Morwood*(2022), will be published by Titan. She's won a World Fantasy, a British Fantasy, an Australian Shadows and six Aurealis Awards; her debut novel was nominated for the Dublin Literary Award. Her work has been translated into French, Chinese, Spanish, Japanese, Italian, Bulgarian and Russian.

Find her at: www.angelaslatter.com,

Twitter @AngelaSlatter

Dr Cat Sparks is a multi-award-winning Australian author, editor and artist. Career highlights include a PhD in science fiction and climate fiction, five years as Fiction Editor of Cosmos Magazine, running Agog! Press, working as an archaeological dig photographer in Jordan, studying with Margaret Atwood, 75 published short stories, two collections – *The Bride Price* (2013) and *Dark Harvest* (2020), plus a far future novel, *Lotus Blue*. She directed two speculative fiction festivals for Writing NSW and is a regular panellist and speaker at speculative fiction events.

Find her at: www.catsparks.net

Twitter: @catsparx

Other Titles by Editor

Discover other titles by Aiki Flinthart at: **www.aikiflinthart.com**

Short Story Anthologies
Worlds in Words
Zookeeper's Tales of Interstellar Oddities
Return
Elemental
Rogues' Gallery

Non-Fiction – Author writing resources
Fight Like A Girl – Writing Fight Scenes for Female (and male) Characters

Blackbirds Sing (Historical fantasy)

The 80AD series (YA Adventure/Fantasy)
80AD Book 1: The Jewel of Asgard
80AD Book 2: The Hammer of Thor
80AD Book 3: The Tekhen of Anuket
80AD Book 4: The Sudarshana
80AD Book 5: The Yu Dragon

The Ruadhan Sidhe novels (YA Urban Fantasy)
Shadows Wake (#1)
Shadows Bane (#2)
Shadows Fate (#3)
Healing Heather (#4)(Romance)

The Kalima Chronicles (YA Sci/Fantasy)
IRON (#1)
FIRE (#2)
STEEL (#3)
A Future, Forged (Prequel)

Sold! (Contemporary Romance/Adventure)

Connect with her on Facebook
https://www.facebook.com/aikiflinthartauthor
Twitter: @aikiflinthart
Instagram: Aikiflinthart

CPSIA information can be obtained
at www.ICGtesting.com
Printed in the USA
LVHW112005080821
694731LV00010B/856